HOW TO SLAY AT WORK

SARAH BONNER

Boldwood

First published in Great Britain in 2024 by Boldwood Books Ltd.

Copyright © Sarah Bonner, 2024

Cover Design by Head Design Ltd

Cover Illustration: Bella Howard

Every effort has been made to obtain the necessary permissions with reference to copyright material, both illustrative and quoted. We apologise for any omissions in this respect and will be pleased to make the appropriate acknowledgements in any future edition.

A CIP catalogue record for this book is available from the British Library.

Paperback ISBN 978-1-83633-532-0

Large Print ISBN 978-1-83633-533-7

Hardback ISBN 978-1-83633-531-3

Ebook ISBN 978-1-83633-534-4

Kindle ISBN 978-1-83633-535-1

Audio CD ISBN 978-1-83633-526-9

MP3 CD ISBN 978-1-83633-527-6

Digital audio download ISBN 978-1-83633-530-6

Boldwood Books Ltd
23 Bowerdean Street
London SW6 3TN
www.boldwoodbooks.com

To Bronwen,
for being nothing at all like Freya

PART I

MILLIE

1

My boss is a stone-cold bitch. But please don't think I hate her; far from it, I admire her. She's an icon. She *slays*. Freya Ellwood-Winter, Sales Director of Serendipity Cosmetics plc, goes through life not giving even one single fuck what people think of her. Just imagine how free she must feel to be so unshackled from propriety and the normal rules that govern our social contracts.

Of course, I would rather she wasn't my boss. I'd rather *I* wasn't the person being summoned into her office at 7 a.m., before I've even been able to take a sip of my coffee or change out of the trainers I wear for my commute.

She doesn't bother with any pleasantries. 'Samantha has quit.'

'Oh?' I reply, wondering if Freya will elaborate.

She doesn't. 'We leave for Paris in a few hours.'

'We? As in—'

She cuts me off with a stare and a sigh. 'You will obviously take over Samantha's workload.' This conversation is undeniably a complete waste of her time.

'Right,' I reply, trying to keep my tone neutral, as if this is a reasonable request from her and not an utter piss-take. I mean, it's an overnighter, what if I had plans for this evening? Plans that don't involve an impromptu trip to France. And don't get me started on the fact that I now need to learn the ins and outs of the deal with C'est Magnifique. 'I'll need to go home to get my passport.'

The look she gives me could turn a person to stone. 'Well at least you can jog there,' she says as her gaze sweeps down to my footwear.

I message Sam on my way to the tube. I need to know what happened; did she get fired? Or did she finally reach breaking point and tell Freya where to stick the job? If that was the way it happened, I wish I'd been there to witness. Sam doesn't reply.

The flat is quiet as I let myself in; Lissa must still be asleep, the vat of cheap wine she drank last night still cradling her in its languid embrace. The place is a mess, Lissa's stuff strewn everywhere; there's even a pair of her tights hanging off the lamp in the living room. We're total opposites: I'm tidy and ordered – a neat freak, Lissa calls me – but she's an absolute slattern. We've lived together since we were teenagers – sharing a room at the home and then this flat – and I've finally learned not to let it get to me. Plus Lissa is currently temping for a fashion PR company and having samples all over our communal space makes it much easier for me to borrow things. Like the fabulous Louboutin heels that are lying incongruously under the breakfast bar in the kitchen. They'll be perfect with the black L. K. Bennett dress that's been hanging in the hallway for almost a month.

I scribble her a note on the fridge. She's notoriously dreadful at reading text messages or WhatsApp, but she's a creature of habit who needs a milky coffee every morning, so she always sees the little magnetic whiteboard. Then I carefully pack my little carry-on case, pluck my passport from its home in the small safe in my bedroom, and head back to the office.

Lissa messages me just as I'm rehearsing the final touches of the pitch I will give our Parisian clients.

> Ooooh! Look at you! International jetsetter xx

Lissa has always had this thing about business travel. She thinks it's exciting and glamorous and a perk. A fucking perk! The next twenty-four hours will swing between absolute boredom and horrendous stress in luxurious settings that cannot be enjoyed. I will live in constant fear that I'll say something outlandishly offensive in my terrible French, or order something in a restaurant that is delivered to the table still alive and squirming. And all the while under the watchful and ever-judgemental eye of Freya Ellwood-Winter.

I've worked for Freya for almost two years as her Bid Analyst. Technically I'm meant to write pitch packs for potential high-value clients and brand collaborators, but most of my time is spent as a glorified PA, running seemingly random errands for her while she makes vague promises about future opportunities if I prove myself. Sam is – was, I guess, seeing as she's quit – the Bid Manager, the one who accompanies Freya as she jet-sets all over the place. It might sound more senior – and it is, of course – but the reality is Sam takes – took – a lot of meeting notes and spends – spent? Who the fuck knows – most of the rest of her time booking ridiculously specific hotel rooms and making all the travel arrangements. I guess I do both of these jobs now. And I guess there won't be a pay rise any time soon. This will be dressed as an opportunity and I'll take it, make some sycophantic noises about how I relish the challenge and then bitch about it to Lissa later. Welcome to office life in the twenty-first century.

At twelve minutes past eleven, Freya suddenly appears at the door to her office and announces we're leaving in five minutes. I scramble into action mode: I call a town car, shut down my computer, gather my things, and run downstairs to ensure I'm ready and waiting at sixteen minutes past. I watch the clock behind the receptionist as it ticks forward.

Seventeen past. Eighteen past. Nineteen past. I need to pee. Three more minutes pass; I could've nipped to the loo but it wasn't worth the risk that the lift doors would open and she wouldn't find me waiting. I'll have to hold it, feeling as if I'm about to burst, until we arrive at St Pancras.

The uniformed town car driver pops his head into the reception area. 'Pickup for Millie Brooks?' I stretch my face into an exaggerated grimace at him. He's driven us before and he knows what my expression means. 'I'll wait in the car,' he says with a huff.

It's twenty-nine minutes past before Freya steps out of the lift without even a sniff of an apology for saying five minutes when she meant twenty. 'Are you coming, Camille?' she asks as she strides past me.

My name isn't Camille. Millie is short for Millicent – I was named after my grandmother, who began calling me Millie when I moved in with her to avoid the confusion of *two* Millicents – but I don't correct Freya. It's easier not to. And what is a name anyway? I'm being facetious; names are incredibly important, they define the very core of who we are. Millicent means 'brave strength', something I have had to learn the hard way. Freya technically means 'noble woman', but it was also the name of my neighbour's aloof husky who considered herself far above giving anyone any affection. She looked like a wolf and had the teeth to match. My boss couldn't have a more perfect moniker in my opinion.

Freya spends the first hour of our Eurostar journey quizzing me about the clients we're meeting this evening and the details of the proposal. I've had about two hours to get my head around the deal, but she can't help herself from nit-picking about the tiny little things I get wrong.

'They launched C'est Magnifique *four* years ago, not three.'

'It's the *second* largest youth beauty brand in France.'

'It's pronounced Mar-tan, not Mar-tin. It's *French*.'

I find myself making more and more of these micro-errors, probably in direct correlation to the pressure on my bladder as I still haven't been able to go to the toilet. Thankfully, lunch arrives and Freya starts devouring her starter. I manage to excuse myself to wash my hands before I eat.

'You were a long time, I've almost finished eating,' she says as I slip back into my seat opposite her. She's already eaten her starter and half her main course. I was gone for less than five minutes, but she has this thing – I was going to call it a talent, but it seems a rather odd thing to celebrate like that – for being able to eat incredibly quickly, as if she's merely inhaling the food rather than eating it. I went on a date a few months ago with a guy who ate in the same way. He told me it was an old boarding school habit, but Lissa did some Google searching and discovered he'd spent two years in prison for identity theft. 'That'll be why he eats like that,' she'd said with an arched eyebrow and self-righteous smirk. 'I told you he was trouble.' He was hot as hell though, and sometimes we all need a bit of bad boy in our lives.

Almost as if she knows I'm thinking about her, my phone begins to beep as a stream of messages comes in. I like to consider what I'm going to say before I compose a single and well-formed message. Lissa, however, messages like her phone is directly plugged into her stream of consciousness, randomly pressing send at whim before she continues to type. I fumble with my phone, trying to put it on silent as I offer Freya an apologetic smile.

But Freya stares back at me, finally putting down her knife and fork and crossing her arms. 'We might be eating, but you are still at work, Camille.'

'Sorry,' I say quickly, and slip the phone under my napkin so the offending item is out of sight. But I hate myself for apologising, and for buying into the whole corporate 'all my time is work time' bullshit. She has literally dragged me to Paris with zero notice and now she's begrudging me having a friend send a few texts over lunch. It's not like I'm going to clock off at 5 p.m., the meeting with C'est Magnifique is over dinner and doesn't even begin until eight.

It takes twenty minutes for the taxi to take us from Gard du Nord to the Marriot Champs-Elysée. It's been a long time since I was last in Paris and I stare out of the window at the buildings with their stone facades and black wrought iron balconies.

'My grandmother brought me here once,' I say as we pass the Palais Garnier, home to the Paris Opera. 'Although I slept through the performance. I think I was a bit young for opera.'

Freya doesn't even look up from her phone. 'That's nice,' she says dismissively.

I keep quiet for the rest of the journey, drinking in the sights and opening the window a crack to allow the scent of freshly baked bread and coffee to waft into the car from the plethora of streetside cafes. The May sun has warmed the pavement, bringing the city to life around me. We turn onto the Champs-Elysée, the Arc de Triomphe in the distance, and pull up in front of the Marriot. I remember Sam – Freya always called her Samantha, but she thought that made her sound like a Sex and the City character and always went by Sam to the rest of us – spending almost two hours on the phone last week trying to wrangle a specific suite Freya wanted. You may have figured by now that my boss is rather exacting in her tastes. Sam never said if she resolved the issue and I hadn't thought to ask, it was her problem after all and I had plenty of my own to worry about at the time.

'I assume you sorted out the correct suite,' Freya says as she pulls up the handle of her roll-on case and heads towards the entrance, leaving me to pay the taxi driver. Right. Well, I guess Sam's problems are now my problems. I cross my fingers as I try to catch up with Freya.

Somehow Sam had pulled off the suite and Freya almost breaks into a smile as the receptionist hands her the key. My room, of course, is not a suite. I'm in one of the cheaper rooms the hotel offers – which even then is so expensive it makes me feel a little queasy; I could pay my share of the rent for over a month with that kind of money – but I do have a tiny little balcony. At least I'll be able to sneak an illicit cigarette without having to come down to the street.

'We will meet at seven thirty in the Atrium Bar,' Freya tells me, before heading to the bank of lifts up to the rooms. Then she stops and turns towards me, raising her voice to ensure I can hear her across the space. 'Make sure you look a little more put together for dinner.' She waves the hand she is holding her room key in at me, motioning not to something specifically wrong with the way I look, but that *all* of me needs some attention.

I send a silent plea for strength to the sky, before trotting dutifully after her.

As soon as I've closed the door of my room, I unzip my little case and pull out the bottle of wine I had stashed in there. Thank God for the Eurostar not having any liquid restrictions. It's warm; but warm Prosecco is better than no Prosecco, plus it isn't like I'm picky. I pop the cork and pour a generous measure into one of the little glasses wrapped in hotel-branded tissue paper from the bathroom. The door to the balcony slides open to reveal a space no larger than a yoga mat, the world's smallest table and two chairs squeezed into the space. It's bourgeoise and ridiculous and an absolutely perfect place to watch the last vestiges of a spring afternoon with a glass of wine and a Marlboro.

The smoke hits the back of my throat and the headrush hits me like an old friend; I trap the involuntary groan behind my lips. I know old-school cigarettes aren't fashionable any more, but my grandmother was never without a Marlboro or even a brightly coloured Sobranie and I find the smell comforting; it's the scent of home and a life that had almost made sense. I can see the Sacré-Cœur in the distance and I step forward to lean over the balcony railings to look at the street below. Unfortunately, my room looks over the rear of the hotel, so there isn't much to see.

Except a woman dressed all in black: black leggings, a black hoodie – slightly incongruous in the early-May warmth – and black trainers. Is that... but of course it is, her almost white blond hair reflects the sun even though her long bob is scraped back into a stubby pony tail. Freya pulls on a black baseball cap as she hurries down the alleyway, looking behind her as if to check she isn't being followed.

What the actual fuck is she up to?

2

I smoke four Marlboros back to back as I wait to see when Freya returns, soothing my throat with another glass of Prosecco.

Just as I'm grinding the last cigarette into the minuscule ashtray, I hear my phone beeping from inside the room. *Shit, I didn't message Lissa back.* She has a tendency to get pissy about these things, even though she so frequently ignores my texts, the queen of double standards.

Now, I know I'm meant to have an army of friends and lovers and people who send me stupid GIFs and memes and links to random Reddit threads about skateboarding dogs. But I don't. I'm very much team 'small and exclusive friendship group', not the kind of person who collects acquaintances and hangers-on. That's how I know the person messaging me is Lissa. It quite simply can't be anyone else. Especially since Reggie and I broke up. Well, he dumped me because all I ever did was work, but I was having doubts about our relationship before that, so our separation was effectively mutual.

Ooh la la, how is it? Are you having the best time?

I'm sitting on my balcony chain smoking.

With champagne?

Warm Prosecco *grimace face*

Close enough. Are the men gorgeous? Have you
found a paramour yet?

If she was with me, I'd have rolled my eyes and made a face like I was about to vomit. Lissa has this whole fantasy about meeting an attractive stranger and having a night of unbridled passion leading to an illicit affair. Unfortunately, this results in a monthly incident where she will end up doing the walk of shame, or knocking on my door to ask for help in the removal of said attractive stranger, who never ends up looking quite as alluring in the cold light of day. I decide to call her instead of trying to type quickly enough to get a word in edgeways; I can see she's already writing something else.

'Buongiorno!' she says as she answers the phone.

'Italian, but close enough,' I deadpan.

'Is it fabulous?'

'Question,' I say and she waits for me to ask it. 'If you saw someone in an alley, dressed all in black on a warm afternoon, what would you think they were up to?'

'Something nefarious, for sure.'

'Right? I mean, it's weird?'

'Maybe they're an assassin, casing out the place?' she suggests, always prone to over-dramatising a situation.

'It was my boss.'

'Oh.' She sounds disappointed. 'You had to ruin it.'

'She was wearing leggings, and a hoodie, and a baseball cap.' I try to pique her interest again.

'And trainers?'

'Well, yeah.'

'She was probably going for a run.'

I reach for yet another cigarette and light it, taking a deep drag. Lissa is probably right. Freya is very private about her life outside of work, only sharing the barest minimum. All I know is she has an apartment slap bang in the middle of Covent Garden – not that I'm jealous – and she doesn't seem to have a husband or kids. I guess she could be a runner. But then I see a black-clad figure enter the alleyway. 'She's coming back,' I hiss into the phone, despite the fact that I'm too far away for Freya to hear me from the alleyway.

'Is she sweaty?'

'I'm like five storeys up,' I say, frustrated I can't see more closely.

'Your phone has a zoom function...' she makes it sound like I'm a moron. She's generally the scatty one, the one who surprises me at her ability to navigate the real world, but sometimes she's a straight-up genius who doesn't even realise it. I open the camera and snap a series of photos, then I enlarge her face. 'Well?' Lissa asks, sounding quiet and tinny without the phone pressed against my ear.

'She is definitely not sweating.' But then I peer over the edge of the balcony again. She's squeezed herself behind one of the huge bins stored where the alleyway opens into the rear courtyard of the hotel and is staring up at one of the other rooms. I tuck myself down a bit so she won't spot me if she turns in my direction. 'She looks like she's up to something,' I whisper into the phone.

I fall silent as she climbs onto the roof of the bin, crouching low before springing up to grab the railing of the first floor balcony above her. In an impressive display of upper-body strength, she pulls herself up, then stands on top of the balustrade to grab the railing of the second floor balcony. 'Jesus...' I whisper to Lissa.

'What's going on?' she almost shouts into the phone.

'My boss is...' I start but I'm struggling to put what I'm seeing into words. 'She's... like... climbing up the balconies,' I say eventually, but it doesn't do the spectacle justice. It's like she's Spiderman. But some kind of modern feminist parkour take on Spiderman.

'Are you *drunk*?' Lissa asks in mock horror.

'Of course I'm not drunk. I have a meeting in...' I check my watch. 'Shit! My meeting is in like forty-five minutes. I need to get ready.' I go to hang up then add 'Love you' before I press the button to end the call. I hear her say 'Love you' back before I cut her off.

At seven twenty-nine I'm standing in the Atrium Bar, dressed in the L. K. Bennett dress and Louboutin heels, my long brown hair in a classically chic chignon, make-up understated but flawless. There is literally nothing Freya can criticise about my appearance.

At seven thirty-nine I'm still standing in the Atrium Bar and Freya hasn't turned up yet. I suppose it might take her a few minutes to get ready after scaling the outside of the hotel. I'm starting to wonder if that's what I really saw. I mean, it's just too ridiculous. I should have taken a video of it, even if just to prove to myself what actually happened.

At seven forty-nine I'm *still* standing in the Atrium Bar and I'm debating calling Freya to ask where the hell she is. We cannot be late to this meeting. Am I meant to just go alone and then make up an excuse for why she's late? What do I say? *Oh, sorry Freya is a little late this evening. I just watched her climbing up the side of the hotel using the lovely wrought iron balconies like a ladder. But I'm sure it was nothing and she'll be with us any moment.*

I'm being ridiculous. She's probably already there, probably came down to the bar at seven twenty-six, found I wasn't already waiting and went straight to the restaurant to prove a point.

At seven fifty-four I make the decision to go to the restaurant; it's only a few minutes' walk and so I'm perfectly on time. Freya isn't there. Enough is enough. *Where are you?* I text her from my work phone as I'm shown to the table. I watch the screen as it confirms the message was delivered and wait for the three little ellipses to show she's replying. They don't come.

I'm interrupted by the arrival of Nicolas and Julien, the Martin – Mar-*tan* – twins who were semi-famous models in the early 2000s and who now run C'est Magnifique. I introduce myself as Sam's replacement.

'No Freya?' Julien asks with a raised eyebrow.

'She's just running a few minutes late.'

'Is she sick?' Nicolas's voice drips with faux concern. 'She has not had an accident, no?'

'Oh no, no,' I say with conviction. But... what if she had? What if – when I was having a quick shower as I rushed to get ready so I wouldn't be late – she fell? What if she's lying in that alley, no one any the wiser about where she is? No. I'm being ridiculous, catastrophising, spinning a story out of nothing but fear and paranoia and some kind of morbid fascination with people dying in gruesome ways that has followed me since I was a child.

'Shall we begin without her?' Nicolas asks, as he raises a finger to signal to the waiter that he wishes to order.

'Of course,' I reply with a smile, despite the fact my insides have turned to jelly and my brain to mush. I guess I'm going to have to negotiate this deal on my own. It's only a ten million pound contract. Nothing to worry about. Apologies: I get snarky when I'm nervous.

I gulp the wine that appears at my elbow. I'm going to need it if I have any hope of making it through the next few hours.

I don't want to blow my own trumpet, but I do pretty well over dinner. The Martin twins and I hash out a slightly refined deal – one well within the parameters I know Freya would expect – over an extremely good chateaubriand, and then we have creme brûlée paired with a glass of sweet Sauternes for dessert. They insist on walking me back to the hotel, despite it being mere minutes away, before hailing down a passing taxi for themselves.

'It has been a pleasure, Miss Brooks,' Julien says as he kisses my cheeks three times in that bizarre way that is somehow both shockingly familiar and horrendously awkward at the same time. 'Please pass our regards to Freya. Such a shame she couldn't join us. I wanted to congratulate her in person for that phenomenal presentation she gave in Boston last month.'

Despite the height of the Louboutins, there's a spring in my step as I head into the hotel and I contemplate treating myself to a glass of champagne. And by treating myself I obviously mean that I will charge it to the room and make Serendipity – that's the company I work for in case I haven't already said – pick up the tab. There's a hum in the air as I cross the reception area, a crackle of something I can't quite put my finger on.

But then I walk into the atrium. Guess who's sitting at the bar? OK, I know that wasn't exactly difficult, of course it's Freya. Just sitting there as cool as ice, as if she didn't fail to turn up for the meeting and leave me to deal with everything by myself. My blood rises as I watch her casually sipping from the cocktail in front of her. I want to slap her, but I also want to tell her that I sealed the deal on my own. I want her to be proud of me. I'm such a fucking cliché.

'Are you OK?' I ask her, as I slip onto the stool next to her.

'Of course, Camille,' she says. 'Shouldn't I be?' She genuinely sounds like there is no reason for me to even ask that question.

'You didn't show up for the meeting.' It's not an accusation, I sound like an abandoned dog left at the shelter by the person who was meant to give him a forever home. *Eughh, what is wrong with me?*

'But I'm sure you got them to sign.'

'Yes. And I only had to give away another ten percent.' I wait for her to look impressed.

'You gave away *ten percent*?' She doesn't seem impressed. She seems... incredulous.

'Only ten, yes.' I can hear the uncertainty creeping into my voice.

'Oh, Millicent.' It's the use of my real name that sends a chill up the back of my neck. 'We'd already negotiated as low as would make commercial sense.'

'Shit.'

'Quite.' She takes a long slug of her drink and motions to the bartender for another. Then she takes a deep breath, letting it out slowly as she turns to look at me head on. 'I suppose it would be best if I tell the Board I was the one who negotiated the deal. I'll tell them it was a deliberate strategy to bring the Martin brothers on board to encourage partnerships with some other brands.'

'But—' I begin, but she cuts me off.

'It's done, Millicent. Let's not talk of it again.' Her voice is laced with disappointment.

I want to tell her that it is all her fault anyway. That she should have been there. That I was only brought into this deal a few hours ago. That there is no way it should be considered my fault. But instead I order a Chambord Martini and we sit in silence as we drink.

Half an hour ticks past, as I grow more and more angry that she fucked me over and then somehow made out like I was the one in the wrong. *Screw this!*

'Freya,' I start, 'where were you this evening?'

'I was with you, finalising a deal that *I* have the authority to negotiate, while you kept notes of the conversation. Notes that I'm expecting on my desk by close of play tomorrow. I suggest you spend the Eurostar journey home writing them up.' And then she slides off her stool, scoops up her bag and walks away from me. Leaving me sitting at the bar, my mouth hanging open in disbelief. That woman has some serious gall.

I wait five minutes to ensure she won't possibly still be waiting for a lift, and then make my way back to my room. There is still enough – very, almost unbearably – warm Prosecco left for another glass and I take it out onto the little balcony for a nightcap and a final cigarette. The alleyway is bathed in blue light; when I lean over the balustrade a little I can see a police car at the other end of the narrow space. Two men in black, the word POLICE emblazoned across the back of their jackets, are shining torches around the bins, searching for something. A German Shepherd in a police harness is with them, nose to the ground, tail swishing slowly from side to side as he works. Then suddenly he turns and looks directly at me, his eyes glowing red. He lets out a low growl and then returns to the job at snout.

What are they looking for? I slip back into my room and grab my phone. I didn't delete the photos I took of Freya earlier and I pull them up. Zooming in on one I notice something in Freya's hand. It looks like a pill bottle, one of those orange plastic ones with the white lid. In the next photo she's slipping it into the pocket of her leggings, causing an unsightly bulge on one hip. I flick back to the first picture, zooming in further to see if I can read what's written on the label. But there is no label.

What was in that bottle?

And what are the police searching for in the middle of the night in the exact same place I watched Freya climb up the side of the hotel?

3

Somehow I manage to sleep through the alarms I set on my phone
– or, more accurately, I switch them off in my sleep – but thankfully
I arranged for coffee to be delivered to the room at seven and the
room service waiter is extremely persistent in knocking on my door
until I drag myself out of bed.

'I hope your night wasn't too disturbed, Ms Brooks,' he says in
English but with a trace of an accent as he places the tray on a small
table by the door. He turns and must see the confusion on my face.
'With the ambulance and then the police outside.'

'Ambulance?'

'One of our guests...' he trails off and clears his throat. 'Such a
shame.'

'Are they OK?' But it's pretty obvious from the look on his face
that no, they are very much not OK. 'Who?'

But he shakes his head. 'I can't say any more,' and then he
thrusts the room service slip towards me for my signature.

As soon as the door closes behind him I reach for my laptop
and open Google. I type in the name of the hotel and hit the *News*
icon. Three hours ago, France 24 ran a story about the tragic death

of an American businessman and someone has helpfully already snipped the segment and posted it to YouTube. The newsreader is impossibly perky given this went out at 5 a.m., but her co-host is almost comatose. I'll try not to see it as an indictment of just how much harder women have to work to be considered equal to their male counterparts.

'At nine o'clock yesterday evening, a body was discovered in a suite at the Marriot Champs-Elysée. The man, who we can now confirm as Cody Gelber, CEO of InterBank LLC and a regular feature of society in both New York and Paris, is believed to have been alone in his room at the time of his death. Early reports indicate the drug fentanyl may have been involved, amid suggestions this was suicide.'

Fentanyl? I call Lissa, half expecting her not to answer but pleasantly surprised when she does.

'It's the middle of the night,' she tells me.

I go to make a snarky comment, but to be fair it is only 6 a.m. in London. 'Question. How easy is fentanyl to get hold of?'

'Err... do we need to have a chat about something?' Her voice is hard and I hear a slap in the background, followed by the rustling of bed sheets as she sits up. 'You do not, ever, mess with that shit.'

'Jeez, Lissa. I'm not trying to score, for fuck's sake. What the hell?'

'So why are you asking?'

'Just. Well, someone died in the hotel last night. The news is saying it was a fentanyl overdose.'

'I thought you were staying somewhere swish? Not some crack house. That said, it's actually pretty easy to get hold of if you have money and contacts.' There's a giggle in the background and then that sound of a slap again. 'Stop it,' I hear her whisper under her breath.

'Are you—'

There's another giggle, slightly louder this time.

'Lissa. Did you answer the phone while you're having sex?'

'Not like *sex* sex,' she says, innocent as pie. 'Just a little bit of fun.'

'You are a disgrace,' I tell her, but my tone is light, imbued with a touch of laughter. This isn't the first time she's answered the phone while she has company, just another thing I've got used to over the years.

I spend another half hour googling Cody Gelber, painting a picture of a man well known as a purveyor of capitalist hedonism: prone to excessive spending, excessive drinking, and excessive partying with a veritable harem of beautiful women. Wealthy, generous, and not that unattractive – especially if you like your men with the appearance of well-weathered leather – he was the kind of man who was invited to all of the most prestigious events. But under that artificially whitened smile is a hint of something else, something wrong, something wicked. I can sense it in his eyes, in the way the photos show him resting his hand on the base of whichever woman he is entertaining's spine. This man is a predator.

Now, I know mental health is a silent killer, that you cannot possibly look at someone and have any idea of the demons they battle. Trust me when I say I have more experience of this than anyone should have; I was only six when my father succumbed to his darkness. But Cody Gelber doesn't seem like the kind of man who would barricade himself in his hotel suite and take a huge dose of fentanyl. If he'd been found with a bevy of women, dead from an accidental overdose of MDMA or some other chemsex drug, that would have tracked. But this whole situation doesn't seem to make sense.

On the drive to Gare du Nord, Freya barely speaks to me, her eyes hidden behind a pair of grossly oversized sunglasses like an ice-blonde Audrey Hepburn. But as soon as we're seated on the Eurostar she takes them off, folding them carefully and placing them next to her MacBook.

'Did you write up those notes from the meeting?' she asks, with a hint of exasperation, as if she's pre-empting me saying I haven't.

Of course I haven't. It's nine in the morning – I'm not a stickler about these things by any stretch, but my contract does actually say my hours are nine to five-thirty – and the meeting was last night, for fuck's sake. But I swallow my irritation. 'I was going to use the train journey.' Which was actually *her* suggestion in the bar last night.

'Right. Well, I suggest you get cracking then.' She pauses for a few moments. If it was anyone else I'd assume they were silently debating if they should say something more, but given this is Freya, it's far more likely the pause is purely for dramatic effect. 'I'm doing you a favour here, Camille. You understand what the Board's position would be if they knew you'd given away such a huge margin, don't you?'

I swallow. I would be fired. Summarily, no chance to tell my side of the story. And then everything I've been working toward for so many years would be lost, disappearing in a puff of iniquitous smoke. 'Thank you, Freya,' I say and open my laptop to write the absolute bullshit she wants me to spread.

I'm about halfway through this farce when my phone beeps with a message. I glance up at Freya, but she has headphones in, eyes half closed and her head resting against the back of the seat. I wonder for a moment what she's listening to. But at least she has no idea I'm receiving random messages from Lissa.

The WhatsApp message isn't from Lissa. I don't recognise the number, the profile picture a plain black circle. I debate deleting it, it's probably spam. Or something dodgy. To be fair, the most likely scenario is it's some guy's dick. But curiosity gets the better of me.

An image opens on my screen, a plain blank sheet of paper with a sentence written on it in thick black block capital lettering:

RUBEN CHAMBERS AND NOW CODY GELBER. CONNECT THE DOTS...

What the hell? I open a browser and type Ruben Chambers into Google. In November last year, Ruben Chambers was found dead in his Milan apartment overlooking the Parco Alessandrina Ravizza. He was a Professor of Economics at Bocconi University, beloved by his students and fellow faculty members who described him as 'the best in the business' and who expressed their distress in the days following his death.

I check the message again, or at least I try to. It has disappeared, vanished into the ether. I remember Lissa showing me how to send self-destructing picture messages on WhatsApp; it's actually super easy, you just tap the little icon with a 1 in it. I'm sure it said 'connect the dots'. Suggesting there is something linking this Ruben Chambers and Cody Gelber. But Ruben's death was absolutely a murder.

He'd been found on his knees, a single bullet through his brain. An execution, the press had called it. I scroll through a few more articles, each of them confirming the details. The gun was most likely a Beretta 92FS, the standard issue pistol for the Italian military. It was unclear if it had been fitted with a silencer, but given the lack of reports from his neighbours it was considered highly likely. The gunman left no prints, no DNA, no clue as to their identity. They were never found. Although the file remains open, the working hypothesis is that it was a professional job. No leads. The trail cold.

But if it was a professional job, then why was Ruben a target? Everything I read about the case suggests he was simply a mild mannered and well-respected professor who devoted his life to teaching economics. I mean, sure it might not be the world's most exciting job, but it shouldn't be the kind of career that would get you killed.

Perhaps it was something in his private life. Something that connected him to Cody. Did they move in the same circles?

I sigh and crack my knuckles – yes, a terrible habit but it helps me think. What has any of this got to do with me? I click on yet another article, this one from the day the story first broke. The 24 November 2022. Something snags in my brain; I remember that date.

I search my work emails. And there it is. On 24 November last year, Freya and Sam were in Milan for the Making Cosmetics trade show. Freya was the keynote speaker and I'd been helping ensure all went to plan from London, making sure everything was perfect with her outfit and the transport and checking the venue had the right version of the slides for her presentation.

The date should be seared onto my memory as it was an absolute shit-show. The car failed to turn up to take Freya and Sam to the Milano Convention Centre – apparently known as MiCo, which made the whole thing more infuriating as I didn't understand all the abbreviations – and then the taxi they flagged down took them on a convoluted route that ended up with them stuck in a huge traffic jam. And then the venue didn't have any oat milk for Freya's latte and she lost her shit at the poor barista who was trying to help her.

It had got worse as the day progressed and afternoon turned to evening. The restaurant couldn't find their reservation and I had to try to find an alternative at stupidly short notice, which was almost impossible as the city was so busy. I was meant to meet Reggie's parents that night, he had this whole thing planned with dinner and drinks at Clos Maggiore – yep, only one of the fanciest places in

London – but I was two hours late and they'd already finished eating when I arrived.

'It's fine,' he'd said. But the pout told me it wasn't.

'I'm sorry,' I told him. 'You know what Freya's like.'

'It isn't worth it, you know.' But that was where he was wrong. Of course it's worth it. I will put up with anything, do anything, go anywhere for this job. I will bitch and moan and scream in frustration, yes. But I'll do it. Nothing matters except clawing my way up the hierarchy at Serendipity and making it to the Los Angeles headquarters.

I banish Reggie from my thoughts and sit back in my seat as the importance of the date sinks in.

On 24 November 2022, Freya was in Milan on the same day a man was murdered.

On 3 May 2023, Freya was in Paris on the same day a man apparently committed suicide.

I raise my eyes and watch her over the rim of my laptop.

Surely it's nothing more than a coincidence.

4

Freya opens one eye and stares at me. I quickly avert my gaze. Shit!

'Was there something you wanted to say?' she asks, a gentle sigh tinging her voice as if she's utterly exasperated by me but trying not to show it.

'Err... No... Of course not,' I stammer, cursing myself for being such a blithering idiot.

'Do I have something on my face?' She arches a single eyebrow in the way I have never been able to.

'No. I...'

'Have you finished writing the minutes of the meeting?' She puts out a hand and makes a flapping motion.

I've been so busy googling Ruben I haven't made any more progress. 'Um. Almost,' I say, praying she doesn't ask to see what I've done.

She huffs and shakes her head. Just slightly. Just enough for the sense of her disappointment to course through me and turn my cheeks pink. 'Please don't make me regret allowing you to take on some of Sam's responsibilities,' she says, her words slow and careful.

I won't, I've got this. But I don't say it out loud.

I need this job. I don't say that out loud either. *Whatever it takes.*

'Just get it done.' Her tone is bored, dismissive.

I turn my attention back to my laptop and the meeting notes. In this moment I hate her. Loathe the way she treats me. Despise the tone she uses when she talks to me. I sneak a look at her, at her perfect white blond hair and thousand pound suit and demeanour of absolute fucking grandeur. I hate her and I admire her and there are times when I want to be exactly like her and then I hate myself even more than I could ever hate her.

Cody Gelber keeps nagging at me. Who was this man really? And why did he choose to kill himself in a hotel room? That isn't normal, surely? How many people commit suicide in a place they know some poor chambermaid will find them? Actually, that probably isn't fair, I doubt the thought of who will find your body is exactly a priority when you're staring down the barrel of your own existence.

Although I'm meant to be finishing the made-up minutes of the meeting, I can't help myself from bringing up Google. Cody Gelber had everything going for him. Or at least that was the way it seemed. Which makes me wonder if it really was suicide.

'You know I can tell you're not working on those minutes?' Her sharp tone cuts through me and I instinctively click out of Google.

I stare at Freya over the top of my screen. Is she tracking my laptop? Looking at everything I've been looking at? Can she see what I'm searching? My heart pounds in my chest and I can feel a cool film of sweat building on my lower back. Or is she just seeing the guilt stamped all over my face?

'Are you going to share?' she asks, clipping the words. 'Whatever it is must be very interesting if it's dragging you away from the work I have expressly requested?'

I feel like a chastised school child, asked to read the note I've been passing between my friends. Not that I was that kind of naughty in school. Or that popular. Sorry, it's a bad analogy. But *you* probably were popular enough to have secret notes in class so let's just say it was like that and move on.

'Just please do the work you're paid to do,' Freya says, bored with the conversation already.

It's also a complete lie because – exactly as I expected – I've not been offered a new title or the commensurate pay rise associated with the increased workload I'm taking on. Lissa is going to go ape shit when I tell her.

When we get back to the office I'm thrown into meeting after meeting, taking so many notes my hand begins to cramp and curl into a claw. I have no time to continue my internet stalking of Cody Gelber or Ruben Chambers, even as my brain sits and stews on the puzzle.

By the time 6 p.m. comes round I'm exhausted, ready to get home, order some kind of greasy takeaway and sink a bottle of wine. I change into my trainers, feet screaming in relief as I release them from the stupid heels I've had them crammed into all day. When did someone decide that women should wear high heels? And when did someone decide they were the most appropriate choice for corporate women? I bet it was a man. Although it could have been a woman who hates other women: it's not like the business world isn't littered with them. The whole 'I had to suffer to get where I am, so you must suffer too' thing really gets to me. All that girl power my generation was promised and it all turned out to be a fucking lie. A fallacy as other women smashed the glass ceiling and immediately boarded it up again to ensure no one could follow.

Lissa and I live in Clapham, just off the Common in a little flat we can barely afford. And only because the landlord gave us a huge discount when we offered to do all the home improvements it needed in exchange for reducing the rent. It was a total mess and we spent almost three years working every weekend to make it into a home and now it's perfect, big enough for the two of us and not too far from the station.

The tube is rammed. As usual. I turn my head to avoid my nose ending up in some man's armpit as the crowds push onto the train and force us into even closer proximity. There's a guy to my right who reaches around me to grab hold of the hand rail, his hand grazing my bum for a moment. I whip my head round to stare at him, but he's looking away, seemingly oblivious to his infraction.

But no. There it is. His hand is no longer on the rail. I try to move forward out of the way, but there's nowhere for me to go. The weight of it increases, fingers twitching slightly as he grows in confidence. I turn suddenly, ignoring the fact that I knock another passenger off balance. The hand clamps hard onto my buttock and squeezes forcefully.

Do you know what? I am done with this shit today. 'Get your hand off me, right now,' I demand, raising my voice over the hubbub of the carriage.

He turns to face me. 'Sorry, love? What was that?' He smirks and I want to punch him.

I raise my voice even higher. 'Get your fucking hand off me.'

'Which hand?' he says with faux innocence as he squeezes again, this time hard enough I think he might leave a bruise.

The tube comes to a stop and he squeezes again before pushing his way through the crowds to exit the carriage, leaving me standing there fuming. The absolute audacity of him. I stand with my mouth half open as another wave of people pushes on board. No one else bats an eyelid at the fact I just got groped in public in the middle of rush hour.

'Did you see him?' I ask the woman next to me.

'Who?' she replies with an almost imperceptible shrug.

'That guy. He was standing here before?'

'Sorry.' She shrugs more obviously this time.

I'm about to say something else – because how is it possible that some guy can grope me on the tube and walk away as if he did nothing? – when I spot her. Sam. As in the Sam who used to do my job. The Sam who apparently got fired for reasons I have no idea about. Just standing in the next carriage, dressed in baggy jeans and the same vintage TLC T-shirt Lissa has been coveting for years, a pair of chunky headphones around her neck.

I stare at her but she's not looking at me. I need to talk to her, ask her what the hell happened, make sure she's OK. Actually, that last bit is a tiny lie. She hated the job and complained constantly so no doubt she's absolutely fine about the situation. No, I need to know what she did to get herself fired so I can make sure I don't repeat her mistakes.

At the next station I push my way off the train and hop into her carriage. But she's not there. As the train moves away again, I see her walking down the platform of Stockwell station, head down, not looking at me. Does she live round here? Perhaps I can find her address in the Serendipity files and go visit her, ask the questions I need to ask?

As soon as I'm off the tube, my phone beeps with a stream of messages. It's Lissa.

> Drinks

> Meet me in Be At One

> Now

> Or at least as soon as your tube gets in

> Love you

I groan a little as I read the messages. I just want to go home and have a shower and put on my pyjamas.

It will do you good

Lissa messages. I sigh. She's probably right. Alcohol and company versus takeaway and lonely sadness.

Stop debating and start walking to Be At One

I laugh a little – out loud so a few people turn to look at me like I'm a lunatic, which is nice – and start walking to meet her.

* * *

'I'm assuming you're paying for the drinks, little miss moneybags,' Lissa says with a grin as she picks up the cocktail menu and starts flicking through it.

'Errr...' I start, my face twisting into a grimace.

'Oh hell no.' She puts the menu back down and stares straight at me. 'Do not tell me you didn't secure a pay rise for this new job?'

'Well... I... It's just...' I peter out.

'Did you even *try* to negotiate?' Her stare hardens.

'I...' But I can't lie to her about this.

'For fuck's sake, Millie!' She picks up the cocktail menu purely so she can throw it down again. 'What the fuck?' She picks it up a second time and slams it down even more forcefully. 'You're letting her walk all over you!'

'It's complicated,' I say, but my voice sounds thin in my ears. I'm not even convincing myself at this point and I feel my shame and self-loathing begin to crystallise.

'Complicated? Jesus Christ! How the actual fuck is it complicated to ask for more money to take on more work? It's like...' she waves her hand angrily as she gropes for the word. 'It's like you're a fucking masochist. Like you enjoy that bitch walking over you.'

'It's not like that. I need this job, remember? *We* need this job.'

She looks a little contrite at that last bit.

'And yes,' I continue, 'she might be taking the piss a little bit—'

Lissa snorts loudly. 'A bit?'

'OK. A lot. But it's about the long game. You know that as well as I do.'

'Do you really think this will help you get to LA?' Lissa drops her voice slightly, her anger and disappointment in me dissipating and being replaced with hope.

I nod. 'This new position gets me in front of people, gets me seen. Noticed.' I raise my eyebrows. All that matters is that I eventually get offered a role at the Serendipity headquarters in Los Angeles. I think that's why there's a part of me – probably too big a part if we're honest – that wants to be like Freya. Women like her – ruthless egotists with zero compassion – get the promotions. Playing nice doesn't work in the corporate world, we all know that.

'Promise you're not just being shafted?'

I nod.

'Promise she's not going to use you and then fire you and you'll end up even further away than ever before?' Lissa sounds like a concerned parent. Or at least how I would imagine a concerned parent to sound, how they sound in the movies being my only basis to work from.

'I promise. I just need to ride it out, not rock the boat.'

This time it's Lissa's turn to nod. So much of our communications remain unspoken, as if we're twins instead of best friends. I guess that's what comes from living with someone for so long.

'Right then,' Lissa says definitively, signalling an end to this train of conversation. 'I guess I will pay for the drinks and then you can tell me all about your boss scaling up the side of the building.'

'It was nothing,' I tell her quickly. I don't want her to worry, that's my role in our relationship.

'By which you mean it was absolutely something but you think I'll only disapprove even more about this current job situation?' She says it with a hint of dry humour as she raises a hand to motion to the bartender, flicking her black hair over her shoulders and pasting a flirtatious smile on her face to ensure she gets his full attention.

I don't say anything as I pick up the cocktail list to choose something suitably strong. I can't tell Lissa my suspicions about Freya. I can't tell her what I suspect about the man who died in my hotel last night. Or that Freya was in Milan the night another man was killed. Lissa doesn't need that kind of stress, I don't want her to spiral again. And besides, it's probably nothing. I mean, it isn't like Freya killed them both. That would be ridiculous. Ridiculous and stupid and so ludicrous it doesn't bear thinking about.

So why is it the *only* thing I can think about?

5

Lissa insists on more cocktails and I distract myself from thinking about Freya by telling her about the gropey man on the tube.

'Eughh. Creep!' She's incensed. 'I am so sick of this crap!'

I nod. 'Me too.'

'Did you kick him in the balls?' she asks with a glint in her eye.

'No. The train was too packed for me to get enough space for a decent leg swing.' I say it without even a hint of sarcasm.

'So you punched him instead?'

I roll my eyes at her. We both know what I did. Or rather what I didn't do. Because you don't, do you? You move away, if you can, and if you can't you might say something, like I did today. But it's not like anything happened to him as a result. He walked away as if he'd done nothing at all.

Lissa reaches out and squeezes my hand, her eyes telling me she understands exactly what happened, exactly why I did what I did, that none of it was my fault, that I'm brilliant and strong and no one can break me. 'One day...' she says eventually, 'one day I will kick one so hard his balls disappear back inside him where they fucking belong.' There is so much venom, so much pure and unbridled anger in her voice it sends a shiver up my spine. 'One day.' This last part takes on a dream-like quality, as if she's playing a movie in her mind and finding the whole scene really rather satisfying. Then she pats my hand a few times and straightens her shoulders. 'Shots!' she exclaims playfully, as if she hasn't just been saying she would cause serious bodily harm to someone.

This is one of the – many – reasons I love Lissa. She can go from sad and mournful, to full on vigilante, to warrior queen, to party girl in the space of just a few minutes. She's a whirlwind you cannot contain and any time spent in her presence is full of unexpected surprises. And fun. Normally far too much fun, and certainly far more than the situation demands.

I, on the other hand, am prone to overthinking everything. And being eminently sensible. 'I have to work tomorrow,' I reply with a wince, knowing Lissa isn't going to accept this as an excuse.

'Boring!' she exclaims, so loudly a group of guys at the next table swivel their heads in unison to stare at her. 'Besides...' she begins – now, Lissa doesn't wear glasses, but if she did she would have pulled them down her nose slightly to peer at me over the top – 'can you even call it work if they don't pay you?'

'Ha ha.'

She giggles and sticks her tongue out a little. 'Oh, come on! Just one little shot of something. Pretty please? For me?' She gives me the puppy dog eyes and as usual I capitulate.

'Just one.'

'Of course.' But there's a mirror behind her stool and I can see she's crossed her fingers behind her back.

She knows I can't resist indulging her and I know she manipulates me. But I can't help myself, especially after everything that happened. I just think she deserves to be happy. And right now she's on a high, one I couldn't forgive myself for pulling her down from.

The bar is running a special offer on something called a Raspberry Kamikaze: a shooter made from vodka, raspberry liqueur, and lime. It's surprisingly delicious, sweet and sour and with exactly the right level of kick. Four shots later and I feel like my limbs are moving through water. It's not an unpleasant sensation, especially after the tension of the last thirty-six hours.

'Oooh!' Lissa suddenly exclaims. 'I didn't tell you about my hot date.'

'Do you have to give me all the details?' I ask, pulling a face.

'You're such a prude! How are we friends?'

'I'm not a prude.' But I'm protesting too much, because I am, in fact, a prude. But maybe that's just because Lissa took all the non-prudiness – which isn't a word, but I don't know what the right antonym would be – for both of us.

'We fucked on the stairs,' she tells me with a salacious wiggle of her eyebrows.

'We live in a flat,' I say, trying not to form a mental image.

'We have stairs.'

'Err... no. There are *communal* stairs that lead up to the flat.'

'Same thing.' She shrugs and takes a swig of one of the beers she ordered last time she got us a round of Raspberry Kamikazes.

'But anyone could have seen you.' I try not to sound shocked, but fail. I mean, I *know* what she's like, but I still struggle with the idea that anyone would want to risk someone like Mrs Peterson from the next-door flat stumbling across them in such a compromising position. But don't think I'm judging her, because I'm not, not really anyway. It's not that I have some kind of fundamental disapproval, it's that I can't understand why you'd want to.

Her eyes twinkle as she leans forward slightly. 'That was kind of the point,' she whispers with a grin.

I shake my head in mock disgust.

'You wouldn't love me any other way,' she tells me. She's right.

She's been my best friend for so long I have no idea who I'd be without her in my life. 'So,' she says and puts down her beer, 'do you want me to tell you all the details, a blow by blow – if you pardon the pun – of exactly what happened, or are you going to tell me what's eating you up instead?'

'I'm fine,' I say, a little too quickly and the look on her face tells me I've made a fatal error.

'Well, in that case.' She sits back in her seat and cracks her knuckles. 'His name is Tom, or Tim, or John... hmmm... something short anyway. And he's something boring in the city, like an accountant or an actuary or something. Anyway, he's fit. A bit over six foot and was one hundred percent on the rugby team at university; he has that V-shape thing with the broad shoulders and the tiny waist and the arse like an absolute peach. We met in Disrepute, you know the adorable place in Soho, and I immediately knew we were going to fuck. Like rabbits. Just over and over and over again. So, the first time was the stairs. And then we went into the flat and fooled around on the sofa for a bit. I mean, just wow, what that man can do with his tong—'

'Alright!' I can't take it any more. 'Please *please* stop!'

Lissa collapses into a fit of giggles. When she finally composes herself she picks up her beer, shakes it slightly, and then motions to the bartender for another. She looks at me and I nod. She raises two fingers at the bar man. 'Right then. Spill. What's really going on with you?'

'Nothing.'

'Don't do that, Miss Brooks.' She looks directly at me. 'You forget that I know you almost as well as you know yourself. Something's on your mind and you know how I feel about secrets.'

'Honestly, Lissa,' I tell her. 'It's nothing.'

'Well, in that case I'll go back to my story about hot boring Tom. Or maybe it was Paul... Anyway, we were in the show—'

She's interrupted by the bartender placing our drinks on the table, and I take the opportunity to try to compose my thoughts, to corral them into some kind of order. I'm trying to find the right place to even start, the right words. But in the end I get out my phone and bring up the news from this morning and the body found in my hotel.

'Um. Who's Cody Gelber?' she asks. But what she really wants to know is why I'm showing her this story.

'The guy who was found dead in my hotel last night.'

'Right, the fentanyl guy.' She carries on reading the article. 'Suicide?'

'Apparently.'

'You didn't... you know?' She gives me a look as if I might not have realised she was asking if I slept with him.

'Of course not! I was at a meeting and then Freya and I had a drink in the bar and then I went to bed. Alone.' I add the last word and give it extra emphasis.

'So...'

'Freya didn't make the meeting and, by the time I met her for that drink, Cody Gelber was dead.'

Lissa looks at me, confusion etched into her face. 'I don't get it.'

I take my phone back from her. 'I got sent a message. One of those disappearing ones. You know, a picture that you can only see once before it's gone.'

'A picture of...' she looks horrified.

'Oh no, no. Not of *him*.' We both pull the exact same face at the idea of someone sending pictures of a dead body. 'No, it was a message written on a piece of paper.'

'Oh, phew! Who sent it?'

'That's the thing. I don't know. It wasn't a number saved in my phone. There was no name on the WhatsApp profile. It could've been anyone.'

'And? Jesus, Millie, what did it say?'

'Sorry. The message told me to connect the dots between Cody and someone else.'

'Who?'

I tap my screen a few times. 'Him,' I say and slide the phone back to her.

'Ruben Chambers?'

'He was murdered. In Milan. On 24 November last year. Freya was at this trade show that same day. It was the same day I was meant to meet Reggie's parents for the first time.'

'The one you were hours late to and he was a total prick about it. Fucking Reggie.' Lissa had never liked him and had made no apologies for her honesty in the matter. She hands my phone back to me. 'I don't get it.'

'The trade show Freya was at, was in Milan. She was there, in the same city, when Ruben died. And she was there, in the same hotel, when Cody died.'

'But Cody was suicide.'

'They think that because the door to his suite was locked from the inside.'

The realisation dawns across her face. 'Ohhh. Ohhh. Your boss was climbing up the balconies. She could have... Holy fuck!'

'Yep.'

'So you think Freya killed these men?'

'I don't know what to think.'

'Jesus shitting Christ, Mills. Your boss is a fucking serial killer.' Her blue eyes flash in the lights of the bar, her mouth open in a near perfect 'O'.

* * *

The next morning, Lissa wakes me up just before six thirty with a mug of coffee. 'I've been thinking about your boss issue,' she says, sitting on the edge of my bed. Somehow, despite us not getting home until after midnight, she looks radiant, fresh faced like she's had nine hours' sleep, a yoga session, and a green juice.

'Liss,' I groan, trying to bury myself further under the duvet. 'My alarm hasn't even gone off yet.'

She sighs and stares at my phone for a moment. Suddenly it bursts into life with a chorus of chirping birds. 'There you are.' She sounds smug, like she's been waiting to get the timing perfect. 'Now, listen to me.' She waves at the coffee as I struggle to pull myself into a sitting position. 'So, Freya was there when those two guys got killed right?'

'Right.'

'But that's only two.'

'What?' I'm still half asleep and I have no idea where she's going with this.

'That's only two. And you need to kill three people to be classed as a serial killer. So...'

'So?'

'So what if there are more than two?'

'What? You mean... what if she really is a serial killer? Like a proper one?' There's a hint of disbelief in my voice. I mean, maybe after a few shots it might have seemed like there really was a link between Cody and Ruben, but that was just the Raspberry Kamikaze talking. And earlier in the day my paranoia. Tiredness. Anger that Freya fucked me over with the C'est Magnifique account. I've been under a lot of stress the last few days.

'Exactly. What if she's been leaving a trail of dead bodies everywhere she goes?' Lissa takes a sip of her own coffee. 'Someone is sending you messages. What if *that* is what they're trying to tell you?'

6

I try to put Lissa's theories to the back of my mind as I arrive at the office, an ibuprofen masking my hangover, and start jotting down a list of all the things I need to get done today. The list is fucking ridiculous, almost two pages long, just task after task after task and some of the things I don't even know where to start with. Last week I was in control, quietly competent as I powered through my work, not quite slaying it, but not too far off. Now I'm adding Sam's stuff as well, I'm starting to realise I don't have a clue. I need to speak to her, and not just to find out all the gossip over why she left. I need to ask her how she managed to do everything, ask her what some of the abbreviations and acronyms mean on her files.

I send her a few messages over the course of the morning, but none of them even deliver. WhatsApp shows me nothing but a single grey tick so I know it's sent.

At 1 p.m., Freya stalks out of her office. 'Get me a salmon poke bowl,' she barks at me before turning on her heels and returning to her desk. She could have picked up the phone, but she must get a kick out of making me jump as she shouts across the office.

I sigh and pick up my bag. At least I can have a sneaky cigarette on my way to the little staff canteen, which serves an unusual array of lunch options. I take the lift down to the basement level, where deliveries are made and where the few remaining of us smokers gather when it's raining. I can hear the water on the roads as cars zip passed on the streets outside.

'Millicent,' one of the other smokers says with a subtle nod of his head as he sees me.

'Kieran,' I reply and repeat the head nod. Kieran works in HR and was the very first person I bumped into when I started at Serendipity. And when I say 'bumped into', yes, I am meaning literally. As in, I walked straight into him, almost knocking him over and causing the pile of papers he was carrying to go flying. I'm sure it looked almost comical to an outsider, but I was mortified. Even more so when he kept turning up during those first few weeks. He was even the one who led Orientation. Which was just a fancy word for the day-long corporate bullshit-fest everyone is subjected to in order to learn the vision and the mission statement and all that other crap about the company. You might have guessed that I didn't exactly buy into the whole spiel, even if Kieran looked especially earnest while delivering the materials.

Now Kieran sidles up to me, looking around as if to check no one is listening to what he's about to say. 'Are you OK?' he asks quietly and a blush blooms across his face.

'Of course.' Even though it's a blatant lie: I'm tired and stressed and this morning's To Do list has grown arms and legs and I have no idea what I'm doing or how I can ever hope to fit everything in. Plus the ibuprofen has worn off. Not to mention – well, you know – there is the small matter of my potentially psychopathic boss.

'Is there... ummm...' he runs his hand through his hair, the sun glinting off the copper tones so it almost looks as if he's wearing a crown. He clears his throat and continues. 'Well... is there any...?' he trails off and shifts his weight to his other foot.

Please don't say it. Please don't ask if there is any chance I want to go for coffee or lunch. It's not that he's *un*attractive, but now is most certainly not the time and turning him down would be super awkward. And I'd never be able to borrow a cigarette again. I wait for him to pick the sentence back up.

'I'm not going to ask you out,' he says.

'What?'

'That's what you were thinking.' He smiles ruefully.

'I wasn't.' But my protestation sounds too loud and we both hear it. 'Sorry,' I say, at a normal volume this time.

'I was only going to ask if there's anything I can help with. In an entirely professional context, of course. I work in HR, remember. I might be able to help escalate getting a new analyst hired for your team.'

'You can do that?'

'It's my job.' He shrugs.

'Thank you. That would be brilliant.' I mean it, he's offering me an absolute lifeline.

'And congratulations. On the promotion.'

I make a face.

'No promotion?' he asks, sounding unsure. 'I thought you were taking over Sam's role?'

'I've taken over her workload.'

'Oh,' he says and grimaces. He understands exactly what is going on, of course he does. 'But it's not been made official?'

I shake my head.

'Look, Millie. I can't promise anything, but let me see if there's anything I can do, OK?'

'Thank you. That would be amazing!' I want to hug him. But of course I don't. I don't want him to get the wrong idea.

He grins. Hmmm. You know I said he wasn't *unattractive*? Perhaps I was being a little too harsh. Not that it matters though, I guess.

We both grind our cigarette butts out and move back towards the door. 'You and Sam were friends, right?' he asks as he reaches for the handle.

'I thought so.' There's a sadness in my tone.

He drops his hand and turns to face me, head slightly cocked. His eyes tell me to elaborate.

'It's just she's not returning my messages.'

'You're worried?'

I nod. Yes, I *am* worried. Why did she just quit like that? What if...?

'Perhaps you should visit her? Make sure she's OK?'

'I... I don't have her address.' I wince as I say it. I mean, can I even classify her as a friend if I don't know where she lives?

'Look. I probably shouldn't... you know, data protection and all that...' he trails off.

'You have her address?'

'Sometimes it's handy to have a friend in HR,' he says simply.

'I don't want you to get into trouble.'

He glances around as if checking for eavesdroppers, then leans in conspiratorially. 'I'm a rebel at heart.'

* * *

Later that afternoon, I'm trying to wrangle the minutes of yet another meeting into some semblance of shape when a shadow looms in front of my desk.

'I have a 3 p.m. with Freya,' Kieran says with a grimace.

'You do?' I ask and pull up her calendar. 'You do,' I confirm. 'Is that about—?'

'I need her to sign off on recruiting a new analyst.' He grimaces again. 'And ask her to make your role official.'

'Thank you. Although you don't seem particularly enthusiastic about the meeting,' I say with a smile.

'I didn't think I'd actually have to talk to her face-to-face.' He sounds horrified. And terrified. 'I thought all this stuff would be done on email like it usually is.'

'I guess I'm going to have to treat you to coffee to say thank you,' I say with a playful edge. *Where did that come from?*

'And cake,' he says. 'Oh, and...' he hands me a bright orange Post-it note. 'Sam's address,' he adds.

'Thank you.' I take it from him and slip it into my handbag. Our eyes meet.

'I don't have all day.' Freya's voice breaks the moment.

'Good luck,' I whisper to Kieran.

'I think I'm going to need it.'

* * *

According to the address Kieran gave me, Sam lives in Fulham. In a block of entirely nondescript flats on an ordinary looking road lined with chicken shops, pizza places, and an off-licence with a window display of lurid coloured liquors and imported beers in a rainbow of fancy cans.

I ring the buzzer for 15H and wait. No one answers. I ring again. There are no names listed against each buzzer – I mean, this is London after all – so I check the Post-it again. It's definitely flat 15H, Kieran's handwriting is very neat, no chance I'm misreading it. I try a third time.

'For fuck's sake!' A man's voice shouts through the intercom. 'Who the fuck are you and why the fuck do you keep ringing my buzzer? If you're some little shit who's forgotten their keys, you can fuck off.'

'Um. Sorry,' I say into the intercom, wincing a little at how oddly posh my voice goes when I'm put on the spot. 'I'm looking for Sam?'

'I'm not Sam.'

'No. Sam Mulligan?'

'I'm not Sam.' He repeats it more forcefully this time.

'No, I understand that. She's a friend of mine. This is her address. Flat 15H?'

'I'm not Sam,' he says it a third time.

'Yep, understood. But is there a Samantha Mulligan who lives with you?' I try to keep the exasperation from my voice but don't manage to.

'Nope. And just like I told the other one... fuck off.'

I turn away from the intercom, shoulders slumping forwards. It's getting dark and the wind picks up suddenly, blowing cold air in my face and sending a shiver down my spine.

Loud chatter in the street catches my attention. A group of youngish lads – late teenagers probably – dressed in tracksuits and sparkling white trainers round the corner. They have that unique swagger of a pack of boys who think they're men, who think respect is a weakness, and that fear and intimation makes them 'madlads'. I duck into the porch area a little further so they won't see me.

But they climb the steps towards the door. I'm trapped. Nowhere to go, nowhere to run. I try not to look directly at them, face down, hair hanging forward to cover my features.

'You alright there?' one of them asks me.

'Yes, thanks, fine,' I say quickly, desperate to run, to get away from them as fast as possible.

'Sure?' He takes a few steps towards me.

'Ahum,' I reply, willing him to leave me alone.

'You need to get in the building?' One of the others has opened the door with his key card and the rest of the group file inside.

'I was just looking for a friend, that's all,' I say, the words tumbling fast from my mouth. 'But apparently I have the wrong address or the wrong flat number because there is a really grumpy guy on the intercom and—'

'Flat 15H?' he asks. 'Miserable fuckwad. Only moved in yesterday and he's already threatened to call the cops on my little bro.'

'Er. Yes.'

'So, you're looking for Sam?'

'You know her?' I sound surprised. Well, I am surprised. Sam was all Grey Goose trainers and Sisley skincare. I doubt she was hanging around with guys like this.

'She was helping me with my Maths coursework. I'm doing A-level and it's hard. Gonna be tricky getting the grades now she's gone.'

'Gone?'

'Knocked on my door late on Tuesday to say she was moving. Sudden. Weird. I think she might have got herself in a little bit of trouble, you know.'

'What kind of trouble?'

'I couldn't say.' He shrugs. 'She never had a boyfriend, or girl-friend, or nothing. Not as far as we knew anyway and we know everything that happens round here.'

'Do you know where she went?'

'She said something about going home.' He shrugs. He seems to shrug a lot, as if the world doesn't really matter to him. I feel bad for judging him so harshly just a few minutes ago. 'I dunno. It sounded off.'

'Home?'

'Well, she's not from round here is she?'

Isn't she? I'm starting to realise I know nothing about her. How can I possibly have worked with someone for almost two years and know nothing about them. 'Do you know where home is?'

'Birmingham.' He says it like I'm dumb.

'She didn't have an accent.'

'Your boss-bitch told her to fix it.'

'Ouch.' That sounds exactly like the kind of shit Freya would do.

'Yeah. Look, if you find her, can you tell her thanks? For everything she did for me. I didn't say it the other night. I was mad at her leaving. Told her she was giving up on me. I regret it.'

'I'll absolutely tell her if I find her,' I promise. 'Did she say anything else? About where she was going? Anything at all you think might help?'

'Just home. Which I guess is Birmingham. Erdington. I've got a cousin who lives there so I remember. Opposite the massive cemetery.'

'Your cousin or Sam?'

'Sam. Why do you care where my cousin lives?'

'Thank you,' I say and turn to leave.

'Promise you'll thank her for me,' he calls to me as I walk down the steps.

'Of course.'

But I don't add the last bit. *If I find her.* Because I have a gnawing sensation deep in my gut – and my gut is almost never wrong when it makes itself this clear – that I'm not going to find Sam. Something has happened. I can feel it in the air around me, in the cool breeze blowing yesterday's newspapers down the street, in the flickering of a lightbulb as I walk back toward the tube station.

I spend the rest of the evening playing dumb games on my phone in an effort to keep my brain occupied and avoid thinking about everything that's been happening. I make it through to 10 p.m. and decide to head to bed. Tomorrow's another day and perhaps I'll wake up in the morning and everything will miraculously make sense.

But just as I'm cleaning my teeth, my phone beeps with a WhatsApp message. It's the same number as before, the same plain black circle in place of a profile picture. I open it to find another photo: black words scrawled on a piece of paper in thick pen. A photo that disappears as soon as I've seen it.

THERE HAVE BEEN AT LEAST FIVE...

7

'There have been at least five?' Lissa asks as she makes us coffee the next morning.

'That's all it said,' I reply. 'But five what?'

'You're kidding?' she asks, handing me a mug of something very dark and with the consistency of sludge. She has this habit of making me coffee "a la French" as she calls it. She went on two dates with this guy who said that was how 'real French' people drank it. Even though he was from Norwich.

'You think it's... oh!' I suddenly realise. Forgive me, I'm a little tired still this morning, OK?

'Yep. Five victims.' She elongates the final word, adding a hiss to the end.

'But who's sending the messages?' I ask and then take a sip of the sludge. It makes me gag, but I try to cover it up. Shit coffee made by someone else is still infinitely better than good coffee you have to make yourself.

'Holy fuck, Millie. I thought you were meant to be clever?' She stares at me and I feel instantly small and insignificant. I hate being called out like that. I can feel myself freewheeling, desperately trying to think of something witty that will make her love me again. Why am I like this? So eager to please all the time? It's exhausting.

'I... err...'

'It's rhetorical, you doughnut!' Doughnut has been her preferred slur since the first day we met. It cuts the tension instantly. 'Anyway. The messages are obviously from Sam.'

Despite the fact she's standing in the kitchen in llama patterned pyjama bottoms, a hoodie that looks suspiciously like my ex-boyfriend's, and a sleep mask from a JetBlue flight pushed up on her forehead, she sounds so authoritative I instantly believe her. Of course they are! I bet you'd figured it out too. Fuck, I need to get my act together.

'Do you think that's why she disappeared?' I ask Lissa. 'Or do you think...?' But I can't put the thought into words. Not out loud anyway. Not without potentially manifesting those words into something that could actually be real. Did Sam find out about what Freya had done? Did she discover Freya really was a serial killer? Did she find actual evidence? Did Freya make sure that evidence...?

A knife slashes through my vision and dings into the wooden chopping board in front of me. I scream, darting back from it.

Lissa laughs, like an evil Disney villain. 'You're on melon duty, babes,' she says.

'What the fuck...' I stare at the knife and then shift my gaze to her.

'You were starting to catastrophise, your brain conjuring up too many pictures of what might have been and you know you'll only freak yourself out. So crack on with something useful, hey?'

'But I was saying—'

'I know exactly what you're saying. But you need to keep your head. If it's Sam sending the messages, nothing bad can have happened to her. Now,' her tone turns serious, 'I'm not saying that she isn't in danger, but she has to be OK at the moment. Right?

Now, let's start by following her clues and find the other three victims. And then we'll go from there. OK?'

I swallow down the feeling of bile in my mouth and pick up the knife, the blade glinting in the harsh overhead lights Lissa keeps talking about changing for something more bougie.

She catches my eye and winks. 'We're a team remember.'

I smile back. 'You and me forever.'

* * *

I arrive early to the office on Monday. Freya isn't here; she's been invited by the Institute of Sales Professionals to a round-table brunch event. It's entitled Empowering Individuals to Build Trusted Team Networks. The irony that the biggest bitch-boss in the business has been asked to pontificate on how she raises team morale is not lost on me. But this is what I mean about her being an icon; and we all know icons get away with stuff the rest of us never would. Anyway, it means there's no dragon breathing down my neck and so I use the opportunity to get digging.

Most of Freya's business trips were dealt with by Sam, I was only drafted in to help when things were too hectic for one person to deal with. I could probably get access to the business travel system via an IT request. But that could take weeks, the IT Department can be somewhat flaky. Unless...

I hurry over to the desk Sam used to occupy and open the top drawer. Inside is a jumble of pens and pads of Post-its and other office detritus no one ever really uses. And a small leather notebook. Gotcha!

Ten months ago, Serendipity decided to crack down on computer security and instigated a new password policy. We had to change our passwords every thirty days, using a combination of letters and numbers and punctuation marks, and couldn't repeat the same ones in any twelve month period. It was a total disaster and everyone kept forgetting their passwords and locking themselves out of all the primary systems they used.

Good sense would have been to revert back to a simpler system or install some kind of block chain software. But Serendipity didn't do that. Instead they sent everyone a little black leather notepad with the Serendipity logo embossed on it in rose gold foil and a notecard suggesting it was the perfect place to jot down password reminders. Yes. Seriously.

I never used mine, but I remember Sam sighing with relief and immediately writing down every single password she could think of. But at least now I can get into the TravelPro system and look at all the flights and hotel rooms Sam booked for Freya for the last couple of years.

There are so many trips. Freya goes away at least once a week, sometimes twice, and so there are hundreds of trips to scroll through. I don't even know what I'm looking for. How is this going to tell me if she killed someone while she was there?

Jesus, can you hear yourself? The rational part of my brain takes over and I start to think more logically. Once I have a nice neat spreadsheet – don't judge me, I like order and precision and Excel is a lifesaver – I start to search the internet.

On 21 June 2022, Freya was visiting a new supplier in Dubai. Also on 21 June, Spencer Balmforth, a senior executive with Miller Harding Inc, jumped from his fortieth floor hotel room at the Emirates Tower.

On 28 September 2022, Freya took some very important clients out for dinner in Amsterdam. The next day a body was dredged from the Herengracht and later identified as Ethan Donahue, an American hedge fund manager who was visiting family in the Netherlands.

Freya has been in the same place, and at the same time, as a

series of unsolved murders and apparent suicides. Is it simply a
coincidence? The result of looking for a pattern and finding one,
even though it's just chance, some quirk? Maybe she's merely a
harbinger of doom.

Or is it far more sinister than that?

Desperate for nicotine and a distraction, I head out for a
cigarette. Kieran enters the smoking area within about fifteen
seconds of me lighting up.

'Millicent,' he says with his customary nod.

'Kieran.' I return the nod.

'Did you find her?' he asks, sidling closer to me so we can whisper. 'Sam, I mean.'

I angle myself to face him. 'Nope. She's moved.'

'Moved?'

'Some kid in her block of flats said she went home.'

'What, back to Bristol?'

'Birmingham,' I correct him.

'Bristol,' he reaffirms.

'Birmingham.'

'Definitely Bristol.'

'The kid said Birmingham. Erdington. It's a suburb. Opposite
some massive graveyard.'

'She went to school in Bristol.' His forehead creases as if he's
trying to pull up a particularly tricky memory. 'I can see her CV.' He
holds up a finger to stop me from interrupting him. 'Yep, definitely
Bristol. Ashton Park School. Blackmoors Lane, Bower Ashton,
Bristol.'

'Do you have a photographic memory or something?' I ask.

'Kind of.' He blushes a little. 'I can generally remember details if
I've seen them written down.'

'Must have been useful when studying,' I say, masking the jealousy in my voice. I have a habit of forgetting key details. *Mind like a sieve*, my teachers used to say. Of course, remembering the dates of the kings and queens of England was perhaps not a huge priority to eight-year-old me, but hey-ho.

'Why do you think I ended up in HR?' he says with a grin. 'Had to put that first-class classics degree from Cambridge to good use.'

'Do you really have that?'

'Yeah. It seemed like a good idea at the time. Totally useless in the real world, but it does help me to pick up girls.' He raises his eyebrows at me.

'It does not,' I give him a playful shove.

'No, it doesn't,' he confirms and looks bashful. 'Although, you did promise me a coffee.'

'Can you get the address of Sam's family home?' I ask.

'That would cost you a beer at least.'

'Six p.m. in the Fox Lounge?'

He nods.

'It's a date,' I say.

'It's not a date.' For a moment I feel slightly crushed, but then he smiles at me and I feel my stomach flip. Do I fancy Kieran?

* * *

At the bar, I buy him a pint of – horrendously overpriced – beer and get a glass of – even more horrendously overpriced – wine for myself. Once we're safely ensconced in a little booth towards the back of the space he starts talking.

'So I did some digging,' he says before taking a long drink of beer, watching me over the rim of the glass, his eyes never leaving mine.

'Digging?' I maintain eye contact. There's something in the air.

'About Sam. So it turns out she went to school in Bristol like I'd thought.' There's a hint of pride in his voice. 'But she went to uni in

Birmingham, well Aston Uni anyway. Lots of students live in Erdington.'

'I guess that explains it then.'

'Ah, but,' he says and put up a finger. 'Here's the thing.' He pauses as if waiting for my encouragement.

'Carry on,' I indulge him.

'She applied for two jobs at Serendipity. Once four years ago, for a job in Marketing. And then again two years ago. She didn't get the first one. But she did get the second. Obviously,' he adds quickly.

'So...' I'm not sure why this is interesting, although his slightly sing-song voice – he's from Wales, not sure if I mentioned that before – is having an effect on me I wasn't really expecting.

'Samantha Mulligan went to Ashton Park School in Bristol. But she also went to Hall Green Secondary in Birmingham.'

'One for A-level and one for GCSE?'

'Both A-level.'

'Weird,' I say.

'Isn't it. Almost like one of the CVs was made up. Or both of them of course.'

'You think she lied?' If I sound scandalised it's because I am. You don't lie on a CV.

'Yep. She had better grades the second time. And a degree in a more relevant subject.'

'Still Aston Uni?'

'Yes. I guess it's easier to control a small lie than a big one.'

I don't tell him how right he is about that. 'She must really have wanted to work at Serendipity.' *I* really wanted to work at Serendipity. So I worked my ass off for years and years to make sure I would be the most qualified, most impressive candidate I could be. It pisses me off that she lied her way in.

'She must really have wanted to work with Freya Ellwood-Winter,' he says, his tone dry.

'What do you mean?'

'You'll need to get me another beer before I tell you,' he teases.

I get us another round. 'OK. Spill,' I demand as soon as I return.

'Well she applied to Marketing, right?'

I nod.

'Guess who was the head of that team at the time?'

'You might need to work on your delivery of secrets as it's quite obviously Freya Ellwood-Winter,' I tell him. Then I feel immediately guilty as he looks crushed. 'Sorry,' I add.

'That's OK. You're right. So, Freya turned her down. But she was offered a different job at the time. The PR team needed an analyst to work for Peter Burrows.' He raises an eyebrow.

'No shit? Peter Burrows? She was offered a job with Peter Burrows and she turned it down?' Peter Burrows is a legend. The kind of boss who has your back and makes sure you're seen by all the right people, giving you credit where it's due to help you work your way up. I would've killed for the chance to work with him.

'Yep. Apparently Freya felt Sam didn't meet the educational threshold required,' he says it in her clipped voice, a near perfect imitation that makes me snort wine out my nose. I really hope he didn't notice. 'But Peter didn't care. He said he thought he saw a spark in her.'

'So how did no one notice that she doctored her CV?'

'We're kind of busy in HR, you know,' he says. 'Besides, I wasn't working there when the first application was made, so I didn't see both.'

'Because you would have remembered.'

'Of course I would. But no one made the connection and the original application was archived.'

'Didn't Freya realise?'

'Hundreds of people apply for every entry level role. I sift out the ones who are blatantly unqualified, but that still leaves fifty or so for her to look at. You think she'd remember one person from over three years ago, who she made a sneering dismissal of after looking at her CV for about five seconds?'

'I guess you have a point.' I take a sip of wine. 'Who in their right mind would want to work for Freya?'

'You do.'

'No. I do work for her. But that doesn't mean I want to.'

'Touché.'

'It doesn't make any sense...' I trail off, lost in thought as my mind whirls through a series of possibilities, each more ludicrous than the last.

'No it does not.' There's an edge to his tone, which makes me start a little. He sounds almost angry, pissed off, like Sam duped him and it was personal.

'Is there a way to check?' I ask. 'Find out which one's the truth?'

His smile is sad. 'Neither is the truth, Millie. Sam lied and now she's disappeared off the face of the world.'

Perhaps I should tell him about the messages? But then I'd have to explain what they said, about Freya and my suspicions. He'd think I was a lunatic. And I kind of don't want him to think of me like that.

'I'm worried about her,' I say instead.

'Me too,' he replies, the anger gone from his voice and replaced with a sadness. 'Promise you'll let me know if you hear from her?'

I nod and I hate myself for lying. But something isn't adding up here. Who really is Sam? And what has happened to her? Despite the smile on Kieran's face and the warmth of wine in my belly, there's a chill in the air, a cool hand on the back of my neck, a blanket of foreboding settling across my shoulders.

8

'Do you have an ESTA?' Freya demands as soon as I walk into the office the next morning.

'Umm...' She catches me off guard and I fail to answer properly.

'An ESTA. To get into the US. Do you have one?' She doesn't add *for fuck's sake* onto the end of the sentence but she may as well have.

'Yes,' I confirm, properly this time. Lissa and I went to Miami last year to visit an old friend and I remember renewing it before we went.

'Good,' Freya says and then turns to head back into her office.

'Err... can I ask why?' I call after her.

She stops in her tracks and I see her take a deep breath, as if she's trying to contain her annoyance. 'Because we're going to New York tomorrow.'

Of course we are.

Jesus fucking Christ.

I put my bag down and go to take off my jacket. But I stop as the door to her office swings back open again.

'I need one of the prototype new PALETTES kits to take to New

York. I trust that won't be a problem.' It isn't a question. It's never a question. And as far as she is concerned it won't be a problem.

Is it a problem? Of course. But right now my biggest issue is that I have no idea what Sam has booked for tomorrow, and I'm certainly not even booked on a flight.

It turns out that no one is booked on a flight. Because no one – read Freya, obviously – thought to actually tell anyone she wanted to go to New York. There's nothing in her diary – or even in Sam's as a placeholder – and there's no record of a meeting having been booked. There isn't even an email in her inbox. There's literally nothing to suggest we need to go to New York tomorrow.

I take a deep breath before I knock on the door to Freya's office.

'What!' she barks and I steel myself for a bollocking before I push open the door.

'I'm just confirming the details for tomorrow's trip,' I say, holding a notepad on which I have scribbled all the questions I need to ask her.

She narrows her eyes slightly. 'I gave all the information to Sam,' she says and then turns her attention back to her computer screen.

But Sam isn't here, is she? 'I understand that.' I keep my tone level, pushing down all the irritation and praying it doesn't randomly burst to the surface. 'But unfortunately, I can't seem to find her notes.'

Freya looks at me with utter disdain. I feel my insides shrivel a little. 'I'm having a late dinner with Marcos De Silver. I need to be back in London on Friday.'

'Thank you. And—'

'You can figure out the rest, Camille. I'm very busy here.' She stares at the door instead of me. My signal to leave. I won't be getting anything more from her.

Luckily Marcos De Silver – pretty sure that isn't his real name –

has an assistant who has enough detail for me to piece together the evening plans. All I have to do is organise flights and a hotel and a car to take her there. Oh and find a prototype new PALETTES kit, which is like rocking-horse shit, of course. I'm assuming it's for one of Marcos De Silver's kids. Or possibly his new, and very young, girlfriend. She's literally just turned twenty-one and the thirty-three year age gap is pretty much all the press can talk about. She's basically the perfect target market for the upgraded PALETTES make-up range Serendipity is launching next season.

Apparently he made all his money as a stock broker back in the day, before deciding to – and this is a direct quote from his own website – 'devote his life to the appreciation of beauty in all its forms'. Yep, I too vomited a little into my own mouth the first time I read it. Freya and Marcos have been friends for years and meet at least twice a year for dinner. He gives her insider knowledge on who is doing what in the industry and so she claims it as a business expense.

I don't need to be there for the dinner. It isn't exactly the type of evening where one takes notes and writes up formal minutes. Instead she will insist I run ridiculous errands around New York City. That is why she wants me to accompany her.

If we can even get there. There are no first class seats on the British Airways flight from Heathrow. For a second I debate booking her business class and then laugh softly to myself. As if she would accept that. In the end, I get lucky with an American Airways flight that actually lands a little earlier into JFK so it won't be as hectic when we arrive.

I book a suite for Freya at The Langham and a standard room for myself. And then – buoyed by everything else I've already achieved – I try to find a PALETTES prototype.

No one in R&D has any, nor does Marketing, or anyone else in the wider Sales Division. I'm about to declare it a bust when I get a call from Araminta, the PA to the UK Production Director.

'What happened to Sam?' she asks, the second I answer.

'I don't know,' I reply, possibly a little snarkier than I should have but I'm knackered.

'Shame.'

'What can I help you with, Araminta?'

'I'm actually the one offering to help you. Unless you're going to be a bitch. I have a new PALETTE prototype and I heard you were looking for one.' Araminta has a reputation at Serendipity for liking to trade. In secrets and scandal mainly. If there's a rumour of an office affair you can guarantee you'll find Araminta's fingerprints somewhere on the gossip chain.

'Freya wants one,' I reply. But I already know Araminta isn't just going to give it to me.

'That's nice.'

I know she's waiting for me to make an offer. To tell her what I might be prepared to give her for the prototype. The problem is that I have no gossip. Or at least I have no gossip anyone would take stock in. I hardly think revealing my suspicions of Freya's... out of work interests – is that a good description? I don't know, but let's run with it – would get me very far with Araminta.

In the end I take the direct approach. It'll probably save us both a lot of time. 'Just tell me what you want for it. It's late and I'm tired and I want to get home.'

'That isn't how this works.' I can hear the smirk in her voice over the phone. She loves this; being in a position of power over other people.

I call her bluff. I put down the phone, disconnecting the call.

She rings back ten seconds later. 'I think we got cut off.'

'No, I hung up on you. I'm not playing.'

'Kieran's phone number,' she says hurriedly. 'Kieran in HR. You smoke together, I've seen you.'

'You want me to give you his phone number?' First, his work mobile is on the intranet. Second, we're not at school any more: if she fancies him she can ask him out herself.

'That's my price,' she says tartly.

'Deal.' Kieran will probably hate me, especially as he's told me a number of times that Araminta terrifies him. At least I know he doesn't reciprocate her feelings.

I get home at 10.30 p.m. I'm utterly exhausted, but I still have to pack and make sure everything is sorted for the trip tomorrow.

'No way? New York! You lucky bitch!' Lissa screeches at me when I tell her my travel plans.

'Aren't you missing something?' I ask her, as I gingerly sniff the armpit of a Claudie Pierlot dress that is hanging in my wardrobe. I know I've worn it at least once, but it's dry clean only and I can't afford to pay fifteen or even twenty quid every time I want to wear it.

Lissa just shrugs and throws herself onto my bed.

'My boss? And her...' I search for the right word.

'Proclivities?' Lissa suggests. 'Or is that only weird sex stuff?' She sits bolt upright. 'Oh my god. Is it a weird sex thing?' She makes a face. 'Do you think she fucks them first and then waits until they're all nice and sleepy and then...' She pauses for a moment and then suddenly claps her hands together, the sound reverberating around the room.

I don't really know what to reply if I'm honest.

'What's that spider? The one who bites the male's head off right as he ejaculates?' she asks.

'She bites it off so he *can* ejaculate,' I correct her. Please don't ask how I know this stuff. 'But anyway. I don't know if it's a sex

thing. Or a psychopath thing. Or a... I don't know... what other kind
of *thing* might it be?'

Lissa shrugs.

'But I...' I trail off as I fold a T-shirt and place it in the little case
I'm taking.

'I know, Millie.' Her voice is gentle. 'But all you need to do right
now is your job. Ace it. Be brilliant. Show her what you're capable
of. And then, soon, I promise, we will get you that big shiny promotion and off you will go to La La Land and never have to see her
again.'

'You think I should just pretend I don't even suspect a thing?'

'Absolutely. That is the only way to play this. Smile, be nice,
make her think you're another sycophantic fool who worships the
ground she walks on and who ABSOLUTELY ONE HUNDRED
PERCENT does not think she's a serial killer.'

'But what if she figures it out?' My voice is small. Scared. It's so
easy for Lissa to be ballsy. She isn't the one travelling with Freya.

'She won't. You're cleverer than she is, Mills. You know that. I
know that.'

'Yeah,' I say, but I don't sound convinced.

'One more year. At most,' Lissa tells me.

I nod. 'And then freedom.'

'Freedom,' she repeats.

I've never flown first class on a transatlantic flight before. It's a
revelation. The seat is huge and actually converts into a proper flat
bed, complete with a duvet. I'm even offered a pair of pyjamas. I
mean, I obviously don't accept them, can you imagine what Freya
would say? But it's cool to be offered. Not that this is meant to be a

review of the flight, sorry about that. But the best bit is that I can't see, or hear, Freya from my seat. Seven hours of blissful silence await me.

By some kind of miracle, there isn't a queue at Border Control and we sail through the airport. There's a car already waiting for us and the uniformed driver is the perfect blend of cool professionalism and frustrated New Yorker, leaning on his horn almost constantly. I'm still feeling relaxed from the flight and the three glasses of champagne – actual proper champagne, not cheap and slightly warm Prosecco – as I settle against the leather interior of the luxurious town car.

But of course my peace is shattered as soon as Freya opens her mouth. Well, actually she doesn't even speak, she just hands me a page torn from her Smythson notebook. A list of items and store names.

'Umm...' I say as I start to read the list.

'It's a shopping list.'

'For me?'

She rolls her eyes. 'No, for Taylor Swift.'

'Right.' I knew she'd have a few tasks for me, some errands to run. But I'd been hoping to do *some* sightseeing, maybe squeeze in a little trip to one of the museums or galleries. But the list is so long there will be zero chance of me doing anything except schlep from place to place picking up all the ridiculous things she wants.

'There are a few things on the list that are personal,' she says, seemingly ignorant to the fact that I'm a Bid Manager and not a PA. 'Especially the jewellery. You'll need to tell them you're me when you collect it.' She reaches into her purse and pulls out a credit card. 'And use this to pay for everything.' She hands it to me, the platinum card smooth against my fingertips.

* * *

Yes, I'm a fool. There. I've said it now so you can stop thinking it to yourself. I realised forty minutes ago as I rang the bell to Trinity Bespoke, a very exclusive looking jewellery store in the shadow of the Rockefeller Center, and told them I was here to pick up the necklace.

'What's the name please?' an overly chirpy voice had asked.

'Freya Ellwood-Winter,' I'd replied.

'Come right up, Ms Ellwood-Winter.' The door buzzed and swung open to reveal an entrance corridor of pale marble and gilt accents. It was quiet and cool like a museum.

I was treated with reverence, almost bordering on deference. The necklace was brought to me on a silver platter for my inspection, then spirited away to be appropriately packaged for the trip home.

And now I'm standing outside, the necklace in a bag slung around my wrist so I cannot possibly drop it, a cigarette curling smoke into the air as I suck nicotine greedily into my lungs.

I'm an alibi.

Or more accurately, I'm creating an alibi for Freya. If – and I'm going to keep thinking *if* until my horrendous suspicions are confirmed, just in case I am being ridiculous – another body turns up, Freya was at Trinity Bespoke. 'Oh of course. Ms Ellwood-Winter came to collect a custom necklace we had made specially for her. Yes, the records show it quite clearly. You can see the credit card transaction.'

Holy fucking shit.

Another body is going to drop.

Should I try to stop her? Try to get some evidence? Go to the police?

And say what?

Someone else has been killed and I've helped to make it happen.

I think I'm going to be sick.

9

There's Wi-Fi on board our return flight from JFK. I spend the entire trip constantly updating every news site I can find.

BBC News. Refresh. Scroll.

USA Today. Refresh. Scroll.

Washington Post. Refresh. Scroll.

To Google to look for new results. Search 'murder NYC'. Search 'body found New York'. Search 'man dead Manhattan'.

Nothing.

Begin cycle again.

BBC News. Refresh. Scroll.

USA Today. Refresh. Scroll.

Washington Post. Refresh. Scroll.

To Google to look for new results. Search 'murder NYC'. Search 'body found New York'. Search 'man dead Manhattan'.

Nothing.

By the time we begin our descent into Heathrow I'm starting to think I've got it all wrong. That Freya wasn't out killing someone while I picked up her necklace and created her the perfect alibi. It's 8 a.m. here in the UK, the country beginning to wake up, kettles being flicked on in every kitchen in every town. In New York it's still the middle of the night. But surely a morning murder would have been discovered by now.

Passport control is a typical nightmare, the queues stretching out of the main hall and back into the corridors. Freya and I stand shoulder to shoulder, jostled by the crowds as we inch closer and closer to the front of the line and the automated gates.

I can feel Freya bristling next to me, no doubt thinking this is all my fault, that there should have been something I could do to avoid this debacle. Trust me that I have tried. There was a premium service once and I would have booked it had it been available. I have zero desire to stand in this queue either.

It takes over half an hour before I can see light at the end of the tunnel. The literal tunnel as we're still in the corridor, waiting to enter the main passport control area. I haven't been able to check my phone, I mean, I hardly can when she's standing right next to me, can I? Let's just imagine how that would go down:

'Oooh, what are you doing?'

'Just checking to see if you murdered someone while we were away.'

It doesn't exactly work, does it?

So anyway, I don't see the news break. But Lissa does and messages me immediately, obviously in her trademark drip feed of information:

Jim Handley

Bludgeoned

Manhattan apartment

Yesterday morning

Morning as in NYC time

No witnesses

No suspects

Well officially at least

I take a sideways look at Freya. At my boss who may have spent yesterday morning beating the life out of a man in his Manhattan apartment.

I paint a neutral look on my face, but inside I'm screaming.

Holy fucking shit!

Is it all actually true?

I don't go back to the office that morning. It's Friday so I'm meant to. Even though I've arranged for a car to pick Freya up and take her to her apartment on Macklin Street in Covent Garden, where she will conduct a handful of meetings from her palatial home office, *I'm* still expected to be in the office and representing the team.

But I need a shower. I need to wash the city grime from my skin, wash away the feeling that I am complicit in all of this.

And Lissa and I need to discuss our strategy.

'DKAs!' I shout as I open the front door of the flat. DKAs – technically 'Dominique's Kouign Amann' – are basically a caramelised croissant, with flaky layers and this crispy sweet crust and they are absolutely delicious. I made a little detour to Dominique Ansel's bakery on Spring Street while I was running errands for Freya. I would've brought back the infamous cronuts but they only last a day and they'd have been ruined by now.

Lissa has also played hooky from work and the proper coffee machine is already in overdrive to accompany the DKAs. She's also done a tonne of research already into Jim Handley and I spot a notepad next to her laptop covered in doodles and her extraordinarily messy scrawl she calls handwriting. I peer at it but can barely make out any of the words.

'I'll translate,' she tells me as she places the coffee on the table and grabs a roll of kitchen paper to use as napkins. I hand her a DKA and she takes a huge bite. Her face breaks into a perfect picture of beatification, as if this is the true taste of heaven on her lips. 'Holy fuck!' she exclaims, her mouth still full. 'That is the absolute tits.'

'Told you,' I reply. I take my own bite, relishing the sugary crunch of the edge.

We both finish eating in silence, neither wanting to start discussing murder and mayhem while we're enjoying our pastries.

But eventually we're done, crumbs wiped from mouths and swept from the pockmarked surface of the kitchen table Lissa picked up from a car boot sale last January. It had come from the home of someone with little kids who'd drawn all over it in felt tipped pens, the ink bleeding through the wood. Lissa varnished it, sealing in the kids' scribbles forever. It looks cool. And very far removed from the functional yet artistically devoid kitchen area from our teens.

'Shall I tell you about Mr Handley?' Lissa says.

I nod as I sip my coffee.

'Aged forty-three. Successful. Attractive.' She turns her screen so I can see a picture of a tall man standing at the top of a mountain somewhere, the sun reflecting off the snow. He's wearing a dark blue ski jacket, goggles and woollen hat in his hand, nonchalant smile on his face. His impeccably handsome face. This man wasn't just 'attractive', he looks like a model.

'What did he do?' I ask, unable to drag my eyes away from the picture.

'Plastic surgeon.' She raises an eyebrow as she says it. 'I think he might have been availing himself of the company discount. Let's just say that ten years ago he was slightly less Ken-doll.' She taps a couple of keys on her laptop to bring up another picture to show me.

'It's still him, but also, kind of not,' I say as I squint at the screen. 'The nose is different.'

'And the jaw line,' Lissa says. 'And he's definitely having botox.'

'Hair replacement therapy?' I ask, his hairline was receding slightly in the older picture but in the ski one he has a full head of thick glossy black hair.

'I'd say,' Lissa confirms. 'He has gone to a *lot* of effort.'

'Had,' I correct her.

'Oh yeah.' The mood in the kitchen dips as we both realise that we aren't talking about some guy who has his life ahead of him. We're talking about a ghost. A dead man.

'So he was a plastic surgeon. Was he married? Kids?' I ask.

'No kids. No wife. String of girlfriends. And a pretty explicit profile on Grindr.' She motions downwards in case I wasn't aware that the explicit profile included some *intimate* photography.

'So he was bi?'

'Guess so,' Lissa shrugs. She's never felt the need to categorise things, to put people into boxes based on who they want to sleep with. 'It's weird how people get so obsessed about other people's sex lives,' she told me once. 'Like, what kind of perverts are they?'

'What else?' I ask.

'He had an apartment in Manhattan, close to everything, all the nightlife and restaurants and stuff. Liked to spend his summers in the Hamptons and his winters in Aspen. Went to the gym five times a week, seeing a personal trainer at least twice. Bought his suits from Cad & The Dandy, his watch from Patek Philippe, and his girl-friends' necklaces from Tiffany on their birthdays. Didn't smoke, drank Parkers Heritage Bourbon, ate quinoa in the week and steak on the weekends.'

'So he was basically a walking cliché?'

'Yep. On paper at least,' she adds. 'I mean, who knows what else he was doing that he didn't put on his social media or his CV?'

'You said he was bludgeoned?' I grimace a little, *bludgeoned* is such a visceral word.

'Yep. Blunt force trauma. In his apartment. He'd been to the gym that morning, gone home to shower and get ready for work. The time of death is estimated at between 9 and 11 a.m. local time.'

'Exactly when Freya had me pretending to be her.'

'She what?' Lissa's voice echoes around the kitchen.

'She had me pick up something personal, told me to say I was her so they wouldn't worry about giving it to me.'

'You created her alibi.'

'I guess so.'

'Fuck! Fuck!' Lissa says.

'Hey, calm down. It's not—'

'She's made you an accomplice,' Lissa interrupts me, her eyes flashing. 'You have suspicions and you've covered up for her. You could be considered an accessory!'

'Of course I couldn't. I'm just an innocent employee running errands for her boss.'

'Who you think is a killer and yet you haven't gone to the police.' She sounds matter of fact. Laying out the truth I've not wanted to see. But I can't avoid staring straight at it now. *I* am meant to be the one who catastrophises and blows things out of all proportion. If Lissa is doing it then it must be serious.

'So what do we do?'

'We need to be careful. Make sure there can never be any question of your suspicions. If anyone finds out you even thought for a moment she was a killer, you could be in trouble. This has to stay just between us, OK?'

'Who else exactly did you think I was going to tell?'

'You can't go to the police. Not now. That ship has sailed, Millie.'

She stares at me, her eyes wide and pleading over the table. She's right. I'm stuck.

My boss might be a killer and I'm powerless to do anything about it.

'So what next?' I ask, my voice small in the kitchen.

'Well...' I can see from her expression that all this is challenging her mental capacities, her brain whirring as she tries to think of something.

'Rock. Hard place.' I tell her.

'Don't be defeatist, Millicent.' She mimics our house manager, who was stern and serious and who we were both absolutely petrified of when we were fifteen.

I pull a face and fake a shiver. Well, it's a fake now, but for years after we left the home I would twitch involuntarily every time I even thought of the old bitch. It took a lot of therapy to get over it. Which is kind of ironic seeing as she was in charge of our "pastoral care".

'I've got it!' Lissa exclaims. 'A three-stage process.' She looks excited, like she's found a new game and is itching to play it. The problem is that when she gets like this, it's normally me who ends up being the loser in the game. 'First stage: you need proof. Absolute, irrefutable proof. This is all nonsense if it does turn out to be a coincidence.'

'Fair enough. So, I get the proof. Then what?'

'Well, in the meantime, we get cleaning. Make sure that there is no possible way for you to be accused of being an accessory or an accomplice.'

'And then?'

'Then we lay a trap. One that will expose her as the villain she is, while...' She pauses for a moment, eyes sparkling, 'while you come out as the greatest employee of all time. One who is guaranteed that promotion to the fancy LA office.'

'So she ends up in prison and I skip off into a wondrous sunset.'

'Exactly.' She looks proud of herself. As well she might.

'You are a fucking genius, Lissa Readman.'

'Yes, I am.'

We're still sitting at the kitchen table drinking coffee and feeling rather smug about Lissa's three stage plan, when my phone lets out a loud beep.

I pick it up and stare at the number.

'Who is it?' Lissa asks.

'That same number as before,' I reply, tapping the screen to bring up the picture message. It's the same as the others, block capitals in black ink on plain white paper. 'I guess you just went to New York,' I read to Lissa. 'Be careful.' The last two words are underlined three times, the thick lines almost tearing through the paper.

I turn my phone to show Lissa and she visibly pales in front of me. Neither of us feels quite so smug about our silly little plan any more.

10

On Monday I'm in the office by five thirty – yes, in the morning – and it's only just getting light. I don't think I've ever got in this early before, the coffee shop I pass en route to the tube station was only just opening.

By the time Freya comes in, I've done almost every task on my To Do list. It's amazing how productive I can be when I'm focused. But my self-satisfaction doesn't last very long.

'Expense reports,' she says, not bothering with any pre-amble. No 'Oh how was your weekend' or 'That blouse is a good colour on you'. I mean, not that I expected her to, but I just want to make sure you understand what I have to deal with on a daily basis. And, of course, why I'm so quick to believe she really is a psychopathic man-killer.

'Expense reports?' I reply, confused as to what she's actually asking for. Or demanding at least.

'They're due by close of play,' Freya replies, as if that is a full explanation.

'Right,' I say to her back as she walks towards her office.

Guess who used to do the expense reports? Yes, of course it was

Sam. I really need her advice; I know they go to Corporate and I really cannot afford to screw them up. So I try to call her but all I get is a message: *the number you have called has not been recognised.* I try a WhatsApp message but that fails to even send.

It feels like an invasion of her privacy, but I'm desperate and so I pull up Twitter so I can DM her. But her Twitter profile @Sammy_-Mulligan no longer exists. That's weird. Who the hell deletes their Twitter profile? I know we all threatened to when Elon Musk took over and fucked it all, but no one actually did. I check Instagram and it's the same story. She didn't use Facebook – we're not in our 40s – and had never got into either TikTok – who has the time to make videos? – or LinkedIn – no, I don't care that you found an apparently fascinating article about corporate leveraging.

There is one final place to look. And it makes me feel oddly icky, like this is the ultimate invasion of privacy. I open Catfished, a website that allows you to find someone's profile on dating sites. It's super useful for vetting the guy you think might be a catch but who might also turn out to be running multiple apps and searching for dodgy hook-ups on niche sites. I type *Sammy M* into the search bar as that's the name she tended to use. Hundreds of Bumble and Tinder profiles appear in the results. It seems Sammy M is the kind of name that is popular with students looking for sugar daddies. Who knew. But as I scroll down the list, I don't recognise any of them. It looks like Sam has deleted her profile from all the dating apps too.

It's like she's disappeared. Dropped off the face of the Earth.

Where is she?

Without Sam's help I need to find someone else to show me what I'm meant to do with the expense reports. Luckily, Kieran is a creature of habit and so I know exactly where he'll be at 9.55 a.m.

'Millicent!' There's far too much joviality in his voice this morning. Perhaps it's the bucket of coffee he's holding in one hand, taking alternate sips of caffeine and drags on the cigarette burning between his fingers.

'My favourite HR person,' I say. He smiles at the moniker.

'I guess you need a favour? Another one.' His eyes twinkle as he speaks.

'I need to do the expense reports. Sam used to do them and I have no idea what I'm doing. I've tried to message her to at least ask where I should start but she's completely AWOL.'

'You still can't find her?'

I shake my head. 'I've tried calling and messaging and then...' I drop my voice. 'This is odd. All her social media's gone.'

'Gone?'

'Yep. Just, poof. Vanished. Gone!'

'All of them?'

'Yep,' I confirm. 'I mean, that's odd, right?'

'Very.' His brow furrows and he looks almost pained.

'What is it?' I ask, a touch of concern in my voice.

'It's just... you don't think something's happened to her?'

'Like what?' But dread claws at my stomach.

'I don't know.' Then he smiles at me. 'Gosh, listen to me! What an idiot!' He laughs, but it sounds hollow, almost forced. 'I'm sure she's fine.'

But the seed is well and truly planted and I'm not convinced.

'Tell you what,' he says, grinding out the cigarette and yeeting the coffee bucket into the bin, 'how about I show you how to run the reports?'

'Would you?'

'Of course.'

I won't go into detail about the reports, but rest assured they were as boring and time consuming and absolutely soul destroying as you're imagining them to be.

Although Kieran does try to make them seem less dull and less complicated, pulling a chair close to mine at my desk so we can both see the screen. He smells of pine and musk – obviously some kind of cologne – but with a hint of grapefruit underneath.

'Does all that make sense?' he asks me after about an hour of his teaching.

'Yep,' I reply. Even though I'm not sure all of it has gone in. But at least now I have a vague idea and I'm sure I can fill in the gaps.

'Promise? It's just I need to be getting back to my desk. And I don't think I want to be here when Freya returns.'

'Absolutely. I'm fine. Thank you,' I tell him.

'Anytime. For you, anyway.' He blushes a little.

'I see there is a lot of work going on.' Freya's voice cuts through our gentle flirting.

'Good afternoon, Ms Ellwood-Winter,' he says as he gets up and walks away.

She really is an absolute buzzkill.

An hour later and I pop out to grab some lunch. Just a prawn sandwich mind, nothing fancy. After lunch – which I obviously eat at my desk because these fucking expense reports aren't going to do themselves – Freya returns from her meetings.

'Haven't you finished them yet?' she asks, folding her soaking wet umbrella and hanging it on the coat rack where it drips into my trainers I wear for my commute.

'I just have a couple of queries for you,' I reply.

She pauses in front of me. 'Well, go on then.'

'Right, well... there isn't a charge for dinner in New York.'

'Marcos paid. Next.'

'Um. How did you get from the restaurant back to the hotel?'

'Taxi.' She says it like it's so obvious. Like how else would she possibly have travelled.

'But there isn't a charge for one.'

'It must be a mistake.'

'I reconciled the company credit card.'

'I must have paid cash,' she says, then shrugs.

'Do you have a receipt?' I'm really trying to sound level and non-confrontational and like this is all entirely reasonable. I mean, it *is* entirely reasonable.

'I don't know, Camille. I really don't have time for this.'

'It's just, if you paid cash and there isn't a receipt then I can't get a reimbursement for you.' I wince inside as she turns to stare at me.

'Whatever, Camille. It was probably fifty dollars.' She makes a motion like fifty dollars is nothing. Oh to be that dismissive of enough money to pay my phone bill for the month. 'Anything else?'

'You're sure it was cash?'

'Yes! Jesus, Camille. Who gives a shit?'

It might seem like nothing but Freya Ellwood-Winter just lied to my face. I know for a fact she didn't pay cash for a taxi from the restaurant to the hotel. She used a pre-paid dollar denominated Mastercard. Given the way she uses me like her very own PA, she's given me access to her work email account. The other day I saw an email message pop up that I thought was weird. So I went digging a little more and found she had this pre-paid card with surprisingly lax security and a password I was able to guess on the second try. The charge was clear, and it was for a lot more than fifty dollars. She didn't go straight to the hotel: the fare was almost one hundred and ten dollars. She took a significant detour.

Perhaps to scope out a certain person's apartment? To make a plan for the following morning when she went to Jim Handley's place and caved his head in?

It gives me an idea though. I can use the expense reports to look for anomalies. For times when a taxi was the wrong amount, or she hired a car or took a late-night subway journey. Anything really that suggests she wasn't just propping up the hotel bar or having an early night in a plush hotel. And they go back a long way in time. I can see exactly where Freya was on almost every day for the last six years. This might give me actual concrete proof.

After I've sent the reports off to Corporate, I decide to treat myself to a fancy coffee and head out to the place across the street. I need air and space and to feel the sun on my face in a way that lets me know I'm still human. It's amazing how little natural light you get working in an office, even in the summer when the sun hasn't fully set as you leave for the night.

Just as I get to the front of the queue I feel a shiver cross the back of my neck, as if someone just walked over my grave. Or as if someone is watching me. I spin round and almost head butt the guy standing behind me.

'Watch it,' he says, his eyes flashing fire and his stance changing immediately to the defensive.

'You were kind of close,' I say and give him what we call the 'Lissa stare'. Lissa taught me how to do this when we were fifteen and it's the kind of life skill everyone should learn.

He glares at me for a moment as if he's debating whether to start an argument. But then his body language softens and he takes a teeny tiny step backwards.

I smile sweetly and go to turn back to the cashier. But then I see a flash of bright scarlet red, the exact shade of the Macintosh rain coat Sam bought from a charity shop in Chelsea and was madly in love with. I push past the people behind me, desperate to get out of the little cafe and onto the street, apologising as I stand on people's feet and they tut around me.

I push open the door, calling 'Sam!' at the top of my voice as I tumble out into the brilliant sunlight. But she isn't there, just a hint of scarlet turning the corner and disappearing.

It must have been someone else.

* * *

That evening, Lissa and I eat dinner in the kitchen, nothing special, just goujons and chips, but sometimes we like to pretend we're fancy by laying the table and drinking wine from the posh crystal glasses we thrifted last year.

We've just cleared the plates when my phone beeps. Lissa looks at me as I sink back into my chair, the phone in my palm.

'Another one of those messages?' she asks.

I nod and take a breath before I open it. A single sentence on a sheet of paper:

Be careful, don't let her know you're digging…

I turn it to show Lissa.

'Reply back,' she demands, even as she's reaching for my phone to do it herself.

'Are you OK? I'm worried about you, Sam,' I repeat the words as I type them and hit send.

The reply comes quickly.

I'm OK. But now I have to burn this phone

Lissa makes a face. 'Seems a little melodramatic.' She twerks an eyebrow at me. 'Ask her where she is.'

Where are you?

I type the words as Lissa nods her approval.

My phone beeps again and I read out the message. 'I can't tell you. Just be careful. This is serious. Say hi to Lissa for me.'

I look up in time to witness the blush bloom across Lissa's neck.

'Something you want to tell me?' I ask her.

'Nothing ever happened,' she says quickly.

'Right,' I reply, not believing her for a moment. I want to talk to Sam properly, all this messaging and cryptic clues is boring me now. But the call fails to connect.

'She burned it?' Lissa asks.

'I think so.'

Lissa takes a deep breath. 'All because you mentioned her name? I mean, maybe she's uber-paranoid, but... I'm starting to worry now.'

Something in her tone tickles up my spine. 'Me too.'

PART II

FREYA

11

So, you want me to start with the whole New York taxi thing? OK. I guess it's not the worst place to begin. Maybe not the best either, but there we are.

Despite what I told Millie, I didn't pay cash for a taxi from the restaurant. I intended to, of course I did, the little stack of bills was already in the pocket of the black trench coat I'd checked into the cloakroom at the maître d's insistence. Some little shit must have stolen the money, because when I went to pay the fare my fingers closed round nothing but the silk lining. I panicked, little mistakes like that can end up costing everything. I couldn't pay for the cab with my corporate card without someone sticking their beak into my business. I know Lucas would probably have smoothed things over, but I think it's best to be cautious. Especially with Sam pulling her vanishing act.

Anyway, I have a pre-paid Mastercard I've used a couple of times to do things like hire a car or book online train tickets. You know, things you can't pay for in cash. The stupid thing was I wasn't doing anything particularly nefarious, or not obviously anyway.

The driver waited outside The Kitty-Kat Klub for twenty minutes while I went inside to pick something up from one of the girls. Then I went back to the hotel and changed.

Half an hour later, I walked a few blocks from the hotel and flagged down a yellow cab, giving the driver an address in the West Village. This time I did pay cash. This was definitely a journey that wanted zero paper trail.

Lawrence Handley had been hiring girls euphemistically described as *escorts* twice a week since his third wife left him six months ago. It didn't take much to find his regular girl and slip her a few thousand dollars to stay at home for the evening. No doubt she'll be going back to him later this week, trying to keep the bile from filling her mouth as he ruts on top of her. No doubt he will weep afterwards, feign love for his big brother taken so cruelly from him.

Ironically – given he was the brother of one of New York's finest plastic surgeons – Lawrence hadn't aged well. He was like a caricature of the middle-aged, overly privileged, overly indulgent white man. A disgusting slug with a penchant for silk dressing gowns and girls young enough to be his daughter.

'You're not Starr,' he said as he opened the door and found me standing there.

'She couldn't make it.' I adopted an accent, my voice almost a purr as I leant closer towards him. 'But she told me exactly what you like, you naughty naughty boy.'

I watched as his eyes flared and a gentle blush started to spread across his fleshy neck. 'Come in.' He stepped backwards and opened the door wider so I could slip into the apartment. He craned his neck out into the hallway to ensure no one saw me enter. He really didn't need to worry about that. No one saw me come in and they wouldn't see me leave either.

The girl at The Kitty-Kat Klub had given me the small vial of

GHB all ready to slip into a glass of whiskey for him. 'Cheers,' I said, making direct eye contact with him as he knocked the entire glass back.

Five minutes later he was snoring on the sofa. I held my breath as I loosened the ties of his dressing gown and tried to avert my eyes as I wrestled his bulk from the pair of matching silk boxer shorts he was wearing. In his bedroom I selected a tie from the array in his closet. Bright crimson. The colour of fresh blood. He was so out of it he didn't even move as I wrapped it round his neck and pulled it tight. Tight enough that he would wake up in the morning with a hoarse voice and an angry looking bruise. Starr had been very clear about his predilection for erotic-asphyxiation. I gouged my nails down his chest a few times for good measure, drawing deep welts on the first pass and blood on the second.

I didn't wait around afterward. But he would have woken up a few hours later, his limp cock still in his hand as if he fell asleep straight after the act. He would have been confused. He would wonder if something was slipped into his drink. But he'd think it was part of the fun. And even if he thought perhaps it wasn't part of the fun, well, he's hardly going to tell anyone is he? I did debate sticking something up his arse, something suitably embarrassing, just to be absolutely sure he would stay quiet, but frankly he was too heavy to move into a position that I could do it.

I generally don't like to embroil other people in my plans. I don't like to make use of so-called *innocent bystanders*. But let's be honest, sometimes men like Lawrence deserve to be humiliated, deserve a little touch of their own medicine. I've already made my peace with it.

The next morning I walked the ten minutes to the Flatiron District. Used the set of keys I lifted from Lawrence's kitchen drawer. Let myself into Jim Handley's apartment.

Little Jimmy had done well for himself. Very well.

His fancy apartment looked out over Madison Square Park, the Empire State Building and other icons of the Manhattan skyline in the distance. There were always lots of pretty young women flocking around him. He had finally sorted that weak jaw line that had plagued the Handley family for generations.

Jimmy didn't recognise me at first. I was sitting on the sofa as he let himself into his apartment.

'Who are you?' he demanded. Voice deep and rich. Almost seductive. He must have found a speech therapist.

'Hi Jimmy. Long time, eh?' I said, reverting to my original accent.

I watched as the realisation dawned on him. As it blended with the understanding that I wasn't here on a friendly house call. 'What do you want?' he asked, terror distorting his voice.

'Oh Jimmy. You know exactly what I want.'

'I don't.' He'd been almost petulant. It wasn't very becoming.

I smiled. A slow and languid smile. A predator's smile. 'I'm coming for all of you, Jimmy.'

He blanched and then began to look round himself in a panic. He was searching for anything he could use as a weapon.

A few years ago he'd won a rather prestigious award for his pioneering work in designer vaginas. He had coined the specific look he recommended 'The Handley'. The award was a huge block of very heavy resin, although not, you'll be pleased to know, in the shape of one of those 'Handleys'.

It was chunky, the weight of it a comfort in my hand.

I was quick. I've been training for a long time.

He tried to dodge the first blow.

But he never stood a chance.

* * *

I walked west, through Chelsea. Tossed the keys into the Hudson. Bought coffee and a bagel from a street cart. Walked back to The Langham through the crowds in the city. The sun on my face.

I felt calm.

Peaceful.

Satiated.

I always felt like this. Afterwards. As if I'm completely untouchable, like no one could even get close to me. As women we spend so much time looking behind us. Holding our keys between our fingers. Praying the guy across the street with the leer on his face is just a little creepy and not a killer.

If only you could taste the power I feel. It's intoxicating. Addictive.

Trust me, I think you'd like it.

Perhaps I should rewind a little? I'm not sure how much you already know.

Yes. I killed Jim Handley in New York.

Cody Gelber didn't commit suicide in Paris. Even if that's what it looked like. You have to mix up the MO.

Ruben Chambers? It wasn't some kind of professional hit. No one paid me. The kick on that Beretta though, Jesus!

Do I enjoy it? You know, it's funny. Not ha-ha funny, I'm not a lunatic. It's weird funny. Unexpected funny. I do enjoy it. In a way at least. It's... soothing. Calming. Better than yoga certainly. Perhaps murder is the cure for the current feminist rage pandemic sweeping through my generation. Perhaps it's better than alfalfa sprouts and ninety percent dark chocolate and genteelly described 'female pleasure stimulators', which cost over two hundred pounds a go and look like something from a sci-fi film.

Maybe if we all went and snuffed out some lousy little man we'd all feel so much better. We could treat it like therapy.

But no. I get it. I'm just being blasé because it's easier. How many of us joke around to mask the truth of what we feel inside. The reality of our existence. The lives ruined by shitty men and an even shittier society that enables them. Encourages them. Eggs them on to destroy us for their own fun.

I'm merely taking back control.

Wresting it from them, despite how god-damn hard they try to hang on to it.

It's getting easier though. They have come to fear me. Come to understand what I represent. What is going to happen to them when they realise not just who I was, but who I am now.

After Millie's slightly loaded confrontation with me about the New York taxi situation, I decide to go and see Verity. I want to tell her about New York. She'll be so excited to know Jim Handley has been ticked off the list.

'You're so lovely,' the woman on reception tells me as I sign my name in the little book. 'Always coming to visit, even after all this time.'

Verity has no concept of the passing of time. To her it might as well have been yesterday. She isn't aware we waited over two decades before we even began. Maybe it's kinder this way. Oblivion preferable to the knowledge your life is over, meaningless, all purpose destroyed in a single act.

As far as Verity knows it's still 1999. Bill Clinton is still in the White House. Christina Aguilera's *Genie in a Bottle* is still dominating the charts. The iPhone doesn't exist. *Friends* is still the undisputed favourite show. We're all wearing baby-doll dresses and bandana tops and chokers. I think I envy her. Or at least, there are moments when I do.

There is the odd time I hate her. Yes, I know I shouldn't say it. But I'm being honest and sometimes I do hate her.

I hate the burden she creates. I hate the guilt she fosters.

She is the embodiment of my failure.

12

When I was snooping around Jim Handley's fancy Manhattan apartment, I found something very interesting. A parcel was lying on his kitchen counter, one he hadn't opened, but it was obvious from the sloshing noise when I shook it that it was a bottle of some kind of liquor. Written on the back was the sender's name and address. How sweet that Kai would still send his old buddy Jim a gift after all these years. Especially all the way from Finland.

To be honest, if I'd known Kai Helve had returned to his native Helsinki I would've planned this for the middle of winter. January probably. When the sun doesn't rise until half nine and sets again six hours later.

But no. It's June. This morning the sun rose at 4.56 a.m. and won't set until 9.38 p.m. this evening. It is almost impossible to find enough dark to skulk around in. How is a woman meant to kill a man under these conditions? And I can't wait until the seasons turn. It's two weeks since I killed Jim and I don't want to wait any longer. Kai should count his blessings as this death will be quick and quiet and not cause any more ripples. The others can be splashier. More Avant Garde.

Kai works for a bank. All very dull, except he did get sent to some rather exotic locations. He used to be in Venezuela, where he was effectively untouchable. There are certain places it is not worth the risk. I mean, I have alibis, I'm not stupid. But there are some places that are less on board with the idea of democracy and innocent until proven guilty and all the other benefits we enjoy as part of a modern country. There are also some countries who refuse to send you back to your home nation to face trial. Would you risk it? Ten years for manslaughter in a UK prison, out in five years for good behaviour, is one thing. Fifty years in a Thai hellhole where no one knows your name is quite different.

But Kai could have had the grace to move to Finland in the winter. This level of daylight is ridiculous. But anyway. You don't want to hear me bitching.

Without the assistance of darkness, I'm going to need to figure out how to kill Kai in the bright sunlight of the Finnish summer. Luckily the national pastime of sweating one's balls off in a sauna gives me an idea. Did you know there are one point eight saunas per capita in Finland?

I came to Helsinki once for Christmas. It was a long time ago, probably about fifteen years. My boyfriend's family lived in this apartment that looked out over the harbour. Which was completely frozen over, a solid sheet of bright white ice jutting up to the horizon. As soon as daylight broke, a whole herd of completely butt-naked men suddenly ran out of a hut on the pier and threw themselves into holes bored out of the sea ice.

'What the...' I'd exclaimed.

Aimo laughed. 'It's a tradition. Twenty minutes in the sauna. Five minutes in the water.'

'But it must be freezing.'

He shrugged. 'You get used to it.'

'You've...'

'Of course.'

The sheer masochism of it. Apparently it's good for your circulation. Fuck that. I'll take the two hundred pound a go Augustinus Bader's The Rich Cream, thank you very much.

But here's the thing. People die. Going from eighty degrees of heat to sub-zero cold can send your body into shock. Trigger a fatal heart attack. Especially if you're pre-disposed to one. Or if there are other extenuating circumstances. Like cocaine or ecstasy. Unfortunately Finland has some pretty draconian drug laws and I don't have good enough contacts.

Luckily though, the Finns do like a drink. And that's going to have to do.

Millie excused herself after dinner with what she euphemistically described as 'tummy trouble'. Ipecac in a cocktail will have that effect, but I couldn't risk her knowing where I go tonight. I'm taking extra precautions, my paranoia up a few notches. It's for the best. I'd been getting lazy and sloppy. Sam should never have even thought to look.

It's three thirty in the morning when I let myself into his flat. This is what I mean by it being a pain in my backside that it's June and so it has to be this time when it is still pitch black outside. I needed the cover of darkness to crawl into the basement window and now I can take the servants' elevator up to his apartment. His building is old and has been modernised in some respects, but not in others. In his kitchen is a walk-in pantry, although there is very little of the way of food inside, and at the back is the metal door to the elevator.

I risk walking around the flat and find him fast asleep in his bed, snoring softly, his bedsheets rucked around his waist. But then I retreat to the elevator. There is no way he will find me in here when he makes breakfast in the morning, and nor will he hear the sound of my breathing through the heavy metal door.

As soon as he leaves for work I start my preparations. The first thing is to check Kai's sauna is working. Which of course it is, no self-respecting Finn would allow theirs to be out of action for long. Then I start on the ice. I'm going to need a LOT of it. He has one of those old-American style fridge/freezers that creates ice at a rate of about three pints per hour. Every hour I harvest it and put it into the main freezer to stay frozen. It's dull and monotonous. I won't tell you too much detail.

But anyway, by the time he comes home from work at 7 p.m., I'm ready. The sauna has been heated to a perfect eighty degrees and I've drawn him a freezing cold bath, using about half the ice I prepared earlier. The rest is still in the freezer, proof that this is the kind of thing Kai does regularly. I wait until he's locked the front door of the apartment, sliding across all four locks like a security-obsessed lunatic even though the old staff elevator is literally an open door to the flat. Isn't it funny, the things we do to make ourselves feel safe, even though they're ultimately completely ineffectual in reality.

I listen as he takes his shoes off, hangs up his jacket, puts his car keys into the faraday box on the sideboard. He takes short shuffling steps into the living room, his socks muffling the sound of his feet on the polished wood floor.

'Hi Kai,' I say with a wave from my position on the sofa.

Kai was one of my favourites. Back then. He had dirty blond curtains and we all thought he looked like Nick Carter from the Back Street Boys. And he was charming and witty and generally less of a twat than most of them. I've always wondered if there's another world where things turned out very differently. But they didn't and now things are only going to end one way.

'I... err...' he says, not yet fully appreciating his predicament. He looks vulnerable. Like a little lost boy. Despite being almost six foot and over forty. I could spare him. But then I think about Verity and my resolve hardens.

Ice cubes clink against the crystal of the glass in my hand, bobbing in the black liquid of the Salmiakki Koskenkorva I'm drinking. It's bitter and sweet at the same time and surprisingly delicious. Inspired by this story last year of a man who tried to drug his wife by mixing Nytol with this stuff, I've added some of the liquid sleep-aid to the glass I've poured for Kai.

'Come here, Kai.' I pat the seat next to me.

He pauses, unsure of what he should do. Surely he's seen the news. Seen what has happened to Cody and Ruben and Jim.

'Please Kai.'

It's like he's unable to refuse. But I know it's fear taking over from his rational brain. When you've killed as many arseholes as I have you start to realise 'lamb to the slaughter' isn't just a pretty euphemism. It's the truth. They say you will fight to the death for your life. You hear the stories, chewing your arm off, gloving your hand – thank you Stephen King for that image in *Gerald's Game*. Stories of the human capability to refuse death. But you never hear the stories of those who know the game is up. Who stare down the barrel of their own mortality and decide to go quietly into the night.

'How did you find me?' he whispers as he sits down. I hand him his own glass of Koskenkorva and the confusion sweeps across his features. 'What's this?'

'A nightcap. The first of many. And to answer your original question, I went to see little Jimmy Handley.'

He pales slightly and takes a sip of his drink. His mouth twists into a grimace. 'This tastes odd.'

'Just drink it, Kai.'

He takes another sip. 'Why now?' he asks softly.

'Verity.'

Confusion sweeps across his features and his eyes beg me to

elaborate. He already knew it was about Verity, but he isn't understanding me.

'Verity woke up,' I whisper.

'She's awake?'

'Yes. You should have been paying more attention.'

His shoulders slump slightly as he begins to collapse in on himself. He knows what Verity's consciousness means. What will happen next. There is only one way this chapter of the story ends.

Unless he wants to fight me properly.

But he's already given up.

'Drink up, Kai,' I tell him, motioning to the glass of black liquor.

'It doesn't taste like Koskenkorva,' he says, but takes a sip anyway.

'All of it, Kai.'

He does what he did back when the other boys made him drink a raw egg. He holds his nose and tips the entire contents down his throat.

'Good boy,' I say and take the glass from his hand. I pour him another large measure. This one will taste like Koskenkorva should, I don't want to give him too much of the Nytol. I don't want it to be too *quick*.

'Poison?' he asks.

I smile. 'No, Kai.'

His lip quivers as if he's about to sob. 'Then... H... H... How?' he eventually manages to ask.

'Oh, Kai. Did you really think I was just going to poison you? That you could drink a little bit and then it would all be over? Drift away into a dreamless sleep?'

I smile at him, lips stretching over teeth. A wolf appraising the captured animal in front of her. Men can be such fools sometimes.

Kai Helve isn't found for four days. And only because the continuous running of his sauna eventually causes a fuse to melt and the whole building loses power. The building manager sends an electrician to fix the problem as he's bored of the complaints from the other residents. I could have switched it off, but I felt that leaving it on added to the whole tableau of a man having a few too many drinks and his sauna/ice bath combo ending in a terrible tragedy.

What a sad indictment of your life. To only be found because someone else is being inconvenienced. No one wondered where Kai Helve was for days. How long would it have been if that fuse hadn't gone? Although, he did live in an apartment so eventually someone would have wondered what the smell was. Perhaps a week. Maybe ten days. I'm not really sure to be honest. It's not something I want to dwell on.

I make a mental note to make sure I have a protocol established. That I would be found before... well, you know what I'm getting at. No one wants to be the body eaten by their cat. Or, even worse, someone else's cat. Twitter is full of people posting pictures of the neighbour's cat taking liberties; lying on their sofa, sitting on the kitchen counter. Adding #NotMyCat like it's hilarious. I don't want to end up a #NotMyCat meme. An involuntary shudder passes through me.

13

A week has passed since Kai and the post-kill high is morphing into a desire to plan the next.

I'm making progress. Good progress. Excellent progress. There are now only two more names on the list.

Lawrence Delaney.

Gregory Fuller.

Gregory will be last. The *pièce de résistance*. The most important one of them all and the one I will enjoy the most. I've spent a lot of time thinking of the most creative way, the most theatrical way. Do I want to make a statement? I think I do. But only if I can still walk away; I'm not a total fool.

But before Gregory there is one other.

Lawrence Delaney: I'm coming for you.

I get to the office at 7.30 a.m. and find Millie is already at her desk, seemingly absorbed in some spreadsheet. She's been getting in early a lot recently, this is the third time this week and it's only Thursday. What's brought on this change in her level of commitment?

'Good morning,' she says as she sees me.

I don't reply. It isn't a good idea to become friendly with your team. It's better if they hate you and have no desire to spend time with you when they don't have to. Or, heaven forbid, want to share secrets and niceties.

I'm sure she's told you how much of a bitch I am. Oh don't be coy, I know exactly what they all think of me. I'm not upset about it, I cultivate their disdain, their hatred. I want them to go home to their spouses or flatmates or whoever they live with and tell them how awful I am. How I have made unreasonable requests of them, forced them to work too many hours, to perform tasks outside their job description.

Why? As in why do I want them to hate me? Two reasons.

First, you do not get to be an industry icon and sit at the big boys' table if you play nicely. That's just a fact. We might pretend progression is all about hard work and determination, but that's bullshit. It's about results and it's about who knows you can deliver them. It's about taking the credit for the good, and firing someone when results don't materialise. It's about schmoozing with the guys at the top and you can only do that if you produce the goods. So I need a team that works hard and works fast and will push themselves to the edge for the chance to gain my approval. Is it manipulative? Yes. Do I care? What do you think.

Second – and to be honest this may be more important in the overall scheme of things – I need them to speculate that perhaps I sleep in a coffin, or drink the blood of babies, or ride on a broomstick, or whatever other pedestrian insult they can think of. Quite simply, for all the time they think I'm a bitch, they probably don't think I'm a killer. Sam was an oversight; and one I won't make again. Lucas is still looking for her, but to no avail. I'm trying not to think about it but she's a loose end just waiting to snag on a nail and unravel everything.

Determined to assuage any suspicions from Millie, I don't reply to her pleasantries. Instead I wait until I've crossed to the door to my office before I turn. 'Where is the new analyst, Camille?' I lace the question with a mix of disappointment and despair. And yes, of course I know Millie is short for Millicent.

Millie looks at her watch. 'It's only seven thirty.'

'Well, *we're* both here,' I say pointedly before turning away and walking into my office.

Millie reaches for her phone, no doubt to call the new analyst and find out where she is.

The new analyst doesn't turn up. It was her fourth day. She didn't even last the week.

I call Lucas to demand that he sorts it out.

'Perhaps you could try being a little bit nicer to them,' he says. I think he means to sound sarcastic, but it comes across with a bitter edge. A little rich for the man who still hasn't been able to track down a wayward former Bid Manager. It isn't like it's easy to disappear these days.

'Lucas. All I need is an analyst who doesn't run away after less than a week,' I tell him, making no apologies for any role I play in their fleeing.

'Of course. But, just maybe go a little easier on them. That's all I'm saying.'

I sigh. 'I'll try,' I say eventually. 'Just arrange for someone who isn't a total imbecile.'

This morning I have a very boring international sales round up to attend. Thankfully it's online and so I'm able to do other things in the background. Zoom gets a lot of hate, but it does mean I don't have to physically sit in a room with all these morons. Before remote working became popular, I would have had to pretend to be at least vaguely interested in what the Serendipity sales lead for Canada had to say about eye make-up trends. Everyone strap in,

Patricia's about to tell us 2023 is the year of face jewels. Someone kill me.

I position my personal laptop out of shot of the Zoom camera on my work computer, check the internet connection is going via the VPN and then open a new browser. I have a few details to check.

Lawrence Delaney is married to Katerina Jansen, the first female CEO of München Bank. She is fierce and fearless and brilliant. We could have been friends. If she didn't have such shitty taste in men.

Lawrence Delaney was voted 'Most Likely To Succeed' by his high school. But no one ever said what it was they thought he might succeed at. He wore the moniker like a badge of honour. But the truth was that he was a snake. The kind of guy who would befriend anyone he thought might be helpful to him.

Does he love Katerina? I highly doubt it. Most narcissists only really love themselves. And Lawrence is the epitome of a narcissist. You know the type; always convinced they're special, that they deserve only the very best, that the rest of the world will bow unto them. That every woman wants to fuck them. And most of the men too.

He did have charisma. I will give him that. Even back when we were teenagers people would look to him as a leader, defer to his opinion on things. If Lawrence wanted to play a game, everyone else jumped on the band wagon.

Anyway, I digress. Back to the now. The Delaney-Jansen residence is in Starnberg; the wealthiest town in Germany, about thirty minutes south of Munich on the shores of Lake Starnberger. A little slice of Bavarian paradise. If you're a millionaire at least.

Katerina is old money German. Proper old money. The type with a sprawling country estate that eats all the cash in upkeep and so the Gen X or older Millennial offspring end up in banking and law to try to fill the gap in the coffers. Delaney on the other hand is new money. His grandfather set up some company making widgets in the Deep South – Alabama to be precise – and amassed an absolute fortune. Delaney has a modest trust-fund but his family always expected him to work hard and make his own way in the world. Instead he married Katerina and now lives off the proceeds of her hard work. He's been very lucky, she's *exceptionally* good at her job.

I find a spread about the couple in *View* magazine. They look so smug. So perfect. The villa a masterclass of muted interior design that oozes class. They have two children who both attend exclusive Swiss boarding schools. Thank heavens for small mercies. You can't kill a man in a place his children might find him. I'm not a monster. I have standards, limits. Moral boundaries.

You might laugh, but it's true. I have a code.

No collateral damage. Yes, I will admit Jim Handley's brother could perhaps be considered an innocent bystander caught in the crossfire. But the way he treated the women he hired was reason enough to humiliate him just a little bit. To be honest he probably deserved a lot worse. Now, there is a caveat on this one: self-preservation will trump the code, but it's preferable to just never let yourself be in that position.

No witnesses. I don't mean this in the literal sense that no one can see me. That's not a code, that's just basic self-preservation. I mean no one else needs to see them die. So, no pushing in front of a train, for example. Imagine being that driver. It doesn't bear thinking about.

No children. By which I mean their children can't be the ones to find them. A child shouldn't bear the sin of the father. It isn't fair and it isn't right and it will not happen on my watch.

No mercy. When I come for them it is too late for clemency. There will be no point in them begging for their lives. Most of them will. Of course. It's the simplest of human functions. To beg and plead and implore and grovel and try to bargain with any god you can think of, even those you've previously shunned. Most but not all. Kai didn't fight back. He could have stood a chance against me, but he didn't even try. He always was weak, eager to follow orders. I remember how many times he did what Lawrence told him to without even a second thought.

No patsy. This one is very important. You don't let someone else go down for your crime. There are ways to kill and get away with it: an unsolved murder, an accident, a suicide. They are all permitted. Setting up another for the fall is not.

14

I've known exactly where Delaney was living for years. It's always good to stay up to date with where the people from your past are living. And social media has made it so easy, almost stupidly so. Anyway, once he married Katerina there was no chance they would live anywhere other than Bavaria and so all I've needed to do is periodically check she hasn't divorced his arse.

Unfortunately Munich is hardly the epicentre for youth beauty and cross-over products, which would naturally provide partnership opportunities with Serendipity. In order to hide this trip in my business travel I'm going to have to be a little creative.

In the end it takes me almost two weeks to find a suitable excuse to go to Munich. 'I need to visit Alle Farben,' I tell Millie.

'Alle Farben?' she asks, pulling a face. 'You mean the shops who sell the same ten items but in like a thousand different colours?'

'Yes.' I sound confident, but the look on her face is saying this isn't my finest idea.

'Why?'

'Because colour is the next trend.' I state it as if it's fact. It isn't, but it could be.

Millie narrows her eyes slightly as if she's mulling this over. 'Where is their head office?' she asks.

'Munich. Set up a meeting with Stefan Trammell. Next Tuesday.'

'Have you met before?' she asks as she jots down the detail.

I smile briefly. Stefan Trammell and I met at a gala dinner in Berlin last year. He's fairly attractive, albeit in a slightly uptight way, but he's also a raving misogynist who believes in very old-school gender roles. He was at the gala with his wife, a simpering fool in a long-sleeved and high-necked dress who barely talked to anyone and refused to make eye contact with any of the men, including the waiters.

Stefan refused to take my business card, despite my senior role at Serendipity. 'Oh, I'm sure Alle Farben and Serendipity wouldn't have any commonality,' he'd said, the condescension in his tone more than apparent. It was nothing to do with Serendipity and everything to do with me being a woman. This truth was made even clearer when I bumped into Mrs Trammell in the ladies' room a little while later.

'My husband and I have very strong beliefs,' she said in stilted English as she washed her hands, looking at me in the mirror. 'We believe in a certain order, a rule to things.'

I should've walked away from her, but I couldn't help myself. 'You think I should find a husband and stay at home to raise some babies?' I said as if it was a joke.

'I think you are an aberration,' she said with the righteous conviction of the brainwashed.

'Good to know,' I replied.

'And an abomination. You will be punished in the next life.'

'Excellent.' I smiled at her and then allowed the smile to slide from my face. 'Now here's what I believe. Your husband is a dinosaur and eventually his kind will go extinct.' I assumed she's a creationist who thought God created the fossils to test his followers' conviction.

'I will pray for you,' she said, drying her hands. 'One day you will realise the emptiness of this life you have created for yourself outside His love.'

Here's the problem though with being a pompous prick who is too convinced nothing can touch him. The economy doesn't give a flying fuck about traditional gender values and certainly puts zero stock in your trad wife. Alle Farben is sailing close to the edge, their cashflow critically poor and unable to withstand many more hits. They *need* a deal with a bigger company who can inject some capital into their flailing business. And the Alle Farben Board wouldn't give a shit that I'm a woman. Stefan will have no choice but to meet with me.

You know, even if I wasn't planning this trip as a cover to stalk Delaney, I'd be looking forward to it. Maybe next time I'll take Millie and hand over the account to her to manage. It would kill him even more if he had to deal with not just a woman, but a young and pretty one without director in her title.

* * *

I take the Murnau train from Munich Hauptbahnhof to Starnberg, dressed like a tourist in a Disney sweatshirt – fucking Disney, like I'm not a grown ass adult – and carrying one of those stupid miniature backpacks in a cheap nylon material. My hair is tucked into a cap, my face free from make-up, and I'm wearing a pair of unbranded sunglasses. I'm good at being invisible when the need arises. No one will pay me any attention.

The train pulls into Starnberg at 11 a.m. It's warm, sunny. Almost balmy. My feet are sweating in my hiking boots. I strip off the sweat-shirt and tie it round my waist. Then I start walking.

The Delaney villa is just outside the town, right on the lake for which Starnberg is named. The view's pretty impressive, sun glinting off the turquoise water, and the forty-five minutes' walk feels almost pleasant. If you're into that kind of thing – which I was, once upon a time, anyway. It gets hotter as the hour hand creeps towards twelve and I pause to take a long drink of water from the bottle in the silly backpack.

You can approach the house from the main road or from the water and so I cut down an overgrown path to the edge of the lake. No one ever walks this route and overgrown foliage covers the *Privateigentum: kein betreten* signs. For a moment I wonder if I'm too exposed, if this is too risky. What if someone sees me? What if someone stops me and asks why I'm here, why I'm ignoring the no trespassing messaging and just ploughing on? I guess I'll just have to claim innocence. Use an American accent and claim stupidity and a lack of modern language classes at my high school.

But no one stops me and the path leads to the perfect look out spot, the whole Delaney villa laid out before me. Remember I said Lawrence was voted 'Most Likely To Succeed'? Well, succeed he did. In finding himself a rich wife to leach off anyway: this place is impressive by anyone's standards.

Apparently Katerina's inheritance is tied up in some monstrosity of a castle that costs millions to maintain and allows very little disposable cash to flow to her. So it's lucky she's brilliant. And even luckier for me that she works such long hours, leaving the villa at six thirty in the morning and not returning until at least 8 p.m. Or at least that's what she always says in interviews.

Which leaves Lawrence with a lot of free time. And it would appear he's using it to full effect today, lounging by the pool in a pair of age-inappropriate speedos like the archetypal trophy husband. He stands up and stretches, his gaze drifting over the water. He twists from left to right twice, then bends over to touch his toes, bouncing a few times. Then he straightens up and looks out over the lake again.

The edge of the patio juts over the water, a white stone balustrade to prevent an accidental fall. That could work. A little tumble over the side, the angle just unfortunate enough to hit his head on a jagged rock before he falls into the water, too confused to swim to safety.

Or the swimming pool. A dive in, the angle miscalculated so he breaks his neck hitting the surface. Hmm. Maybe scratch that one, it's too difficult to mimic the right injury. And too difficult to force him to do it to himself.

But then the sound of an engine breaks the silence and a huge arc of water splashes over the balustrade. The engine noise cuts out, giving way to the sound of laughter. A few moments later a tall man appears, leapfrogging over the wall with ease. 'Arschgeige!' he yells at the top of his voice in heavily accented German.

I tuck myself back into my hiding place. There's something frightening in the man's tone, a sense an argument is about to happen.

'Arschgeige!' Lawrence replies with the same tone.

But then the two men meet in the middle and embrace, slapping each other on the back, the sound of it ricocheting around the patio.

'Fuck. It's good to see you, Dünnbrettbohrer.' The stranger says to Lawrence, reverting to English, except for the final slur. It means *driller of thin planks*, basically someone who takes the easy way out and does the bare minimum. It's fitting.

'You might not think so after I've told you why I invited you over,' Lawrence replies as he walks to the bar area built next to the pool. It has a thatch roof like a tacky tiki bar, but somehow manages an aura of class. Perhaps it's the sheer scale of expenditure lavished on the space, with its driftwood bar and matching stools with burgundy leather seats. He moves behind the bar and pours them both a pint of a pale lager. 'Prost,' he says clinking his glass against his friend's.

'So, spill it,' the stranger says, sliding onto one of the stools. He takes a long drink as he waits.

'Katerina is having an affair.'

'No way.'

'Yep.' Lawrence sounds both upset and pissed off and with more than a hint of entitled child.

'You have proof?' The stranger pauses. 'Oh. Right. That's why I'm here.'

I'll save you the boredom of listening to the rest of their conversation. It went on for some time, deconstructing every conversation between Lawrence and Katerina, every phone call she'd taken, every time she stayed late in the office. Lawrence is a whiny bitch who totally under-appreciates his wife. I don't blame her for looking elsewhere for a little validation.

It's a pain in my arse though. Now I'm going to have to find a way to kill him that can never backfire on Katerina. If she is having an affair she'll be the primary suspect. Did I include that one when I told you the code? That you can't pin it on anyone else specifically? That's not fair. Think how you would feel if you were accused of a murder you didn't have the satisfaction of actually undertaking. Imagine spending your life in prison with the knowledge that, while the bastard is dead, you weren't the one who got to do it?

Anyway, this knowledge means I need to do some more thinking. I need a better plan, something more intricate, more time consuming. I'm pissed about it. Although I have always loved a challenge. And it means I can come back with Millie and make fucking Stefan squirm some more, so it isn't all bad.

But for now my trip is over and I need to head back to London.

Just so long as I get this done before mid-August. There is still Gregory and I'm on a schedule.

15

There's an envelope sitting on my desk when I get to the office at 6 a.m. on Thursday morning. Luckily I'm so early I've beaten the new turbo-charged Millie here. I used to get so much more peace in the early morning and I resent her for her conscientiousness.

Inside the envelope is a list, printed on the rubbish recycled paper the office switched to in an effort to appear more environmentally responsible. I scan down the lines. It's just a list of some expense reports from the last few years. But then I turn over the sheet and find a Post-it stuck to the back, the handwriting neat and even:

Millie has been digging...

That's all it says. I turn over the sheet again and look more carefully at which reports she's been looking at.

June 2022.
September 2022.

On 21 June, Spencer Balmforth apparently jumped from the window of his hotel room on the fortieth floor of the Emirates Tower. I was in Dubai, visiting the potential supplier of make-up mirrors Serendipity wanted to market to wannabe beauty influencers.

On 28 September, Ethan Donahue's body was dragged out of the Herengracht. I was entertaining some VIP clients at the Restaurant Bougainville near the Royal Palace of Amsterdam.

But perhaps Lucas is just being paranoid. She also looked at July 2021. Now that is a month when I know for a fact nothing happened. I broke my wrist on the 28th of June that year when some idiot pushed me as we disembarked an aircraft and I fell down the last few of those slippery steps onto the tarmac. He claimed it was an accident but I remember the pressure of his hand on the base of my spine before I fell. His word against mine. I didn't bother progressing it.

It must just be a coincidence Millie's been looking at some of the months I was more... well, let's say *active*, shall we? I've been additionally careful since Sam. But I'm going to have to keep an eye on Millie, perhaps be even more harsh on her. Make sure she doesn't start putting two and two together and making anything other than a very dull and staid four. Remember, I want her to think I'm a bitch and never a killer.

I put in a formal request to the IT Department to monitor her internet usage and send the findings directly to me. I want to know what else she might be looking at. And before you think badly of me for spying on my team, it's fairly standard to make sure someone isn't just passing away the day on Pinterest or Instagram.

Then I start to build a proposal for Alle Farben. It's all bullshit of course. There's no way we'll ever actually do this deal, but it'll provide a decent level of cover for the next month.

This is the final element of my code: always have an alibi. By which I'm not meaning a reason that places you nowhere near the scene of the crime. But a reason that means you were in the vicinity for a legitimate and entirely valid reason. You can never really control who might see you, and this saves an awful lot of stress.

Business travel is an absolute godsend and one of the main reasons this job with Serendipity was so attractive. My expenses are almost unlimited and I have absolute autonomy to travel wherever the hell I like in the pursuit of new partnerships and collaboration opportunities. Now, ninety percent of my trips are genuine. Meeting boring men from stuffy and well entrenched companies. It's funny that even in the beauty industry most of the senior roles are taken by men, even though their primary product user is female. It's the same in most industries though to be fair. But at least in beauty it is *possible* for a woman to rise to the top. Turns less heads.

At the beginning of my career, leaving university and staring out at all the possibilities of my future, I'd considered what kind of company to apply for. I was excellent at problem solving, good with maths and I have a naturally analytical brain. I could've gone into construction. And I would've been damn good at it too. But I would have been an enigma. An oddity. Someone who captured too much attention. I wanted a place I could be successful, rise to a senior position, but not end up splashed across the front pages of *Time* magazine or something else that would have made me too noticeable. So definitely nothing that could have made me properly famous.

It's very hard to get away with murder if you're firmly in the public eye.

Millie arrives at seven forty-five. Five minutes later the new analyst comes in, balancing a tray of coffees. There had better be an oat latte for me.

Millie knocks on my door.

'Come in,' I try to sound a little more friendly than usual. Yes, I want her to think I'm a bitch, but sometimes I want to disarm her.

'Jennifer bought coffees from Brew Box.'

I look at her over the screen of my laptop.

'Oh,' she trips over her words a little. 'She got you an oat latte, with an extra shot because Brew Box can be a little weak.' Millie motions to it in her hand.

I reach out and flap my hand. Then I drop the friendly act. 'Next time tell her to ask for only half the extra shot, but I suppose this will do for now.'

She places it on my desk and then walks backwards away from me.

'Oh. Camille,' I say and she stops in her tracks, standing awkwardly like in the shittest game of Musical Statues. 'You remember my meeting with Alle Farben?'

'Yes...' She looks confused, as if she's missed something.

'They're doing interesting things in the nail art sphere.'

'Oh. I'll look into it some more,' she replies.

'Do.'

'Do you really think there's potential there?' She sounds almost snarky. I don't appreciate it, it is her job after all. Or at least what she thinks her job is. The reality is there isn't a commercially viable proposition there. But it doesn't really matter. Just as long as I get the alibi.

Just before she leaves my office, she turns round, the movement quick and decisive. 'Freya, why did Sam leave?' She looks almost surprised when the words leave her mouth. I wonder how long she has been wanting to ask the question. Probably for the almost two months since she took over the role. I'm surprised she's taken this long, although perhaps she's been chatting to her chum in HR.

Lucas and I argued over what we should say about Sam's rather sudden departure. I wanted to say I fired her. Make up a whole gross misconduct narrative. Lucas thought that had the potential to find its way into the gossip network and cause more scandal than we wanted.

'You do not want anyone to dig into Sam,' he told me. 'And you certainly don't want some overly helpful idiot thinking they should find her to offer advice on unfair dismissal. Plus,' and to be honest this had been enough of a clincher, 'you might find yourself at the centre of an HR furore and even I can't protect you from Sebastien Villeneuve.' Sebastien is the Global Vice President of Human Resources at the LA headquarters and the most morally straight and absolutely infuriatingly *nice* man in the world.

He didn't say the other thing. That I don't want anyone talking to Sam about what she might know. About my other interests.

In the end Lucas and I agreed we would just say she quit. Often it's easier to maintain a lie that doesn't stray too far from the truth. 'But I want the inference to be she quit before I fired her,' I'd been adamant. That was my line and I wasn't budging from it.

Lucas had huffed a little, but eventually agreed it was probably better. 'I'll make sure people think you were going to fire her but she decided that would look worse on her CV. What with you being so well-respected in the industry.' He doesn't sound sarcastic, but he can be a very smooth liar when he wants to be. 'It's probably better than people thinking it was because you were being a bitch.'

Or a killer.

Anyway, I repeat the line Lucas told me to. 'She decided Serendipity wasn't a good fit for her.' It's bollocks, a corporate bull-shit soundbite.

'So she left?' Millie asks.

'Officially.' I can't help myself. Lucas will probably have a hissy fit later about just how much that single word inferred.

Millie looks thoughtful, as though she has a whole raft of

follow-up questions. She opens her mouth to speak but then closes it again.

'Was there something else?' I clip the words so it sounds less of a question and more of a dismissal.

'Umm...' but she closes her mouth again.

I cough purposefully and she takes the hint.

'Sorry. I'll... I'll leave you to it.' And then she's gone.

I take a sip of the coffee, bracing myself for it to be too strong with the double shot. But it's perfect. For fuck's sake, I should have kept my mouth shut about only adding half an extra shot. Now I'm going to spend however long it is until this new analyst quits drinking shit coffee.

My bad mood prickles my skin and I find myself scratching at my forearm. I don't know when it started, the itching. It feels like it was always there, waiting, festering, whispering my name in the dark of the night, begging me to scratch *just a little bit*. I would wake in the morning with blood on the sheets, my father's disappointed face at breakfast, my mother insisting we saw yet another doctor.

I snatch my hand away and pull my personal laptop out of the Bulgari leather tote Gabriel bought me last Christmas. It was a breach of the rules, a sign of affection that I refused to tolerate in our purely physical relationship. But the bag was nice, the leather soft as butter, and he really did have an excellent eye for accessories. So, yes, I use it, but only because it's practical and not because I have any feelings for him at all.

Before my hand can creep back to scratch the phantom itch, I open the laptop screen and check the VPN. A little more research into Mr Lawrence Delaney will help. My symptoms have been basically stable for a while now, directly correlating to how I've been managing my extra-curricular activities. Almost as if they're the thing providing the relief, the salve. Mum used to try to push me towards therapy. I wonder what a professional would think of the coping mechanism I've developed?

16

The train takes almost forty-five minutes from Victoria, stopping at a whole host of stations for places no one has ever heard of. The villages of middle-class suburbia. The type of places favoured by the Heads of Department of large organisations who do incredibly boring things like sell insurance or household electrical goods.

I'm one of only a handful of people to get off at Woldingham. It's always the same, mediocre people getting off in a mediocre village to continue their mediocre lives. Of course, not all of them will be mediocre, some might even be extraordinary. But it's easier to look through them, to see them as nothing. Otherwise I might be dragged into the minutiae of their lives, find myself chatting to one of them. Perhaps some of them also visit Burtenshaw House.

It's a short walk from the station and the sun is warm on my face, hinting at the potential heatwave summer we're being fore-casted. But you need to remember it has a huge impact on my personal projects. It affects everything, and can end up being the difference between success and failure. Just think how fewer witnesses there would be on a rainy night versus a balmy one, or how much less conspicuous someone wearing a large coat and a hat is in the middle of a snow storm.

Burtenshaw House is set back from the main road, surrounded by a tall wrought iron fence with an ornate gate that has been retro-fitted with a sensor to open automatically as you get close. But only if you're approaching from the main road. It has retained the faded majesty of its Manor House origins, but there are a few subtle details that hint at its current deployment. The gate that only opens automatically from the road. The sash windows on the upper floors that only open a few centimetres. The CCTV cameras covering every inch of the rather pretty gardens.

It isn't a prison. But it has been designed to keep the residents inside the grounds. For their own protection, of course, as many are prone to wandering, or unable to recognise potential dangers. It's a private facility, and an expensive one. With the price tag comes a high degree of discretion. It's rumoured a minor royal is a patient, but no one has ever confirmed that.

I follow the protocol, waiting for the gates to close behind me before walking further into the grounds. The gravel driveway is lined with tall and slender cypress trees, filling the air with a herba-ceous scent. The place is peaceful, quiet, and I take a moment to breathe it in. There are moments when I envy her, living here. Although of course her experience as a patient is so very different to mine as a visitor. I can leave, for one.

The large stone and brick porch is shaded and almost cool. I pause, psyching myself up to push open the heavy wooden door and step inside. The air is stale, tinged with a medicinal scent, and I gag slightly. It's an involuntary action. The reception area sits a few metres away, leather chairs and antique rugs softening the space but doing little to hide the true nature of Burtenshaw House.

'Lucky Verity. Second visit this week,' the receptionist says, her voice gentle.

I don't respond as I sign my name in the visitor book.

'She's not having a good day,' a voice from behind causes me to jump. It's Nurse Adelaide. One of the few constants in Verity's life.

'Quiet or loud?' I ask with dread at the answer I might receive.

'Loud,' Adelaide confirms.

'The usual?'

Adelaide sighs and nods. 'It's been the same for the past few hours. If you'd called ahead I would've advised you not to make the journey.'

'Have you...?' I don't bother finishing the sentence. My meaning is clear.

Nurse Adelaide blushes a little, her cheeks turning a pink that could be considered rather attractive. If you liked that kind of thing. 'I gave her a little something an hour ago,' she says as her expression shifts from guilt to a faux pained look. She might pretend to find the idea of sedation difficult, but we both know how much easier her life is when she can drug Verity to the eyeballs. But of course she has to wrap it up in the suggestion that it's what is best for the patient.

I play along. 'I think that was probably for the best.'

'Would you still like to see her?' Adelaide asks.

'How lucid is she?' Lucid covering off both the possibility she's so out of it a visit is pointless and the risk she might do nothing but scream in my face as she's done in the past on some of her 'loud' days.

'Fairly, but I'll make sure she's calm,' Adelaide promises.

'I'll wait in the common room.'

Verity is silent when the chair is wheeled into the common room, a grand room with views out over the lawns at the back of the house. You can often see deer and rabbits grazing from the window and Verity finds the wildlife fascinating on her better days.

In light of her animal obsession, I've bought her a present. A copy of *The Last Bear*, complete with illustrations. Her face barely registers as I unwrap it for her and show her. 'See, Verity. It's even signed by the author.' I flick through to one of the illustrations. 'Isn't it pretty, Verity? It won the Blue Peter book award.' A flicker of something that could be a smile curls the edge of her mouth. 'You remember Blue Peter?' I ask.

I spend the next half hour reading *The Last Bear* to her, keeping my voice animated, exactly as you would read to a small child. She shows no sign of enjoyment. No sign she can even hear my voice. But, as I close the book, she suddenly looks at me, eyes like daggers piercing mine. I brace for the scream. But she remains silent. A shiver runs down my spine at the look on her face. Comprehension. She sees me. She knows me.

'I have to go,' I say hurriedly, placing the book on her lap.

And then I'm running. Running away from her. From all she could have been.

From whom she might become.

* * *

Lucas messages just as I'm stepping onto the train.

> Hope all OK with Verity

I don't reply, just close my eyes instead, trying to stop myself from reliving the moment this afternoon over and over. Ice spreads through my stomach. It's been so long, so many years. I never thought she would regain any kind of meaningful capability. But that look... that was something else altogether. Why now? Or can she sense that I'm close? That there aren't many left. That it's almost over?

My plan is to go home, have a shower and a nightcap. Get an

early night. Try to push all thoughts of Verity to the back of my brain. Try to have a rest from it all.

But fate has another plan.

I'm in town xx

Gabriel. I should ignore him. Or tell him I'm busy, that I have plans and they don't involve him.

The Bulgari tote is on the seat next to me and I find my fingertips sweeping over the buttery leather. I cannot help myself. I feel the pull of him.

He's at the bar of the hotel, back straight, shoulders squared. His hair is longer than last time, curling over the collar of his shirt. A book lies open in front of him, a glass of red wine at his elbow. He senses my arrival and turns to look at me.

'You look beautiful, Freya,' he whispers in my ear as he draws me into an embrace. He smells amazing, like fresh linen and earthy forest mixed into one heady scent. I curse myself for noticing.

He motions to the bartender and orders me a Cherry Paloma cocktail. I only drink them with him. He changes me in a way I cannot articulate. And I hate it. But I cannot help myself.

We have dinner in the restaurant. Fillet steak with Béarnaise butter, sautéed red cabbage, potato croquettes. Lemon posset for dessert. The meal is deliciously unpretentious and the perfect match to our easily flowing conversation. We drink white wine even though propriety demands we pair our steak with red. The Sauvignon Blanc is crisp on my tongue.

We talk about everything and nothing at all. We skirt over work, moving instead to films and books and galleries. To friends and family.

'How is Verity?' he asks.

'She's doing well,' I reply. Despite the mood of affinity between us, I don't tell him about that moment of absolute recognition at Burtenshaw this afternoon. Or what it could mean. I change the subject, put us back onto safer ground. 'How's Ava?' Ava is his German Shepherd and the love of his life.

'Gorgeous,' he can't help but smile as he talks about her.

The evening continues, winding slowly towards its natural conclusion. Gabriel and I have performed this same dance many times before.

He looks me straight in the eye as he enters me, whispers my name as he pushes himself deeper, the last syllable dissolving into a growl. I feel the room melting around me until nothing else exists except the two of us. His skin on mine. The weight of him pressing me into the cool cotton of the sheet beneath my back. He is fire and rain and beauty.

His fingers trace the line of my chin as he supports himself on his other arm. I wrap my legs around his waist and pull him closer. He groans, his rhythm speeding up a little as he leans in to kiss me. I close my eyes, hands in his hair, lips on his. Melting together.

'Open your eyes,' he says softly, his voice loaded with lust.

I look at him, breath mingling with his. His hand cups my cheek and he shifts his weight so the other does the same. He's almost squashing me, the sensation exquisite. I shift my hips, just a millimetre, but it's enough to catch the breath in the back of his throat.

I let go. Allow myself to fall.

* * *

I'm lying on my front, the sheet covering me from the waist down, his fingers trailing a path across my shoulder blades.

'Freya?' he whispers.

'Yes?'

'Is there a chance… for us?'

I swallow. I want there to be. I know I come across as the kind of person who needs no one. Who wants no one. A lone wolf stalking her prey. But with Gabriel I crave normality. Stability. Peace. 'It's complicated,' I tell him, unable to say the truth.

'One day?'

I smile. 'Maybe.'

I want to tell him I could love him.

But I don't. Instead I reach out and pull him to me. My kisses are forceful, almost violent. It cannot be love. And I prove to myself it's only physical. It's just fucking.

I do not have feelings for Gabriel.

17

It's not quite two weeks later and I'm no closer to figuring out how to kill Lawrence and not implicate Katerina. I need inspiration.

The flight to Munich is delayed. Millie's sitting next to me in the airport lounge frantically refreshing the flight information on the app on her phone. She's worried we'll be late for the meeting with Alle Farben. Like it matters.

The meeting is nothing more than an introduction, a chance for the prick Stefan to meet Millie. It's doubly good that I'm going to let Millie take the lead on this. First, she'll make Stefan squirm and I will sit and enjoy the show. Second, it'll put her fingerprints all over the deal. That way if it's ever questioned I can simply say it was a training exercise for her. An opportunity for her to show me what she can do. What a shame it'll be a bit of a disaster.

Plus of course I get my alibi, my reason for being in Munich. And if it means at some point down the line I can pull out this failed deal with Alle Farben as an example of Millie's incompetence, which leads to her dismissal from Serendipity, then all the better. It's always good to have back-up plans. Especially as I'm starting to feel concerned about her. She's always around, digging into things, asking questions. Just like Sam.

Sometimes I catch her staring at me. Just sitting at her desk, her gaze drawn to me. I'm not sure she even realises she's doing it.

'You don't think she suspects?' I'd asked Lucas last night.

'Do *you* think she suspects?' he asked in return.

'No.'

'But you're not one hundred percent sure.'

'Sometimes she looks at me like... I can't explain it. Like she's trying to figure me out.'

'She has no idea,' he said. 'We wouldn't be sitting here if she knew. *She* would definitely have gone to the police.' He sounded so confident. And he's right, of course. Millie is exactly the kind of person who would turn me in the moment she had real suspicion. She wouldn't realise she should cut and run like Sam did.

However, I know it is always better to have a back-up plan and that's why I'm making sure I have reason to fire her if I need to. No one ever listens to a disgruntled ex-employee. It's one of the easiest ways to make someone invisible.

We make it to the meeting on time and it goes exactly as expected. Stefan's face when I tell him Millie will be leading the discussions is a picture and I wish I could take a photo of the moment. No doubt he will meet his friends later and deliver a sermon on the destructive power of allowing 'females' in the work-place, while clapping himself on the back for his foresight in selecting a better class of wife. But the best part of it is he still thinks he's in control of the negotiation. He doesn't realise his company is too small, too stale, too staid. I always knew the busi-ness case wouldn't stack up and it's even worse than I was expecting.

'I think we should leave it,' Millie says after the meeting ends and we go for a light dinner at Irmi's, the Bavarian restaurant in our hotel.

'Leave what?'

'The deal with Alle Farben.'

'You do?' I'm going to have to tread carefully. I need to keep them as a potential client to come out another few times. But she can't think it's my idea. It's not like I can fire her for my own mistake.

'It's not viable. We should just walk away.' She's looking at me over the rim of her glass. Is there something there? A hint of... I don't know how to read her and it's making me angry. But I damp it down, plaster my professional mask over my features.

'Have you done enough due diligence?' I ask her, keeping my tone clipped.

'I've done a lot.'

'That isn't what I asked, Camille.'

'Do *you* think we should progress?' she asks.

I pour myself another glass of wine and then sit back in my chair, taking a slow sip as if I'm thinking it all through. Eventually I say, 'I think the economy is tough at the moment. The kind of ROIs we were seeing in previous years have stalled. Profitable deals are further apart, and it's significantly more difficult to get partnerships off the starting blocks. We need to explore the possibility for synergistic benefits that could provide cash flow injections for future fiscal periods.' I know I'm throwing jargon around to sound clever and important. And I know it doesn't actually work. But that's beside the point. I want her to hate me. I want her to think I'm a wanky boss who doesn't really understand the ins and outs of the business. I want her to think she has to double down her efforts to impress me.

'I don't think the potential IRR is sufficiently attractive to justify the risk,' she says.

Did she just try to out-jargon me? 'How many years have you been doing this, Camille?'

She sighs, loudly enough for me to hear her. 'I'll continue to work up the pitch,' she says quietly, the resentment clear in her voice.

I want to shout at her, to tell her not to be so bloody disrespect-ful, that she will do what I fucking tell her because I'm her boss. But instead I take another sip of wine. Something isn't right here. She's never spoken to me like this before, the defiance so close to the surface, sitting just behind her eyes. Instead I say, 'Good. Let's just give it another few weeks. See where we land.'

'I suppose we'll need to come back to Munich.' She catches my eye and smiles, before reaching for the wine to top up her own glass.

'If you think that will be necessary,' I say magnanimously. But it feels like she's just handed me a gift-wrapped box. One that may contain a bomb that will blow up in my face.

When Millie excuses herself to use the bathroom, I make a call.

'Lucas, she's suspicious,' I hiss into the phone the second he answers.

'Who?' he asks, and I hear the sound of a television in the back-ground. 'Just a sec,' he says, but the words are muffled, as if he has covered his phone while he talks to someone else.

'Who are you talking to?' I demand.

'I have someone over.'

'Oh. Well, I'm sorry to interrupt you.'

'No, you're not,' he replies, no real emotion in his words. He's merely stating a fact.

'No, I'm not. Anyway, I'm getting worried.'

'About our mutual friend?'

'She's being difficult. Asking questions.'

'How would she have proof?' He's matter of fact. I like this in him. He doesn't panic or fly into an anxious rage, he's calm and methodical. How, who, what, why: these are the questions he lives by.

'I don't know.'

'You've covered your tracks. Left no loose ends.'

'You're right.' I don't say goodbye, just hang up the phone and place it face down on the table next to me. He's right, I have solid alibis. Some of them she has even helped me with.

* * *

Lawrence Delaney is stalking his wife. And I am stalking Lawrence Delaney. It's almost ridiculous. But I'm a lot better at this than Lawrence is.

Katerina is beautiful. Tall and aristocratic with a bone structure any Greek goddess would have been proud of. She's dressed in a dark green silk dress with a slash neck and asymmetric design most people wouldn't be able to get away with. But on her it looks incredible.

The man she's meeting in the bar of the Nobel Hotel on Landwehrstraße is attractive, attentive, and listening closely to everything she has to say, his hand resting on the back of her chair in a casually proprietary way. Are they having an affair? It certainly looks like it. He bears more than a passing resemblance to Lawrence. Well, I guess Katerina has a type.

I'm sitting at the next table, dressed in a simple black suit and cream blouse, my laptop in front of me along with a large glass of red wine. I occasionally tap the keys and sigh gently. Just another overburdened executive working late into the night on a business trip. I order another glass of wine from the waitress as she passes, affecting a French accent behind my apparently terrible German.

Katerina and her date talk about a range of topics; music and theatre and the places they would like to travel. She doesn't mention her husband or children.

Lawrence is outside the bar, watching his wife and this attractive man from the street. I don't know what his plan is. Is he going to come in, 'bump' into her as if by accident? I should probably excuse myself, find a less obvious spot if he's going to make a scene.

Katerina touches her date's hand and then tells him she is going to the ladies' room.

I decide to take the moment to make my getaway, so I fold away my laptop and slide it into my handbag, before standing and picking up my refreshed wine glass.

'Mademoiselle?' Katerina's date says.

'Oui?' I reply, praying he doesn't want to start a conversation in French.

'English?'

I nod.

'You are here on business?'

I nod again.

'If you would prefer not to drink alone...' he says and places a card on my table, sliding it a few inches until it's directly in front of me.

'Merci,' I whisper as I pick it up and slip it into my jacket pocket. I offer him a shy smile and he returns it with a wink.

Well, well, well. So the handsome stranger is an escort.

Just as I'm walking away, Katerina returns. And then all hell breaks loose.

'You bitch!' Lawrence runs towards her. He's obviously decided not to skulk around outside any longer.

'Lawrence... I...' she starts.

'Shut it, *whore!*' He spits the word in her face. It sounds even more vicious in German.

I melt away, heading towards the foyer of the hotel, but staying within ear shot, thankful to the overly conscientious young Freya who paid attention in her German classes at university.

'Don't speak to the lady like that,' the escort says.

'She isn't a fucking lady. She's a lying, cheating bitch.'

'And you are?' The escort is taller than Lawrence, broader, in better shape.

But Lawrence is fired up with the indignant rage of a man scorned. 'I'm her husband.'

'Oh.'

'Yeah. Oh!' Lawrence shouts, jabbing a finger towards the escort. 'You're fucking my wife.'

'No.' He takes hold of the jabbing finger and pushes it away gently. 'I'm having a civilised drink with a friend.'

'Oh, a civilised drink, is it? Do you think I'm blind?' He whirls around to face Katerina. 'Do you think I'm a fool? I know exactly what you're up to. I can't believe this.'

'I think we should all calm down and take a little breather,' the escort says.

'Oh, do you?' Lawrence's voice has risen almost an entire octave and every single person in the bar has now stopped to watch the argument. 'You think you can tell me what to do? You think you can fuck my wife and then boss me around. Just who the actual fuck do you think you are?' He shoves the escort in the chest.

'Lawrence!' Katerina finally speaks up. 'Stop it.'

'I'm not letting him get away with this.' Lawrence says, giving the escort another shove. 'He isn't going to get away with stealing my wife.'

'Oh for fuck's sake. He isn't stealing me. I'm paying him.'

There is a collective sucked intake of breath as her words sink in with the listening patrons.

'Yes.' She doubles down on her confession. 'This man is an escort.'

'You're...?' Lawrence curls his lip in disgust as he looks at his wife.

'Oh, knock it off, sweetheart. Like you haven't paid for it a dozen times in the last year alone.'

'That's different.' Lawrence sounds genuinely aggrieved. Like he really believes in his ridiculous double standard that it's OK for a man to pay for sex but it's something horrifying for a woman to do.

'I suggest you go home,' Katerina tells Lawrence. Then she reaches for the escort's hand and pulls him towards the foyer where I'm still standing, watching them. I move out of the way as they pass.

One of the hotel security guys nods at the escort. He's obviously known to the hotel and they don't bat an eyelid. All part of the service.

I move further to the side and use the cover of a pillar to peer back towards Lawrence.

He's standing with his mouth hanging open, staring at the retreating back of his wife as she goes off to fuck some guy she's paid for. I really hope she used their joint account.

But then I do something entirely unprecedented. My feet are walking on their own. And then I'm in front of him. There isn't even a hint of recognition on his face. He has no idea what has happened to Jim and Kai and the others. No inkling I'm anyone other than a woman in a hotel bar in Munich.

'Are you OK?' I ask in English, maintaining the subtle French accent I used earlier.

'I... I...' he starts but his mouth is unable to form the words.

'Let's go to the bar next door, OK?' I touch his elbow.

He nods dumbly and lets me lead him outside.

18

Lawrence remains silent as I steer him into the bar next door. It's been decorated to look a bit of a dive, all dim-lighting and shabby furniture, but the patrons are mainly in their thirties and forties, middle management blowing off steam after a day in the office. At least it's busy and the music's loud. No one will give us a second look in here. At the bar, I order two beers and two shots.

'I can't believe her,' Lawrence says, sliding onto a bar stool. 'I mean, he's a stranger.'

'Perhaps that's the point,' I reply, pushing a shot of Jägermeister towards him.

'But... a *gigolo*?' he wails and then necks the drink, slamming the little glass down on the bar once he's done.

I stifle my laughter at his use of the word. It sounds so old fashioned. So odd. I motion to the bartender to get us another round of Jägermeisters.

'Why?' he asks in a slightly more normal voice.

'Why?' I reply, not sure what question he's actually asking.

'Why is she cheating? Why is she using an escort? Why is she paying someone?'

'Do you really want me to answer?' I take a sip of my beer.

'You think it's because I'm bad in bed?' He sounds so incredulous, so utterly taken aback by the idea that perhaps he's a selfish lover who can't please his wife.

'Are you?'

'Of course not.' But his voice is too loud, his bravado so gossamer thin it's see-through.

'I don't mean in a technical way,' I reassure him, placing my hand on his knee for a second. 'I mean perhaps you're emotionally unavailable. That you're not there for her when she needs it.'

'So why isn't she having a proper affair? Hmm? Why is she paying for cock?'

I pretend to blanche a little at the crassness of his words.

He notices my response. 'Sorry,' he says quickly. 'It's just... I love her and now she's done this to me.'

Here's the funny thing. He never once mentions how much the escort looks like him. Like he hasn't even noticed the similarity. Or grasped the significance. I don't point it out to him. Don't tell him that she's chosen to play out a fantasy in which her husband, the man she fell in love with, isn't actually a total dick. She obviously still loves him. It makes me feel a bit queasy.

How can such a brilliant woman be so dumb?

Lawrence and I carry on drinking together into the early hours. Well, I'm sipping beer. He's slamming back the shots like they are going out of fashion. Jägermeister is surprisingly strong, about thirty-five percent, almost as much as shooting neat vodka. His words are starting to slur, his movements messy.

'We could go to your hotel,' he says as the clock strikes one. This is the first time he has made any type of approach on me. I'm almost offended he thinks I would have so little self-respect as to take him home.

Up until this point, my plan was just to stop him from making any more of a tit out of himself. To make sure he didn't decide to go back to the hotel and knock on the door to every room until he found Katerina and her escort. But then I realise what a gift I have almost drooling in front of me as he struggles to keep upright on his barstool.

What if I could get him to take me back to his house? He's certainly angry enough with his wife to punish her in the worst possible way he can think of. Do you remember when I said it was best to find reasons for you to have been in the vicinity of a crime for completely valid reasons? Well, how about putting my fingerprints legitimately into my future victim's house.

Now, I would absolutely expect the Delaney-Jansens have a housekeeper who's extremely fastidious and so it's highly unlikely there would be any of my fingerprints left by the time I kill Lawrence. And I will obviously wear gloves on that final visit. But there is always a chance, a margin of error. *If* my fingerprint, even just a partial, was ever found at the Delaney-Jansen house, this would be my alibi, my get-out-of-jail-free card. Plus it's an excellent opportunity to have a proper poke around where he lives.

'We shouldn't,' I reply, but my body language doesn't match my words as I lean closer to him.

'Live a little,' he breathes beery-Jägermeistery fumes in my face and I force myself not to recoil.

'My work has strict rules about guests in hotels.' My hand slips to his knee and I bite my lower lip.

'Oh.' He looks crestfallen. I slide my hand higher up his leg and watch as his tiny brain lands on an alternative plan. 'You could come home with me?'

Well, that was easy. He really is a fool. 'How far is it?' I ask, my hand creeping another inch towards his – most likely pathetic – dick.

'Not far,' he says. 'I have a driver.'

Not far is a bit of a stretch given it's more than fifteen miles and will take half an hour each way, but the driver creates another layer in my alibi. 'How will I get back?'

'My driver will bring you back; I'm a gentleman.'

He has just invited a stranger to his marital home for a quick fuck to get back at his wife. The very epitome of a gentleman. I pause for a moment as if I might still turn him down. In reality I'm just calculating if I can get enough alcohol down his throat to put him into a coma on the journey to Starnberg. I'm obviously not going to sleep with him.

'OK,' I finally say to him. Whisky should do the trick.

'You won't regret this...' he trails off and a look of confusion crosses his face. 'Umm... oh shit...'

'Freya.' I tell him, feigning a laugh that he'd forgotten my name. He hadn't, he never actually asked. Which is quite lucky, as I *was* going to tell him my name was Francoise. Which would have rather fucked up my alibi plan. Now I just need to fade out the French accent before I meet his driver. No need to over-complicate things and he won't remember the accent in the morning. He doesn't react to my name. Makes no connection to the girl he knew all those years ago.

'Why don't you get us a bottle for the road and I'll call my driver.' Then he leans in, slightly unsteady so he has to grip the edge of the bar to stop himself falling. 'Freya,' he whispers my name as if it's the most glamorous thing he's ever heard. 'Are you ready for a night you won't forget?'

I simper, even as I want to vomit into my own mouth. 'Your wife doesn't know what she's missing.'

Lawrence must have the constitution of a horse, or be a border-line alcoholic, because he's still standing when we pull up outside the house at 2 a.m. He's obviously drunk, but he can still walk. And unfortunately, he can still talk, keeping up an almost constant commentary of the things he wants to do to me when we get inside. Actually, that's not quite true. He has kept up an almost constant commentary of the things he wants me to do to him. He's a selfish pig and I'm not surprised at all that Katerina is with the escort. I envy her at this moment.

Inside the house he leads me down a huge wide corridor. Everything is in neutral tones, but not in a sparse IKEA way. It's subtly stylish, contemporary without being brutalist. If I wasn't going to kill her husband, I'd be asking Katerina who her interior designer was. Lawrence shows me into the living room. More neutral tones provide a sense of muted calm, except for the statement sofa and matching armchairs in a glorious deep blue print, picked through with silver accents like the night sky.

He sits heavily on the sofa and pats the seat next to him. I need a new plan to disarm him. It's staring me in the face. 'Is this your wedding?' I ask. It's a stupid question because Katerina is dressed in white, with a veil and a bouquet of flowers.

He grunts in response.

'Your children?' I point at the large framed portrait above the fireplace. 'You all look so happy.'

'We were.' He sounds sad, almost wistful. Exactly what I was hoping for.

'Do you still love her?'

He pauses for a moment, then he says, 'I don't want to talk about her.'

'Because she betrayed you?'

'Because I...' but he doesn't finish.

I move towards him, sitting a little distance away on one of the chairs. The fabric is more beautiful up close but I try to keep my focus on Lawrence. 'Do you still love her?' I repeat my question.

'Yes,' he whispers.

'I think she still loves you.'

'Then why did she...' he wipes a tear with a brusque flick of his wrist and swallows. 'She's cheating on me.'

'You bought a stranger home from a bar.'

'That's different.'

'Is it?' I pluck a tissue from a chestnut coloured leather box and hand it to him.

Once he starts crying, he can't stop, blubbering like a baby all over the covetable upholstery.

I play the understanding friend. Tuck him up in bed. Let him sleep it off.

Thank God that worked! Now I have a few hours to get to know the layout of the house before he wakes up and I can ask for his driver to take me back to the city.

This has all worked out perfectly.

You might be wondering why I don't just kill him tonight. And I'll admit it's tempting, I've already run through a series of potential methods, how I might get away with it. But none of them are good enough.

There would be two suspects if he was murdered tonight. Myself, which instantly discounts the option. And Katerina. It wouldn't be much of a reach to think she came home and killed him in the midst of a screaming match between them. I won't make her another victim.

I have contemplated the suicide route, he does have an excellent motive after witnessing his wife's infidelity this evening. But it's such a difficult method to get right and I haven't done the planning.

So, he's safe. For tonight at least.

The rest of the Delaney-Jansen home is exactly what I was expecting after seeing the living room. It's large and spacious and elegantly furnished, the odd statement piece used to great effect.

In the basement I discover a gun cupboard – padlocked of course, Katerina would never be that dumb – plus a large wine cellar and a sound-proofed cinema room. The soundproofing could be useful to avoid the neighbours overhearing anything. I make a mental note and continue my exploration.

I hit the jackpot in the kitchen when I find an iPad mini. Lawrence is snoring like a hog and doesn't wake up when I use his thumbprint to unlock it. And there, in a notes document, is the gold. All of their security codes are listed. I now have their Wi-Fi password, Alexa controls, the ability to shut down their external CCTV network. Oh, plus the four digit code to the gun cupboard padlock and the security code for the alarm system.

All I need to do now is find a time that the rest of the family are definitely away.

I'm almost looking forward to it.

Lawrence wakes up at seven and organises for his driver to come and pick me up. 'I'm sorry,' he says quietly, refusing to make eye contact.

'That's OK,' I reply.

'I just couldn't go ahead with it. I know you must have been disappointed.' He sounds serious. Like I spent the night crying over his rebuttal.

'Well, I—'

'It's not personal. You're quite attractive, really. Please don't take my rejection as a sign of your own failure.'

Wow. Just wow. 'I hope it all works out with your wife,' I say, even though I know Katerina will soon be a very happy widow, thankful to whoever it is who helped get rid of her marital baggage.

Alexander, the driver, barely speaks as we head back to the city and I watch the trees sliding past us on the Autobahn. I can only assume he thinks I slept with his boss last night and he'll do everything in his power to forget the mental image he's conjured. He'll never connect me with the brutal murder of his boss in a few weeks' time.

I smile to myself and sink back into the soft leather seat of the car.

'Thank you for the lift,' I say as we pull up outside the hotel.

'You're welcome,' he replies, his tone perfunctory.

She's sitting in the foyer waiting for me.

'Good morning, Freya,' she says, irritatingly chirpy.

'Good morning, Camille.'

'Early walk?'

'I couldn't sleep,' I reply.

'Hmmm...' she says, her eyes travelling from my face to the drab suit and blouse combination. The blouse looks a little crumpled; I have been wearing it all night after all. 'Well, I'm going to have some breakfast. Will you join me?'

'Of course,' I reply, even though it's the last thing I want to do.

The waiter seats us at a table by the window and I swiftly order us coffee and pastries. I don't want to give Millie time to even consider a traditional Bavarian weisswurst and pretzel combination, just the thought of it is making me nauseous. We sit in silence until the food arrives.

Millie takes a cinnamon roll, but leaves it on her plate as she watches me take a bite of my apple slice. 'A friend of mine was telling me about this bar.' She watches me chew for a moment before continuing. 'She said we should go next time we come to Munich. It's only a few minutes' walk from here, next to the Nobel Hotel on Landwehrstraße. Apparently it looks a bit shabby, but they do the best Hugo cocktail in Munich.'

An image from the bar I took Lawrence to flashes into my head. A framed certificate hanging on the wall: *The Best Hugo in Munich.*

She was watching me last night.

19

I watch her closely as we continue our breakfast, analyse every movement, every look, every word she doesn't actually say as she rattles off a stream of banalities. She's waiting for me to say something. She's played the first move and now she can relax as I'm forced to consider my next step.

My brain is working overtime, even as we sit and discuss the relative merits of the different pastries they have served and how they stack up against more international options like pancakes.

I can only bear it for twenty minutes before I put down my napkin and make my excuses.

I hate to admit it but I need some help with solving this particular problem.

The moment I'm back in the safety of my hotel room, I call Lucas. 'It's a fucking disaster.'

'You're sure she saw you?' he says, his voice irritatingly calm.

'Yes.' I stop myself from adding an expletive. 'She mentioned that exact bar I was in.'

There's silence on the other end of the line.

'Are you there?' I ask, kicking my heels off so I can pace the suite more comfortably.

'I'm here.' He sighs and pauses again.

I continue pacing, waiting for him to speak. This is his forte. He will help me fix this.

I stop moving when he finally speaks. 'Why were you drinking with him?' He sounds pissed off with me.

Like I'm the problem here and not Millie sticking her nosy little beak into my business. 'Sorry?' I say.

'Freya. You have to think about damage control. What if someone saw you?'

'They did. That's what I'm telling you.' I say each word slowly so he can understand.

'I don't mean Millie. I mean a witness who will tie you back to him.'

'That isn't the problem. The issue is Millie.' Is he thick? Perhaps hungover?

I hear him sigh again and it makes me bristle. 'You need to fix this,' I tell him.

'And how am I meant to do that?' he asks with more snark than is strictly necessary.

'You'll think of something.'

He's silent on the other end of the line, the only sound a nondescript pop song playing in the background.

'Well?' I ask after a few moments.

'I'm still thinking,' he snaps. There's another pause. Then finally, 'OK. Here's the play.' He suddenly sounds more confident, more like the person I've come to rely on.

'I'm waiting,' I say, if only to regain control of the conversation.

'You're not going to like it,' he says. 'But I think it's the only way.'

'Just say it, Lucas.'

'Right. So this is the story. You couldn't sleep. You went for a walk. Popped into a bar for a late-night drink. Met this guy.' His voice changes a little, 'Please tell me he's at least vaguely attractive?'

'He's not hideous,' I concede.

'Thank Christ,' he says with more positivity. But then he's back to business, 'so you met this guy and had a few drinks. You went back to his. You like him. He's cute. Clever. He makes you laugh.'

I pull a face even though I know he can't see it. 'You think she's going to buy that I want to *date* him?'

'She's going to buy whatever you tell her.' He's stern.

I sit down on the edge of the bed. 'OK. I'll try.'

'I suggest you take her to a bar at the airport. Tell her how much you liked him. Get a little tipsy because otherwise she'll never believe you telling her about him. And then you're going to get even more pissed. Because the bastard ghosts you. Doesn't return your calls and messages. You're upset. He could have been the One.'

'The One?' I scoff, even as my thoughts drift to Gabriel.

'Maybe the bitch is thawing.' He laughs loudly.

'Fuck you, Lucas.'

'Look, Freya. This will work. So he ghosted you. And then one day you'll see a news article. A terribly sad, such-a-waste kind of article. You'll lament what could have been.'

'It won't work.'

'Listen to me.' His voice is hard. Authoritarian. I quite like this side of him. 'It has to work. You need to kill him. And you need to get away with it.'

I hang up without saying goodbye. He's right: I need to kill Lawrence. And I need to get away with it.

Otherwise how can I kill Gregory Fuller?

Our flight back to Heathrow is at six thirty that evening, but I insist we head to the airport early. After security I direct Millie to the NightFlight Bar, with its huge palm trees and glass atrium. I order us both a glass of champagne and then I lay on the charm, just like Lucas told me to. 'Millie's a gossip,' he had told me when he rang me this afternoon to check I was still on board with his plan. 'And she likes justice, she'll root for the underdog.'

'I'm not the fucking underdog,' I'd hissed at him, not bothering to conceal the annoyance in my tone.

'In this you are.' Fuck Lucas. He'd better be right on this.

'I need to talk to you about something,' I say to Millie as we take our drinks to a table furnished with rather utilitarian looking seats, which turn out to be surprisingly comfortable. There is still at least an hour before our gate is announced and so I'm hoping we can get through this whole 'heart to heart' bullshit by then.

She takes a sip of champagne, her forehead creasing a little. 'Is everything alright?' she asks. I hate that question. So vague. So ineffectual at actually eliciting the response you really want.

'It's about this morning,' I say, my hand gripping the stem of my glass. This whole conversation is making me feel weird. I can act like the best of them – I wouldn't have lasted this long if I couldn't fake it – but that doesn't mean I enjoy it.

Millie puts down her glass and looks directly at me, squaring her shoulders a bit. 'Have I done something wrong?' she asks, bracing herself for the answer.

'This isn't about you.' Even to my own ears my words sound too harsh. Too brusque. Why am I always such a bitch? 'Before breakfast. When you saw me in reception...'

'After your walk?'

I allow a smile to flash across my lips. 'We both know I hadn't been for a walk.' I take such a large gulp of champagne my flute is almost empty. I wave at one of the waiters, hoping he'll understand my desire for a fast top-up. 'I was just coming back to the hotel.'

'Oh,' Millie says. 'Oooh,' she repeats, as if my words have finally sunk in. It's an act, but I'll give her a small amount of credit for keeping up the pretence as long as she did.

'I met someone. I don't normally... it's not the kind of thing I usually do...' The waiter comes over and tops up our glasses. He leaves the rest of the bottle on the table and winks conspiratorially at me. I giggle. *Giggle.* Like a fucking teenager and a small part of me dies inside. I hate this. It's stupid and ridiculous.

'Where did you meet?'

'I couldn't sleep. I went for a walk. This bar advertises the best Hugo in town.' I shrug, as if the advertising strap line was just far too tempting. 'He was at the bar. We got talking.'

I wait for her to say something, to pick up the reference I made about the bar she apparently followed me to like some creepy stalker, but she's staring into space, her gaze tracking nothing as she sips her drink. Then eventually, 'Why are you telling me this?' Her tone neutral, if perhaps a little confused.

Why *am* I telling her this. Oh yes, so when I kill Lawrence Delaney she won't immediately suspect I'm the murderer. 'I felt bad for lying to you. It's not professional.'

'Right,' she says. Her tone saying everything she isn't. That it might not be professional to lie, but nor is it professional for your boss to tell you she went out last night and hooked up with some stranger.

'That's... that's not...' I say quickly. She's not buying my bullshit. 'Look, I...' I look at her, wait for her to make eye contact. 'I need your help, Millie. I'm rubbish at this. It's...' I giggle again. 'I like him, OK!'

'You want my... help?' She squints a little as she says it, trying the words out for size.

'I'm a dating disaster, Millie. Help me.' I lean forwards and take her hand awkwardly. 'Please?'

'Help you, how?' She's still suspicious. Perhaps I should rein it in a little.

'Help me not be such a fucking mess. Help me write him a message that won't send him running to the hills.' I drop my voice to a whisper. 'Help me to make him want me.' I avert my eyes quickly from hers. But she's seen it. The desperation. The pleading. I feel debased. Dirty. I will not beg her. But we all know I will if that's what it takes.

Oh, how the mighty have fallen.

'OK,' she says and nods slowly. She runs her tongue over her teeth. 'So you really like him?'

I nod.

'Did you...'

Is she asking if... yes she is, she's making some kind of hand motion. This couldn't get any more uncomfortable.

'Yes.' My voice is high-pitched. Almost a squeak. I'm mortified. So is she, if I'm honest.

'Right.' She clears her throat. 'Now, I'm not sure if I'm the best person to give advice.' She offers me a nervous laugh.

'But you have a boyfriend...' I half-ask. Even though I obviously know all about her little workplace crush.

'Well, no. But,' she adds and raises a finger as if she's about to counter-point herself, 'there's this guy—'

'You like him?'

'He's... nice.' She laughs properly, her eyes shining. 'I didn't realise at first. We've known each other for a while. But just recently I've started to wonder if maybe he's someone. You know?'

Nope. I have no idea. And no I'm not thinking about Gabriel. The way he smiles, the dimples at the base of his spine. The way he says my name...

But to Millie I smile and nod, then I top both our drinks up again. 'Please help me. I'm useless at this stuff.'

She stares at me for a moment. 'OK! I'll help you.' She picks up her glass and motions it towards me. I pick mine up too, tapping it gently against hers, the chime ringing across the minimalistic bar area.

'Thank you, Millicent,' I say, pointedly using her actual name.

She beams at me and relief courses through my veins. Yes, I've just become the weird boss who asks her team for help with her love life. But at least she has no reason to suspect there is anything more to it than that.

PART III

MILLIE

20

What the actual fuckedy-fuck is going on?

I'm sitting in the NightFlight Bar at Munich airport – which is rather pretty with these huge palm trees and purple lighting – and my boss is telling me about some guy she banged last night? This isn't... well, it isn't normal. Not just 'this rather sits outside the boundaries of normal social interaction at work' normal. But 'I think she's trying to befriend me so I don't think she's a serial killer' normal.

I excuse myself and go to the bathroom. I text Lissa.

> She's telling me about her sex life!

vomiting person

> It's weird, right?

shrug

Lissa is obviously busy as she doesn't send another message immediately after the emoji. My fingers pause over my screen. Am I reading too much into this whole thing? I mean, is it possible that Freya did just hook up with someone and is embarrassed I called her out? It can't be that. She's trying to throw me off the scent of something. But of what? I type another message.

> Does she know I know?

How do I know if she knows you know?

Arghhh! Lissa's reply is absolutely infuriating! I know she's just being oblique, seeing how many what-if-she-knows-you-know-she-knows-you-knows she can string together before I threaten to kill her.

> I'm being serious, Liss

OK. Tell me from the beginning

I pause to think about how to put this into a text message.

> She told me she went out last night and met some guy. And that she likes him, and wants my help to lure him in.

Maybe she's telling the truth?

> Really? And she asked if I have a boyfriend...

I send the message and then put my phone down so I can pee.

Did you tell her about your mega crush on Kieran?

> I don't have a mega crush

We both know I do though. I put the phone back down so I can wash my hands.

Does it matter if you date a dude from work?

He's a different department

But the truth is I don't actually know if I'm allowed to date Kieran, or if that infringes some kind of policy.

Have you told him yet?!

Lissa knows I haven't. I mean, how am I meant to do that? Oh, hey, work colleague. Can we bang?

You just ask him for a drink

Lissa writes as if she knows what I'm thinking.

What if he says no?

Have you seen how smoking hot you are?!

She always knows how to make me feel better about myself.

But what if he has a girlfriend?

I'm ever practical.

Threesome?

I'm not sure if she's joking. But it makes me laugh, which gives me the confidence to send Kieran a message.

On my way back from Munich. Fancy a drink tomorrow?

I debate if I should add a kiss on the end or not. I think not. I don't want to come across as weird and desperate.

Yes

A man of many words.

xx

He adds.
Then my phone beeps with a third message.

Sorry. Wasn't sure if I should add them or not...

Fuck it. I throw caution to the wind.

Excellent xx

I send the message and then turn off my phone and head back to the table.

Freya launches into another soliloquy about how much she fancies this guy. She's definitely acting suspiciously. I just need to keep her on side for long enough to figure out what's actually going on. And who this guy really is. There's a disconnect between the words she's saying and the look in her eyes. She doesn't fancy him. In fact, I don't think there's enough vodka in the world to have made her want to go home with him.

So why is she so intent on me thinking she did?

* * *

I am not going to tell you about my date with Kieran.

Oh, who am I kidding? Of course I am, I can't stop smiling!

He's smart and kind and does all the right things like opening doors and not trying to order for me. God, that actually sounds like a pretty low bar when you say it out loud. So, he's a catch because he doesn't order for me? You know I don't really mean that specifically, more that it's a symptom of a wider disregard toward women.

I dated this guy once who tried to order me a sirloin steak because it was 'superior to the rubbish you wanted'. It wasn't; I'd ordered a fillet, which most people agree is objectively better. He also wanted to change how my steak was cooked to well done instead of medium rare because 'it tastes better like that'. It doesn't. He also suggested my skirt was a little short. Reached out to remove my hairband because 'you should really wear your hair loose'. I messaged Lissa about him from the ladies' room. All she sent back to me was a stream of red flag emojis. A whole page of them.

'I assumed you wouldn't want dessert,' he had told me when I got back to the table. We're still talking about the red flag dude, not the lovely Kieran.

'Why?'

'You already had a steak and chips.'

'And you think that's enough food for me?'

'Don't you want to look good?' He said it like he actually thought he was in the right. Like he genuinely thought he was helping me and I'd be *grateful* for his interference. Such a cock. 'So, shall we go back to mine?'

I just stared at him in disbelief.

'I bought dinner,' he said.

'Actually, sweetheart,' I told him, 'you bought half a dinner. I only go home with guys who order dessert.' And then I walked out, leaving him standing open mouthed in the middle of the restaurant. I thought that would be the last I heard from him, but he had the audacity to message me a week later and ask me out again. Deluded fool.

Anyway, I've digressed badly. Back to Kieran. We had cocktails. And steak – fillet steak, cooked exactly how I wanted – with both chips and dauphinoise potatoes because I couldn't decide which to order. We had cheesecake for dessert, and Irish coffees. Then he walked me home, his hand warm in mine.

At my door, he tucked a strand of hair behind my ear and told me he had a great evening and could we do it again on Saturday. Then he kissed my cheek and walked away, turning halfway down the street to turn and wave.

The next morning I practically dance into the office. And then it all comes crashing down when I see that Kieran is in Freya's office, balancing a little notebook on his thigh as she talks to him. His face looks grave, serious. And the worst bit is that he keeps stealing glances towards my desk, not like he's looking for me, but like she's whispering poison about me in his ear.

He leaves her office about ten minutes later, closing her door behind him, shoulders slumped. He crosses over to my desk and gives me a thin smile.

'Everything OK?' I whisper.

'Of course,' he replies but I can tell he's lying.

'Kieran...'

'Meet me outside in five,' he says before he turns and leaves.

I check Freya's diary, she's about to go on a call with the Global VP of Sales and so she won't even notice I've gone. I'll just bring her back an oat milk latte so she'll think I popped out to do her a favour.

He's already there when I push open the door to the smoking area.

He doesn't give me the usual head nod, or call me Millicent. Instead he holds out his lighter to light the end of my cigarette, and

I pause for a moment with my hands cupped around his, savouring the feeling of being so close to him. I have a horrible gnawing sensation our fledgling romance is already over before it really began.

'It was about me, wasn't it?' I say, wanting to be the first to start the conversation. 'Your meeting with Freya?' I add for unnecessary clarity.

Kieran runs his hand through his hair. 'Yes,' he says eventually.

'About us?' I physically cringe as I say 'us', I mean is one date enough to warrant an 'us'?

'Oh.' He breaks into a smile. 'No, no.' But then his face falls again. 'She's concerned you might be...' he trails off, dragging on his cigarette while he thinks of the right words. 'She says you've been working a lot of hours, but not producing more. Not achieving more.' He looks at me, kindness in his eyes. Or is it pity?

'She thinks I'm struggling?'

'She says she's worried you aren't ready for the job.'

Shame crashes over me. I've always achieved. I've always done well. Top of the class and the best exam grades and the first one to be picked for the lead in Youth Theatre productions. I clear my throat. 'Why are you...' I start but then I pause. 'Isn't there like a formal process for this kind of thing?'

'Yes,' he replies. 'But I'm not telling you this formally.'

'So... what is... this?' I motion between us a few times.

'There's something going on. With Freya,' he whispers.

I drop my own voice to match his. 'I don't understand. I thought this was about me?'

'No, Millie. It's about her. I'm not making any records of the meeting this morning because it's not fair on you. There's something not right about her. Have you noticed anything unusual about her behaviour recently?'

He looks concerned and I want to reach out and touch his face.

Which obviously I don't as I'm not a complete psycho. 'She's always been a bit...' I trail off. It feels odd to talk about her while we're on work property. I mean, you can bitch and moan about your boss in the pub, that's kind of a given, but to do so here... it feels wrong.

'You haven't noticed a change?' he asks again.

I want to tell him. I want to tell him that I think she's an actual bona fide serial killer, taking out men as we travel across the world. But something stops me. Probably the desire to see him again and not have him run from the paranoid freak I'm worried he would think I am. So instead I tell him about the man she apparently met in Munich. 'She met someone.'

'Like a guy?' He sounds surprised. And a little grossed out.

'Yep. She told me she really likes him.'

His eyes widen and then he laughs. 'You're serious?'

'I swear, that's what she told me.' All the tension between us is gone and I grin at him.

'Who is he?'

'She didn't tell me his name but I think he lives in Munich and I think he's made her a little...' I raise my eyebrows.

'Wow!' He shakes his head as if not quite believing it. 'But why does she have it in for you?'

'I saw her. Having a drink with him. That's why she told me about him. She's probably embarrassed. It's kind of against protocol.'

'Well, you are the queen of protocol,' he says, a playful edge to his voice.

I take a small step toward him, 'and what's that meant to mean?' I ask softly, my tone flirtatious.

'A little bird told me you went on a date with someone from HR last night.' He flashes me a grin.

'A little bird, hey?'

'I'm just repeating what I heard.' He shrugs and moves another inch towards me.

'Did that little bird say anything else?'

'Only that the someone from HR was very keen on a second date.' He edges even closer, I can feel the warmth of him.

'*Very* keen?' I ask.

'Very,' he says and then leans forwards, his lips grazing mine. 'Oops,' he says with a smile as he moves back from me.

'Oops, indeed,' I say and return his smile.

But then he steps away from me and clears his throat. 'Just promise me you'll be careful with Freya, OK?'

21

I get home from work to find Lissa has turned the living room into some kind of serial killer's lair.

'What the actual fuck is this?' I ask motioning towards what I can only describe as a murder wall. You know the way that the unravelling detective will paste pictures and bits of paper and maps across their walls, joining things together with string? Well, Lissa has achieved something similar with magic whiteboard, Post-it notes, and a bright red marker pen.

'I'm researching this guy your boss apparently went on a date with,' she states matter-of-factly, although the words are slightly muffled by the pen she's holding in her teeth as she stares at the wall.

'Why do you care who my boss is dating?'

'Oh Millie,' she says it like a disappointed parent. Then she points towards the kitchen, 'get the wine. We have work to do.'

I do as I'm told, my hand opening the fridge door for the wine before I even realise quite how placidly I just obeyed her. I pour us both a generous glass and then head back into the living room. 'OK, Liss. Tell me what I'm missing.'

She takes a glass from me and takes a sip before grimacing at the acidity. Well, it was only six pounds a bottle so what was she expecting? 'You didn't think she was telling you the truth about him.'

'No,' I confirm.

'It wasn't a question. Anyway, I figured out who he is.' She puts her glass down on the mantelpiece and then uses it to play a little drum roll. 'Thanks to the wonders of reverse image searching I can confirm that his full name is Lawrence Avery Delaney!' she exclaims, her face turning smug.

'Who is...?' I ask, sinking onto the sofa and slipping off my heels.

'Married,' she says.

'Ooh.'

'Yep.' She nods theatrically at me.

'That could explain why she's being a bitch,' I say. Perhaps she found out this morning and decided that somehow it was my fault? 'Well, even more of a bitch than normal.'

'What did she do?'

'Reported me to HR.'

'No way!'

'It's fine. Kieran realises she's just being a cow and didn't record their conversation. It'll all blow over.'

'Well, I'm glad. But I think you're missing the very obvious question,' Lissa says.

'Enlighten me.'

'So. She met a married man in a bar. And she didn't even really seem to like him. You thought it was a bit of an act.'

'Right.'

She pulls her shoulders back, her eyes on mine to make sure I'm paying full attention to her. 'So who is he really? Who is he to her?'

'You sound like you have an answer.'

'I think he's her next victim.'

* * *

Lissa and I stayed up until almost two in the morning trying to figure out if she's being ridiculous or if there's a tiny chance she's right. I now know everything there is to know about Lawrence Delaney.

He was born in Lincoln, Nebraska in 1980 and went to the Eagle Academy, some private day school about half an hour from his parents' McMansion. All very boring and very white wealthy American.

His sister is prolific on Facebook, with zero sense of the kind of things you should and shouldn't share online. Pictures of her kids. Pictures of their school. Pictures of their friends. Pictures of them on fancy holidays and driving nice cars and buying expensive jewellery. Her entire life lived online, screaming into the void that she had both money and something worth ransoming.

'She is literally asking for someone to kidnap her kids,' Lissa said, shaking her head. 'I'll never understand why people don't understand this shit.'

In addition to sharing her whole life in real time, Lawrence's sister is also overly prone to a bit of #ThrowbackThursday, a series of posts detailing her own childhood, including plenty of information about her 'favourite' brother. As I scrolled though her feed, I watch the pair of them turning from gawky kids to slightly less gawky teenagers: pictures from prom and summers at Camp North Creek and graduation.

I moved on to looking for his own social media foot print. The pictures of his time at Penn State, meeting an attractive woman who would become his wife, the birth of their kids and a handful of carefully curated images as the children had grown up. He led an apparently picture perfect life.

There is absolutely nothing to suggest he might be a potential victim.

I wake up with a start at 8 a.m., panicking I'm going to be late for work, before realising it's Saturday. As I open my door to go in hunt of coffee, I hear the sound of squeaking in the living room. Lissa is writing on the magic whiteboard.

Cody Gelber: 15 Apr 1980
Ruben Chambers: 21 Jan 1980
Jim Handley: 28 Jun 1980

'What are you doing?' I ask her from the doorway.

'Notice anything?' she asks, turning toward me, hands on her hips. She's wearing an oversized T-shirt that has seen better days and a pair of seasonally inappropriate pyjamas featuring dogs in Christmas jumpers. Her hair is piled on her head in a messy bun.

'Did you actually go to bed?'

She ignores the question and instead uses the marker in her hand to underline the year beside each name. 'See?'

'Is that their birthdays?' I move closer to the wall.

'Yep.'

'So they were all born in the same year?'

'Bingo, Millie.'

'Coincidence?'

She gives me a withering look. 'No such thing.'

We go for breakfast in the cafe down the road. Lissa didn't want to leave the flat and the murder wall but I wasn't taking no for an answer. I also insisted she got dressed into something vaguely externally presentable. 'The PJs were clean on this morning,' she'd objected.

'They have Christmas dogs on them.'

'So?'

But anyway, now we're wearing jeans and hoodies and sitting in the cafe eating American-style pancakes and bacon, all dripping in maple syrup.

'Do you think they knew each other?' Lissa asks me, just before she loads another forkful of food into her mouth.

'They grew up in different places,' I say. 'Cody in California, Ruben in Indiana, Jim in Delaware. Lawrence was born in Nebraska.'

'College?' Lissa asks, tapping the screen of her phone with one hand as she scoops more pancake onto her fork.

We sit in silence as we both research. 'Nope,' I confirm, 'all different.'

'Jobs?' Lissa asks through her final mouthful. 'Perhaps like a grad scheme or something?'

'Jim was a plastic surgeon. He would have gone to med school. Cody studied finance and then straight into InterBank as a junior exec.'

'This is pointless,' she says. She pushes away her empty plate in frustration. 'Fuck! There has to be something.'

'We'll figure it out,' I tell her and she huffs slightly.

I finish my breakfast as she sips her coffee. Finally, when I've put down my cutlery and it's obvious I'm finished, she leans forward. 'Millie?' she asks, and her tone sounds different. The frustration gone, replaced with something else. Fear? 'What if we're right?'

'How do you mean?'

'If we're right, she's going to kill Lawrence Delaney.' She whispers it so quietly no one else around us could possibly hear.

'Yes,' I whisper in return.

'Should we stop her?'

Our eyes lock over our syrup-smeared plates, the unspoken words passing between us.

* * *

That evening Kieran takes me to the cinema to watch the new *Guardians of the Galaxy* movie.

'I cannot believe you haven't seen it yet,' he says, with mock incredulity. 'It's been out for ages.'

I don't tell him it's because Lissa would rather stick pins in her eyes than come to the cinema with me to watch a Marvel movie. I don't want him to think she's literally my only friend. Or that she has shit taste. We go for drinks afterwards.

'I wanted to say thanks,' I tell him. 'For yesterday and the whole Freya thing.'

'Do we have to talk about work?' He leans forward to take my hand and a frisson runs up my spine.

'Is this allowed?' I look pointedly at our fingers intertwined on the wooden table.

He strokes my palm with his thumb. 'Is what allowed?'

'Us.'

He turns and looks at me, his eyes focusing on mine as if I'm the only thing in the world. 'Us.' He says it without question. Then he leans forward and kisses me.

I pull back after a few moments. 'But will we get into trouble, at work?'

'Does it matter?' He kisses me again.

'I need my job, Kieran.'

He leans back a little and smiles at me. 'Millie, I wouldn't be here if it would jeopardise your job. I know how important it is to you.'

'Promise?'

'Promise.'

I know it's only our second date. But that feels like a technicality, especially as we've been friends for ages. If you're going to be all accurate, we've known each other for over two years.

At the door to the flat I pull him to me, my kisses hard. 'Come in with me.'

He nods and I unlock the door, almost tripping over the step as I try to walk while still maintaining as much contact with him as possible.

I giggle, picking up Lissa's shoes we knocked over.

'You have a flatmate?' he asks, staring at the mountain of shoes and coats and bags in the hallway.

'Yeah.'

'Is she...?' he grimaces slightly.

'Don't worry. She has good headphones.' I take his hand and drag him through the kitchen to my bedroom.

* * *

In the morning the other side of the bed is empty when I wake up. Has he left? Without even saying goodbye?

I slip on a cotton robe and push open the door of my room, expecting a silent house to greet me. But the kettle is whistling and there's a box of pastries from the bakery down the road on the kitchen table. I push the box open with one finger and breathe in the scent of freshly baked croissants. Plain ones, my favourites. The cross-body bag Kieran always carries is sitting next to them.

He's in the living room. Standing staring at the wall. Lissa obviously spent yesterday evening working on it, there are hundreds of Post-its stuck haphazardly over our thoughts from yesterday, covered in the scrawl she calls handwriting. Yesterday it looked like we were making progress. Now it looks like the handiwork of a deranged lunatic. He turns slowly to look at me. 'What's this?'

His eyes are wide, a look of confusion on his beautiful face.

My stomach drops as I stare at him. My brain scrambling to find an excuse even as my body stands frozen.

'Millie?'

I feel him slipping away from me. I want to tell him the truth. But I can't.

'Morning, lovebirds!' Lissa crashes into the room, back in the Christmas pyjamas. 'Please excuse my wall of horror.' She's loud, exuberant. 'It's a little side project. I am *obsessed* by true crime documentaries and podcasts.' She starts to roll down the magic whiteboard, obscuring all the workings and theories.

Once she's done she turns back to us. 'I'm Lissa, by the way,' she says. 'You must be Kieran.' She winks at him in a way that says she knows exactly who he is. And exactly what he and I were doing last night. 'Oh my god. Look at your face!' She laughs loudly. 'You look terrified.' She walks towards him and slaps him on the back as if they've been friends for years. 'I promise you Millie is *not* obsessed with murder and mayhem. She's the normal one. You know how it is with friends. One of them is always a little...' she makes a face and pokes her tongue out at him. 'But I'm harmless, I promise.'

She takes him by the elbow and leads him from the living room towards the kitchen, glancing over her shoulder at me and winking. I just hope he buys her act. I don't want him to figure out any part of what we're really researching. What we think might be about to happen to poor Lawrence Delaney.

22

On Thursday, Freya and I return to Munich.

I've been trying to avoid her as much as possible. Every time I see her I think of him, Lawrence Delaney, and all the ways she might plan to kill him. What did he possibly do to elicit her wrath? Lissa and I have decided there must be a connection between all the victims. She can't just be floating from city to city, picking victims at random; they have to mean something. But what? Who are these men to her?

She did her usual trick of giving me zero notice for our trip, literally deciding on Wednesday morning we were going.

'You're not going to moan, Camille?' she'd asked with this horrendous smirk when she told me.

'Not at all, Freya.' I'd smiled sweetly as I tried to figure out what her plans were for the trip. Is this it? Is this the trip where she kills him, where she thinks I'm helping to create her alibi? And if that's what she's planning, how am I going to thwart her?

We stay in the same hotel as last time, Le Meridian on Bayerstraße, just a short stroll to the Bahnhof. That evening, in the bar, she tries to talk to me about her love life again. 'He isn't replying to my messages,' she says, staring into her Negroni as if it might give her the answers to her love life problems.

'Oh,' I reply, trying to stay non-committal. Lissa told me to play along, pretend I'm actually buying all this stuff about a love connection. But Lissa isn't here and she has no idea how awkward this whole situation is.

'I think...' Freya pauses for a moment, swirling the drink around the glass, ice cubes chinking against the crystal, 'I think he's married.' She finishes the sentence quickly.

'Oh.'

She looks sad; shoulders slumped, fingers picking at imaginary fluff on her skirt, eyes downcast. But it's so obviously an act. Does she really think I believe this sham?

I excuse myself to go to the bathroom. Not that I actually need to go, but the tension is making my skin crawl and I want to get away from her for a few minutes.

I come back from the ladies' room to find an entirely different Freya.

'He messaged,' she says, eyes bright. 'He wants to meet.'

'But I thought he was married?'

'Separated,' she says quickly. Too quickly. I'd know she was lying even if Lissa and I didn't already have a dossier on Lawrence Delaney and his impressive wife.

'Oh. Well, that's good,' I say, trying to muster a little enthusiasm.

She smiles at me. 'Do you think I should? Meet him?'

'Tonight?' I ask, although of course she means tonight.

'Right now,' she confirms. 'So, anyway...' she pauses to drink the rest of her Negroni and then stands up. 'I'm going to go and get changed...' she makes a motion towards the door.

'Great,' I reply, feigning nonchalance. But inside I'm fizzing. This is it. My chance to find out what is really happening between her and Lawrence.

I'm still at the bar when Freya comes back downstairs from her room. She's wearing a bright red wrap dress and black patent stilettos, her hair brushed to a glossy sheen around her face. She has one of those expensive leather holdalls over one shoulder. It looks full. She glances towards me and I wave, making sure she's seen me sitting here.

As soon as she's round the corner I'm moving. I deliberately wore a pair of black wide-leg trousers and some trainers to the bar, with a simple white T-shirt to keep the look crisp and clean and young. But in my small leather backpack is a lightweight black hoody and a cap to cover my hair.

I follow her, keeping to the shadows as she walks in the waning sunlight down the middle of the street. She's confident, a bounce in her step. She doesn't even glance behind her, no idea that I could be following.

The Engel Hotel is small and exclusive, just off Pettenkoferstraße, favoured by popstars and bohemians – or at least that's what their website says. From the street, I can see the hallway is opulent: all mahogany furniture, deep purple velvet sofas, and burnished pewter. There's a small bar off to the side.

Freya pauses as she reaches the door of the bar and takes a deep breath, checking her reflection in the camera of her phone. Then she swings open the door and walks inside. I watch from outside as she approaches where he stands at the bar, facing away from me. He's tall, at least six foot and fairly broad across the shoulders. His blond hair has been styled with something to give it a uniformed wave, and he's wearing a well cut suit in a mid-grey. She taps him on the shoulder to get his attention, before he pulls her into an embrace.

But then he turns towards the window and I see his face. It isn't Lawrence Delaney.

I stumble backwards slightly at the sight of him. The fuck? Who is he? I subtly take a quick photo of him, this fake guy, and then I call Lissa.

She answers almost immediately, as if she's been sitting with her finger millimetres from the screen of her phone. Which is exactly what I'm assuming she *has* been doing since I messaged to say Freya was on the move to meet her paramour.

'It isn't Lawrence,' I tell her.

'What do you mean it isn't him?'

'I mean, she has gone to meet a guy and he's the same height and build as Lawrence, but it's *not* him. I'm sending you a photo.' I ping over the picture I just took.

'Send me the one you took the other day of Lawrence,' she tells me.

But when I try to find it, it's not there. 'I... it's not there. Lissa, the photo's gone.'

'Gone?'

'All the photos I took last time we were here in Munich have just vanished.'

'Did you delete them? Check your trash.'

'Of course I didn't delete them,' I hiss at her. 'What the fuck?'

'OK. Just chill. The copy you sent me will still be on my laptop. Let me try to figure out who this guy is. Keep an eye on them. What are they doing?'

'Oh.' They're walking into the reception area, laughing. They head towards the bank of lifts up to the rooms. 'I think they're going upstairs.'

'Gross.' She mock gags. 'But it buys us time to figure this all out.'

It takes Lissa two hours to work out who this fake Lawrence is. I'm sitting in a bar just down the road, one with an oblique vantage over the door of the hotel, just watching and waiting for Freya.

'He's an escort,' she tells me.

'A what?'

She sends a link that opens to a company called Bettgeflüster – which according to Google translates as pillow talk – that advertise the utmost in discretion and quality. I find him on the second page of 'available companions', listed with his key credentials including height and build.

He really does bear a startling resemblance to Lawrence Delaney.

'Earth to Millie,' Lissa is saying. I must have zoned out while she was talking.

'Sorry. What did you say?'

'I told you to wait for a few minutes. I'll call you back, OK?'

'OK,' I agree, and sit back in my seat to wait for her to call back.

After a minute, the barman slides a cocktail with multicoloured layers across the bar towards me.

'Oh, I didn't order this,' I tell him.

'I know. I'm playing with some new ideas and I want you to taste test for me.' His English is accented, a melodious quality to it. I appraise him quickly, running him through my 'freaks and weirdos' filter. He *looks* harmless. But when did that ever matter?

'Oh. I couldn't—' I start to say but he cuts me off.

'I'm trying to design a signature cocktail for my wedding.' He looks around him. 'Just don't tell my boss, OK?' He grins at me conspiratorially.

'I promise,' I reply. 'When's the wedding?'

'Two weeks. We've been planning it for so long. I just want it to be perfect for Jannick, he's been having such a shitty year. Now!' He claps his hands. 'Please tell me what you think. His favourite book is *Red, White, and Royal Blue* and I wanted it to be a homage. So, the red is grenadine. But a home-made one, it's delicious. Then the white is a mix of vodka and bitter lemon. Then the blue is curaçao, which is a bit basic, but needs must.'

'Should I mix it together?'

'Of course! Otherwise it will taste like shit!'

I do as I'm told. It's pretty good actually and the colours mix to a gorgeous purple. I give him a double thumbs up and he blushes with pride.

'Thank you,' he says and then goes back to what he was doing, leaving me to wait for Lissa.

She calls me back about five minutes later. 'Millie.' She sounds serious. 'When did you plan this trip?'

'Um. Yesterday, it was a last minute thing.'

'Right... it's just... I rang the escort agency. Markus is available. Right now.'

'OK...' I draw the word out, hoping she might explain what she means.

'Millie. Freya cannot be with him.'

'I watched them go upstairs,' I tell her.

'But I could literally book him. For right now. So she can't possibly be with him any more.'

It's slowly starting to dawn on me. If she isn't with this escort then where is she?

'Mills...' Lissa's voice is quiet. 'We probably should have looked at Katerina's Instagram before...'

I don't reply, I just bring up the profile on my own phone. The reel plays automatically: Katerina and her children beaming from the screen, the caption:

Off to visit the grandparents #BrazilBound.

It was uploaded this morning. I vaguely remember reading something about her parents retiring to a beach-side complex in Brazil. I scroll down to the next post. Yesterday she'd posted a picture of their suitcases all lined up neatly by the front door.

Taking the kids to visit my parents #FamilyLove.

One of her followers had commented:

Yay! You and Lawrence must come and visit!

She had replied:

Lawrence has to stay behind for work. Next time chica *heart*.

Why the fuck didn't we check? Shit!
Lawrence is home.
Alone.
And Freya is not in a hotel with Markus the escort.
This is it. She's going to kill him. Tonight.

There's one significant advantage to having spent the last couple of years as a glorified assistant to a woman who is such a frequent business traveller: I know exactly how to get to Starnberg in the middle of the night. But, as I pull up an app to call a car, I realise I can't just turn up in a sleek sedan. If I'm going there I have to stay unseen.

Luckily, I'm in Germany. There's an S-Bahn – basically like the Underground but cheaper, cleaner and generally more efficient – that goes all the way there in just thirty minutes. And it runs into the early hours.

I call Lissa as I jog to Karlsplatz station.

'Are you sure you should go there?' she asks me.

'It's the only way we'll ever really know.'

'I don't like this, Mills. We should tell the police and get them to go out and find her.'

'Liss, we talked about this. What if they don't find her? What if she's already gone? Or what if we are so totally wrong about all of this, and he's just sitting in his living room in his pants, alive and well?'

'But what if she *is* there?'

'You have everything ready?'

'Yes.'

'Then I will send you the final piece of evidence and we can push the button, OK?'

23

I get to Karlsplatz station just in time to see the S-Bahn leaving.

'Fuck!'

A well-dressed woman who has obviously just got off the train throws me the dirtiest look I've ever seen and I realise I must have sworn out loud. I stifle the British urge to apologise and hurry further down the platform looking for a sign of when the next one might leave. My heart drops when I realise there's a forty minute wait because of how late it is.

I use the time wisely. I pace. Up and down the platform. Allowing my mind to unfurl, thoughts spooling out around me. I have no idea how long Freya has been with Lawrence Delaney this evening. I have no idea what may have already happened, what I'm going to find when I get to the house.

I know Lissa is hoping I don't find her there. She's approached this whole thing as a problem. Something we need to get over. Get past. And then we can go back to the original plan and I can continue to work my way up through the ranks of Serendipity until they finally offer me that coveted role in the Los Angeles office.

But I'm starting to question if I want the role in LA. It's so easy to keep working towards a goal without ever taking stock and asking whether it's still the right thing to pursue. What if there is something else? Another solution?

So this evening I am going to do something I haven't done since I was a little kid. I'm going to let fate decide.

If Freya isn't there and all I find is a man in his underpants watching porn and drinking beer while his wife is away, then I will go home to Clapham and continue to work my arse off to get to Los Angeles.

But if Freya is there?

* * *

Lissa has sent me a map with instructions of exactly how to get from the station to the Delaney house and I study it as the S-Bahn heads towards Starnberg. Apparently there's a trail that runs from the road down to the shore, which should provide a way to get to the house without anyone seeing me.

It's pitch dark, the moon a mere sliver in the inky sky. The air is cool, that crisp cold so redolent of proximity to water, and I can smell the lake. I'm close now. Really close.

I've never been that comfortable in the great outdoors, the idea of hiking and camping has absolutely zero appeal. Every rustle in the distance has me convinced someone is following me, hunting me, waiting to leap out around the next corner. The pathway that runs down beside the Delaney house is unlit and so I use the torch on my phone to ensure I don't trip or – far worse – somehow veer off the path and stumble into some alternate twilight zone. I try to push that thought from my head. Being overly paranoid and obsessing over ludicrous things isn't going to help me right now.

The temperature drops by another degree or so as the path widens and I can see the lake spreading out in front of me, the pinprick stars reflecting off the perfectly glassy surface. The air is still, as if the whole area is holding its breath.

An otherworldly shriek rings out, sending a shiver up my spine. The hair on my arms is raised, but whether from cold or from fear I'm not entirely sure. I turn to the source of the sound; it's coming from inside the house.

Suddenly light spills onto the patio, a golden glow across the white tiles. The swimming pool is a black inkwell, a solid block of nothingness. I hear the shriek again and this time it's louder, closer, even more desperate than before. I can't help myself, I duck down, making sure I'm fully out of sight up here. I drop further, onto my hands and knees, and then finally down onto my stomach so I'm flat to the ground. Crawling forward, I search for a small gap in the foliage, just enough for me to peer through without risking being seen myself. Once I'm happy with the spot, I open the phone on my camera and set it to record, streaming the video to Lissa's laptop back in Clapham.

A shadow jerks in front of one of the windows, like someone running. And then, once more, that shriek. Only this time it's cut short and the shadow crumples to the floor.

Suddenly a door opens, slamming into the wall with enough force I can see the glass in the centre wobble. A man comes crashing out, falling to his knees on the bleached tiles, the cracking sound reaching my hiding place. His whimper carries to me. He sounds utterly broken, pathetic, like an animal caught in a trap.

This is the man she met before. This is the one in the pictures that have somehow disappeared from my phone. Lawrence Delaney is naked. Completely naked – but without even a shred of shame at his nudity – except for a pair of white sports socks, one of them bunched around his heel, almost hanging off. His blond hair is a mess, turned dark around the hairline with sweat, which slicks his body, giving him the appearance of a greased chicken.

He starts and spins on his knees to look behind him. I know it will be her before she comes into view. But I hadn't expected the look of absolute ferocity on her face. Or that she'd be holding a hunting rifle.

She looks wild. Fierce. Athena incarnate.

Freya Ellwood-Winter.

She's here. And there is nothing but murder in her eyes.

A random gust of wind blows in from the lake, rippling across the swimming pool. The movement causes her eyes to flick from him for a moment and he takes the chance to rush at her.

But she's too fast and she raises the rifle, the weight of it seeming familiar in her hands. She has obviously fired one before; there is zero hesitation. Delaney stops in his tracks.

'Please,' I hear him whisper. He drops back to his knees, clasping his hands in front of him like a toddler praying. 'Please,' he begs again.

'This is the only way,' Freya tells him, her voice hard and resolute.

'But I have a family.'

She laughs and it fills the air around the pair of them. Delaney shrinks a little.

'Please.'

'Get up,' she demands.

Delaney whimpers and shakes his head. 'No, no, no, no.' It is a soft keening and it almost breaks my heart. Up until now I hadn't thought of him as real. As a flesh and blood human being with a flesh and blood family and his own hopes and dreams and little quirks. Now I realise how serious this situation is. But surely she's not really going to kill him and we can walk away from tonight?

She's done it before. She's a thousand kilometres away but I can hear Lissa's voice.

Of course Freya is going to kill him.

Unless I can stop her.

I push myself back up onto my knees, taking a deep breath for courage. This is probably stupid. Probably the most stupid thing I have ever thought to do in my entire life. But I can't just lie here and watch an innocent man die.

'Stand up,' Freya demands of Lawrence and I stop moving for a moment before turning back to watch. It feels like it's happening in slow motion, but it must be seconds. If that.

Delaney jumps to his feet, spinning on his toes to face the lake. He takes three steps and then he slips, his body pitching forwards as his foot fails to make purchase and it slides from underneath him.

He falls.

The sound of his head meeting the balustrade echoes around the patio area, folding in to the echo of the snapping sound his neck makes as it breaks.

I turn away and vomit onto the path.

I can tell from up here that he's dead. It must be a survival instinct, the ability to look at a person and know they're no longer alive. Or perhaps it's just the impossible angle of his head relative to the rest of him.

Freya walks over to the body and stares at him for a few moments.

'Fuck!' she hisses. 'Fuck! You stupid fucking bastard fool.' She moves her foot back as if she's about to kick his corpse, but stops herself. 'Fuck. Fuck. Fuuuuuck!'

She takes a few steps back again and cracks her neck. I've seen her do this before she goes on stage to present to a big audience, as if cracking her neck makes her feel more powerful, more confident in herself. It works, because she rolls her shoulders back and pauses, back ramrod straight, rifle held beside her.

Then she turns and walks back into the house, leaving the door wide open.

I creep onto the patio area, being careful not to look too closely at Delaney's twisted form, and hurry to tuck myself into the shadows, looking in through the windows. I can't see her, so I continue to creep round the house until I spot a light shining up from the ground. It's a window to the basement.

Freya is in the corner of a whitewashed room, placing the rifle back into a gun cabinet in the corner. She treats it with a sense of reverence, laying it carefully back onto its hooks. She's just about to close the cabinet when she spots a box tucked away towards the back. She opens it to reveal a collection of handguns, each nestled into black foam. She plucks one out – it's small and I can just make out an intricate silver filigree pattern on the grip – and inspects it carefully. Then she slips it into the pocket of her jacket and returns the box to where she found it before standing up and closing the gun cabinet door. She threads a padlock through the handle and closes it, spinning the numbers to scramble the combination.

The light snaps off as she leaves the basement and I'm plunged into darkness. I retrace my steps around the side of the house. She pauses at the door to the living room, her eyes scanning the scene inside. A porn movie is on screen, his clothes in an untidy pile on the floor by the sofa. A bottle of something I can only assume is lube and a box of tissues complete the image. Whoever finds Delaney will know exactly what he was doing just before he died.

I debate for a moment. Should I go inside and turn off the porn? Remove the lube and tissues? Preserve his dignity just a little. I'm frozen with indecision. I know I should leave, but another part of me is inexplicably drawn to save his reputation.

I should have been paying more attention.

I should have run the moment I realised he was dead and I couldn't save him.

'Hello, Camille.' Her voice is level, almost friendly.

I turn and flee.

24

I've fallen too many times to count. My feet catching on exposed tree roots and brambles, sending me flying with outstretched hands and fear in my heart.

The knees of my trousers are torn, the skin grazed, oozing blood.

My palms are caked in mud.

My lungs burn.

But I can't stop.

I can hear my ragged breath and the blood pounding in my ears. The sound of leaves rustling as I push past them, trying to get away, trying to put some distance between us.

But still she's chasing, like a hound who's picked up a scent. She will not stop until she catches me.

Fuck. Fuck. Fuck. I need to think.

But there's no time for that.

A storm has rolled in over the water and the rain lashes me, turning my hair into wet snakes that wrap round my neck and threaten to strangle me. I can see the lights of the lake shore in the distance, glittering through the prisms of falling rain. That must be the town of Possenhoffen.

Does it offer sanctuary? A place to stop and rest and grab a breath. To allow my heart to slow down and stop trying to escape my ribcage. Or will she follow me there too? Stalk me down the streets with the pretty little gun she stole in her hand, ignoring the screams of the people around us.

Should I turn? Take a pathway away from the lake, wind up into the hills and wait for morning?

I pause for a moment and try to take stock of what I should do. Fear is the devil. Fear makes you stupid.

But dawdling is dangerous. I break into a run again.

As I stumble, I reach my hands out and they rip open on a patch of thorns. I scream into the night, the pain joining with my frustration and sense of utter helplessness. It's all over. Everything. The whole dream for our future.

I think of Lissa. She'll be sitting in her Christmas dog pyjamas, tapping her fingers against the arm of the sofa, waiting for me to call and tell her it's all OK. To tell her that what she witnessed on the live feed was all a hoax and that I'll be home tomorrow and we can put this whole stupid endeavour behind us and concentrate on moving another chess piece into play for our long game.

But I've ruined everything. Stupid stupid girl. I stumble again, as if I've been hit, smacked in the back of the knees by an unseen hand. Stupid stupid girl. I picture *his* face, the curl of his lip as he said those words. *Stupid stupid girl.*

I manage to right myself, but my next step doesn't meet solid ground, the path beneath my feet vanishing as I fall.

Wet mud and mouldy leaves fill my mouth. *Eat dirt* I hear him say. His hands pin me to the ground as he piles it into my open mouth, tears running down my face as I try to push him off me.

Pain flares in my ankle, reverberating up and down my leg. *No one gives a shit what happens to you.*

I try to turn my face away but I can't. A whimper escapes my lips. I'm going to die here.

'Oh do be quiet, Camille.' Her voice rings loud and true, piercing the hallucination and causing the vision of him to evaporate.

I look up and see the outline of her standing over me. She snaps on the torch in her hand and I'm forced to shield my eyes.

So I'm definitely not dead.

'Get up,' she demands.

I try to push myself to standing, but my left leg buckles underneath me and I fall back to my knees.

'For fuck's sake, Camille,' Freya shouts at me.

'Leave me,' I call out weakly. I'm going to die tonight. It might as well be in the dirt and the muck. *Where you belong.*

'Don't be a fool,' she says and then I see the outline of the gun in her hand.

But she puts it in her pocket and jumps into the hole with me.

'What are you doing?' I whisper.

'Rescuing you. You fell into an animal trap. Let's get out of here.' She reaches out a hand and pulls me to standing.

I wince as I put weight on my ankle. 'I think it's broken,' I say as I try to take a few steps.

'Bad sprain,' she replies with unwarranted confidence. 'There's a little holiday cottage not far up the hill. We can rest there until sunrise.'

'I...' I start to say, but trail off. She's unsettled me with her niceness, with her offer to help. There's part of me that wants to go with her, forget she's the same killer I'm running from. I think I might have hit my head when I fell.

'Millicent!' Her tone shocks me from my stupor. 'Come on.' She puts her hand around my waist to support me and heads down the path, her torch a brilliant yellow glow.

I'm close to vomiting by the time we reach the little cottage. It's actually more of a hut, a white-washed wooden structure built deep into the woods and boasting a combined living, kitchen, and sleeping area, with a tiny little bathroom. The furnishings are simple, hewn from a rough wood that gives the air a distinctively nutty smell. The walls are bare, with no pictures adorning them. The only patch of colour is a large red and green woven rug under the coffee table and a few mis-matched cushions on the sofa.

My ankle is on fire, as if someone has taken a red hot poker and rammed it beneath my skin.

'Sit,' Freya tells me, motioning towards a little chair. She pulls a stool over and instructs me to put my injured foot up on it. 'That was really fucking stupid,' she hisses under her breath.

'You...' I start to say but the pain causes my words to dissolve into a hiss.

She turns away and starts opening cupboards, taking out two enamel mugs, some tea bags. She fills a tiny kettle with water and places it on the stove, rooting through three drawers before she finds a match to light it with.

She makes tea slowly, squeezing the tea bags to make the brew stronger. She adds three large spoons of sugar to one of the mugs.

Then she slams it down in front of me. 'Drink.'

'Where are we?' I manage to ask.

'It's a holiday let,' she replies.

'Whose?'

She shrugs. 'I've no idea. But it's empty.'

I look around me at the single room. 'Obviously.'

'I meant no one is renting it at the moment. The owner's been struggling to find tenants. Probably because she's trying to charge over two hundred euros a night for a hut. It used to be part of the network of hiking refuges in the area. Designed for whoever needed it. But then someone got greedy and put it on Airbnb.' She sounds almost wistful. 'They were all over this area. These huts. For people who got caught out with the weather, or were tired, or injured. You used to be able to use them and then leave them. People who hiked would carry a few supplies to top them up.' She looks around her as if she's somewhere else.

'You're a hiker?' I say it with such incredulity she snaps her gaze back to me.

'Why do you find that so surprising?' she asks, pulling out a chair and sinking into it.

'You don't exactly scream mountain person,' I reply.

'I grew up in Boulder.'

'You're *American*?' She has one of the most RP accents I have ever heard. I always assumed she went to some terribly British boarding school, her parents stiff and formal, her childhood full of rigid rules and stultifying routines.

'I grew up all over the place. Army brat,' she clarifies.

She reaches into her pocket and pulls out my phone, the screen a mess of shattered glass. 'Just FYI. You dropped this when you ran.' She places it on the table between us. The atmosphere changes in an instant. Whatever game she's playing I will not be pulled in by her tea and tales of her all-American childhood.

She didn't technically kill Lawrence Delaney. But I know she was planning on it.

Fate intervened this time. But she is still a killer.

And we're still alone in the middle of nowhere.

Plus there's a gun in her pocket.

I look at her and she looks at me and time stretches and yawns between us.

She knows I was watching.

I'm in a cabin in the middle of the night in the middle of

nowhere. Oh, and I suspect my ankle's broken. I am no longer prey. I am carrion. Dead meat waiting for the vulture to circle.

Freya picks up her mug, her nails singing on the enamel, then she blows on the surface before taking a tentative sip. I copy her, the tea hot and sweet. How can I possibly think about that right now?

The silence grows, taking up space in the small cabin.

Just when I think I can't bear it for another moment, that I'm about to explode, she puts the mug down. 'Shall I start?' she asks, her tone level and matter of fact.

I swallow audibly and wait for her to continue.

25

'Do you ever wonder where I go when I leave the office in the middle of the afternoon?'

'Sorry?' I ask, wondering if I misheard her. What the hell is she talking about?

'When I leave the office at 3 p.m. without having a meeting to attend. Have you ever wondered where I go?'

If I'm honest I always assumed it was something boring, like a hair appointment. 'Not really.'

'Well. I take the train to Woldingham. To a place called Burtenshaw House. At least once a week. I try to go on Fridays if I can. Routine is helpful. For Verity.' Her voice cracks slightly on the name.

'Verity?' Who the hell is Verity?

Freya pauses for a moment. 'Verity is my sister. Burtenshaw House is a residential home. For people with certain... limitations. Who can't live on their own,' she adds, looking at me as if to check I understand her meaning.

'She's sick?' I ask.

'That would be a very nice way of putting it, Millie.' She sounds tired, broken.

I struggle with what to say. Am I meant to offer my condolences? Ask more questions? I get a feeling from Freya there's a lot more she's going to tell me. Perhaps it would be best for me just to stay silent and listen.

'Verity and I were always close growing up, even though she's younger. I was five when she was born and used to follow our mum and her round the house, always wanting to hold her.' Her whole demeanour has changed. Gone is the boss-bitch who chews me out for every single tiny little infraction and in her place is someone softer, gentler. 'Do you have siblings, Millie?' she asks.

I shake my head. 'I had—' I start to say that I had an unusual childhood, that the definition of siblings is a curious concept when you're raised like I was. But I stop myself. This isn't about me. Not yet, anyway. 'No. I'm an only child.'

'Verity was everything to me,' she continues. 'And I was everything to her. Maybe it's because we travelled around so much, following Dad from posting to posting. Never staying anywhere for longer than two years, three if we were very lucky. Mum wanted to send us to boarding school. Give us stability. She had all these big ideas about Marlborough College for me and Cheam for Verity. But all we wanted was each other...' she trails off for a moment, her gaze ostensibly resting on her mug of tea, but I can tell it's the past she's seeing.

'We managed to persuade our parents not to make us go. And so we kept moving, every two or three years it would be a new country, a new school. So many army kids go to boarding school; all of Mum and Dad's friends' kids did. We were so smug that we didn't. Wore it like a badge of pride.' She smiles a little, as if remembering something particularly good. 'So what if we had to keep making new friends? Every time we moved was an opportunity to start over, to become someone new and exciting.'

She looks at me. 'Growing up like that teaches you resilience. Teaches you how to walk into a room and grab everyone's attention.'

She says it like it's a positive, but I'm undecided. Sure, it's probably helped her career, but did it contribute to her being completely dismissive of what other people think of her? I might envy that ability, the way she doesn't give a shit about other people's opinions, but it isn't normal.

'Anyway,' she continues, 'when I was seventeen we were living in Boulder. It's a beautiful place and I met this guy who loved nothing more than to spend his days in the mountains, hiking the trails and getting lost in the wilderness.' She sits back in her seat. 'I was obsessed with him. My father thought he was a bad influence.' She raises her eyebrows for a second. *Typical Dad*, she's saying: not realising – or not caring – that I didn't have one to give a shit about me. 'So he insisted I went to Minnesota for the summer. I didn't want to go.'

'What's in Minnesota?' I ask.

'Camp North Creek. You've heard about American summer camps? Seen all the apple-pie movies with smiling kids and group singing and disgusting wholesome-ness?'

'Of course.' I shudder a little. Lissa and I used to play a game called *It Could Have Been Worse*. Going to summer camp, especially if it was a Christian summer camp, was always top of our list of places we would have hated.

'Well, as I said, I was seventeen. I was a junior counsellor. There to help look after the younger ones. Verity had this huge tantrum about me leaving for so long. So in the end our father agreed she could come too.'

She stands up quickly, turning away from me and brushing her hand across her eyes. 'It was my fault.' She says it so quietly I almost miss it.

'What happened?' I ask, gently so as not to spook her.

'A lot of people do two years as counsellors, juniors at seventeen and then another year when they're eighteen. At Camp North Creek there was this group of guys who'd come back for their second year. Eight of them. They thought they ran the place. They lorded it over everyone, but they treated the junior counsellors like we were their slaves.'

'1980,' I whisper under my breath. A year older than Freya who was born in 1981.

'What?' she asks.

'Nothing. Carry on,' I reply.

'One of them became the unofficial leader of the group, and all the others ran around doing everything he asked. No matter what it was. The stupider the better. One night they stole the Camp Director's car and went to the nearest big town for some music festival. Another time they put laxatives in a birthday cake and thought it was hilarious when half the faculty thought they had a stomach bug.'

'They sound like idiots.'

'They were.' She shrugs. 'But he was their leader and they followed him like puppies. Gregory was a classic jock. You know the type. A little bit thick. A little bit hot. A little bit full of his own sense of self-importance.' There's a bitterness to her tone.

'Gregory?'

'Yes.'

'What about Lawrence Delaney?'

'We'll get to him.' She offers me a thin smile. 'But first, I need to tell you about Gregory.' She spits his name.

'You hated him?' I ask.

'Ha!' she says, with a mock laugh. 'I was a seventeen-year-old girl who'd been forced to leave her boyfriend behind to spend my summer helping twelve-year-old kids learn to bake cookies and play softball. So of course I fell madly in love with Gregory Fuller. I thought he was the most perfect boy to ever grace the planet. He looked like Leonardo DiCaprio and this was the summer after *Titanic* came out.'

'Did he reciprocate?' I ask, but I don't really want to, there is something already so familiar about this story, one which has no doubt been told by thousands – millions even – of girls.

She pauses for a moment before she answers. 'Here's the thing about Gregory. He was also more than a little bit mean. A real sadistic streak to him. He toyed with me. Told me I was beautiful and smart. Told me he'd take me to the end of season party and we'd be together properly as soon as we left camp. There was a strict no dating policy,' she adds for clarification. 'But of course everyone was hooking up. One night he invited some of us junior counsellors to a get-together in the woods. We lit a bonfire and sat around taking turns to sip from the bottles of beer the boys had stolen from the petrol station up the road.'

She sits back down, looking at her hands, picking at the bright red polish, lost between the Bavarian hut and the summer of 1998. 'We played Spin the Bottle.' She makes a face. 'He made the bottle stop spinning when it was pointing directly at me.' She smiles, but it doesn't reach her eyes. 'God, I was so full of it! We went into the trees and I let him finger me. I was so cocky as I went to sit back down with the other girls. I was the one he had chosen. The next time he spun the bottle and we went back into the trees, he asked me to suck him.'

She clears her throat and takes a sip of her – now cold – tea. 'I was so besotted with him, I did. And then he told everyone. All the other teen counsellors. They laughed, teased me, pointed and told me I was a slut. I was mortified.'

'I'm sorry that happened to you,' I say, but to be honest I'm really struggling with where this is going.

'It was nothing. Not really. I was seventeen. So what if I gave the boy I fancied a blowie?' She sounds more like the old Freya again, a little more of that trademark 'fuck you' energy emanating from her. 'But Verity was incensed on my behalf. She'd always had this strong opinion of right and wrong. She went to Gregory and all his friends. Threatened to tell the adults about our late-night excursions when we were meant to be looking after the younger kids. It would have cost them their end of season bonuses. We all got a thousand dollars if we made it to the last day of the season, a way to make sure people didn't slope off during the last week.'

'And did she? Tell them, I mean?'

She raises her eyes to meet mine. Pain is etched so deeply into her soul it takes my breath away.

'What happened?' I whisper.

26

Her shoulders slump and for a moment I think she's going to lose it entirely. But then she straightens up and looks directly at me.

'Verity was known for being a bit of a tattle-tale.' The edge of a smile tugs at her mouth. 'I tried to tell her that wasn't the best way to make friends, but she was so earnest and so indignant about injustice. She overheard one of our neighbours once, in the garden, losing his rag at their new puppy for some minor misdemeanour. She climbed up on the garden table so she could shout over the fence.'

Freya stands, mimicking her sister straining on her toes. '"Don't you dare shout at him. He's just a puppy. He doesn't know what you want from him."' Freya sits back down. 'Credit to my neighbour though. He was so chastised he apologised to the puppy. Actually got on his knees to look the puppy in the face and said he was sorry. Verity was so proud.'

Freya sighs. 'But the boys at camp weren't like our neighbour. They hated her for threatening them. I should have stood up for her more. I should have gone to the Camp Director and told him everything that had happened. Perhaps he could've stopped it...'

'Freya, please just tell me what happened.'

'Verity was found on the shore of the lake the next morning. She'd drowned. We thought she was dead.' Her voice has dropped to a whisper. 'But she was alive. Just. Hanging on by a thread.'

'What happened?' I ask, but I think I can tell from the look on her face.

'The camp claimed it was an accident. Said she must have been swimming and got into trouble. She was an amazing swimmer, was on the State team, tipped for the Olympics if she worked hard enough.'

'You don't think it was an accident?'

'Gregory and his minions wanted to shut her up. And they succeeded.' She lifts her head and looks me straight in the eye. All I can see is her pain, her anguish. 'Verity was in a coma and she didn't wake up. My father brought her back to England, found her a place at Burtenshaw House. Shut her away and never visited again. Jesus, he even dumped poor Mum and went and found himself a new wife, had another family and left the rest of us in hellish purgatory. She lay there in silence. For twenty years.'

Her eyes darken for a moment. 'But two years ago something changed.'

'She woke up?' I ask, leaning forward, completely invested in the story.

'She told me the truth, of what they'd done to her. How they'd taken it in turns to hold her head under, laughing as she struggled, pulling her back up to watch her cough up water. But then Lawrence held her down a little too long. When he let her up she was sick. She told him they would regret what they'd done. That she'd make sure of it.' A single tear tracks down her face and she wipes it away angrily. 'So Gregory held her down for even longer.'

'He wanted to kill her?' I'm shocked.

'He thought he had,' she says sadly. 'They *all* thought she was dead. And they left her there in the water. As if she was nothing. As if she didn't matter.'

'The others?'

She looks directly at me. Her eyes flashing rage and righteous retribution. 'Spencer Balmforth. Ethan Donahue. Cody Gelber. Ruben Chambers. Jim Handley. Kai Helve. Lawrence Delaney.'

I swallow, the picture becoming perfectly clear. 'And so you...?' But I trail off, not quite able to say the words.

'For Verity.' She's matter of fact. As if it was the most natural and obvious thing in the world for her to have done. But then her face crumples.

I thought she was a serial killer. Taking out these men for some sick and twisted enjoyment. There was a brief discussion that Lissa and I had about whether it might be a sex thing. Like she was getting off on killing them. But it wasn't like that at all. I can see it now. She looks vulnerable, like a frightened child who doesn't know if she's done the right thing, or if she'll now get in the very worst of trouble for hitting back at her bullies.

She didn't want to kill them.

She *had* to.

For her sister.

I think we can all understand that. Can't we?

'So that's the whole story,' Freya says, splaying out her fingers as if to say *that's it, all of it, every last thing.*

'Except it isn't,' I reply. 'What about Gregory? I'm assuming he's still alive.'

'He was meant to be last.' She sounds deflated. Defeated.

And that's when I realise what's really happening here. She wants my silence. She *needs* my silence. She needs me to agree not to go to the police, not to tell the whole world. To let her remain free for as long as it takes to complete the task she's been undertaking.

I thought she might kill me here in this isolated cabin, leave my body somewhere it would never be found. But I was never a potential victim. She isn't a murderer. Not really. She's a vigilante.

Freya stares at me, waiting for me to decide what I'm going to do. I hold all the power here and she knows it. I stand up, careful not to knock my ankle, and start to hobble away from the table.

'Where are you—?'

'I need the bathroom.' But really I need time on my own to compose my thoughts. Am I really sure I can do this?

In the mirror, the woman staring back at me is covered in blood and mud. It is dried into her hair, caked across her skin.

Her eyes bore into mine. She is an animal. Wild. Feral. Beautiful.

Her savage truth laid bare.

She smiles.

We can do this. We must do this. The voice in my head is strong and confident.

We can't do this. We mustn't do this. The other voice is disgusted.

It's the only way.

No. It's wrong.

Is it really?

I take a deep breath and leave the bathroom. Freya's made another mug of tea for both of us. I can feel the nervous energy emanating from her. She's waiting for me to announce her fate. To tell her what happens next.

She thinks there are two choices.

Choice one is that I go to the police. Tell them I witnessed my boss try to kill a man, that I've had some suspicions about her previous victims but didn't *actually* think they were true. I mean, who even does that? I can play the slightly dumb victim. How I witnessed her chase him and then I tried to run, injuring my ankle in the process. I can cry and wail and tell them I almost died at her hands. My testimony will put her in prison for a very long time.

Choice two is that I don't go to the police. That I forget everything I saw and what I learned about her and pretend none of it ever happened.

Of course there is another way this plays out. She could kill me. Dump my body somewhere. But she had my phone. She'll know I was recording what happened. No doubt she realises I'm clever enough to have already sent the video to someone.

'Drink your tea, Millie,' I hear her say.

I obey and take a sip, she's added even more sugar to this cup and it's almost cloyingly sweet.

'You need it to make sure you don't go into shock,' she says when she sees my expression.

I take another sip, already I'm feeling a bit better. I pause to finish the drink, putting down the empty mug, stalling for time a little as I make my mind up about what happens next. 'Gregory Fuller. You know where he is?' I ask.

She nods, but confusion skitters across her features. 'He lives in Sacramento.'

'What does he do? For work, I mean?'

'Something in life assurance.'

'Is he married? Kids?'

'Twice divorced. His last wife took out a restraining order against him.'

'He was violent?'

'He held my little sister under water until he thought she was dead, all so she couldn't tell on him.' Her tone is deadpan. But the meaning is clear. *Of course a man like Gregory Fuller would be violent towards his wife.*

'So he lives alone?'

'Why are you so interested in Gregory?' she asks.

I lean back in my seat. 'Because I'm going to help you kill him.'

The silence in the cabin is thick and heavy, covering us in a shroud. I can see her trying to make sense of my words and I wait for her brain to catch up.

'You...' She narrows her eyes, 'you... why?'

It's an excellent question, because it isn't just one, there are many layers. Why would I help her? Why would I put myself in danger? Why do I care? What's in it for me? I suppose you're asking the same things? We'll get to that, I promise.

But for now, all I say is, 'For Verity.'

'What about the others?'

'How do you mean?'

'Are you going to the police?' she asks.

I take a sip of tea and smile softly. 'I'm not going to the police.'

There's a notepad on the table. I pull off the top sheet. We all know you never write a note on the pad itself, far too easy for some bright eyed CSI technician to read the imprint of your words on the next leaf underneath.

My handwriting is neat and careful.

Connor Weedon.

Liam Weedon.

I push the sheet of paper towards Freya.

She reads the names under her breath and I relish the sound of them on her lips. 'The Serendipity Chief Executive Officer and Chief Finance Officer?'

I nod.

'I don't understand,' she says.

'I'm going to help you kill Gregory Fuller. And then you're going to help me kill Connor and Liam.'

PART IV
FREYA

27

Well, well, well.

That took a turn I wasn't expecting.

Whoever would've thought little Millicent Brooks would have it in her?

'Why?' I ask.

'Why?' she repeats the question back to me.

'You've just told me you want my help in killing the two most senior people in our company. I think you owe me an explanation.'

She gives me this funny twisted smile, and for a brief moment I think she's about to burst into laughter. Tell me she's joking and of course she's going to the police to tell them everything. I still have the gun I took from the Delaney-Jansen house, the weight of it a comfort in my pocket. But it would be messy, sloppy; the kind of loose end I don't leave. I would have to send Lucas to deal with her flatmate, she's Millie's only real friend and the only person she could possibly confide in. He might refuse. There's always a first time.

Silence grows between us, taking form, so thick I can almost taste it. I wait. Take deep breaths. Try to remember I am the one with the gun.

Eventually she speaks. 'How well do you know them; Liam and Connor?'

'I know Liam a little. Purely in a professional context, of course.'

'Of course,' she echoes. She has obviously heard the rumours.

'Unsubstantiated gossip,' I add. Not that I need to explain myself.

'Started by whom?'

I frown briefly, taken aback. 'You know, no one has ever asked me that before.'

She shrugs. 'So, who started the rumour?'

'Liam Weedon,' I reply.

'And why would the CEO of a company as big as Serendipity start a rumour about sleeping with a junior executive?' There's a playful edge to the question, like she knows the answer.

'I had an idea he wanted to take credit for,' I say it quietly. I'm still livid, even after all this time. It smarts, like a burn. As if he branded me, throttling my career for three years. I've had to claw my way back, inch by humiliating inch. At least Lucas has helped get rid of a few of my most ardent detractors: it's always useful to have contacts in HR.

'Do you know the real origin story of Serendipity?' Millie asks.

'How Liam and Connor had their brilliant idea but no money? So they went to Las Vegas and turned a hundred dollars into almost a million, then convinced some big investors to get on board?'

'That isn't how it happened.'

'Which part?'

'Any of it. Well, except the big investors part. But all businesses have investors so...'

'You know the real story?' I ask, even though it's obvious she does.

'You asked me earlier if I had any siblings. And I said no, which is strictly true. I should have had a brother and a sister. My mother was on her way to the hospital for a scan. She was five months pregnant with the twins.' Millie pauses for a moment, dragging in a ragged breath. 'A drunk driver failed to stop at a junction and they were killed.'

'The drunk driver? Was that—?'

'Oh, no,' she interrupts me. 'This isn't a story about how I want to avenge my mother's killer. A few months after she died, the drunk driver was charged with causing death by dangerous driving. If convicted he would have been sentenced to up to fourteen years in prison. But he didn't serve any of it.' She looks at me and I can see a mix of emotions skitter across her face. 'He was killed in a car accident the day before the case was due in court.'

'Karma,' I say.

'No,' she corrects me. 'Not karma. My father was driving the other car.'

'Oh.' I'm rarely lost for words, but I have no idea what else to say.

'He planned it for weeks. Learnt the guy's routine. Knew exactly where he would be and when.'

'What happened, to your father?'

'He died. It was a head-on collision.' She says it like it was an inevitability.

'He meant to die?'

She nods and a look of absolute pain clouds her eyes. I almost want to reach out and touch her.

But then she gives herself a little shake and continues. 'I was sent to live with my grandmother. But when I was eleven she had a heart attack. Just dropped dead in the kitchen one morning as she made breakfast. And so I ended up at Weedon House.'

'*Weedon* House?'

'As in Connor and Liam Weedon, Serendipity's founders,' she confirms. 'It's a privately run children's home owned by their parents. There's a lot of money in rescuing poor little orphans.'

There must be. Despite always claiming they started Serendipity without any financial help from their family, Connor and Liam benefited from an Edenbridge Academy education, an incredibly expensive public school in the Home Counties.

'Connor was twenty-five when his parents, for some inexplicable reason, decided to give him a seat on the management board of Weedon House. I think it was part of his MBA.' She shrugs, that is obviously not an important detail. 'Liam worked there too, never too far from his big brother. Anyway, they would come to the home once a month and they always brought gifts. The other kids loved them.' She rolls her eyes. 'Kids are stupid. And easily bought.'

I'm starting to realise where this is going. 'Did he...?' I leave the end of the question hanging. We all know what I'm asking.

'Oh, no,' she says quickly. 'It wasn't that. They wanted us to like them. To talk to them and tell them the things we thought they could do to improve the home.'

'Oh. That sounds—'

'Nice?' she interrupts. 'Like they're the "good guys"?'

I'm taken aback by how vehement she is. 'Sorry.' I put up a hand in apology.

'I always kept my distance. There was something off about them, although I couldn't quite articulate it back then. It's like they were pretending, playing at being our friends, waiting for us to become valuable. Like assets-in-waiting.'

I nod. 'That's exactly what Liam is like.'

'Yeah. So when I was thirteen, I started to get into make-up. My parents and grandmother had left me some money and I was given an allowance each month. Enough to buy clothes and phone credit and fund a weekly trip to Boots. It was the highlight of a life that was... well, I was an orphan. In a children's home. So... you know.'

I don't know. Her experience is so far removed from my own I can't even begin to imagine. But I nod anyway and she continues.

'It wasn't make-up for *me* though. I loved doing it for other people and when I was fourteen I joined the local Youth Theatre. I was the one who did everyone's make-up before shows and I loved it. But it was hard to lug everything around, all that make-up was heavy and I didn't have parents to drive me around, I had to take the bus. So I got inventive. I bought a small fishing tackle box and had a friend help me make a series of smaller containers that fitted perfectly inside. We even begged the Design and Technology teacher, Mr Drummond, to let us use this machine he had to mould little plastic pots. Whenever there was a show, I would spend hours figuring out exactly what I needed to take, leaving everything else behind. Streamlined. Simple.'

'PALETTES.'

She looks at me. 'Yep.'

PALETTES is the cornerstone of the Serendipity brand. The thing that gave them a unique selling point to stand out against the competition. PALETTES lets you design your very own, entirely customised, make-up kit. All in a small and easy to carry case. If you want to change your eyeshadow, you just order a new quad of colours and snap it into place inside the main case. The combination capability is endless, and there are three ranges that are compatible with any case, so the system is saleable to teens as well as young professionals and even the more luxury end of the market.

'He stole your idea,' I say.

'Oh, no,' she says. 'When Connor first saw the case he told me it was genius. He and Liam were looking to start a business. They wanted to prove to their parents they weren't losers, that they could make something from nothing. Mummy and Daddy Weedon thought they needed to get a grip, get real jobs, and stop messing around. I overheard their father giving them this huge lecture once, about family and responsibility and being proper men. It was painful to listen to.'

She stops talking for a moment to adjust her position, wincing as she moves her ankle slightly. 'Anyway, Mr Weedon Senior refused to help them start the business. They needed some cash to make prototypes to try to tempt some investors, but of course neither of them had anything in savings and no solid employment history to try to get a loan.' She smiles. 'In the story they tell, they went to Vegas and hit a winning streak, making money from slots and roulette and blackjack to fund the R&D. In truth, they begged and cajoled a teenage girl into giving them her dead parents' inheritance.'

'You gave them money?'

'I gave them everything I had – almost five hundred thousand pounds – in exchange for a fifty percent share of Serendipity. Even the name was my idea. It means an unplanned fortunate discovery. Any time something positive happened to me, I would wonder if it was *because* I was an orphan. If perhaps this good thing was why all the bad stuff had happened before. That perhaps all the shit would turn out to *mean* something. I was fifteen and obsessed with the idea that things didn't just happen randomly, that there must be order and purpose in life, if only we could figure out what it was.'

'What did they do?' I ask.

'They cut me out. Took the name and the idea and all the money I had and built the third biggest beauty brand in the world.'

'So you want to make them pay?'

'Oh, no, Freya. I want to make them suffer.'

The look on her face causes a cold shiver to run down my spine.

'They stole my future. The person I was meant to be. For years I've been scraping by, trying to carve out a place for myself in a world that has failed me time and time again. Do you know what Connor said when he told me I wasn't going to be part of it any more?'

I shake my head.

'He told me that I was a stupid, stupid girl. That no one gave a shit about me. I got angry, started screaming at him, fists flailing. He told me to calm down and shut the fuck up. So I said I'd tell everyone what he did. He laughed.'

'Did you? Tell someone?'

'I tried. But the next day, I was walking up the driveway of Weedon House from the bus stop down the road. I heard a car crunching across the gravel. It pulled to a stop. I didn't look behind me but something in my subconscious told me it was Connor. He dragged me by my hair into the woods that surrounded the house and threw me into the mud. He started kicking and punching, telling me I was a worthless little bitch. Told me that if I said another word he would make sure I didn't talk again. He stuffed wet leaves into my mouth until I was sick.' Her voice is level as she talks, the tone even, almost robotic. It's as if she's relaying a movie she watched from a distance rather than remembering something real. But then her whole demeanour changes and she leans forward, squeezing her eyes shut, the next sentence coming out in nothing more than a whisper. 'And then he told me that Liam was with Lissa. Making sure she knew to stay silent too.'

'Lissa?'

'She was my best friend. She still is. More of a sister, I suppose.' Millie opens her eyes again. 'I want them to suffer for what they did to me. But I want them to die for what they did to Lissa.'

28

There is an anger inside Millie, one she can barely contain. I can hear it in her voice and see it in the way she's sitting, the set of her jaw, the flash in her eyes. Neither of us speaks. I watch the anger grow and shift, morphing into something bigger, something more powerful.

The desire to rip it all down.

To let the world burn.

I think I've been wrong about Millie. I thought she was weak. I thought she was a little bit lazy. I thought she wasn't the brightest. In fact, when I first interviewed her for the analyst role I was convinced she wouldn't get the job.

'Another pretty fool who wants to work in Beauty because it sounds *so terribly super fun*,' I'd said to Lucas, disdain dripping from my words and turning into a parody of the kind of person I thought Millicent Brooks was.

'Perhaps she would be an asset?' he'd replied.

The look I gave him would have withered anyone but him. 'Really?'

He sat up straighter in his chair. 'Just hear me out,' he said, raising a finger. 'Someone who's a bit half-hearted. Maybe she makes the odd mistake. Doesn't check things as well as she should.' He raised an eyebrow at me. 'You see where I'm going with this, right?'

I smiled at him. That was why I'd asked him to apply for a job at Serendipity; sometimes he could be a real asset. I hired Millie to be a patsy in reserve. Waiting in the wings for a time I might need someone a little less than capable, someone to pin a mistake on. She doesn't realise how many times I've used her to create an alibi, like in New York when she went to pick up my necklace while I was with Jim Handley.

But now? I think perhaps I was too harsh in my judgement, or that I was given poor information to begin with. Lucas shouldn't have underestimated her. I'm going to make damn sure he knows about his slip in judgement and what it almost cost me. Insist he keeps an even closer eye on her – if that's possible.

Imagine if she hadn't fallen into that animal trap? Imagine if she'd fled and gone straight to the police? It could have all been over. I deleted the video from her phone, but I'm assuming she streamed it somewhere as she recorded. I'm almost certain there's another copy, somewhere out there, drifting in the ether. I shiver at the thought. I need to keep her on side.

I lean forward, stretching out my right hand. 'Millicent Brooks, I think we are going to make an excellent team,' I say as we shake hands.

The deal struck, we begin the process of getting home to London. Oh, and dealing with the whole Lawrence Delaney issue. With Katerina and the children away, I decide to leave him exactly where he fell. One call to Lucas and he agrees to hop on the next flight to tidy up any loose ends.

'You need to make sure he's found before the children come

home,' I tell him. Well, it is part of the code and there's no point in having one if you don't even try to follow it.

'I'll get a burner and call it in to the emergency services. Claim to be a hiker who got lost and stumbled across his house. Then I'll get out of there before the police show up and want to chat.'

'Excellent. And do a sweep while you're there. Make sure nothing got dropped on the route between the house and hut.'

'Of course.'

After I end the call, I notice Millie is staring at me. 'Who was that?' she asks.

'A friend who'll help to ensure we aren't linked to the Delaney house.'

'We?'

'My friend will check you didn't drop anything in the forest, or leave any fingerprints by the house.'

'Who is this friend?'

'Just a friend. Someone I trust very much.' I don't name Lucas. Now isn't the time for her to find out the truth about him. 'Now,' I say, standing up. 'Do you think you can walk on that?' I motion to her ankle. 'There's an S-Bahn station at Possenhoffen, but it's about a twenty minute walk.'

'I'll be fine.' She's stoic. I can tell from her gait that it's incredibly painful, that every step is agony. But she doesn't complain. I'm impressed, to be honest. And it takes a lot to impress me.

* * *

We're booked on the 15.50 flight from Munich to Heathrow, so there's plenty of time for us to get back to the hotel to shower and change before we meet back in the foyer. Neither of us has slept and even I am starting to feel the effects a little. I read an article a decade ago about high performing people who only need a limited amount of sleep. Marissa Mayer, former CEO of Yahoo, reportedly only slept between four and six hours a night. If she could do it then so could I, and I've trained myself to function on an average of five hours a night, punctuated by occasional all-nighters. It has revolutionised my professional and personal lives.

Millie is obviously used to far more rest, and she yawns every few minutes while we're having brunch. We haven't spoken much since we left the hut as the sun began to rise this morning, just occasional platitudes and banal observations.

'Isn't the weather nice?'

'The S-Bahn is so much more efficient than the Underground.'

'This pretzel roll is delicious.'

Millie yawns again after she sips her coffee, covering her mouth with her hand. Then she tips her head to one side and looks at me.

'What?' I ask.

'You don't have a sympathetic yawn response,' she says.

'Because I'm a cold and heartless bitch,' I reply, keeping my voice neutral. It's not the first time someone has pointed it out. It's always held up as an empathy test, but it's total bullshit. Pseudo-science that people trot out to convince themselves their dog yawns when they do because Fido loves them.

Millie laughs softly, but she doesn't mention it again. Not even when her repeated yawning at the airport causes everyone we come into contact with, from security to the staff at the gate, to mimic her.

I get home early in the evening. I've still not slept, but I stay up, waiting for Lucas. He arrives at my flat a few hours later, coming straight from the airport once he's landed.

'We have a lot to discuss,' I say as I open the door and motion for him to enter.

'I bought you a gift from Austria,' he says, handing me a small wrapped liquor bottle and a bar of Zotter chocolate featuring a squirrel on the wrapper.

'Austria?'

'I could hardly fly in and out of Munich could I? What if I'd bumped into you at the airport?' He sounds a little pissed about the extra effort and it irritates me.

'You didn't need to buy me a gift.'

'Of course I didn't. But yet, here we are.' He smiles.

'Is it an apology?' I ask.

The smile melts from his face. 'I suppose you think I failed to do the proper due diligence on Millie?'

I shoot him a look that says that's *exactly* what I think.

'Respectfully,' he says without even an ounce of deference, 'you were the one in Lawrence Delaney's house, chasing him with a fucking gun. Which I'm presuming was how you were intending on killing him. Sounds messy.'

We stare at each other, standing in my hallway. An impasse reached.

He's right. I'm right.

He's wrong. I'm wrong.

I'm not going to apologise. He isn't either, not beyond a token gesture at least.

He can ruin me. I can ruin him.

I hand the bottle back to him. 'There are glasses in the kitchen.'

He takes it with a smile. This is how we solve our disagreements now. With frosty acceptance and a shot of whatever alcohol we have to hand. We are dysfunctional and absurd but this is my only relationship that makes any sense at all.

I nibble the edge of a piece of the hazelnut-flavoured Zotter chocolate as Lucas pours us another shot.

'Prost,' he says as he hands it to me.

'Prost,' I reply before drinking it. It's sweet and strong and surprisingly good. 'What is it?' I ask, motioning at the round bottle.

'Marillenschnaps? Basically apricot brandy.' He shrugs. 'It'll do. Anyway, I've been looking at that story she told you.'

'And?'

'It seems to check out.'

'So she definitely lived at this Weedon House?' I'm curious that he hadn't realised the connection to the Serendipity brothers.

'It wasn't called that. Not officially, anyway. The legal name was The Youth Trust, a registered charity operating out of the Weedon House estate. That's why we never realised.'

'But Connor and Liam worked there?'

'For the Trust, yes. Connor was a non-exec director, Liam some kind of strategy consultant. They didn't exactly take a hands-on approach and then quit to set up Serendipity.'

'What about Millie's claim that PALETTES was her concept?'

'No way to prove that either way.' Lucas stands up and stretches, cracking his neck and then his shoulders.

'What about proving the money was hers?'

'Now that *is* interesting.' He moves over to the bag he always carries, pulls out a folder and passes it to me. 'I was able to get access to the initial incorporation documents.'

I take the folder. 'He didn't *name* her as an investor?'

'Of course not. But there was no confirmation of the source of the funds. Liam and Connor claimed the money was a combination of personal savings and some winnings in a US casino. But they never filed a tax recuperation claim.'

'A what?'

'US citizens pay tax on casino winnings, but we don't in the UK. The casino will deduct the tax from a big win automatically, but if you're British you can claim it back when you get home. You just need to fill in a few forms.'

'I'm bored of this story,' I say. Who gives a shit about tax treaties?

'Here's the thing,' he says, his voice animated as if trying to reignite my interest. 'If what they claim was true, that they won a massive amount on a slot machine, then the casino would have taken forty percent of it. Tens of thousands of pounds. Hundreds of thousands maybe. They would have claimed that tax back.'

But they didn't. 'There was no casino win,' I say with clarity.

'Nope.'

'Because the money came from Millie.'

'That is one plausible explanation for it.'

'Interesting,' I say. 'Any sign of a bank transfer?'

He shakes his head. 'Not that I can find, but I doubt Liam and Connor would leave that evidence to be traced.'

He has a point there. I doubt we'll ever know for sure, but at least it seems to fit. 'And what about this Lissa?'

'She lives with Millie. Works in fashion PR or something. A bit ditzy, known for getting drunk and some ill-advised liaisons.'

'Anyone we know?'

'Just people she picks up in clubs, or on dating apps.' He sounds judgemental, even though he can hardly claim a moral high ground. 'Apparently she struggles to form lasting relationships.'

I'm not sure I can blame her. 'So you think Millie's telling the truth?'

'Probably.'

'Probably? I need to know she definitely has the appropriate motivation. That she needs my help. We're in a mutually assured destruction scenario.'

He raises an eyebrow. 'A what?'

'When you both stand to lose everything if one of you talks.'

'Oh. Like us?' He gives me his best wolfish smile.

'Exactly.'

'Do you think she'll actually do it?' he asks, stretching his frame along my sofa, making himself a little too comfortable.

'Do you?' I ask in reply.

He pauses, tapping his fingers against his lips. 'There's a fire in her.'

I let out a short burst of laughter. 'A fire?'

He winks.

'Killing takes more than fire,' I tell him pointedly.

'It does.' He pauses. 'I'm not sure,' he says eventually.

'Neither am I.' I'm forced to agree with him. 'I think *she* thinks she'll do it.'

'So what do you want me to do?'

'I don't know,' I say simply. I need more time to think through the repercussions. The what-if scenarios. What if she does? What if she doesn't? 'For now, just watch her. Tell me what she's up to. I'm assuming that won't be a problem for you?'

'Not a problem at all.' He smiles that handsome smile that makes all the girls fall for him.

29

When I get to the office on Monday morning, Millie's already at her desk, tapping away at her keyboard as if nothing has changed. The new analyst hasn't arrived yet, her desk empty and dark.

'Good morning, Freya,' she says when she sees me. Her eyes are clear and bright, no hint of the last few days.

'Good morning, Camille,' I reply, using the same tone I always would.

She gives me an almost imperceptible nod and swallows down a smirk. She's enjoying this, the pretence of normality.

'I apologise in advance but I'm wearing trainers because my ankle is still a little swollen. From falling over jogging in Munich.' She adds the last bit quickly.

'Thank you for letting me know,' I reply.

'Could I get you an oat latte?'

I know that she'll take at least ten minutes, possibly more with the ankle, while she has a cigarette but I could use a quiet start to the morning. A little time to take stock before the day begins. 'Please.'

* * *

She knocks on the door of my office to get my attention and I motion her inside. 'I came in early to do some research,' she says, placing the coffee at my elbow. 'There's a conference in Barcelona in two weeks. I think it would be a good opportunity for us.'

I narrow my eyes, she sounds off. What is she up to?

'The 9th of August,' she says.

'Right?'

'I'll need to book it fairly soon if we want to go. There's another conference in town that week and so hotels and flights will get busy.'

'OK...' I fail to keep the irritation from my voice, she knows I don't give a shit about that kind of detail. I just want to drink my latte and get on with the day.

'The other conference is called Life Matters. It's about life assurance.'

My eyes meet hers. 'Life assurance?'

'Yep. Apparently it's their main conference of the year. Anyone who's anyone in that industry will be there.'

I understand exactly what she's saying. Gregory Fuller will be in Barcelona. 'In that case, I suggest you make sure we've booked in advance. Before everything gets too busy.'

'Of course, Freya. I'll get that sorted this morning.'

I think she winked at me as she left the office. As if we were co-conspirators. Partners in crime. I don't like it.

* * *

'It was her idea?' Lucas asks me later, glancing from me to Millie's desk, where she's sitting very straight, shoulders back, fingers flying over the keys. The picture of efficiency.

'Yes,' I confirm.

'That's good, isn't it? Shows she's thinking about it.'

'I suppose.'

'You don't sound convinced.'

'Do you remember when I hired her? We thought she was a bit of a bimbo.'

'Well, that was your word, not mine. I wouldn't want to get in trouble for using inappropriate language.'

I shoot him a look. If he ever gets into trouble it will be for something far worse than a nominally problematic slur. 'Anyway, she wasn't good.'

'No she wasn't,' he agrees.

'But now look at her.'

He leans a little to get a better look.

'She's proficient and quick and taking initiative. Something's happened in the last few weeks.'

'Maybe the carrot of a promotion gave her a kick? Gave her the incentive to apply herself.'

I let out a little snort laugh. 'You're getting sappy, Lucas,' I tell him.

'Maybe it's her lovely new boyfriend?' He raises an eyebrow as he says it and smiles to himself. 'I hear he's a bit of a catch.'

I look witheringly at him. 'Just be careful. Don't get too attached to her.'

He pulls a face. 'I won't. But it is allowing me to spend a lot of time with her. Trust me, it's all good,' he promises. 'Now, about Barcelona. Gregory made an announcement earlier that he will be speaking at the Life Matters Conference. Something about erroneous claims.' Lucas mock yawns. 'He sounds *very* excited about it. Boring bastard.'

'I'm assuming that's where Millie got the idea.'

'Have you had any ideas yet? On the how?' He asks the question like he's asking what restaurants I might try on a weekend to New York.

'None,' I lie. I've thought about very little else for a long time. Gregory Fuller won't overdose on fentanyl. Or fall from a building. Or die in a senseless accident like Lawrence.

Gregory Fuller will look me in the eyes as he dies. Slowly. Painfully. *Excruciatingly* painfully.

But it needs to be more than that. It needs to be a performance. A ballet. Something that will make him notorious. If there is an afterlife I want him to watch on as his whole reputation is destroyed, as his name becomes synonymous with something shameful.

'Does she share your vision?' Lucas asks softly, pulling me back from my fantasies.

I look at him quizzically.

'Or does she think it'll be arm's length, a gun fired in the dark, poison dribbled into a glass?'

'You make me sound positively Machiavellian,' I say with an edge of laughter to cover just how uncomfortable a truth he has hit on.

'You *are* Machiavellian. And an artist,' he says, before rising and walking to the door. After he opens it, he turns to me and says loudly enough for my team to hear, 'Please let me know if I can assist with any other HR-related issues, Ms Ellwood-Winter.'

* * *

'We will leave in five minutes,' I tell Millie.

'I'll call a car,' she says, picking up her phone from her desk.

A week has passed since Millie suggested the conference to me.

Today we're going to Barcelona. I've organised to meet Petra, the CEO of a large influencer agency and one of the best connected people in the beauty industry, but it's really a thin ruse to cover up our need to undertake some research.

My father – before he deserted us and we never saw him again, even on his death-bed – was a great lover of a mantra. A quippy little sentence to encapsulate some life lesson or another. The kind of shit you see on a motivational poster. However, some of those are very applicable to my current vocation.

If you want to achieve greatness, stop asking for permission.

Don't wish for it, work for it.

Fail to plan. Plan to fail. Now this one is probably the truest thing ever said. Especially when you're trying to get away with multiple murders across multiple continents. Getting caught is not a desirable outcome.

At Gatwick Airport we weave through the crowds of people heading off on cheap package holidays, all tracksuits and sliders and beer breath at eleven in the morning. They spill out of the pub, rowdy and raucous. Millie leads me to Junipers and we find a table in the relative quiet of the champagne bar.

I can feel the energy humming off her. She's jittery, like she's had too much caffeine. She's making me nervous. It's not even midday but I order us a glass of champagne each. 'You need to calm down,' I tell her pointedly.

'I'm fine,' she says, but even as the words leave her mouth she's twisting in her seat, her eyes roaming from person to person as they walk past.

'You're not fine. You look like you're on drugs or something,' I hiss at her.

'I'm fine,' she insists, but her hands are shaking a little and I stare until she sits on them. 'OK. I'm a bit...' she trails off, turning in her chair to look directly behind herself.

'Thank you,' I say to the waitress as she deposits the champagne in front of us. Then I turn my attention back to Millie. 'Drink that. And sort yourself out.'

She physically blanches at my tone and it feels good. I need to make sure I'm the one in control of this situation. I need to lead the narrative. Direct the outcome. Manage the potential fallout. At least I have Lucas to help pick up any pieces that might get dropped. Just so long as he doesn't wimp out on doing what is necessary. Or decide he actually does have genuine feelings for little Millie Brooks.

I glare at her as she drinks the champagne. Then I motion to the waitress for a top-up.

'I'll get pissed,' Millie protests, as the waitress heads towards us with a bottle of Taittinger.

'You will not get pissed on two glasses.' I pause while the waitress pours and then walks away again. 'But I'd rather have you giddy on champagne than looking like you might be carrying a fucking bomb in your hand luggage.'

She looks horrified and turns to check behind her again. 'You can't say that in an airport.'

I ignore her and try to turn the conversation to practical matters. 'You brought your running kit?'

She nods.

'Good. We'll go to our meeting and then when we get to the hotel we'll check-in and then head straight out.'

'Do we have to run,' she asks. I look at her, she's not in bad shape but having watched her try to run from me in Starnberg I know she's hardly a regular.

'It's the best way to learn the layout of the city. If your ankle can cope. And no one bats an eyelid at a woman jogging in Sweaty Betty. It's like an invisibility cloak.'

'OK. But promise you won't take the mickey out of me.'

* * *

The meeting with Petra is dull.

'We could have just met at the conference next week,' she says, over coffee and little custard-filled doughnuts. 'Saved you a trip.'

'We wanted to ensure you had our undivided attention,' Millie says smoothly, and for a moment I'm impressed. There are times when she reminds me of someone. A young woman who could turn on the charm when it was needed, say the right thing to the right person at the right time. I've always been pretty good at getting what I want.

'Besides,' I add, 'I might not be able to attend the whole conference next week. Busy times and all that.'

Millie shoots me a look.

Later on she asks me why I said that. 'Don't we want everyone to think we're at the conference the whole time. Isn't that our alibi?' She's angry, running the words together as if she's trying to get them out before she changes her mind.

I sit back in my chair. We're in my suite, the Sagrada Família just visible in the distance.

'You have a lot to learn about this, Millicent.' I've decided to stop calling her Camille, at least when it's just the two of us. It's probably unnecessary to deliberately antagonise her.

'So teach me.'

I take a breath and look at her. She's so young. 'Are you sure you want this?' I ask, imbuing my tone with mature concern.

'Yes,' she replies, leaning forward slightly so I can see just how earnest she is. Is it an act? A performance?

I shift my weight a little. 'There are many stages. All of them are vital. You cannot skip them. Or rush them. This isn't about the finale. It's like a seduction, the time spent before to make it perfect is part of the ritual. The time spent afterward even more important.'

She nods.

'It isn't enough to get revenge. You understand that don't you?' I ask.

She looks confused. 'Isn't revenge exactly what this is all about?'

'If you go into this thinking that vengeance is more important than anything else you'll spend the rest of your life in a prison cell. Or worse.'

'Worse?'

'There are worse places than prison, Millie. You think Weedon House was bad? You should see the inside of British mental health institutions for those they consider to be "ill".'

She swallows audibly. I'm glad. I'm trying to frighten her, even if I'm not being one hundred percent truthful. A life spent dosed up on diazepam in an institute may indeed be preferable to a high security prison. But I'm not going to end up in either.

'You sound like you're good at this,' she says, slowly, chasing each word with care.

I motion around me. 'I'm here aren't I?'

'Only because I need you.' She says it softly, gently. Without pride.

I cock my head to one side and watch her for a moment. Her words settle in the air around us.

After a full minute she starts to squirm. I continue to watch.

Another minute and the tension in the room reaches a point she can no longer bear it. 'I only meant—'

I interrupt her. 'I know exactly what you meant. But you're wrong, Millie. You do need me. Without me you haven't got a hope in hell's chance of pulling any of this off. But I'm not free because you *allowed* me to walk. You know that don't you?'

'I... had...'

'No. Millie. You did not. I was always one step ahead of you. I always had a back-up plan. A way to get away if you had made a very different offer.' I'm lying. But so what. She just needs to be convinced that I'm the master. That she's merely the apprentice.

She needs to remember who is the fucking boss here.

30

We go for a run. I was going to cut her some slack, but now I relish in the obvious discomfort she's in as she tries to keep up.

'Why can't we just walk?' she asks as she huffs next to me.

'Because tourists walk.'

'So? Can't we just be tourists?'

'You want to kill him in the middle of Las Ramblas?' I ask with disdain. 'Or maybe in front of La Pedrera? Perhaps in the Picasso Museum?'

'No... I just—'

'The idea is that no one even sees you, they see a runner and their brains move on. If I run through the back streets, through a residential area, past a school, no one cares. But if I walk those places, perhaps with a coffee clutched in my hand, people wonder where I'm going, who I'm going to meet. I become a real person and it only needs one nosy neighbour to fuck up your whole life.'

We're still running. Well, I'm running. Millie is gasping and griping and unable to hold a conversation even at this frankly pathetic speed.

'How... are... you...?' she splutters out the words.

'I run every single day without exception. Thirty miles a week minimum.'

'Wow... that's...'

'It's called discipline.'

But a few minutes later I slow to a stop and give her a few minutes to catch her breath. I don't want her to collapse and cause a scene. And while my gliding past someone in black lycra might not raise an eyebrow, a sweating Millie wheezing like an asthmatic might give someone cause for a second look.

'Sorry,' she says as her breathing starts to slow. 'I would have started training earlier if I knew.'

'When did you decide on this?' I ask.

'This as in...?'

'Revenge.'

'I've thought of nothing else for over ten years,' she tells me.

I know she's being figurative. But again I see that fire in her. It smoulders in a different way to how mine blazes; maybe slow and steady will help her to stay in control.

I look around as I stretch my calf muscles. We're not far from the beach, in an area that has seen better days. There's a bar with boarded up windows and an abandoned-looking food truck. Opposite the concrete parking area is a large single-storey building with no windows.

I point to it. 'I think this used to be a night club.'

She pulls a face. Apparently her generation doesn't go clubbing like mine did, eschewing drinking in a sweaty throng in favour of coffee shops and side hustles. I feel the faint stirring of an idea.

'Tell me what you see, Millie.'

She looks around at the litter skittering across the barren ground, the oppressive sense of abandonment. She shrugs.

'I see an opportunity.' I smile at her. 'This place could be perfect.'

I wait until we're back at the hotel – showered and changed and sitting in my suite – before I tell her my plan. I've already turned it over and over in my head as I got ready and I think it has merit.

I've ordered us room service and we wait until it's arrived, keeping our conversation to the everyday and the professional. A sharp knock on the door rescues me from Millie's boring story concerning some spreadsheet, which I'm sure she's very proud of and wants my validation about, but I quite frankly couldn't care less.

The wheels on the trolley squeak slightly as the uniformed waiter pushes it into the suite.

'You can just leave it there,' I tell him, already reaching for the leather wallet to sign the slip. I'm impatient, keen to get on with the main part of the evening. All this wasted time is making me itch.

Millie starts removing cloches, squinting at the array of dishes I've ordered. It's just simple tapas: patatas bravas, albondigas en salsa, chorizo a la Sierra, gammas al ajillo; and a sharing board of jamon iberico, olives, manchego cheese, and freshly baked bread. A bottle of red wine and a bottle of white complete the spread.

'No sangria?' Millie asks, sounding like an ungrateful child who's been given the world but still wants something else.

'We aren't at Tapas Revolution,' I tell her, referencing the British chain restaurant. I don't think she gets it.

Once we're sitting at the table, the food spread in front of us and the wine poured, I begin to tell her my plan. I feel like a teacher, a mentor. I feel inspiring and powerful and I like it very much.

'There are some key components in the planning stage that are vital,' I tell Millie. 'Obviously the timing: when you will do it. You need to find the optimal point between a guarantee of success and the best chance of remaining undetected. Our window is narrow, we only have the forty-eight hours when both us and Gregory will be in the city and he will be at his conference for a large chunk of that time.'

'I'm assuming it's best to do it on the second evening?' she asks.

'Yes. And then we need to think about place, the where part of the equation.' I pause to take a sip of wine.

'His hotel,' Millie offers.

'No.' I'm firm. It's a stupid idea.

'Why not? Fentanyl wasn't it? In Paris?'

'Which is exactly why not.' I think I'm going to have to go over the absolute basics. 'You cannot do the same thing twice. That is how you get caught. Being in the same city as an accident, or a home invasion, or an overdose is one thing. Who is going to ever look for that pattern? But being a guest in the same hotel when a guest dies of a fentanyl overdose *twice* is too much of a risk. You need to remember that once is bad luck, twice *might* be a coincidence but it could also be considered suspicious as hell.'

Millie chews some bread, swallowing before she speaks. I hate watching other people eat. I hate the sound of other people eating even more. 'Why don't you just tell me your plan, Freya? You've obviously already thought of one.'

'Fine.' I clear my throat. 'Earlier we ran past an abandoned night club. Now, I have been researching Gregory, learning what he likes, what he wants, what he desires.'

'He likes art galleries and Shakespeare and fine dining.'

'No,' I correct her. 'Those are the things he tells the world he likes. The version of himself he projects. What he really wants is to feel important. Like he has been chosen. And he wants to feel that his prowess is recognised.' I raise my eyebrows slightly.

'Prowess?' She sounds like she's never heard the word before.

'Skill. Talent. Call it what you will.'

'At what?'

'Gregory Fuller is a poker player.'

'Is he any good?'

'No. But he thinks he is. He thinks he's good enough to play with the big boys. More explicitly, he thinks he's good enough to play in the underground tournaments. The ones that are invitation only. Highly exclusive.'

'So... we're going to stage an underground poker tournament?' She curls her lip slightly.

'No, Millie.' Jesus! 'We're just going to invite him to one ostensibly being held in an old abandoned nightclub.'

'Oh.'

After we've finished eating, Millie clears the table while I set up my personal laptop with its VPN. She comes to stand behind me, leaning in to peer at the screen. I try not to bristle at her close proximity. But I can't bear the feel of her breath on my cheek.

'Why don't you drive?' I say, standing up and gesturing to the seat.

'But... I—'

'It's not rocket science. All you're doing is posting to a Reddit thread. It's all done in code, so if you stumbled across the sub you'd think nothing of it. But it's a place where people swap details for various tournaments and competitions.'

'Ummm... how do you know this?' she asks.

'Research.'

'Do you play?'

'No. But Gregory does. And therefore I know all about it.'

'OK.'

'We need to make Gregory think he's been invited to a competition while he is here in Barcelona. Then we will provide him with the details of the location, luring him to the abandoned club.'

'But won't the invitation be traced to us?'

'Of course not. Besides, the police are going to think he's the victim of a vicious drug cartel's retaliation, a case of mistaken identity that ended in tragedy.' You remember I said I wanted his death to make him notorious? Well, I've had a better idea. I don't want him to be remembered for *anything*. I want his death to be considered utterly pointless. And what could be more futile than dying by mistake? A life cut short for no reason other than him merely *looking* a bit like someone more interesting.

* * *

The day after we return from Barcelona, the predicted heatwave begins to boil across Europe, grinding everyone's patience to a halt. Apparently it could last for two weeks before it breaks.

In London the tarmac begins to melt, trains are cancelled, schools are closed, and fires begin to break out across arid farmland. The papers take the opportunity to smear images of young women in bikinis across the front pages. There's a scandal when a tabloid runs a headline of *Hot-Hot-Hotties* and one of those girls turns out to be fourteen. A whole host of people on Twitter scramble to deny they're paedophiles. There's the usual bullshit argument about teenage girls and hebephilia and demands that their parents do something about the way they are dressing in 'overtly seductive' ways. If my father was still alive he would probably be one of them. One of his old cronies, George Allanday KC, *is* one of them. *Quelle surprise.* After being caught on camera making lewd remarks about the Hot-Hot-Hotties girl, he posts a long tirade about the state of the nation and how the 'woke left' have created a liberal parenting nightmare. He doesn't offer an apology for being a pervert.

The heat is making me prickly. Fractious. More prone to allowing things to piss me off in entirely irrational ways. I know I'm being even more of a bitch than usual. But if anyone wants to point it out they can fuck off.

'I'm warning you, Lucas,' I tell him, after he accuses me of being unreasonable.

'I just think...' but he trails off, his hands raised in front of him as if to ward off a physical blow.

'We are not postponing.' He's had the fucking gall to suggest we put the Gregory plan on hiatus until the heatwave is over.

'Wouldn't it be better to make sure you have a cool head? And what if he decides not to come to the conference anyway? Or the flights are grounded?'

I look at him. 'Obviously then I will postpone.' Idiot. You can't kill someone who isn't there. 'But I want this done.' I *need* this done. Time is running out.

'Just don't do anything rash,' he tells me, wiping sweat from his forehead.

'Ha!' I reply. Sometimes I think he has no fucking idea.

Gabriel messages me that evening to tell me that he's in town. *My hotel has aircon*, he adds. I can imagine the flash of humour in his eyes as he wrote that. But I can't allow myself to get distracted.

An hour later I'm lying on the crisp white sheets of the Four Seasons Park Lane, revelling in the frigid air. It's so hot outside that sleep would have eluded me at home anyway.

'You seem preoccupied,' Gabriel says as he stands up and moves towards the mini-bar to pour us another drink.

'Just busy,' I tell him.

'You know you can talk to me.' There's a tenderness to his tone.

'I know,' I reply. Even though of course I can't. Not about the way I feel about him. And certainly not about my plans to kill Gregory Fuller.

31

Our flight to Barcelona for the conference is delayed by almost two hours. Luckily the airport is air conditioned. But it's also rammed full of imbeciles. People who don't understand that if you're pulling a wheelie suitcase behind you, you need to be a little more careful about your turning circle. After the third person runs over my feet I'm ready to kill someone right there in the middle of the terminal.

Millie has nailed her heatwave travel wardrobe with a floaty dress and sandals, her hair twisted into a messy bun. She looks cool and almost ethereal and I fucking hate her. I can feel the sweat dripping down my neck, pooling at my lower back. My own hair is twisted into a classic chignon, the pins digging into my scalp, making me want to scream.

But I am a swan, no one will ever know my discomfort. My jealousy. I glide through my life as other people admire me. At least until I can shut myself in the bathroom and luxuriate as I swipe glorious wet wipes across my skin.

We finally land in Barcelona at 8 p.m. It's still boiling hot, the outside temperature almost thirty degrees. It hits me in the face the second I walk off the aircraft, so stifling I almost stumble.

'Jesus,' Millie whispers next to me. 'It's even hotter than in London.'

I mumble in agreement.

'You don't think...' she trails off, but her tone makes her meaning clear.

'No. He'll be here,' I hiss back. He has to be.

There's a nightmare queue at immigration and I'm subjected to listening to a group of blatant Brexiteers in front of me moaning about the delay. 'What did they think they were voting for?' Millie asks softly.

I ignore her. I don't want a scene. I just want to get to the hotel.

An hour later and we're finally free of the queue, heading out of the terminal in search of a taxi.

At least the Spanish have an idea of how to deal with the heat and we find every window and door is closed, blinds drawn, people keeping out the heat instead of trying to create a false movement of air into their homes.

As the taxi takes us to the hotel I'm suddenly struck with a realisation. The streets are empty. Quiet. As if the place is a ghost town. Millie notices the same thing, 'It's dead,' she tells me.

'It's perfect,' I reply. With everyone inside and all the doors and windows closed, the chances of anyone seeing us, anyone noticing anything, is rapidly diminished. This could be heaven-sent.

'Except we can't go for a run,' she says with a hint of a smile. 'Only a lunatic would do that in this heat.'

We don't need to run. I already have the whole thing in hand. It's perfect in its simplicity. Via Reddit, Millie has already piqued Gregory's interest in a potential tournament happening tomorrow night. He's a fish circling the hook, eyeing up what he thinks is nothing more than a juicy worm.

We've deliberately booked to stay in the same hotel as the employees from – the imaginatively entitled – Assured Life Corp, even though most of the beauty industry is staying at the far nicer W on the beachfront. But needs must.

The Hilton has put on a drinks reception in the bar area and I spot Gregory Fuller sipping beer in a crowd of the dullest, most insipid men I have ever seen. Dressed in so many shades of grey they may as well be in a black and white movie; even their complexions are pallid.

'Should we?' Millie asks, motioning towards the bar. 'Or will he recognise you?'

'Unlikely, but we'll sit in the corner,' I reply and nod to an empty table tucked away from the boring men.

Millie goes to the bar and she's beaming as she carries two lemon-drop Martinis back to the table. 'You will never guess what I have,' she whispers as she places the glasses down.

I don't indulge her with an answer.

She smirks and opens her handbag to reveal a small plastic wallet on a dark grey lanyard. She glances around before leaning closer to me. 'It's Gregory's pass for the conference.' She pauses and then adds, 'and the key to his room. He left it on the bar.' She looks very pleased with herself.

'And what exactly are you going to do with them?' I ask.

'I'm going to scope out our victim.' She picks up her cocktail and takes a large sip. 'Keep an eye on him and text me if he makes a move.' And then she puts down the glass and she's gone.

I sip my own Martini, trying to quell my irritation. Am I pissed because it's a clever idea and I should have thought of it? Pissed because it's a stupid and frankly unnecessary risk? Or just pissed because it's hot and I'm tired?

Ten minutes pass. How long does she need in his room? But then I notice the pack of grey suits has shrunk. Gregory is no longer at the bar and I spin to see him at the check-in desk, the pretty receptionist handing him a key with a smile.

Shit! I text:

> Millie get out of there now. He's coming up

The message doesn't deliver. I try to call her phone but all I get is an automated message that the call can't be connected.

Shit. Shit. Shit. If he finds her in his room it's all over. She'll have linked us indelibly to him and there'll be no way we can kill him this week. And the window of opportunity is closing fast. What if I can't get to him quickly enough?

I can't even try to beat him to the room, I don't know which floor he's staying on, let alone the room number. I down the rest of my Martini and reach for the remnants of Millie's. She's on her own and all I can do is hope she hasn't just fucked everything up.

An hour later and I'm going out of my mind. Where the actual fuck is she? If he found her in his room, what would he do? Would he just assume it was a hotel screw up; that she was allocated the same room as him? It happens all the time. Or would he think she had stolen his room key and was trying to rob him? But then he'd have called the police and they would be here by now.

Another five minutes pass. Finally the lift pings and opens to reveal Millie, smiling in that floaty sun dress as if nothing is wrong. She detours towards the bar on her way to the table and I watch as she hands in the lanyard to the barman like she just found it.

'Where the fuck were you?' I hiss as she slides into her chair.

'He came back to the room.'

'I know. I tried to call you to warn you but your phone was off. What the hell happened?'

'The room was one of those interconnecting ones, with a little space between the two rooms. I managed to hide in there and had to listen to him practise his speech for tomorrow about ten times.'

She rolls her eyes. But then she sees the expression on my face 'What? It was fine.'

'You nearly got caught.' I deliberately clip each word. 'You put the whole thing in jeopardy. This is why we plan meticulously. Why we don't deviate.'

'But nothing happened.'

'You were lucky.'

She stares at me for a moment, as if she wants to say something more, but then she nods. 'You're right. I was lucky. I promise I'll stick to the plan.'

'Good.'

I try to keep my relief under wraps. We're still on track. I don't want her to realise just how worried I was, just how important killing Gregory Fuller tomorrow really is.

'I'm sorry,' she says, not meeting my eye. 'I thought I was helping.'

'No harm done,' I reply, keeping my tone magnanimous.

'I got carried away. I... I'm nervous.' The last word barely a whisper.

Sometimes I forget she hasn't done anything like this before.

Was I nervous, the very first time? Of course. I didn't let it stop me though.

She'd better pull her shit together for tomorrow.

* * *

Millie and I spend the next day at our own conference, pressing palms and chatting to as many people as possible. Millie is jittery but she turns it to her advantage, talking to potential clients and collaborators, charming them, setting up almost a dozen meetings over the next few weeks. I watch her, waiting for her chirpy facade to crack, but she manages to make it through the day.

As the afternoon bleeds into evening, we're invited to a plethora of different after-work drinks receptions in various bars around the city. We graciously accept them all. They will form our alibi if we need one, even though we won't actually attend most of them.

At 6 p.m., the conference organiser sends out a waiter with a tray of ice-cold white wine to lubricate the delegates and encourage them to stay at the venue and mingle a little longer. Millie leaves to freshen up for the evening. 'Amateur,' I say to the woman next to me, and roll my eyes. 'Everyone knows you roll straight from here to the first party.'

'Her first?' The woman, who I recognise from events in previous years, asks.

I down my wine and reach for another glass. 'Yep.'

'These kids have no stamina any more.'

I clink my glass against hers in agreement. An hour later we're still making idle chitchat as people start to drift to the bar across the street. 'Shall we?' I ask her.

She doesn't notice when I slip out of the bar, she's far too engrossed in conversation with the Martin twins from C'est Magnifique I just introduced her to. She's on her fifth glass of wine in less than ninety minutes. She'll have no chance of remembering the exact time we were together this evening.

First alibi secured, I head back to the hotel to meet Millie.

Wine sings in my veins and the setting sun paints fire across the sky.

God, I'm looking forward to this.

32

At 8 p.m. Millie and I meet in my suite. She's wearing this rather fabulous Grecian-inspired strappy dress in a soft grey, with a full skirt to just below the knee. I'm still in the same staid linen shift dress I wore all day and I hate that I feel like a maiden aunt next to her dazzling youth. I'm only forty-two for Christ's sake, but in our age-obsessed world I'm starting to feel side-lined.

'You're not getting changed?' Millie asks, and I can see that she's judging me.

'No one gets changed,' I reply, keeping my tone cool and superior. 'Everyone except you went straight to the first bar.'

'Have I...' she trails off, looking stricken.

'I told people it was your first conference. They think you're an amateur.' I shrug. 'It's fine. We'll have to pop in at another party later, though.'

'Thank you.'

I don't tell her that she's probably done us a favour. When people see us for a few fleeting minutes later they will definitely remember us, especially the guys. Our alibi is gaining strength.

'Do you have everything?' Millie asks, glancing at the impossibly small bag I'm carrying.

I don't honour the question with an answer. 'Let's go,' I say instead.

Gregory's room is at the other end of my corridor, on our route to the lifts. A frisson runs through me as we pass it. Behind that door he is probably in the shower, primping and preening as he prepares for what he thinks is an evening of poker against an impressive team of adversaries.

Poor Gregory. So innocent. So unaware of what's coming.

Half an hour later we're ready for him.

The inside of the abandoned club is boiling hot and the stench of decades of sweat and spilled alcohol hangs heavy in the air. In the centre of the dance floor is a single wooden chair, a coil of ultra-fine rope lying next to it. A throne waiting for the guest of honour.

In my late teens I spent the summer working in a nightclub on the island of Mallorca. My memories of that time are pretty hazy, a montage of days at the beach, nights serving rum and cokes, drinking shots with the customers, swimming in the sea under the stars. And the time a fight broke out between some local guys and a bunch of lads on a stag holiday. Within thirty seconds, my manager, the DJ, and three other barmen were armed with baseball bats, breaking up the fight before it escalated to murder.

'Where the hell did they come from?' I'd asked, motioning at the weapons they brandished.

'They're everywhere,' my boss replied. 'Did no one show you?' He sounded concerned.

I'd shaken my head and so he'd taken me on a tour.

The abandoned club in Barcelona had used a similar range of hiding places. The baseball bat now in my hands was concealed within the built-in sofas next to the dance floor. I enjoy the heft of it, the feeling of raw power in the smooth wood. I'm confident in my ability to deliver a blow that will incapacitate him but not kill.

My Apple Watch vibrates. It's 9 p.m.

Showtime.

Fifteen minutes pass and I'm starting to get nervous.

'He'll be here,' Millie tells me, keeping her voice low.

'Shhh!' I don't need her chirpy cheerleader bullshit right now.

'Sorry.'

We're standing on either side of the rear door to the club, the same door Gregory was instructed to use when he arrived for the tournament. The baseball bat in my hand is getting heavier and I swap it to rest on my other shoulder.

Another few minutes pass, but I resist the urge to look at my watch.

'You definitely said nine?' I ask.

'Yes.'

'You're sure?' I'm regretting allowing her to post the final information to the Reddit thread. What if she fucked it up?

'You checked the message before I posted it.' She sounds irritated.

'You could have changed it.'

'I'm not an idiot.'

I hold back a retort.

We wait until quarter past ten.

'He isn't coming,' I'm forced to concede, my voice bitter.

Millie exhales slowly. 'No. I don't think he is.' There's an edge to her voice; I think it's worry. I don't try to placate her.

In the distance a siren pierces the silence. 'We should get out of here,' I say, resting the baseball bat against the wall.

'I... I...' Millie starts to say and I wait for her to finish. 'I'm sorry.' It's barely a whisper.

'And what, exactly, are you sorry for?'

'That he didn't come. That we haven't... you know.'

'I thought you were apologising for failing to get him here.'

'I... but that...'

'I don't want to talk about it. Let's go back to the hotel and see if we can find out what the hell has gone wrong,' I say as I cross the dance floor to collect the rope from by the chair. I coil it carefully and tuck it into my clutch bag.

Millie doesn't say a word as we walk back to the hotel. But I can tell she wants to.

There are two police cars outside the Hilton. A pack of grey-suited men hover in the entrance to reception.

'What happened?' Millie asks one of them as we get close and can see the nervous energy rolling from them all.

He shakes his head and turns his back to her.

'Hey,' she grabs his shoulder and turns him back to face her. 'What the hell is going on?' Her voice is high-pitched, panicked. He recoils slightly from her.

'A friend of ours,' the man says, as if that is any type of explanation at all.

'A friend of yours, what?' Millie demands.

'He's gone. Disappeared.' The man falls silent. We aren't going to get any more out of him.

Luckily, the receptionist is in a chatty mood.

'Apparently some of the guys chartered a yacht for the evening. Thought it would be cooler out at sea,' she tells us. 'One of them didn't make it back. They think he must have fallen overboard. No one even noticed until they got to the harbour.'

'He's dead?' Millie asks.

The receptionist nods.

'Jesus,' Millie says softly.

'Yeah. Poor guy. He seemed so nice. We were chatting last night, he'd lost the key to his room.'

Millie spins to look at me.

I don't say a word until we're back in my room, the door firmly shut behind me. I want to be alone, but Millie has followed me like a fucking puppy.

'So he's dead,' she says as she sinks into one of the chairs by the mini-bar.

'Looks like it.' There's no emotion in my words.

'You don't sound pleased.'

'You want me to be pleased?'

'He's dead. Isn't that what you wanted?' She looks so innocent standing there in her pretty dress, a stupid smile on her stupid face.

The anger hits me, coursing through my veins. 'I didn't want him dead,' I hiss at her. 'I wanted to kill him. He was mine!' I spit the words in her face and she recoils at my fury, pressing herself back into the chair. 'Mine! Do you understand? He was the one I have dreamt about for years.' I take a few steps away from her, spinning on my heels and starting to pace. I know I should rein myself in, but I can't stop. He was meant to take this anger, but now he's... he's... gone!

'I'm sorry,' she says gently. 'I just—'

'You just what?' Spittle flies from my mouth. 'You just what?' I repeat.

'I'm sorry. I just thought...' she trails off. 'I thought you'd be happy that he was dead. I thought that was what we were trying to achieve. I thought we were a team.'

I laugh in her face. 'You thought we were a *team*. Like this is some kind of club. A sisterhood?' I make it sound ridiculous. Stupid and juvenile.

'No, I just thought we were helping each other.'

'I didn't need your fucking help. This isn't about you!' I'm really shouting now.

'OK, OK. Calm down, OK?'

'It. Is. Not. OK!' I raise my hand to strike her. I can feel the adrenaline coursing through me, the monster within me tearing at the bars to the cage I have so carefully constructed over the years.

But then she does something unexpected. I want her to beg me not to hurt her. I want her on her knees, grovelling, broken. But instead she puts her hand on my shoulder. 'I understand,' she whispers, her eyes soft and gentle. 'I understand.'

And then I let her take me in her arms, rocking me gently as I sob.

'It's going to be OK,' she whispers in my ear. 'It's over now.'

And she's right. It is over.

'You can tell Verity they are all gone.'

My heart swells at the thought. I picture the look on her face when I tell her.

Yes. It's all going to be OK.

We go to one of the parties. It's my idea. I need to get out of the hotel room. And I need a drink.

'You don't have to do this,' Millie whispers in my ear just before I push open the door to the bar.

'Freya!' The woman from earlier, now absolutely plastered, spots me and flings her arms around me. 'I thought you'd gone home!'

'We went to Valentina's,' I tell her as I extricate myself from her embrace. I resist the urge to wipe her touch from my skin. 'This is Millie.'

'The virgin!' the woman exclaims and Millie blushes. 'We need to get more wine in you,' she adds and drags Millie to the bar, chattering away to her as if they've known each other forever.

Ten minutes later I slip out the rear door of the bar, cutting down an alleyway and back on to the main thoroughfare. I don't know exactly what I'm looking for. But I'll know him when I see him.

He's on his own and looks a little lost. His face breaks into a smile as I approach. Or perhaps smile is generous, more of a sneer. He thinks he's in control of our tête-à-tête. He thinks he is going to be the one taking advantage of me.

He doesn't realise I'm leading him to an abandoned warehouse.

The baseball bat is still resting against the wall.

The lightweight rope is still in the little clutch bag I'm carrying.

Lucas comes to my apartment the day after we return from Barcelona, armed with a magnum of my favourite British sparkling wine.

'He's definitely dead?' I ask him as I open the door.

'Yes,' he replies. 'Guessing it wasn't what you'd hoped for though?'

I don't reply, just step to the side so he can head into the living room and open the wine. I'm over it. The whole thing with Gregory. He didn't suffer. He didn't scream and writhe in agony, begging for mercy or his mother. I am completely over it. If I say it often enough, perhaps it will be true.

Lucas sprawls across my sofa, feet dangling over the end of the arm. 'Gregory Fuller fell from the Aphrodite while his colleagues enjoyed an early evening tipple,' he says reading from a news article on his iPad. 'Apparently the entire life assurance community has been *rocked* by his death.' He scrolls for a few moments. 'Jesus, this dude's actually crying.' He turns the iPad to face me. One of the grey men from the drinks reception was interviewed by a news station this morning and didn't hold back his emotions.

'Drowning isn't an easy death,' he says, reaching out to take the glass of wine I'm offering.

'No,' I reply. He may have suffered but it still wasn't me holding the knife. Although at least I can tell Verity it's over.

I go to Verity the next day. The train is roasting hot, like an oven slowly cooking a stew until there is nothing but mulch in the pot. My mother was the queen of the stew. Every few months I'd come home from school to discover an ungodly smell emanating from the kitchen. 'Freezer surprise for dinner,' she'd call out as I tried to slip into the house unnoticed. 'Freezer surprise' was literally a stew made from all the stuff she'd failed to label properly and which languished uneaten in the bottom of the freezer. It was vile. Funny the things you remember, isn't it? I haven't thought about that for years.

Burtenshaw House is air conditioned, the icy cold offering blessed relief as I walk into the reception area.

'Is she awake?' I ask as I sign in. I want to tell her everything.

'She's awake but quiet,' the nurse replies as she leads me down the corridor towards Verity's room. 'Shall we go to the common room?'

'I'd rather see her alone today.'

'Of course,' she says, pushing the door open.

Verity is sitting staring out of the window, shoulders slumped as if she can't fully support her own weight, hands hanging in her lap.

'Your sister is here to see you,' the nurse says, affecting a false sing-song tone like Verity is a toddler. 'Isn't that wonderful?'

Verity turns her cold eyes to me, her expression remaining neutral. There is no recognition there, no sign she knows who I really am.

The nurse touches my shoulder gently as she walks away. *I know it's hard*, the contact says.

'Hello Verity,' I say and approach her slowly, carefully, the same way you approach a wild animal whose behaviour you don't fully trust.

I sit on the edge of her bed, my eyes roaming her face, searching for any sign of life.

'Do you remember what happened that night, at camp?'

A tiny light of something flicks on inside her.

'You do remember, don't you?'

The light grows brighter.

'And you remember what I told you I'd do. About the boys who were there?'

'N, n, n,' her mouth tries to form a word but she can't.

'It's all done, Verity. They're all gone. Every last one of them.'

I take her hand and squeeze it. 'You know what that means, don't you?'

For a moment I feel her squeeze my hand in return. But then she throws her head back and howls. The sound ricocheting off the walls.

The nurse comes running in, pushing me away from her. 'There, there, Verity, calm down.' She turns to me, a look of panic etched across her face. 'What happened?'

'I... I... don't know,' I stutter. 'We were just chatting and suddenly...' I motion to her, the keening getting louder and louder.

'I think it might be better if we call it a day,' the nurse says. 'Sorry.'

'That's alright,' I say, standing up and smoothing my dress down over my hips.

The alien sound spilling from Verity's mouth goes up an octave, morphing into something more akin to a scream. It follows me down the hallway and out into the baking wall of the heat of the summer.

I tick off a mental list of their names:

Spencer Balmforth.

Ethan Donahue.
Cody Gelber.
Ruben Chambers.
Jim Handley.
Kai Helve.
Lawrence Delaney.
Gregory Fuller.
That is all of them.
The end.
I draw a line under them and move on.

* * *

The heatwave continues unabated. But it is far worse across the US. Eighty million people are living under a heat warning, a third of Missouri is officially in drought, and Death Valley records temperatures in excess of fifty degrees. Yet still no one talks about climate change.

Millie has reverted to her old, slightly sloppy work self. It's probably the heat.

Lucas, however, is proving himself to be a great asset. He has come to my office under the pretence of sorting out some paperwork, closing the door behind him to ensure Millie can't overhear our conversation.

'Liam and Connor's deaths are going to create a power vacuum,' he says, perching on the edge of the sofa in an attempt to look appropriately meek and earnest for Millie's benefit. She keeps sneaking peeks at him through the windows.

'Are you listening, Freya?'

'Of course.' I snap my attention back to him. 'There will be a power vacuum at the top of Serendipity.'

'Who takes the spoils of war?' He says it like he's intoning a mantra.

'What the fuck have you been reading?' I ask.

'The first person who arrives to claim them,' he tells me, his face breaking into a proud smile. 'It's from a book about military strategy in the middle ages.'

'Brilliant,' I reply, deadpan. 'But back in 2023?'

'Back in 2023, Freya Ellwood-Winter has a unique opportunity to be in the right place at the right time to take advantage of that mad scramble for power.'

'Because I know it's coming.' Oh, Lucas is good. I'm currently the Sales Director. It's not a *bad* level to be at my age. But I want more. Much more. This could be a chance to leapfrog up the career ladder.

'Exactly. But you need to be very, very sure there is no suspicion that you had any idea.'

'Why would anyone think that?'

He stands up and moves directly in front of me. 'I know you're planning on pinning this on Millie.' His tone is almost gentle.

He's right. Of course.

No one will trace a connection between those eight dead men and myself, all records from Camp North Creek were destroyed, and after Verity's 'accident' none of the men ever admitted publicly to having spent the summer of 1998 in Minnesota. But don't you think that when the CEO and CFO of the same company die there will be an investigation? More so as they're brothers. The blame needs to sit with someone. It sure as hell won't be me.

'You don't approve?' I ask Lucas, raising an eyebrow.

'I think it's risky,' he says without emotion. Not even a trace. It makes me wonder what he isn't telling me.

'Elaborate.'

'Well, when your, whatever her role is, Bid Manager, kills Liam and Connor, don't you think someone might question if you had an idea it was going to happen? Especially if you use it as a catalyst for your own career.'

His logic is weak. I can see the holes in it a mile off. 'Oh my god. You like her, don't you?'

'No.' But he answers far too quickly. Far too emphatically.

'You need to pick a side.'

'You know I'm always on yours,' he replies. 'I just want to make sure there are no issues. If you're going through with this it has to be flawless, zero chance it comes back to you.'

I pause for a moment. If he does actually have feelings for her, might he try to stop me? Ruin the whole plan? I cannot afford the distraction of a potential saboteur. 'OK.' I put my hands up, palms forward. 'You win.'

He looks puzzled. 'I win?'

'Yes. I promise Millie will walk away after it's done.'

'Good. Well in that case, I have an idea for you.'

Serendipity has a *Women in Power* programme. Of course it does. It's a huge corporation where ninety percent of the revenues come from female customers. The Board, however, is overwhelmingly male. And white, but they haven't cottoned on to that one yet, or at least they don't think it's necessary to make a public declaration in favour of change.

Every year, twenty women from across the company are selected for their potential to take senior roles. Note how I say senior roles and not Board-level roles, because apparently it's about creating a pipeline for the future, not actually putting women in the seat of power.

You might be able to tell from my tone that I'm not in favour of all this shit. It pays lip service to a problem. It's performative bollocks. All it leads to is claims of women being cherry-picked without paying their dues. Claims of them not being good enough. Clever enough. Talented enough. Hard-working enough. All the jealous mediocre men start to point fingers at the women who do better than them and claim it was reverse sexism. If anyone ever asked me, and of course they never do, I would tell them it isn't because women *can't* get into the top roles. It isn't that they *can't* win at the professional game. It's that most of them don't want to play when the deck is already so stacked against them.

And even those who still want to play baulk when they realise the true nature of their competition. Do you know how many CEOs are psychopaths? It's a lot. Some estimates are around the twenty percent mark. It's a role that attracts a certain type of person: someone who is driven, meticulous, unperturbed by the idea of other people's suffering. I've had my eye on the job since I graduated from my master's programme.

Lucas wants me to nominate Millie for *Women in Power*.

'Just think about it,' he says. 'You nominate Millie and you can both travel to LA for the big gala dinner. Have a personal introduction to Liam and Connor. You'll be on the radar as the kind of person who nominates their team, who raises up the next generation of talent.' He grimaces a little as he spits out the corporate spiel.

'You read the handbook, I suppose?' I ask drily.

'Come on, it's perfect,' he says. 'Can't you just put aside your own personal gripes? It'll pay off.' He makes prayer hands at me. 'Please. Then you can take me to LA with you.'

I sigh. 'But won't the *Women in Power* dinner be a little high profile?' My tone is mocking. He's the one who keeps telling me to be more careful.

'I'm sure you'll think of something. A way to deflect the attention from both of you.'

I smile at him. The fool. He's just handed me the perfect idea. A flawless way to pull this off without any suspicion of my involvement. And I can tie up the final loose end at the same time.

What? You didn't really think I was going to let Millie walk away, did you?

* * *

Millie's nomination to the *Women in Power* programme is accepted. Of course it is, I wrote it. She almost cries when I tell her.

'I... just... I don't know what to say,' she says.

'It means we'll be going to LA next month,' I tell her.

'I... wow. The *Women in Power* programme is such an honour. It's iconic.' She's gushing and it makes me feel uncomfortable.

'That is where we'll do it,' I say pointedly.

'It? Oh.' The realisation crushes her joy and I feel a little more like me again. '*That's* why you nominated me.' Her voice is quiet.

I could tell her that of course I thought she should be nominated on merit. Say that she's very talented and has a brilliant future in front of her. It would be a lie. I debate for a moment. And then I put the lie into words. 'Of course that isn't why I nominated you,' I tell her, forcing a smile onto my face and a touch of laughter into my voice. I don't lie because I feel sorry for her, or want her to feel good about herself. But if she's giddy and thinks she's the dog's bollocks, it will make it easier for her to act the part of excited junior staff member.

Once the dust has settled, the rest of the world is going to deify her as the innocent victim on the cusp of greatness. She may as well bask in that glory while we get there.

I watch her dance out of my office and immediately pull out her phone. I wonder who she'll call first. Her best friend? Or Kieran Lucas?

34

Exactly four weeks after the death of Gregory Fuller, Millie arrives at Heathrow with red-rimmed eyes as if she's been crying all night.

'Trouble in paradise?' I ask her.

She stares at me for a moment, as if debating how much she should tell me.

I lean in to her a little. 'Given what we're about to do, it's probably best if you decide to trust me,' I say, touching my voice with a hint of conspiratorial friendliness. 'Besides, I know you've been dating someone from the office.'

'You know?' She looks stricken.

'Lucas told me.'

She looks puzzled.

'Sorry. *Kieran* told me.' I've called him by his surname for so long I sometimes forget he's Kieran to everyone else. 'He was worried you'd get into trouble and so thought it would be better if he was honest,' I add.

'He... I didn't know he'd done that.'

'He told me if anyone got into trouble it needed to be him.

Serendipity is fairly lax about this kind of thing, but it's technically not allowed.'

'Oh. He told me it wasn't a problem.'

'I think he might have just been telling you what he thought you wanted to hear.' My words are pointed.

Her shoulders drop an inch. 'Yeah,' she says softly. 'Not that it matters, I guess. I broke up with him.'

'Oh.' I already knew they'd broken up, Lucas rang me last night. But I'd assumed *he* had dumped *her*. 'Are you OK?' It's a stupid question given the state of her.

'No.' She sounds wretched. 'I really liked him.'

'So why did you dump him?' Sometimes people make no sense at all.

'I can't lie to him. I can't go out to LA and do what we're going to do and then go home and pretend it was nothing. I... I just *can't*.'

'I understand,' I tell her. Even though she's being melodramatic and ridiculous. 'And perhaps it's for the best.' If only she knew the things I know about him. Would she still want him then?

'Do you think so?' Her voice is small and childlike.

'Millie,' I say seriously, 'what we're going to do to Connor and Liam, it changes you. You'll need time afterwards. To figure out who you become.' I'm only offering her empty platitudes but she's lapping them up.

'So I did the right thing?'

I decide to give her the hard truth. I sigh loudly, as if I'm debating saying the next part. 'I think you're going somewhere much more exciting and sometimes we need to cut the hangers-on from our coattails.'

'You're right. I don't need him.' She says the words but she doesn't really mean them. Not at this moment anyway. At least it's enough to force her into action and take a trip to the Clinique counter for someone to sort out her obvious lack of sleep.

Because this is the *Women in Power* programme and it's all about visibility, we're flying to LAX with Virgin Upper Class. I've been sent a series of instructions about the photos we need to take to ensure the corporate social media machine can gain maximum traction from the event.

'Is this really a good idea?' Millie whispers to me as I snap a few pictures of us in the Clubhouse at Heathrow; the thick marble bar top and pink chairs will no doubt make the vapid girls in the Marketing Department screech with delight. 'I mean, all this shouting about the fact we're going to LA.'

I sip my Bellini. It's far too sweet for my liking, but it seemed an innocuous choice given it's 11 a.m. and this is technically a work trip. Hard liquor might have raised an eyebrow from Corporate. 'We're hiding in plain sight. It might actually be genius.'

'Might?' she asks, her voice taking on a squeaky quality.

I stop myself from rolling my eyes. She's absolutely not cut out for this and she needs to get a grip, stop flip-flopping between happy and sad and nervous and excited and distraught over Lucas. 'Would you suspect us?' I ask.

'I guess not.'

'So pull yourself together.' I'm a little stern but no more than is necessary given the situation.

She pauses for a moment and I can see her debating what to do. But then she rakes her fingers through her hair and shakes it to lie properly. Picks up the cocktail and turns slightly towards me. 'Cheese,' she says and plasters on a fake smile. In her fitted Ralph Lauren dress and killer heels, she looks every inch the young female exec Serendipity is after. The Clinique girls performed a miracle, even if we'll claim the products are part of the new PALETTE range for the Instagram post.

* * *

A limo collects us from LAX airport and takes us to The Peninsula Beverly Hills on South Santa Monica Boulevard. Millie stops in the entrance hall to look around, entranced by the sheer opulence of the place. I've been in enough hotels like this to see through the veneer; it's all an illusion, designed to make you think you're one of the special ones. One of those touched by God's hand – or whatever deity you believe in – or deserving of the fruits of your endeavour. Because all stupidly wealthy people believe their status is either their birth right or a direct result of their own hard work. It's all a fallacy. There is nothing to it but luck and a strong enough stomach to claw what you want from the jaws of the person it was originally given to.

For once, Millie has a better suite than I do. Well, I suppose this trip is all about her. Hers looks out over the lush, almost tropical, gardens, with a wraparound balcony and a hot tub. Mine overlooks the car park. Still, it'll do. It's not like I'm going to be spending much time here.

The main gala is tomorrow evening, but tonight is a smaller reception for those of us who have travelled internationally. Millie knocks on the door of my suite just before 7 p.m.

'Wow,' I say involuntarily as I open it. She looks stunning. Gone is the somewhat meek Millie with her slightly demure fitted shift dresses that sit just below the knee. It isn't that she doesn't usually dress well, there are standards for my team, but generally she looks normal. Pretty, yes, I suppose. But still normal.

Tonight she looks like a siren. Her dress is short and black and studded in sequins. It hugs her curves, highlighting the width of her hips and the length of her legs.

'Are you sure it's suitable?' she asks, pulling the skirt down a little and shifting her weight from foot to foot.

'You look...' I trail off. I hate giving people compliments. It makes me feel weird. But I swallow it down. 'You look sensational.'

'Sure?'

'Absolutely.'

She doesn't realise it yet, but in that dress, and with her hair in a sleek ponytail, she bears a striking resemblance to Connor's former assistant and recently ex-girlfriend. According to the gossip train, which thankfully Lucas is party to, Brittany was offered a job last week in Singapore and didn't hesitate to take it, leaving poor distraught Connor behind.

Perhaps Millie and Connor can mend each other's broken hearts? Or at least it's a nice narrative. And yes, I know that dangling Millie in front of him is regressive. And yes, in theory, this whole trip is meant to be a celebration of female professional talent. But who the hell are we kidding? The best way for Millie to get close to Connor is to make him think she might be interested in sleeping with him. We all know it.

The dress and hair and make-up also act as another layer against the possibility either Connor or Liam remember her from Weedon House. Millie has assured me she's changed beyond recognition, that siren-Millie is a million miles from lying-in-the-dirt-teenage-Millie.

'Let me just grab my bag and we'll head down,' I tell her. This evening's reception is on the terrace of the hotel. Millie thinks tonight is just a research opportunity. An evening to get to know her opponents before tomorrow and the main event.

Poor Millie. She has no idea.

I've met Liam, the CEO of Serendipity, a number of times over the years and he spots me the moment we walk into the room, beelining towards me. There was a time, maybe four years ago, that a rumour was sparked about us having a slightly illicit affair. It was all a fabrication. He wanted to discredit me. Take the glory for an idea I'd had that made Serendipity a tonne of money.

Yes, I know that makes me sound like a bitter old bitch. But it's the truth. My career stalled at the same time as I was tarred as the 'hussy'. Not my choice of descriptor, but I overheard a few members of the Board having a gossip. I nearly moved on, cut my losses with Serendipity and hitched my wagon to a different star. But then Lucas, who can occasionally be wise beyond his years, sat me down and told me to look at the bigger picture. Serendipity is an opportunity and the thing with Liam was nothing but a blip.

'He'll have forgotten about it soon enough,' Lucas had told me and it seems he was right. Because Liam has the fucking audacity to act as if he's done nothing at all wrong and we're the best of pals.

'Freya!' he says, as he approaches, arms wide, expecting me to step into his embrace. I hold my breath as I do so. I do not like to play nice with the men I will kill.

'May I introduce you to Millicent Brooks?' I say as I extricate myself. 'She's my nomination to the programme.'

'Millicent,' he says, holding out his hand to shake hers, before pulling her into an awkward hug. 'It is an absolute pleasure to meet you.'

'The pleasure is all mine,' Millie replies smoothly. I listen for any hint of hatred in her voice but there is nothing. She's flawless.

'You must come and meet Connor,' he takes her elbow and tucks it into his, leading her towards the back of the terrace. I follow politely, swiping a glass of champagne from a passing waitress and downing it in a single gulp.

This is the riskiest part of the whole plan. Everything hinges on neither brother recognising Millie. If they do it will be game over. Her motive will become clear and everything will crumble.

'I promise that won't be an issue,' Millie had said when I pressed her about it.

'This is serious.'

She'd sighed and told me to wait and see. The next morning she placed a photograph on my desk. It was old, yellowed and curling at the edges. The girl was maybe fourteen. She had blond hair and blue eyes. An overbite that made her front teeth look bigger than they were. I stared at it, tracing the lines of the girl's features. And then I looked back at Millie, took in her dark hair and green eyes. Her perfect teeth that were a little too white to be wholly natural.

'This is you?'

She nodded.

'OK. So you look different.' And then it dawned on me. 'What's your real name?'

'Millicent is my real name, after my grandmother. But I was known as Laura at Weedon House. It's my middle name. There was another Millie.' She smiles sadly. 'Well, she was Camille, but known as Millie.'

I'd felt a pang of something. Guilt? Possibly. Anyway, there was a small part of me that felt a little bad about calling her Camille for so long, given what had happened. But I wasn't to know at the time, so I'm not going to obsess over it.

'Laura Brooks?' I asked.

'Laura West,' she confirmed. 'Brooks was my grandmother's surname. My mother's maiden name. It made more sense when I left Weedon House to use it. I wanted a clean break. To put everything that had happened behind me. Move on with a fresh start.'

Now, as she walks towards Connor I do something I haven't done for a very long time. I cross my fingers behind my back. It's a silly superstition and one I don't believe in. But sometimes you need all the help you can muster.

'Connor!' Liam shouts to get his attention. 'This is Millicent Brooks. She's from England and I think the two of you are going to hit it off famously.'

Connor turns to look at her and something in him changes. For a moment I think it's all over.

But then he blushes. It isn't recognition. It's lust. Pure and simple. Men can be so god-damn predictable. Successful men even worse.

Liam leans in to me. 'We're going to have a little after party in one of the suites. You and Millicent will have to join us.'

Oh, yes. Men are so very predictable.

'We'd be honoured,' I whisper back. At least Liam has no interest in me like that. I did always wonder if that was the other reason he fanned the rumour of our affair. It certainly stopped the speculation about his own preferences, and he remains firmly stuffed in the closet even now.

I take out my phone and subtly tap out a message to Lucas.

> Game on.

He took the bait?

> Of course he did

And Millie?

> Oh she is positively lapping up the attention

It's cruel and I know it'll hurt Lucas, but I'm in that kind of mood. I always get spiky when I'm this close to a kill. It's 8 p.m. By midnight this will all be over.

Liam and Connor will be dead. The apparent victims of a robbery gone bad. The perpetrator a lone gunman who broke into their hotel suite to steal the contents of their safe.

And poor Millicent Brooks. Caught by a stray bullet. Cut down the night before her life changed into what would have been a fairytale.

PART V

MILLIE

35

Connor's hand is resting on my lower back and I want to scream at him to remove it.

But of course I don't. Tonight is all about playing nice, getting to know the things he likes, what he drinks and eats, if he has any bad habits beyond an ill-advised predilection for the women who work for him.

All the little details of his life that I can use to bring him and his brother down.

I'm still finalising the nuances of the plan. But it will be something spectacular. Almost poetic.

Freya has suggested using a gun. She says it'll be clean and fast, less likely to go wrong. I don't disagree with her, of course she's got far more experience with this than I have. But since the moment I decided how this would end, I've been thinking about how I want to make them suffer.

And how I want the world to think they suffered.

Not for me but for Lissa. I know I'm taking away her chance for retribution by doing this and it makes my heart ache. But I also know she'd never have the stomach for this, she wouldn't be able to pull the trigger – metaphorically or literally – when it came to it.

The Weedon brothers need to pay for what they did to both of us. I didn't tell Freya all the details of what Liam did to Lissa. Connor's a vicious bully, but Liam is on another level. He had so much pent up rage, so much anger coursing through him, coiled like a snake about to strike. He lost his mind with Lissa.

It's been a long journey for the woman I love more than a sister. Years of therapy interspersed with periods of pretending everything is absolutely fine and there's nothing wrong until the moment she broke again. For the last couple of years she's been seeing a very talented artist who has covered some of the scars with interlocking flowers in an array of gorgeous colours. It's helped her self-esteem, at least a small bit. But hers is a journey with no certain destination.

Lissa needs to feel, when this is all done, that justice has been served. She needs to think that someone somewhere made them suffer in a way commensurate with their crimes against her personally. This will be her closure. Her chance to move on. If she doesn't get that then all this is for nothing.

You see, vengeance is about the wrongdoer getting what they deserve. Or at least that is what vengeance should be to any vaguely normal and well-adjusted individual. A month ago, Freya turned on me in that hotel room in Barcelona. That was when I realised the truth about her. It wasn't enough that Gregory was dead, even though drowning is a frankly terrible way to die. She needed to have been the one holding the knife. For Freya, it was about killing. But, thankfully, Lissa is nothing like Freya.

I could have told her what I was going to do. I could have told her I was going to kill them and buy our freedom that way. But I know how she would look at me, the pain in her eyes as she looks at the woman who replaced the frightened little girl and sees a killer instead. She wouldn't forgive me. It's bad enough that I will never forgive myself without losing her in the process. She can never know what happens.

Back when we were still basically children, we discussed the idea of killing them – more than once if we're honest about it – when the nights were cold and dark and sleep eluded us. And then we went on holiday when we were twenty, to a little hotel in the icy desert of Swedish Lapland. Fuelled by aquavit and the sheer fucking desolation of the place, we plotted the ultimate demise of the two men who had tried to destroy the both of us and very nearly succeeded. But in the light of the morning, we had shrugged off the blanket of our steaming hangovers and made a new plan.

'We will not stoop to their level. To their savagery,' Lissa had said. 'They will pay, but not in cruelty.'

'How then?' I'd asked.

By this time Serendipity was a multi-million-dollar business empire. Lissa had looked at me, a glint in her eye. 'They took what we loved. We will do the same. We'll destroy their passion. The thing they consider their lives' work.'

'Serendipity?'

'Yep.'

'How?' I asked. We spent the rest of the holiday making a plan. One of us had to get a job with the company and I was the one who'd got good enough grades to get into a decent university. The next semester I started to knuckle down and ended up with a first-class degree. A summer of interning helped to make me eminently employable, and eventually I was in a position to try to get promoted up the Serendipity ranks.

I had thought it would be enough: to infiltrate them, become one of them, and then tear it all down from the inside. I revelled in the idea of sabotaging the company and leaving them sitting in the ruins of their empire. In my head the plan took on an almost mythical quality, with Lissa and me standing in judgement over their sins.

It was what got me through the bad times. The days when I wanted to walk out of the building and tell them where they could stick their stupid fucking shitty little job. You know what it's like, don't you? To be stretched to breaking point and only hang in there because of necessity. Because you need to pay your rent and your bills and afford to eat, because you want a better future, because you studied too long and too hard to get here and no one is going to bully you, god damn it! Because you deserve to be taken seriously and treated with some respect and you know that if you quit now you'll only have to start again at the beginning. Since when has a career been an exercise in if you can reach a high enough level before you snap? Perhaps the desire for revenge is what made me strong enough to make it to Bid Manager.

But then I realised who I was really working for. I don't mean Serendipity, I mean Freya Ellwood-Winter.

Stone cold bitch.

Serial killer.

Icon.

She has showed me what's possible if you unleash some of the anger. If you allow the animal inside to break free for just a little time. I'm going to kill Liam and Connor and I'm going to revel in the fact it happens by my own hand.

But then I will stuff the predator back into her cage, lock the door on that side of myself. And finally I will draw a line under the girls we were. Laura West and Mel Anders. Lissa and I can move on, leave the past behind us and become the people we want to be. Will I stay at Serendipity? Take advantage of this *Women in Power* programme and ask for a promotion? Or shall I leverage it to get a better job, take Lissa somewhere different, like New York? We could be proper city girls who live in Manhattan and shop at Macy's and eat pizza by the slice and bagels loaded with cream cheese.

'Millicent?' Connor pulls me back to the present, with a concerned look and a hand snaking round my waist in a way that makes my skin crawl. I force myself not to pull away from him and scratch his eyes out for being so fucking revolting.

'Sorry!' I affect a sing-song tone that rings in my ears, mocking me. 'I was miles away!'

'It's a bit much, all of this,' he says, waving around the opulent room. 'All this glitz and noise and every woman sharpening her nails.' He laughs at his own joke and inside I curl my lip. He leans in, his breath tickling the skin on my neck. 'It's the same every year. Liam and I joke about this being less *Women in Power* and more Jealous Bitches in Power-suits.' He laughs like a braying donkey.

'Oh I'm sure everyone is here to support each other,' I say, with a smile.

It makes him laugh harder, and he flaps a hand as if to say *give me a moment to pull myself together*. It wasn't even funny. But I guess that's the problem with men like this; women always laugh at their jokes and their worlds become distorted. Like that time Elon Musk took an actual sink to the Twitter office and said 'Entering Twitter HQ – let that sink in', like he was a comedy genius and not a weird little kid who had bought the entire fairground because some of the more popular kids told him he wasn't allowed on one of the rides.

Connor composes himself and then replaces his arm around my waist, turning me round to face a group of women standing in a huddle a few metres away. 'You see them?' he asks, not waiting for my response. 'They're your competition. The women who stand between you and a seat at the big boys' table.'

'Shouldn't that be the big *girls'* table?' I ask, sweetly.

He doubles over in mirth again. I want to kick him in the balls. 'You're adorable,' he says eventually, straightening back up. 'They're all watching, you know?' he whispers in my ear. 'Can you tell? They pretend to be chatting, asking each other about their lives, their husbands, kids, cats. Making polite small talk about university and graduate schemes. But all they can think about is how my hand is on your waist, my words in your ear, my attention on you alone.'

'Why me?' I ask softly.

'Because you're not like them.'

My hackles go up, the hairs on the back of my neck standing to attention. 'What do you mean?'

'You're different. I can see exactly who you are, Millicent.' He sweeps my hair across my shoulder and I stand stock still, unable to move as his words linger around us.

I want to ask him what he means by that. Does he know who I am? Who I was once upon a time as he kicked dirt in my face. Is this whole thing over before it's even begun, the plan foiled before I can watch the pain dance in his eyes?

His fingers spider down towards my hip and I hold my breath, waiting for his punchline, for the world to crash around me. 'You're vulnerable,' he says. 'A fragile doll.' The way he says fragile makes me feel sick. 'But you're also fierce and feisty and brilliant.' He leans down, his lips just millimetres from my ear. 'You see now? How your rivals watch?'

I can sense their eyes have turned to me.

'They're jealous. I've chosen you, Millicent. Because you're special. Because you're everything I want.'

'I...' I try to respond but he's so close I can feel his breath on my skin.

'Shhhh,' he whispers. 'You don't need to say any more.'

I close my eyes, force myself to be strong. He doesn't know who I am. He's just a man who can't help himself. All he cares about is that I'm his chosen one. He never even stops to consider if I choose him in return.

I hate this and I hate him and I hate myself for acting like a simpering bimbo. But haven't we always done this? Or rather, been forced to do this? Trade ourselves for the satisfaction of some guy who hoarded all the resources and will only share if we compel him to? I look around the room at all the painted women and sub-par men. This is meant to be a business party, a meeting of equals, a collection of some of the best minds in Serendipity. But it might as well be the court of some distant king demanding everyone preen for his personal amusement.

'This is boring me,' Conner says, waving a hand around the room. 'Shall we have a smaller gathering upstairs with just a select few of us?' He nods his head towards his brother and a handful of others.

'Getting away from all the people watching sounds like an excellent plan.' I tell him and he grins at me.

'Oh yes, I think I'm going to enjoy a more intimate party.'

The way he says *intimate* is terrifying.

Oh, how I am going to enjoying killing you.

36

Liam and Connor have taken the Grand Suite and it sprawls across the upper floor of one of the hotel wings.

Three bedrooms. Four bathrooms. Cream carpet so thick my heels sink into the pile. Silk upholstery on the multitudinous sofas and armchairs in elegant shades of duck-egg blue and grey. Heavy dark wood furniture with a twist of Scandinavian elegance. Lamps dotted all over, casting soft shadows across the space.

Apparently it's considered to be one of the most luxurious suites on the west coast. I'd tell you how much it costs if I had any idea, they don't exactly put the price on their website.

Freya excuses herself to make a call, her eyes meeting mine for a split second. There's something in the look I don't quite understand. Sadness? Maybe even longing? I don't know. But it makes me think of betrayal.

And then I look at the scene through her eyes. Try to see what she sees, think what she thinks. That last part is quite frankly terrifying given what I know about Freya and what I've seen her do recently. But here we are, at a private party with the two most powerful men in the company, men who could make or break us.

It hits me, smacking me in the face with the force of a sledgehammer.

How could I have been so stupid?

I've been thinking about this like we're out here to do some vigilante shit. But she has nothing against these men. So why is she here helping me?

She isn't.

Of course she isn't. She's here because there's something in it for her.

I turn to where she's standing, watching her lips move as she speaks to someone on the other end of the phone. She catches me watching and turns away slightly. I feel the pieces shift into place.

When I kill Liam and Connor, I will create a corporate storm. These men think they're invincible, untouchable; they believe they will live forever. I would bet everything I have on them not leaving behind a robust succession plan that transfers power to pre-selected and carefully vetted individuals. It will be a bun fight. And Freya knows it's going to happen, she'll already have begun to move her own pieces. How far is she planning on leaping up the corporate ladder in the midst of the chaos? Earlier I saw her whispering in the ear of the current VP of Sales; he would be my best bet as a new CEO, leaving that VP role empty, all ready for an ambitious Freya Ellwood-Winter to slide into.

Fuck!

I whisper it out loud as the puzzle zooms out and the rest of the picture comes into focus.

She's setting me up.

They will say I'm a lone ranger.

But how many murders will she try to lay at my door?

Lawrence Delaney. Will she suggest it wasn't an accident? Suggest the German police look at the CCTV of who exited from Starnberg S-Bahn station that fateful evening?

Kai Helve. I didn't leave the hotel in Helsinki. Struck down by a stomach upset that lasted a full twenty-four hours. But do I have any proof of that?

Jim Handley. I created her alibi myself when I claimed to be her to collect that necklace when he was killed. Where will she say I was?

Ruben Chambers. I was meeting with the Martin twins from C'est Magnifique when he died. But how accurate is a time of death? Is there a way she can say I killed him before I went to dinner?

Cody Gelber and Ethan Donahue and Spencer Balmforth?

Or she could just make sure I'm killed in the crossfire.

It feels like time slows to nothing, the world suspended in a moment that reaches from here to eternity. The temperature drops noticeably and goosebumps appear across my forearms.

I can't breathe.

Something is about to happen.

I excuse myself from Conner and the others, desperate to find a way out of this mess. Just off the kitchenette I find one. The hand that smashes the glass of the fire alarm doesn't feel attached to my body; I see it as if it belongs to another, even though the scar on my thumb is the same one I've looked at for two decades. There's a pause as I look at it, marvelling at the exquisite beauty of the puckered skin.

And then the ceiling erupts with a high-pitched beep. Three in a row and then a moment of silence. The three beeps repeat and pandemonium breaks loose.

We congregate outside the front of the hotel, standing on the cobbled driveway beside the fountain, staring up at the cream stone facade with ornate black Juliette balconies.

The air is still hot, the humidity of the summer night high. Around us people are milling about in various states of dress, woken from sleep and hurried outside into the midst of collective confusion. A rumour goes round that someone is trapped inside. That the fire is real. That there's smoke filling the corridors. Suffocating.

The sound of fire trucks in the distance intensifies the whispering around me.

Connor is pissed off. 'No one will tell us anything, for fuck's sake,' Something akin to a growl escapes his lips. He hates not getting his own way. 'What are we meant to do?'

Liam comes over. 'What's happening?' He says it like he expects his brother to have the answers.

'I don't know,' Connor tells him.

'Fucking ridiculous,' Liam says and stalks off to shout at some poor underpaid person who has no ability to do anything other than listen to him. I feel bad about it, I've been that person and I hate that I've contributed to making their shitty shift even shittier.

And their night is only going to get worse. There's a group of guys behind me bitching about how they should have gone to Vegas instead of 'this shithole'. 'Heads are going to roll when my father finds out about this,' one of them says and the others cheer. Pricks.

Ten minutes later Liam is back. He's angry, I can see it shimmering just underneath his skin. 'There's no fucking fire,' he says.

'Then why did the fire alarm go off?' Connor demands.

'How the fuck do I know?' Liam replies.

'I would have assumed you asked?'

Liam huffs and disappears again to find out. Seeing the two of them like this is fascinating. I don't think I'd really appreciated before that Liam was *such* a lapdog, literally doing whatever Connor commands as if he were his master. I've always put the whole blame for what happened to Lissa at Liam's door. But what influence did Connor have. What did he tell Liam to do?

'Some fucker set off the fire alarm,' Liam says as he returns to us. 'The firemen say it was the one inside our suite.'

'An accident?' I ask, innocence personified.

Liam shrugs. 'I don't know. But whoever it was has ruined it all. What a fucking disaster.' He motions around himself to us standing in front of the hotel. It's completely melodramatic; it's hardly the end of the world. Besides, if I was right, he was going to die this evening. We all were. Not that his reprieve will last long.

Half an hour later, an announcement is made that we're allowed back inside. But the party atmosphere has gone.

'I'm going to head to my room,' I say loudly, making sure Freya hears me as well.

'You want to continue where we were?' Connor says, his eyes hungry.

'We have a long day tomorrow,' I remind him, trying to inject a little flirtation into my voice. I want to get away from him but I can't piss him off. 'But perhaps in the evening?' I raise an eyebrow and he grins back. 'Maybe somewhere a little more... fun?'

'Fun? Do you have somewhere in mind, Millicent Brooks?'

The pricks moaning about Vegas have given me an idea. A way to take control of the situation and put myself on the front foot against Freya.

I was going to try to be subtle, but I'm too tired to play games. I lean closer to Connor, eyes locked on his, and bite my bottom lip softly. 'Well, I have always wanted to go to Vegas.' I raise my voice slightly as I say Vegas, making sure that Liam hears.

'Oh yeah! Vegas, baby!' Liam shouts, stretching his arms out like the fucking messiah. I think he may have taken a bump of something, there's so much nervous energy coming from him. I knew he'd like the idea of a Vegas trip, he's been rumoured to have a problem with gambling, but it's hardly uncommon in his circle.

'Well, I guess we're going to Vegas then,' Freya says. She shoots me a quizzical look and I shoot my own message back. One that tells her this is a good thing: an opportunity for us both. But really it's because I need to keep one step ahead of her. Control the narrative. Avoid becoming a victim here.

As we file back inside the hotel, I look behind me to the people still milling around out front. A flash of auburn catches my attention and my heart snags. He's facing away from me, but the man reminds me so much of Kieran, the same broad shoulders and small waist, similar height, one hand running through his hair.

Was it only yesterday I broke up with him? It feels like an age. I thought things were going well, that perhaps we were heading towards somewhere good. But it was built on a lie. And yes, I know we all lie at the beginning of a relationship. About who we really are, hiding the bad and promoting the good. That's just life. But plotting to kill someone – two people, but I don't think that's much worse if I'm honest – is so much more serious than something like saying you graduated from university when in reality you dropped out in the second year.

He's lied to me too. I know he has, there's been a few times he's said something and then something different another time. Once a look of abject panic crossed his features when he realised his mistake, but I ignored it and pretended I didn't notice.

Perhaps our relationship was always fated to end.

'Millie,' Freya's voice is hot in my ear as she slips into the lift with me.

I turn so I can see her more clearly. 'Hi Freya.'

'Are you OK?' she asks, leaning forward a little as if she's genuinely concerned about my well-being.

'I'm fine,' I say brightly, shoving down my thoughts of Kieran, squashing them against my thoughts that this woman is trying to set me up. When did my whole life become such a fucking mess?

'This was all rather... inconvenient,' she says quietly.

'Oh yes.' I smile brightly. 'Such a shame to have to cut the party short.'

I watch her carefully, looking for any sign of her actual plan for the evening.

She gives nothing away.

I absolutely do not trust her.

37

I won't bore you with talk of the business aspects of the trip. It was dull enough for those who profess to love Serendipity and everything the company stands for, who claim to live and breathe the values and embody the corporate culture of our brilliant overlords. That's Connor and Liam in case you didn't get that from my sarcastic tone.

The gala afterwards is an overly formal and incredibly boring affair, involving a six-course meal characterised by lukewarm food, rubbery chicken, and burnt coffee to finish. There are mutterings of dissatisfaction around our table. I'm too distracted to join in, my mind reeling with possibilities of what the next twenty-four hours may hold.

I've thought of a hundred options, a hundred ways this could all play out. But none of them work. None of them feel right. Plus, I have to make sure that whatever happens, Freya cannot turn it back on me. Make me a scapegoat, or another victim.

Last night, I know I stopped her from doing *something*. I suspect that if I hadn't smashed the glass on the fire alarm I wouldn't be sitting here listening to my colleagues moaning about the lack of a vegan option *despite it being California, for heaven's sake*. If I'm totally honest I'm exhausted. By the false smiles to everyone. The false flirtatious banter with Connor. The false pleasantries being exchanged with Freya. The false conversation I had with Lissa earlier.

She had rung while I was getting ready for breakfast and I thought about letting it go to voicemail. But in the end I answered. She'd only have given me shit otherwise.

'Hey Lissa,' I tried to sound cheery.

'Have you seen them?' No *good morning*, or *how are you*.

'Yes.' I keep the lies to the minimum, it's easier to keep track that way.

'And?'

'They have no idea who I am.'

'And?'

'It is taking all my resolve not to kill them.'

Lissa laughed. I did too, although it sounded fake as it echoed around my suite.

'Are you OK?' she asked softly. The same voice you use with a frightened puppy.

'Yeah,' I said eventually, exhaling with the word.

'I'm worried about you.'

The truth is I'm worried about me too. But I didn't say it to Lissa. I didn't want her to fret. And I didn't want her to ask questions I didn't have the strength to answer.

* * *

The formalities of the *Women in Power* bullshit-fest are over and now the main event can begin. But first we have to get to Vegas.

I've never been on a private jet. Of course I haven't, I mean, who actually has?

I've seen them on TV and in films of course, but nothing prepared me for the ridiculous opulence of having a plane designed to your own personal specification. We live in a world on the cusp of burning, and rich boys take jets to Vegas. Connor and Liam think it's a sign of their wealth. I think it's a sign of them being complete dicks.

Everything inside the jet is either a deep obsidian black or a brilliant white and it actually hurts my eyes a little to look at it. There are nine of us on board: obviously myself and Freya, plus Connor and Liam, then two guys who are non-exec directors and their girlfriends, plus a stern-looking woman who I think is from Legal.

'Janine,' she says, shaking my hand in a rather overly formal way given we're boarding a jet to Vegas.

'Millie,' I reply.

'Oh, I know. Connor talked about you a lot earlier.' She reaches into the inside pocket of the fitted suit blazer she's wearing and pulls out something that makes me realise I've judged her completely wrong. She might look stern and favour a firm hand-shake, but Janine is here to party.

'Um...' I say, looking at the small bag in her hand.

She waves it towards me.

'Oh... no. Thank you,' I add hurriedly, 'but no thank you.'

'No one will judge,' she says, hitching her shoulder up in an exaggerated shrug. 'We're not working any more. This trip is strictly off the clock.'

The flight is short and, only fifty minutes after we leave behind the lights of LA, I look out the window to see a spot glowing in the desolate darkness of the desert. The spot grows brighter as we get closer until suddenly the giant hotels of the Las Vegas strip come into view, surrounded by the suburbs, glistening like diamonds scattered on the ground.

It is gaudy and tacky and magnificent all at the same time and it almost takes my breath away.

'First time?' Connor asks as he plonks himself into the seat next to me.

'Yeah,' I say, my voice more of an excited whisper than I would have liked.

'You know the story of Serendipity, don't you? Why we called the company that?'

I shake my head, even though I know exactly why they called the company Serendipity and it bears no resemblance to any of the official stories. Lissa and I came up with the name. We called ourselves the Serendipity Sisters, because although the events in our lives that led us to Weedon House were horrendous, at least we found each other. 'Serendipitous, wasn't it?' she'd said, about three weeks after I'd arrived. Found family is still family after all.

'So. We were in Vegas,' Connor starts to tell me, this fallacious look of pride on his face as if he genuinely believes his own bullshit. 'Me and Liam and a few other friends. It was the weekend of Thanksgiving and the place was packed, the whole city just heaving. People everywhere. Amazing. For months we'd been saving every penny we had to get the business really off the ground and we decided to let off some steam. Something drew me to it, I still can't explain what it was. But this slot machine whispered my name as I walked past.' He drops his voice and runs a gentle finger down my arm as he says almost coquettishly, 'Connor. Connor. Play me. Tonight might be your lucky night.'

I can't help myself and I shiver at his touch. But, this being Connor, he takes it as a good sign and continues to stroke me with all the pressure of a feather duster. It's creepy and inappropriate and I want to slap his hand away, but I don't. God, I hate this!

'I won on the second spin. Over a hundred thousand dollars, well, closer to two hundred but the fuckers took a chunk of tax right there in the casino. Robbing bastards.' His accent slips on those last words and I hear the British-ness bleed through the smooth American drawl he's affected over the years. He shifts in his seat slightly, the leather creaking. 'But that isn't the end of it. The casino took so long with all the paperwork that we got bored. Liam put a hundred dollars into another machine. Won another hundred grand. I had a few lucky spins on roulette and played a couple of hands of blackjack while the casino sorted out his win.' He chuckles to himself. 'I still can't quite believe it. We just couldn't lose, made a small fortune. Enough to launch Serendipity. You get it?' he asks, leaning in to me.

I smile. 'I know what serendipity means,' I say, with absolute seriousness.

He howls with laughter. Actually howls. It's so disproportionate to the joke; but then I remember that about him. It's like his humour radar is off, a little broken maybe, making him think some things are absolutely hilarious but not allowing him to find mirth in things that leave the rest of us in tears. When we were teenagers, Lissa said that was the moment she realised he was a psychopath. The number of times since then she has lamented not trusting her gut about him, not telling me to stay away and never get involved with his grandiose vision.

'It's a good story though,' he says, as if he's waiting for my validation.

'It's a brilliant story,' I reply and watch him visibly relax. I'm not even lying, it is a brilliant story. It's a complete fabrication.

We land and are escorted to a stretch limo, driven by a man in a uniform so starched I'm surprised he doesn't cut himself on his lapels.

'Where are we staying?' I ask Connor.

'Somewhere very special,' he says with a raised eyebrow.

OK. Not what I asked. 'Any more of a clue?'

'You'll love it. It has everything you could ever wish for. And then some more.'

Do women really find this stuff alluring? Are they impressed by rich pricks flashing their money around? Lissa always said I was missing the fancy gene and that I was just fundamentally unable to enjoy the nicer things in life. She's wrong. I am able to enjoy them, but I think the leap from fancy to stupidly fancy isn't worth it. Like you can go to McDonald's and have a cheeseburger for a pound fifty and it's good – don't call me basic, you like it too. Or you can go to Five Guys and have a burger for seven pounds and it's *really* good. And then you can go to Burger and Beyond in Shoreditch and have their Bougie Burger for fifteen pounds and it is excellent. But how much better is the eighty pound – yes, eighty! I'm not exaggerating – burger from Gordon Ramsey's place in Harrods? Is it five times better than the Bougie? Of course it isn't. At that point you're just being an ostentatious twat who's spending the money because you want people to know you have it, not because the product you're buying is fundamentally better.

Anyway, I apologise. I'm getting side-tracked, focusing on things that just aren't important. Right now I need to get my head back in the game and remember I'm planning to kill the two men I'm currently drinking champagne with. And that my boss is a serial killer who I suspect is trying to set me up or even have me killed. And I dumped my boyfriend and now I regret it. No. He's definitely not important right now. Jesus Christ, Millie. Pull your shit together.

We check into the hotel – the big surprise being that it's Caesar's Palace, which is where Connor and Liam apparently had their original winning streak – and then something unexpected happens. I'd assumed there would be some kind of continued party, us all drinking in their suite or gambling in the casino. Or something at least – it's just gone midnight and we are in Vegas. But Connor fields a call and his entire face turns white, like he's seen a ghost. He calls Liam over and they share a whispered conversation that looks serious, both of them hissing at each other, their body language frantic.

'What's happened?' I ask as I sidle up to Freya.

'How the fuck am I meant to know?'

'Sorry,' I say, taking a step back from the venom in her tone.

'No, I'm sorry,' she says and snaps a smile onto her face. It's obviously fake. 'It's been a long couple of days.'

'Yeah.'

Connor strides over to us. 'I'm sorry. There's been...' he trails off, the expression of joviality sliding off his face for a moment. 'Look.' He turns the charm back on, but not fast enough that I can't tell he's rattled. Something has happened. I need to find out what. 'I'm sure it's nothing. So... well, we're going to all check into our rooms and get some rest, OK? Recharge.' He smiles again. 'Have a long lie in and then reconvene tomorrow to get this party started again.'

I just about stop myself from wincing at his frat boy impression and instead imbue my voice with concern. 'Is everything alright?'

'Yes,' he says, too quickly. 'Everything's fine. Just tired. You know.' He smiles a final time and then leaves us.

Freya and I have adjacent rooms on the 20th floor of the west tower. Liam and Connor are sharing a suite on the east side of the hotel.

'What do you think that was all about?' I ask Freya as we step into a lift. She might be my competition, but she's the only person I actually know in the city and none of this is sitting right. 'Connor seemed...' I grope for the right word.

'He was shitting himself,' Freya says matter-of-factly, studying her reflection in the mirror at the back of the lift.

'Yes.' She's right. It wasn't tiredness, or anger. It was fear. 'But why?'

Connor calls my room ten minutes later.

'I don't want you to be alarmed,' he says, no trace of pleasantry in his tone.

'Err... OK?' I reply, obviously now extremely alarmed.

'There's a man outside your door.'

'A what?'

'Calm down. He's mine. I mean, I've hired him. He's a bodyguard.'

'What the hell's going on?' I demand.

'There was a bomb threat to The Peninsula Beverly Hills,' he says and then pauses, like I'm meant to fill the silence. But I don't, too busy trying to process his words. 'We should have been there tonight. Or at least we would have been if we hadn't decided to come here.'

'A bomb...'

'In our hotel, Millie.'

'You think...'

'Someone is out to get me, Millie.' His fear is visceral. He's many floors away but I'm sure I can smell it coming off him.

'And me?' My voice is quiet.

'I'm not taking any precautions,' he says. 'You're safe though. Just... get some sleep, this will all look better in the morning, I promise.'

I put the phone down. Then I pick it back up, checking for the dial tone to make sure the call had definitely disconnected.

Then I scream into a pillow.

This is a fucking disaster. How the hell can I kill them when they have bodyguards looking out for not just them, but tracking my every move as well?

Fuck.

Fuck.

Fuuuuuck.

38

I message Lissa to let her know I'm in Vegas. However much I've lied to her these past few weeks, we still have a rule about making sure we know where the other is. Then I try to sleep but it's practically impossible with everything that's been going on over the last few days. That and the fact my circadian rhythm is doing a very convincing job of bullying my body into believing it's actually lunch time and I've not even had breakfast. I guess it *is* two in the afternoon in London, even if the sun's only just rising here.

My room looks out over the Strip and it's oddly quiet at this time, almost peaceful, the neon starting to fade as it gets light. But I can't enjoy the view. I'd thought coming here would give me the upper hand, open up a series of opportunities I wouldn't have found in LA. After all, *anything* can happen in Vegas. But now I'm here and I still don't have a concrete plan. And now there are body-guards involved. And Freya. Always Freya, stalking me in the shadows.

Should I confront her? Just lay it out that I suspected what she was planning before I set off the fire alarm? Is honesty going to serve me well in this scenario or is she simply going to deny it and find a new way to get to me? In some ways it's a comfort that there's a big burly man outside my door, despite the issue he might cause me.

And what about the bomb at the other hotel? Who planted it? What were they planning? None of it makes any sense.

I have a shower, the bathroom so ludicrously well-appointed I'm forced to take pictures for Lissa. I must also remember to sweep all the little bottles of shampoo and body lotion into my case before I leave. She'll kill me if I don't return clutching a plethora of random toiletries to add to the collection she keeps in a storage trolley in our slightly musty bathroom.

As I'm dressing, my stomach rumbles so loudly it actually takes me by surprise. Which I know sounds ridiculous and cliched, but it's true. The last thing I ate was at the gala dinner, but I barely touched it. And all I ate the day before was the world's most pathetic salad so I would look good in the sequin-studded dress. How fucking depressing that thought is, not eating to look good for some guy I hate with more force than should be possible.

I need to eat. There's a room service menu but there isn't anything on it that takes my fancy. Besides, a simple breakfast of pancakes and cafetière – when you add on the service charge and a tip – would be almost fifty dollars and that feels like daylight robbery, even if I could just charge it to Connor.

I peek out the tiny peep hole in the door. There's a huge guy outside, feet planted apart as he faces down the corridor. I'm trapped. I can't leave the room. My stomach growls again.

Hang on... why *can't* I leave?

Because of a bomb threat.

Because of a bomb threat to the CEO of the company I work for.

Because of a bomb threat to the CEO of the company I work for, in a different hotel.

Because of a bomb threat to the CEO of the company I work for, in a different hotel, in a different state.

Because of a bomb threat to the CEO of the company I work for, in a different hotel, in a different state, which someone called in after we'd left for Vegas.

Why would someone call that in?

Jesus. I'm a fool. Not *someone*. It was Freya. I should've realised last night when she didn't seem at all surprised about there being no party when we got here. She needed to buy herself some time to come up with a new plan.

I need to get ahead of her again. But first I need to eat.

I throw on a simple sun dress and sandals, apply the minimal amount of make-up I can get away with, and sweep my wet hair back into a ponytail. Relieved to see that I look like any other tourist heading out for coffee, I grab my bag and pull open the door.

'Morning!' I call to the man mountain outside my door.

'Miss,' he says, acknowledging me with a nod. It's the same thing Kieran does and it makes my heart skip for a second.

'I'm going for breakfast,' I say, keeping my voice light and friendly.

'I can't let you do that, Miss.'

'I'm not asking permission,' I reply, flashing him a smile before checking I've shut the door properly behind me and the lock has clicked into place.

'But—'

'I promise I'll stay in the hotel, in the public areas. I'm just going to get something to eat and a coffee. OK?'

He puts a hand up in surrender.

I turn to walk towards the lifts and hear him chunter something under his breath. It sounds a lot like 'another stubborn British woman'. So I guess Freya's already up. I pick up my pace as I walk the seeming mile to the lifts – the hotel is fucking huge – keen to see if I can track her down somewhere nice and public. I don't really feel like risking being alone with her at the moment.

I consult a map on my phone – just another sign of the sheer scale of this place – and decide to head to Brioche on the other side of the main casino floor. Most of the table games are quiet at this time in the morning, just a few people playing what I think is blackjack and some old guys clustered around a big table throwing dice and making no sign if they're pleased or otherwise at the number they land on. There's an interesting combination of scents in the air; stale smoke and cologne and spilt drinks and I'm thrown back into a memory hidden for over two decades.

I'm standing next to a table, barely tall enough to see over it so I can't be more than about six. A hand rests on my shoulder and I look up at an undefined face. I know he's smiling but the edges are blurred. 'Go and see if there're any crisps in the kitchen, sweetheart,' he tells me. It's my father. My breath catches as I realise this is it. The last memory. The very last time I was ever with him. There weren't any crisps. 'Well then, sweetie,' he says, 'I guess Daddy had better go and get some.' He never came home. The crisps were a ruse, an excuse to leave me with my grandmother while he went out and deliberately drove head on into the car of the man who killed my mother.

In the casino I squeeze my eyes shut, trying to reconjure the image of him. It was so long ago and I was so little I cannot fully recall his face. Just a sense of him, like a ghost. If only I can... I try harder, breathing in the scent that so reminded me of him. But it's pointless, the moment has gone.

An odd sensation roils over me like a wave; I need to sit down for a few moments and let the blood rush back to my head. I haven't felt like this for a long time. But at least there are plenty of seats around here. I pull out a chair behind a slot machine and lean forward, my hair hanging down in front of my face.

That's when I hear them, standing on the other side of the machines, the electronic jingle as they spin the virtual reels.

'What took you so long?' It's Freya and she's pissed off.

'I had to hire a car and drive three hundred miles. We can't all get whisked away by private jet,' her companion replies. *That sounded a lot like...* no it couldn't have been.

'There's no need for that. We need to figure out what the hell we're going to do. Your bomb plot was a fucking disaster. He hired bodyguards.'

'What are you talking about?'

'The bomb threat at The Peninsula Beverly Hills. Jesus, what the fuck were you thinking?'

'It had nothing to do with me.'

'You didn't call it in?' She huffs loudly.

'Why would I do that?'

'Well, anyway. The window is closing. What the fuck am I meant to do?'

'I... I don't know,' he stumbles slightly over the words.

'Your job is to fix things, Lucas,' she replies.

'I'm not a miracle worker. Even I can't fix this shit, Freya!' he says barely containing the edges of his anger.

I sit up slowly, careful not to let the blood rush from my head too quickly or I'll pass out. I peek through a tiny gap between the slot machines.

She has her back to me, her sleek bob gleaming in the chandeliers adorning the ceiling. He is facing me.

Kieran.

Mr Kieran Lucas. HR Manager. Ex-boyfriend. Apparent friend of Freya. What the hell is going on?

'You need to find me a way out of this,' she hisses at him and I watch him physically blanche.

'I'll do my best,' he manages to reply before she pushes past him and stalks off into the casino.

He rubs his face and then smooths his hair down, the exact same motion I've watched him do a hundred times. Why is my – admittedly ex- – boyfriend standing in the middle of a Las Vegas casino discussing my boss's murderous plans?

He takes a deep breath. 'I can see you, Millie.'

My heart leaps into my chest and I look behind me. But he's already taken the few steps around the bank of slot machines.

How does he know? How much does he know?

He doesn't say anything and the silence grows between us.

But then he closes the gap between us and I'm in his arms, his whole body pressed against me as if we're both drowning. 'Jesus, Millie. Thank God you're OK,' he says into my hair. 'I couldn't bear it if you'd gotten involved in all this.'

I stand absolutely still, barely even breathing. 'What... Who... Why...?' I don't have the words to say what I need to, to raise the questions I want to ask him, especially as I have no idea who he really is and what he knows. The spell breaks and I push back against him, palms flat on his chest. 'Kieran,' I say as I step backwards. 'What the fuck is going on?'

'Oh Millie. I was so worried.' He pulls me close again and I allow myself to melt against him. 'Freya,' he whispers urgently, 'she's... there's something you... oh, God!' The final word is strangled.

He knows. How does he know? But I stop myself from asking a million questions. I have a feeling he is about to answer them all.

'Freya is a killer,' he says. 'Fuuuck,' he almost breathes the word out, 'I can't believe I'm actually saying this. She was going to kill Liam and Connor. And you, Millie.' He wraps me tighter. 'She was going to kill you.'

I stay silent. I knew she was going to try. But how does Kieran know?

'That's why I'm here, Millie. To rescue you.'

39

I push him away again and look at his face. He seems almost giddy. With relief? Or something else? Do I know this man, or is he someone else entirely? At this moment he could be anyone. And if he's working with Freya can I even trust him at all?

'I think you need to tell me everything,' I say slowly, trying to keep calm, trying not to allow my brain to run away with me, not to think of all the ways he may have betrayed me.

'I'll tell you everything, Millie, I promise. Let's go somewhere quieter,' he looks around him. 'Somewhere more private. You have a room?'

I do. But there isn't a hope in hell's chance I am taking him upstairs. 'Let's walk instead,' I say and turn to leave, betting he'll follow me.

'Millie,' he calls out, but I ignore him and keep on walking. I don't care if Freya sees us, but I have a feeling Kieran does. If he's here to 'rescue me' then he's going to have to take the risk. Halfway across the casino I feel him fall into step next to me.

We walk in silence out onto the Strip. A wall of hot air slaps me in the face: it's like walking out into an oven, even though it's only just dawn. I sniff the air, marvelling at how dry it is, so very different to the hot humid weather back at home.

'So,' I say. 'Let's start with the basics. Why are you here?'

'I'm here for you.' He stops and grabs my arms to turn me to face him. 'Jesus Christ, Millie! I'm trying to protect you!'

'Protect me?' I ask, meeting his gaze and hardening my stare.

'You're treating me like a stalker. Like I'm the bad guy. Are you listening to what I'm saying? You're at risk.'

'And you're here to save me?' I sound more than a little sarcastic.

'Yes!' He rakes his hand through his hair, shifting his weight from foot to foot. 'Jesus Christ, Millie! You've really got yourself tangled in a mess. Freya isn't who you think she is.'

'Oh, so you're protecting me from Freya?'

He sighs loudly, as if I'm exasperating. 'Freya is a murderer and she was going to kill you.'

I look at him. 'I know.' There is no emotion in my voice.

'You know?' He tilts his head slightly.

'Of course I fucking know.' The realisation hits me. *He's seen the murder wall.* He has been in my house, seen the wall, laughed when Lissa told him it was just a little project she was working on. 'You know that I know: you've seen the wall.' My tone is hard, brittle.

'Well... I—'

'Shit!' I cut him off. 'Have you been spying on me? For her? Did you wheedle your way into my life to keep tabs on me?'

He turns pale.

'Just tell me the truth, *Lucas*.' I spit his surname at him.

He pauses for a moment and I can see his indecision chase itself across his face. 'OK. I'll tell you everything.' He motions towards the replica of the Trevi Fountain, Oceanus surrounded by the Tritons and horses. 'Shall we sit?'

'Not out here. You can buy me breakfast.' I need a few minutes' silence as we walk to work out what I'm going to do next.

We go to Hash House A Go Go in the Linq Hotel. A restaurant with a specialism for 'twisted farm food' – whatever the hell that is meant to mean. I order griddled French toast, even though there's unlikely to be space for food in my stomach any longer, alongside the knot of nervous energy butting up against the ball of fear and an entire jar of butterflies. Basically, I'm a mess and I think I might be sick when I try to eat. But otherwise I'm going to pass out, I'm already feeling dizzy from lack of food over the last few days.

'So,' Kieran says as soon as the waitress has taken our orders. We're tucked into a small booth, so close our knees are touching. He spreads his fingers wide on the wooden table.

'So?'

He huffs out a breath. 'So, the truth is that I help Freya.' He says the sentence quickly, his shoulders slumping as he finishes. Eyes cast down so he doesn't have to look at me.

'Why?'

I can see from the way his face is twisted that he's chewing the inside of his cheek. He doesn't answer.

'Does she have something on you?' I ask softly.

He lifts his chin and his eyes meet mine. They're full of emotion; pain and remorse and something else I can't quite pin down. He offers me the briefest of nods. I want to reach out and take his hand, tell him it'll all be OK, that we can get through all of this together. But I don't. I still don't trust this isn't some kind of performance.

'Millie,' his voice is soft. 'How much do you know?'

I debate where to start. And how much I should tell him. Does he need to know about the disappearing photo messages and that Lissa knows too? Or my suspicions Sam is involved? I could just say I figured it out, that there was enough to raise suspicion. But I would be lying, and if I hadn't had the messages I would never have realised what Freya was doing right in front of me. It's Occam's razor, isn't it? If your boss occasionally acts a bit off you assume they're stressed, or got a shitty night's sleep, or perhaps even had a terrible date. You don't jump to *ooh, perhaps they're a serial killer and I should match their business travel to unsolved murders and suicides.*

I wait as the waitress serves our drinks, and then add four sachets of sugar to my coffee. Kieran raises an eyebrow as he watches. 'Don't tell Lissa,' I say.

He makes the sign of the scout's promise. 'Your sugar secret is safe with me.'

I stir in some cream and then take a tentative sip. The sweetness coats my tongue and I let out a tiny involuntary moan. 'Sorry,' I blush as I realise it was audible.

'It's adorable,' he says softly, but then he slides his eyes away from me, a gentle blush creeping up his neck.

'You want the honest answer?' I ask softly.

'Millie,' he reaches out to touch my hand for a moment. 'We need to be honest with each other. You need to trust me, OK?'

Do I trust him? Of course I don't.

Do I still have feelings for him? Of course I do.

Is there any future for us? I doubt it.

Shall I tell him the truth? I can't see any other way.

'I got a message,' I tell him, placing my palms flat on the table. 'On my phone. I don't know who it was from. It appeared and then vanished as soon as I read it.'

'What did it say?'

'It told me to connect the dots between Cody Gelber and Ruben Chambers. And then another message arrived, to say there were others.'

'And so you went digging?'

'What else was I going to do?' I ask him and he nods in agreement.

'But you didn't go to the police.'

'I couldn't risk my job.'

He tilts his head to one side and appraises me. It makes me feel exposed, as if I'm sat in this restaurant completely naked. He takes a sip of his coffee then asks, 'Do you know who sent the messages?' But there's something in the question, in the way he asks it. Like he already knew about them. Like he knows exactly who's sending them.

I pause and look at him. I want to trust him. I want to tell him everything and have him tell me that he understands and that we're a team and that he forgives me for everything I've done and everything I'm going to do. But something stops me. 'What aren't you telling me, Kieran?' My tone is serious.

'Nothing,' he replies.

'Bullshit.'

'Sam,' he whispers.

'What about Sam?'

'Fuck!' He thumps the table with his fist so hard another group turns to look over at us. 'Sorry,' he calls to them. 'Fuck,' he says again, more quietly, turning his attention back to me. 'Is it her? Sending you the messages?' There's a hard edge to the question and I feel myself shrink back from him a little.

I don't reply.

'She's even more of a fool than you are, Millie.' He shakes his head a little, his hands clenching into fists and then releasing, pulsing as if he's trying to decide what to do next. 'She... Sam, I mean... she isn't who you think.'

'What do you mean?'

'You remember the whole multiple applications for the job at Serendipity thing?'

'With the different CVs? Yes, I remember.'

'I think Sam is a journalist. I think she came to Serendipity looking for a story about terrible bosses.'

'Well, I guess she found one,' I say softly.

'I promised Freya that Sam had disappeared. That she'd been clever enough to realise how precarious her situation was and had gone to ground. But instead she was sending you messages, stirring things up, digging in places she shouldn't have been. Fuck!' Again he slams his fist onto the table.

'Hey,' I say. 'Calm down, OK?'

'I can't calm down,' he hisses at me. 'Sam should have kept her mouth shut and left it alone. Instead she's drawn you into all of this.' He stops talking and just sits there, staring at nothing in the distance, his face almost blank.

'Kieran?' I lean in to him, concerned. 'Kieran?'

His eyes meet mine and he swallows loudly. His next sentence is barely a whisper. 'I don't think Freya will let you walk away.'

Ice-cold fingers caress my arms as his words hang heavy between us.

I wait. Twenty seconds pass. Then another ten. Finally I speak. 'I think I can get us both out of this.'

'Both?'

I nod. 'Do you know what happened in Barcelona?'

'With Gregory and him having that accident before you could...?' he trails off, raising both eyebrows but not saying the word.

'After that.'

Confusion skitters across his features. 'After?'

'We went to a party. But Freya only stayed for about ten minutes before she slipped out of the side door. I followed her.'

'Where did she go?'

I lean in to him so I can drop my voice even further. 'She walked around for a while. It was like she was looking for something.'

'Looking for what?'

I swallow. 'She was hunting.'

'Hunting?' He says it loudly and I grab his hand to shush him.

'She found this guy and they had a little chat. I was too far away to hear what they said. Then he followed her to this abandoned club. The same place we were planning on killing Gregory.' I pause and pull up a news story on my phone, placing it face up on the table so Kieran can read it.

'"Unidentified male found dead in derelict building",' he reads the headline out loud.

'No one knows who the guy was. And no one really seems to care,' I say sadly. Whoever he was, he was still a person. He may have left behind a family, friends, people who loved him.

'You know who he was?' Kieran asks.

I shake my head. 'No. But I have proof it was Freya who killed him.'

His eyes meet mine.

'This is how we *both* get away from her,' I tell him. 'You need to tell her that I have this proof and if she pulls any shit, any shit at all, it gets sent to the police.'

'She'll kill you.' He's matter of fact.

'Then it gets sent to the police.'

He nods, understanding I've left nothing to chance. 'And me?' His voice is small.

'You buy my way out and then I tell her to let you walk away or I'll release the proof anyway.'

'OK.'

'We have a deal?' I ask.

'Yes.' He smiles at me and his whole demeanour shifts. The scared little boy replaced with someone confident and full of purpose. 'Now, you go back to the hotel and you sit there and do nothing. I'll go and see Freya.' He takes out his wallet and removes a small stack of twenty dollar bills. 'This should be enough for breakfast,' he says as he lays it down on the table. Then he stands up and turns back to face me. 'I think I love you, Millie,' he says, but his tone is grave and eyes dark. Then he walks away without looking back.

About thirty seconds later the waitress brings over my French toast and his order of sage fried chicken and waffles.

'Everything alright, honey?' The waitress asks, looking at the empty seat in front of me.

'Oh, work emergency,' I say, affecting a bright and breezy tone. 'Any chance you could box these up for me?'

'Sure thing,' she replies.

A few minutes pass before she returns with a brown paper bag and a coffee tray with two large takeout cups in it. 'You take care, honey,' she says as I thank her and leave.

Kieran's words dance inside my head. *I think I love you, Millie.*

Will he change his mind about me when he realises I'm still going to kill Connor and Liam?

40

The man mountain is still standing vigil outside my hotel room when I get back from breakfast.

He visibly sighs with relief when he spots me. 'Good breakfast?' he asks with a smile.

'Decided on takeout,' I reply, trying to sound cheerful even though the last hour has been a whirlwind of emotion and I'm still processing everything. All I want to do is go and lie in a darkened room and let my subconscious sort everything out into nice neat little boxes. 'Oh,' I say, reaching into the paper bag in my hand. 'I thought you might be hungry.'

I hand him one of the boxes from Hash House A Go Go and his eyes widen in delight. 'What's this?' he asks, peering inside.

'Just chicken and waffles.' I shrug as if it's nothing. Which it is – I mean it's just breakfast, it's hardly like I've bought him a house – but the smile that creases his face suggests this is a pretty rare occurrence for him.

'Thank you, Miss Brooks,' he says with sincerity.

'No worries,' I reply, pressing my key against the reader. The door beeps and I open the door, turning to smile at him once more. 'Just don't let anyone in, OK?'

For a second he looks like I've slapped him round the face, but then he realises I'm joking. 'Of course not, Miss. You're safe with me.'

Perhaps it's the breakfast – the French toast was delicious – or the lack of sleep finally catching up with me, or the jet lag, or – and I do think this might be having a disproportionate impact if I'm entirely honest – the fact someone genuinely does want to kill me, but I decide to lie down on the bed for a few moments... And wake up three hours later.

The sun streams in through the window, causing tiny dust particles in the air to perform a languid ballet, slowly drifting in the air, twirling and swirling in a never-ending dance. I stay lying down, just staring at them. Until a knock at the door rips me from my trance.

'Miss Brooks?' It's the bodyguard. 'Miss Brooks?'

'Hold on a sec!' I call out, my mouth dry.

'Oh, thank God!' he says as I open the door. 'I thought... I thought...' he shakes his head as if clearing an unwelcome mental image. 'Never mind. You're OK.' Then he squints a little and leans to look at me more closely. 'You *are* OK, aren't you?'

'Sorry, I was asleep. Must have basically passed out.' I smile briefly, but my hackles are up. There is danger in the air. Or perhaps I'm just disoriented from waking up so quickly.

'I just wanted to tell you... well, Mr Weedon – Connor Weedon, that is – has...' he looks uncomfortable. 'He no longer thinks I'm needed.' He adds the last bit quickly.

'Oh.' I don't really know what to say. 'Did he say why?'

'Above my pay grade.' He shrugs but there's a sadness in his eyes. 'I didn't want to just leave.'

'Thank you,' I say and I mean it.

'Are you going to be alright?'

'Yeah.' I sound braver than I feel. That danger in the air feels like it's creeping closer.

He reaches into his pocket and then hands me a card. 'Call me, OK? If you think there's something...' A pained look flashes across his face. 'Just, no heroics, OK?' He smiles. 'I don't live too far and my son just got his learner's permit so he's always looking for places to drive me, so I can get here.'

'Thank you.'

'Be careful,' he says and then turns to walk away.

I decide in a split second, 'Hold on!' I call to him as I grab my bag from the little table just inside the room. I jog to catch him up, my footsteps muffled by the thick pile carpet. 'The casino is calling,' I joke as I join him in the lift. But we both know it's because I don't want to be alone in an unguarded room. Especially as I still have no idea who actually did call in that bomb threat.

I weave through the crowds on the casino floor, watching grown men reduced to tears at the roulette wheel, marvelling at the whooping joy of the woman who looks like she won a small fortune playing some kind of poker.

'Thirty-five thousand dollars,' someone says to me with a conspiratorial wink, gesturing at the woman sitting behind a tray of purple chips. 'Each of those is worth five hundred dollars,' they add. It's a funny atmosphere, simultaneously congratulatory and jealous, pleased for the woman but bitter it wasn't them instead. It's just like life, I guess; winners and losers, but we all have to keep up the veneer that we're genuinely happy for each other. I felt the same thing at the gala the other night, people congratulating me on my nomination while at the same time taking in every inch of me, looking for the flaws, the things they can unpick later as they whisper to themselves that *at least they don't have sticking out ears, or a big nose, or nothing in the chest department.* I learnt a long time ago that the things people take from you – the things they notice and nit-pick and judge – are much more a reflection of who they are and not the other way around.

I get a message from Connor.

> Dinner. 7pm. Old Homestead. Drinks from 5pm at Alto

There is no 'would you like to join us?' Or 'it would be a pleasure to enjoy your company', or even a cursory 'sorry about the whole bomb threat thing, why not join us for dinner and we'll see how we can move on from this?'. Just an order to attend.

Let's think about it this way. If I was just an ordinary girl, over for a business meeting, who meets a guy she is apparently kind of into. And then I get swept to Las Vegas, promised a brilliant party and the potential to get to know this man better. But then – and here's the good part – I'm bundled off to a hotel room and a guard's placed outside my door because there's been a potential threat discovered at the hotel we should have been staying in. What the actual fuck do they think I'm thinking? If I was normal I'd be freaking out right now. Hell, I *am* freaking out right now and I am so far beyond normal given the last couple of months.

I look at my watch. It's 4 p.m. I'd better go and get ready for the evening.

After all, I do still need to figure out how I'm going to kill them.

You didn't think I'd forgotten about that now, did you?

I know there's something wrong the second I push open the door to my room. The air feels different, charged somehow.

Plus, she's taken off her stilettos and left them just by the entrance.

'Just get inside and close the door,' she hisses at me from where she's sitting on the small sofa in the corner of the room. She's helped herself to a gin and tonic from the mini-bar and I involuntarily wince as my subconscious tots up what that must have cost.

'What are you doing here, Freya?' I ask. Which isn't the real question. The real question is how she got in the room in the first place.

'I asked reception for a key. We're all under the same booking.' She shrugs, answering as if she can read my mind. 'Wasn't that what you were really asking?' She arches an eyebrow at me and then reaches to pick up the gin.

Screw it. I go to the fridge and take out a miniature bottle of white wine, it's going on Connor's account anyway. 'What's going on?' I ask her, perching on the edge of the bed. It's awkward and I immediately feel at a disadvantage.

She takes a sip and studies me, her head slightly cocked to one side. 'Oh come on, Millicent. Let's not play games here.' She smiles at me and I recoil a little at the sight of her bared teeth.

'I don't think I'm the one who's been playing games,' I say, flicking my hair from my face before shifting my weight slightly to find a less precarious position.

Freya tilts her head back and laughs, the throaty sound filling the room. 'Can you hear yourself?' Her tone is scathing but also imbued with humour. I can't get a handle on her. And it makes me even more nervous.

We stare at each other, neither saying a word. The atmosphere is charged. A storm is brewing. Freya breaks our stalemate. 'OK, Millicent, how about we play Truth or Dare?'

'What?'

'You must have played Truth or Dare before?'

'Of course I have. But why the hell do you want to play it now?'

'Don't you want to know the truth, Millicent? Isn't that the only way we can move on? The only way we can finish this?'

I'm silent.

'Don't you want to finish it, Millicent?' Her words are more of a purr. Her eyes meet mine.

She can see into my soul.

She finds only darkness.

'That's good, Millicent. Let's begin.' Her eyes widen for a second and then she takes a large drink, staring at me over the rim of the crystal. 'Truth or dare?' she whispers, the words drifting in the gulf between us, waiting for me, goading me.

'Truth.'

'Do you love him? Kieran?'

I'm taken aback by the question. 'I... err...'

'The truth, Millicent. Isn't that the whole point of the game?'

'Yes.' It's little more than a whisper, but it comes from the heart, a pure truth.

'Do you want to be with—'

'Isn't it my turn to ask the question?' I interrupt.

'Just answer me, Millicent. If you love him, don't you want to find a way for you to be together?'

'Yes.'

'You know he's been helping me?'

'Yes.'

'Do you disapprove?'

I stop and think for a moment. *Do I disapprove?* I don't know how I feel to be honest. He covers up for her. But what other choice does he have? Besides, look what I've done and what I want to do. I've spent months with Freya, alternating in my views of her.

Boss. Killer. Icon.

Do I abhor this woman or adore her?

And if I can't decide, how can I even dream of judging Kieran?

'I don't know,' I say eventually. It's non-committal but it is the truth.

'OK,' she replies thoughtfully. 'Fair's fair, it's your turn to ask me.'

'Truth or dare?'

'Truth.'

I'm about to ask my question when there's a knock on the door. I look at Freya and she offers me a slow and languid smile.

'Shall I get that for you?' she asks, unfolding her legs from underneath her. She crosses the room in a few steps and opens the door a crack, not waiting to make sure who it is before returning to her chair.

'Millie?' Kieran's face appears. 'Millie?'

'Oh, just get in and shut the fucking door,' Freya demands brusquely. 'Now then, where were we? Oh yes, Millie was just about to ask me a truth.' She smiles as Kieran moves to sit on the other chair.

I clear my throat and weigh up my options. I might only get one question so I need to use it wisely. I need to understand her motivation, why she does what she does. She killed that stranger in Barcelona so it isn't just about revenge. Was any of it? Or has she been lying to me the whole time? In the end there's only one question. 'Who is Verity?'

Freya leans back slightly as if surprised at what I've asked. Then she grins and takes a sip of her gin and tonic. 'Hmmm. Who is Verity?' She repeats the question, a hint of humour in her tone. 'Well, then. Verity is our sister.'

'*Our* sister?' I ask.

Freya reaches out and puts her hand on Kieran's shoulder. 'I take it my baby brother didn't introduce himself properly?'

'Your brother?'

'Little Kieran took my mother's maiden name after the divorce. I used to take the mickey out of him for it, called him Lucas, but it stuck as a nickname.'

'*That's* why you help her,' I say to Kieran, my voice soft, the truth still not quite sinking in.

'I was only a toddler when those bastards hurt Verity. What they did ruined *everything*.' There is so much pain and anguish there. 'Freya made them pay for what they did.'

'But it wasn't just them,' I say.

'Ah yes.' Freya says, even though it wasn't her I was talking to. 'Your little theory that I killed some homeless guy in Barcelona.'

'It's not a theory.' I sound confident.

'Isn't it?' Her smile is cool and a creeping sensation skitters down my back.

'I have proof.'

'Do you?' Freya tilts her head, appraising me. 'You know you can't lie in a game of Truth or Dare.'

'Fuck you, Freya.'

'Nice retort.' She smirks and I want to slap her. 'You don't have proof, Millie.'

I don't reply. But she's right. I have no proof, only my own witness statement. If I tipped off the police would they find evidence of her on the body? I have no way of knowing.

I was so sure Kieran was on my side, full of righteous conviction that I could win against Freya. It was all a lie. She's not just one step ahead, she is miles in front of me. And she has been since the beginning.

'Well,' Freya says, standing up and stretching her arms above her head. 'This has been a pleasure. But we came here to do something. Something that benefits us all.'

'Liam and Connor,' I ask, my voice no more than a whisper.

'Yes,' she replies. 'So, I think it's time I ask the final question. Millicent Brooks. Truth or dare?'

I study her face, her raised eyebrow, the tug at the corner of her mouth that could be either a smile or a smirk. I have nothing left.

I've played every hand and she has won every time. I throw caution to the wind. 'Dare.'

'Excellent. I was hoping you were going to say that.' She clears her throat and then reaches out a hand, pulling me up to stand directly in front of her. 'I dare you to kill Connor and Liam.' She squeezes my hand, her bones grinding against mine. 'And I dare you to try to pin it on me.'

PART VI

SAM

41

Lissa leans across the aisle. 'Are you sure about this?' she asks. She's turned a slightly green shade, almost puce, and her knuckles gleam white where she's gripping the arm rests.

'About Millie? Or about this, more specifically?' I wave around me.

'We're in a tiny metal cylinder about to trust a stranger not to crash into the sea,' she says through clenched teeth.

'Would it help if I told you a lot of the journey is over land? We go up over Greenland rather than straight over the Atlantic.'

She shoots me a look that says it very much would *not* help.

'It'll be OK,' I say softly and reach out a hand to her. It's awkward, the flight was almost full and so we had to take seats on either side of the aisle. She looks at me with a hint of a smile and then leans back against the headrest, squeezing her eyes shut. Her grip on my hand tightens as the aircraft begins to push back from the stand.

'If we die, know I will haunt you for eternity for making me do this.'

'I don't think a ghost can haunt another ghost,' I reply.

'Ha ha. I'll find a way.' A tiny whimper leaves her lips as the plane lurches forwards.

Being in the aisle seats means we can't see out the window and so the sudden acceleration down the runway takes us both by surprise. Now, Lissa is obviously a bad flier. And I'm playing it cool because I don't want to make things worse for her. But the truth is that I hate flying. I hate the queues, and the stupid rules about how much toothpaste you can carry, and the waiting for the gate number to be called, and the fact that the person sitting next to me is always the one with dubious personal hygiene or who relishes invading my personal space.

Every trip I took with Freya was torture, stuffing down the fear and the discomfort and the irritation so she would never guess I didn't 'just love all the travel'. It was absolutely exhausting acting like I wanted to be a 'Serendipity girl', pretending to like the shoes and the designer labels and the champagne in nameless bars and the hours spent entertaining potential clients. Always being bright and happy and competent.

I'd promised myself I wouldn't get on another plane for a long time.

But we need to get to Millie. Before she does something she can't take back. And because I know exactly what Freya Ellwood-Winter's capable of.

I've always been fascinated by the power dynamics in major corporations, and I had an idea for a piece exposing the real-life Miranda Priestlys, the women who made *The Devil Wears Prada* look like a documentary. The concept was solid and I figured if it was juicy enough I would finally get my by-line in *The New Yorker*. Possibly even win a Pulitzer, although I knew that would be a long shot. But a girl can dream, can't she?

I had feelers out across a range of industries, searching for someone who would make an ideal subject. And then all of a sudden I started seeing Freya's name everywhere. She was speaking at this conference, at that dinner, even had a few interns gossiping about her in a city bar. She had become an icon almost overnight. And everyone thought she was an absolute bitch. She sounded perfect.

But it turned out that getting a job at Serendipity was harder than I'd thought. It took two attempts before I was offered a job working directly for Freya herself. And, Jesus, was she a bitch! I wasn't expecting her to be a serial killer though. That was quite the revelation. I noticed a little discrepancy in one expense report, and with a tiny tug at the string the whole thing collapsed in front of me. I traced her involvement from Spencer Balmforth to Ethan Donahue to Cody Gelber.

I'd already gained the interest of an editor at a major newspaper; but the second I told her what I'd discovered, I was shot down.

'That would be libel,' she told me in no uncertain terms. 'You can't accuse her of being a serial killer, for fuck's sake.' She said it like I was an idiot, a fool who wouldn't be able to back up her claims.

'So I need to get her arrested first?'

'It doesn't work like that. You know this, Sam. You need to tell the police, hand over every shred of evidence you've uncovered. Then they'll arrest her. But you can't run an article after that, using the evidence you handed over. Every hack will have access to that information.'

'Shit!' She was right of course. The only way to run the story was to release the information into the public domain. There would be no exclusive, no award, no accolades.

'Walk away from it, Sam.'

But I couldn't. I kept digging. Until Freya got suspicious about what I knew. She caught me late one night, sitting at my desk in the office because my internet at home had gone down and I was too impatient to lose an evening of research. So I went to the office and didn't realise she was standing behind me as I dug into Cody Gelber's life. She'd cleared her throat, making me jump and instinctively click out of the website I was on. But she'd seen. I could tell from the look in her eyes that she knew who I was looking at and that I'd finally connected the dots she'd been trying to obfuscate for so long.

'I'd better...' I stuttered, desperately trying to slide my feet back inside the trainers I'd slipped off under my desk. Then I grabbed my laptop and my bag and ran. I thought she'd chase me, my heart pounding as I almost threw myself down the stairs in my effort to get away from her.

It was late spring but there was still a chill in the air as I ran out of the door, throwing it open with such force I was surprised it didn't fly off its hinges. I didn't look back until I was inside the safety of the busy pub opposite the office. It was rammed, the after-work crowd already drunk and raucous. I watched as Freya pushed open the door I had flown through less than a minute previously; she peered into the street, looking left and then right as if trying to determine which direction I'd run in. But then she turned her eyes to exactly the spot where I was. There was no emotion on her face, she may as well have been a robot. It was chilling.

So I disappeared. I've been an investigative journalist for almost a decade so I know how to hide. And I know to be prepared to slide away without leaving a trace.

But I *still* couldn't walk away. I sometimes wonder if there's something wrong with me. You're meant to run from trouble, seek an easy life, find the path of least resistance. But I run towards danger, and I will always find a way to make things more complicated. So I messaged Millie. Told her to connect the dots. Told her there were other victims. Followed her. Watched her.

I assumed Millie would dig far enough to find something

concrete. She was always such a goody-little-two-shoes she was bound to go to the police with the evidence. But she didn't. I was so blatant in my messages there was no way she didn't understand what I was saying. So why didn't she go to the police? Why hadn't they swooped in to raid Freya's home and office?

In the meantime I carried on looking at unsolved murder cases and missing persons, matching them against the archive of Serendipity expense reports I downloaded from a cafe close to the office. The company was so lax about security, I was still able to log on to their systems even though I'd left months previously.

What I discovered was horrifying.

I needed to warn Millie to get the fuck away from Freya and Serendipity. I needed to tell her to run as fast as she could. Immediately. But then I saw the Instagram posts of the fancy trip to LA for the *Women in Power* event. And so I went to find Lissa.

She was sitting on her own at the bar in Be At One, sipping a bright orange cocktail and scrolling on her phone. I knew who she was, we'd met a couple of times over the years at Serendipity drinks and other bits of corporate bullshit I attended to maintain my lie.

'Hey Lissa,' I'd said, sliding onto the bar stool next to her as if this wasn't the girl I'd had a crush on since the very first time we met.

I thought she'd smile, perhaps even flirt a little. Instead she went white as a sheet. 'Holy shit, Sam. Where the fuck have you been?' The words hissed under her breath, her lips inches from my ear, her hand gripping my arm.

'I don—'

'Freya!' She was off her stool now, standing so close to me I could smell the banana undertones of the perfume she was wearing. 'We *know*. But we thought something had happened to you. I thought something...' she trailed off, a blush creeping up her décolletage.

'*You* know?' I put a heavy influence on the 'you'.

'Millie tells me everything.'

I hadn't factored that in to be honest. I've always been a bit of a loner, never really putting down proper roots for long enough to make any true friends. I have a little brother but we're about as different as two people can be. It never occurred to me that Millie would tell Lissa.

But then Lissa had sat back on her stool, her whole body language changing in front of me. The confident, almost urgent woman from a moment ago morphing into someone who looked tired, a little broken. 'Or at least she *used* to tell me everything,' she whispered with an air of desolation.

'What's happened?'

Lissa's eyes met mine and I could sense her searching my soul, the twitch in the corner of her eye as she tried to determine just how far she could trust me.

She must have found what she was looking for. 'I think something's going on. And I don't mean Freya. I mean Millie. I think...' she trailed off, looking around her. When she spoke again she sounded wretched. 'I think Millie might be about to do something really stupid.'

'What do you mean?' I asked.

'We didn't go to the police because Freya had made Millie an accomplice; inadvertently, of course. We needed to make sure Freya didn't try to take Millie down with her.'

I nodded. It sounded like the kind of thing Freya would do.

Lissa continued, 'But... I think... Oh God!' She wailed. 'This sounds so stupid and I'm sure this isn't what's really been happening and I'm just being absolutely ridiculous and you'll tell me I'm being silly.' She took a huge intake of breath. 'I think Millie is helping Freya, like on purpose this time.'

It wasn't what I'd expected her to say. 'What? Why?'

'I think they're planning something together.' She grabbed my hand. 'Promise I can trust you?' Her eyes burned into mine.

'Of course.'

'Millie has gone to Los Angeles with Freya.'

'The *Women in Power* event.' I nodded, I knew she'd gone.

'Connor and Liam Weedon.' Lissa spat the names, her fingers digging deeper into my flesh.

'What about them?'

And then Lissa told me everything about their years at Weedon House. Millie certainly has a motive to want the Serendipity brothers dead.

We hit a patch of turbulence over the Arizona desert and Lissa reaches across the aisle to take my hand as the plane drops and my stomach flies into my mouth. She turns to look at me and in that moment I realise what it is to have someone to care about.

But before I can dwell on Lissa, we need to get Millie home safely.

And I have no idea what we're going to find in Vegas.

42

The flight lands in Vegas at 3 p.m. local time, which is basically the middle of the night back home. It's been thirty-five hours since Lissa last heard from Millie, when she was sent a whole load of photos from her hotel room.

As expected, our bags are the last to be offloaded from the flight. It's the same thing that happens every damn time and another reason I hate flying. We should have just taken them as hand luggage, they were small enough. But eventually we're outside the terminal; the heat is fierce and there's a dry wind, like being blasted in the face with a hairdryer.

'I'm still not getting through to her,' Lissa tells me, looking worriedly at her phone.

'WhatsApp?'

'Not delivering.'

'Have you tried her work number?'

She looks at me. 'I'm not going to dignify that with an answer.'

It's fair enough. Given how much she managed to figure out about Freya, I don't have much to teach her about this world I've lived in for so many years.

We take a taxi to Caesar's Palace, the gnawing feeling in the pit of my stomach increasing as we inch closer and closer.

I'm scared. Scared of what we might find. Scared of what it might do to Lissa. Losing Millie would tear her to pieces.

'Do you think she's OK?' Lissa asks softly, her voice touched with trepidation. She's not that much younger than me but in this moment she looks so vulnerable. So fragile.

'Yes,' I reply with more confidence than is warranted. I don't add 'I think' or 'I hope', but the extra words hang in the air, twisting in the wind.

After we get out of the taxi, Lissa tells me to stay where I am with the cases.

'Why?'

'Because I need to get the key,' she tells me like I'm being deliberately dense. 'How can I ask for a replacement key if I look like I haven't checked in yet?'

'Replacement?'

'For Millie's room. Jeez, are you jet-lagged or something?' Then she leaves me outside and swans into the hotel, her whole demeanour changing to someone with an aura of absolute entitlement.

Three minutes later she's back outside, a key card in her hand.

'You did it?'

'Obviously.' She grins at me, and for a tiny moment I see a wholly different Lissa; one who was dealt a very different hand in this life.

'How?'

'I told them I was part of the Serendipity party. Said I was sharing a room with Millie. They barely batted an eyelid.'

Once again I'm impressed and we head inside to the bank of lifts.

'Floor 35,' she tells me. 'This place is massive.'

The carpet in the corridor from the lift is so deep our little cases are almost impossible to wheel. But Lissa doesn't seem to notice, striding down the hallway reading the room numbers as we pass them. '3512, 3514, 3516, 3518, 3520, Jesus Christ, how many fucking rooms are there, 3522, 3524. Here!' She stops suddenly and I almost walk into her.

'What's wrong?' I ask.

She turns to face me and the terrified young girl has returned. 'I've been trying to hold it together,' she says softly. 'But... what...?' she wrinkles her nose as if trying to stop herself from crying.

I leave my case and take a few steps toward her. I take both her hands in mine, her palms are slick with sweat and I can see how fast her heart is racing from the pulse in her neck. 'It's going to be OK,' I tell her, looking directly into her eyes. 'OK?' I raise both eyebrows.

She nods quickly, a couple of almost imperceptible movements of her head.

I take the key from her hand and press it against the lock. It beeps and I take a deep breath before I push the handle down and allow the door to swing open.

The room is dark, the blackout curtains drawn, the light from the corridor barely illuminating the space. I reach for the switch and suddenly the room is cast in brilliant white light.

'Tell me what you can see,' Lissa whispers from outside the door.

My eyes sweep the space once more before I answer. 'Nothing.'

'What do you mean nothing?' The panic evident in her voice.

'I mean, it looks like the maid service has been and no one's come in since.'

She pushes me out of the way gently to peer inside, at the white linen stretched perfectly over the bed, the row of little wrapped glasses on the sideboard, the ice bucket and tongs, the brand new slippers next to the wardrobe. 'She isn't here,' Lissa says, and she stumbles slightly as the truth of the words hit home. Millie isn't lying dead in a pool of her own blood. Millie hasn't been strangled, or shot, or stabbed, or killed in any of the other ways Lissa has obviously been imagining during our flight.

I rescue our cases from the hallway while she collects herself, pulling them into the room and tucking them into the little alcove by the door. I have no idea where we'll actually be staying, but it's hardly a priority at the moment.

'What now?' Lissa whispers, sinking onto the edge of the bed.

'At least we know she's still here, at the hotel.' My voice is muffled because my head is in the wardrobe, taking stock of all the things I can see. I recognise a pair of heels Millie always wore in the office and the carry-on case she used for work trips. 'It looks like she unpacked,' I say extracting myself.

At that moment I hear someone clear their throat in the hallway beyond the closed door, and then the tell-tale beep as the lock is deactivated. I breathe a sigh of relief that Millie is here.

But it isn't Millie who walks in. It's Kieran Lucas. I act without thinking, throwing myself into the door to close it behind him, trapping him inside the room.

'Sam?' he says as he looks at me, confusion painted across his features. Objectively I understand why Millie was attracted to him, he's a good looking guy if that's your thing, but there's something just *wrong* about him. Or maybe it's because I know what he does for Freya.

'What are you doing here, Kieran?' Lissa asks from further inside the room.

He looks from her to me. I can see him thinking. Plotting. Trying to figure out what is really going on here and how he can take advantage of the situation.

I sigh deliberately. 'Really? You're just going to stand there and say nothing?'

'I'm here for Millie. She's—'

I cut him off. I can tell from his faux concern that he's lying through his teeth and I can't be bothered with it any more. 'We know she's in danger from Freya.'

'She isn't in danger from Freya. She's in danger from herself.'

I hear Lissa suck in a breath. 'No,' she whispers.

Kieran laughs. 'I guess Lissa already figured out that Millie isn't here for a holiday.' His tone is nasty, close to sarcasm.

'Where is she?' I demand.

'How would I know?' he asks, spreading his palms wide as if he's innocent in all of this.

It was obvious when I took a step back and thought logically. How Freya had remained undetected for so long. How she had gotten away with so much without ever becoming a suspect. She had help. Someone who covered for her, smoothed over the cracks, made sure there were no loose ends. It didn't take long to discover exactly who Kieran Lucas was. Freya's baby brother. What wouldn't he do for his big sister?

'Just tell me where she is.' Lissa's voice is almost a hiss, and I look at her, her face a picture of pure hatred.

'But that would be far less fun,' he replies with a smirk.

I hate him. He's a bully; a cruel and vicious tormentor who likes to watch the suffering of others. He's also a chameleon; brilliant at blending in, at saying and doing the 'right' things to avoid detection.

As my fist makes contact with his nose two things cross my mind simultaneously. First how fragile the human body is as flesh and sinew flatten against my knuckles. And second how no one ever warned me how painful punching someone in the face would be. Oh, and a third; the sucking noise, like removing a wellington from a mud slick.

'Fuck!' he half-screams as his hands fly instinctively to protect his shattered face. 'What the f—'

'Don't play with us, Kieran,' I say, trying to keep my voice steady as I shake my hand to calm the burning sensation.

'Yeah,' Lissa adds, unfolding from her stooped position and getting to her feet. 'We're done with games.' My heart squeezes at the sight of her standing up to him.

'I think you should sit down and tell us everything,' I say, motioning to the sofa. It's leather so it doesn't matter if he drips blood on it.

'You broke my nose!' But he moves towards the sofa almost dutifully.

I wonder if he's just so conditioned to doing what he's told that he'll obediently comply with any request made with authority. 'Tell us everything.'

For a moment he looks like he'll refuse. But then he opens his mouth and begins to talk. 'Millie found out about Freya enjoying a certain... niche... hobby.'

'That's an interesting way to put it,' Lissa says.

He ignores her. 'Anyway, Millie decided not to go to the police. But in return for her silence, she wanted Freya to help her get revenge on these guys who fucked her over when she was a teenager. When *you*,' he motions at Lissa, 'were teenagers.'

'Connor and Liam,' Lissa says, almost spitting their names. 'We were just kids. Orphans. No one cared about us. No one believed us.'

'What's Millie planning?' I ask Kieran, even though I think I already know the answer.

He laughs silently, before wincing. He does have a busted nose after all. 'She thought she could kill them and walk away as if nothing had happened. She thought Freya would help her.' There is so much disdain in his voice I want to punch him again. He smiles his disgusting twisted smile. 'Poor little Millie doesn't even know she's already lost everything.'

'What the hell is that meant to mean?' Lissa says as she moves to stand over him.

'I made Freya promise not to lay all her kills at Millie's door. That was her original plan, but I convinced her to spare Millie the shame,' he says. 'But then the little slag decided to dump me. No one dumps me.' He is bitter and angry. 'So now I am going to make sure that, when she kills Connor and Liam, she will be the primary suspect. The evidence will lead the police to all her other kills. All eight of them. Millie is about to become the most notorious female serial killer the world has ever known.'

43

'We need to stop her,' Lissa says, turning to me.

'How?' I ask. I look back toward Kieran. 'What evidence? What have you done?'

'You know I help her.' It isn't a question. 'You know I *fix* things.' He's condescending and obviously enjoying this. 'How to fix murder?' He doesn't even pause. 'You make it look like it isn't murder. An accident. Suicide. A case of being in the wrong place at the wrong time. Or you find a patsy.' He grins and wipes a drop of blood from his nose before it falls. 'You're too late. It's all over. As soon as Millie kills Connor and Liam, the ball starts rolling and it cannot be stopped.'

'You're enjoying this,' Lissa hisses and I can see that her anger is rising, the tension visible in her shoulders, the vein in her temple pulsing.

'Oh you have no idea,' he says, and it's almost a purr, almost sensual.

'And all because she dumped you?' I don't even bother to hide my disgust.

'Maybe she should have been more appreciative of the time I gave her.'

'You sick bastard,' Lissa says.

He tilts his head to one side and stares at her. 'You stupid cun—'

He hasn't finished forming the words before she launches herself at him, slapping and punching him. A low wail escaping from her lips.

I should intervene. Drag her off him before she really hurts him. Instead, I wait for her rage to subside slightly and then touch her shoulder. 'We still need him to tell us where she is,' I say softly.

She moves away, wiping blood from her knuckles on a tissue plucked from the box on the side. I take her place in front of him. 'Tell me where Freya and Millie are. Tell me how to stop this.'

'No.'

'Tell me or—'

'Or what? What exactly do you think you can do to me? You broke my nose, let her slap me round a bit. But that's all you've got.'

'You think I'm stupid, don't you? You think I'm a fool. That I'm a junior hack reporter who was scrabbling round for a story and found something I can't even use.'

'You know you can't publish a libellous piece about Freya.' There's that smug self-satisfaction again.

'No. But I can publish a piece about how you've been covering up for a murderer. I have proof of your involvement in doctoring reports and records, I can show your sticky digital fingerprints all over things where they shouldn't be.'

'Bullshit.' He sounds cocky, but his eyes say otherwise.

'You can pin everything on Millie. But I can make you an accomplice. You were her boyfriend after all. Think of the plethora of infamous couples you can join. The Wests. Bonnie and Clyde.' I smile at him and shrug as if I really don't care what happens to him. 'Your life is over.'

I watch him attempt to process everything, the concentration flickering across his broken features as he tries to find a way out of this mess. He closes his eyes for a few seconds. When he opens them, he stares numbly at me. 'Just tell me what you want.'

'How do we stop Millie?'

He sighs loudly. 'Get my bag,' he motions to the stupid bag he has carried everywhere for as long as I've known him. I hand it to him and he reaches inside to pull out an iPad mini.

'That's Millie's,' Lissa says, pointing at it.

Kieran flips open the cover and taps in the passcode. The screen lights up to show a feed from a small camera. 'This is the living area of the suite Connor and Liam are staying in. I was coming here to put the iPad back in Millie's room.'

'So the police will think she's been spying on them?' I say.

'Correct.'

'So...' I raise an eyebrow at him.

'There's more than one camera.' He taps the screen and brings up a different image, a long sleek bar in the background. But in the foreground there are two men on their knees, hands on their heads. It looks like an execution. And to one side stands the executioner. Millie.

Kieran reaches into the pocket of his shorts and pulls out a room key, offering it to me. 'I don't think you have much time.'

* * *

Connor and Liam's suite is on the other side of the hotel. We leave Kieran in the room to contemplate the shit I could rain down on his life. Lissa and I run down the corridor before furiously pressing the lift call button, as if repeated smashing will bring the lift faster, as if it might sense our desperation.

We dash across the casino floor to the entrance to the other tower, weaving through the throngs of people having the time of their lives. A few look up from their gambling to see what the commotion is, but no one tries to stop us.

'That one,' Lissa says, gasping for breath as she points to a bank of lifts labelled Palace Suites. There's already a lift on the ground floor and so we dive in, repeating the earlier button smashing in the hope the doors will close faster and begin the ascent.

I look at Lissa. 'You OK?' I ask.

She nods. The lift comes to a stop. 'Let's do this shit,' she says.

At the door to the suite we pause, unsure what we're going to find when we open it. Are we too late? Will Millie have already killed them? Will she already have played her hand from a deck that's so firmly stacked against her?

Lissa presses the key card against the lock and pushes the door open slowly. The entrance to the suite opens into a wide reception area, all marble and gilt and mirrors reflecting ourselves back at us. One is angled differently and I can see Millie. I tap Lissa on the arm and point towards the mirror. She nods.

'Millie?' Lissa calls out gently, the same tone you would use on a wounded animal. 'Millie? It's Lissa. I'm coming in, OK?'

Lissa walks slowly and carefully down to the end of the corridor and turns the corner. I follow her, but stay just out of sight of the others. I don't want to spook Millie, to panic her into doing something really really stupid.

'Millie? Give me the gun, Millie,' Lissa says in that same soft voice. 'Please Mills.'

I watch as Millie turns towards her and Lissa moves forward. 'Liss... I...' Millie starts to say, then tightens her grip on the gun. 'They need to pay for what they did to us.' Her voice is cold, devoid of all emotion. This is not the same Millie I knew and it's frankly terrifying.

Connor and Liam are still on their knees, hands still on top of their heads. But what I couldn't see on the video stream was the tears tracking their faces, the dark stain on Connor's trousers, the way the muscles in Liam's legs are trembling, but whether from fear or the awkward position I can't tell. These are men who believe Millie is more than capable of pulling the trigger. I wonder how long they have begged for their lives. Long enough they've now grown silent? Long enough they're resigned to their fates?

'I'm getting bored.' The clipped words cause an almost Pavlovian response and I unconsciously straighten my shoulders and brace for her criticism. Freya Ellwood-Winter is dressed in a striking black bodycon dress and skyscraper heels. Poised, calm and in absolute control. 'You came here to do something, Millie,' she says. 'Finish this.'

Millie's hand shakes a little as she readjusts her grip on the gun and recentres the muzzle on Connor.

'Connor first,' Freya whispers, the words dripping from her lips as smooth as honey.

'No!' Lissa shouts and runs to Millie, grabbing her wrist and twisting the gun from her grasp in a simple easy movement that I think takes them both by surprise.

'Lissa. It *is* Lissa, isn't it?' Freya says with authority. 'Give the gun back to Millie. She needs to do this.'

'No,' Lissa replies. 'This isn't how it was meant to be.' I can hear the hitch in her voice. A shiver runs up the back of my neck. 'Millie, this isn't only your fight. You can't decide on your own how they pay.'

Millie steps closer to her and I watch an entirely unspoken conversation pass between them in a split second.

Behind me the lock beeps softly and the door slowly swings open a few inches. Kieran slips through the gap without making a further sound. He holds his finger up to his lips and I nod in reply.

I return my attention to Lissa as she breaks eye contact from

Millie. Then she raises the gun and points it at Liam. 'Liam, do you know who I am?' she asks strong and clear.

Liam nods from his position on the floor.

'And I assume you've already figured out who Millie was back then?'

Liam nods again, and tries to shift his weight slightly.

'And what do you have to say? To us.'

Liam's gaze flicks from Lissa to Millie and then to Freya.

'Nothing? You're going to say nothing?' Her hand holding the gun shakes. 'Maybe I should kill you. After all, you killed me. Took everything I was, everything I thought I could be, and ground it into the dust.'

I'm holding my breath, waiting to see what she does.

What would I do if I were her?

What would you do?

Would you kill the men who ruined your life?

'Oh for Christ's sake!' Freya is impatient. She reaches for a small clutch bag on the glass coffee table and withdraws another gun. 'Am I going to have to kill them myself?' she asks, stroking a finger across the top of the barrel. 'How about I start with Connor? This is your gun, isn't it? How poetic to be killed by your own weapon.'

'No.' This time it's Millie stepping forward.

'Camille. You should never start a game you aren't prepared to play to the end.'

'This isn't a game,' Lissa says. 'This is our lives. Our...' she motions around herself, 'our everything.'

Freya throws her head back and laughs. 'Oh, so very sentimental. How noble.' She clears her throat before calling out, 'Sam. I know you're out there. Come and join us.'

My feet are moving before I even process her words – see what I mean about Pavlov? – and Kieran, who is far more conditioned than I am, almost pushes me out of the way. But I stop him, turning to stare at him so fiercely it roots him to the spot, still out of sight of the others.

'Well, well, well.' Freya says, motioning the gun towards me in a languid motion. 'Looks like we've got ourselves a little party.'

She smiles as she moves towards Lissa and takes the other gun from her. 'Here's what's going to happen,' she says. 'We're going to play a game.' Her smile grows broader. 'You two,' she says to Connor and Liam, 'might want to sit cross-legged instead, this must be torture on your knees.'

They shift into a different position, looking relieved at the momentary reprieve.

'That's better,' Freya says. 'Now then. How about we all play my favourite game? Truth or Dare. I'll answer first.'

I seize the moment. 'Truth or dare, Freya?'

'Truth.'

I was hoping she would say that. I pause for a few moments, allowing the tension in the room to build. When I speak, I ensure my voice is level, my words clear and crisp. 'Who was the first person you attempted to kill?'

Freya starts slightly. *Gotcha.* After Gregory's apparent death, Freya stopped her weekly pilgrimage to Burtenshaw House and I began to wonder why. All it took was a single phone call, my best Ms Ellwood-Winter impression, and a friendly nurse who was ever so concerned that I was avoiding visiting Verity because of her 'accusations'. I pulled on the thread and the whole sorry story unravelled in front of me.

'Perhaps you're more clever than I thought, Sam,' Freya says and then waits a few beats. 'The truth is I thought she was dead.' She lets out a short, self-deprecating laugh. 'But then she came back to life. Which was really rather inconvenient. Especially if she ever regained enough consciousness to become a credible witness. I pushed the blame onto a group of dumb rich boys whose families would do anything to sweep controversy under the carpet. For years it was my story against the eight of them. A classic "they said/she said" and no one really wanted the palaver of trying to figure out who was telling the truth and so we all walked away.'

'Except Verity,' Millie adds.

'She's starting to come back. To recognise people and the world around her. You can see why I had to get rid of those eight boys.'

Millie lets out a single soft laugh as she realises exactly what really happened. 'They weren't the ones who hurt her. They were the ones who witnessed *you* holding her under the water.'

Freya shrugs. 'I wanted to know what it would feel like. And if I could get away with it.'

There's movement from the hallway and Kieran steps into view.

Freya pales and for a moment the gun trembles in her hand.

'You? You were the one who hurt Verity?' His voice almost breaks on the words. I almost feel sorry for him.

Freya adjusts her grip on the gun and the tremor stops. 'Oh, Lucas,' she says, dripping with derision. 'You must have realised I enjoyed it.' She smiles in a way that sends a shiver through me. 'Didn't you ever wonder?'

'I thought it was revenge. For what those men did to *our sister*. I thought...' he trails off, shoulders slumping as if the weight of the truth might squash him.

But there is still more he doesn't know.

'Freya,' I say and she turns her attention to me. 'Truth or dare?'

'Isn't it someone else's turn?'

'Truth or dare?' I repeat.

'Truth.'

'How many have you killed?'

We stand in silence, the question hanging between us. Then she hitches a shoulder and says casually, 'Dozens.' As if she's just confessed to eating a few extra jellybeans and not mass murder.

'Thirty-eight,' I say. Or at least that was the number I found as I dug further and further back into her past.

'That many?' Freya raises an eyebrow and looks rather pleased with herself. 'Bit of a waste to use a Truth or Dare question when you already know the answer,' she says as if this is still just a game to her. 'But at least one more won't hurt.' She turns and pulls the trigger.

EPILOGUE

On 9 August 2023, Gregory Fuller stood in front of the podium and took a sip of water. He cleared his throat as he looked over the room, at the sea of grey-suited men and women, all of whom waited patiently for him to begin his keynote address. This was the pinnacle of his career and he had dreamt of this moment for over a decade.

'Ladies and gentlemen,' he began, relaxing a little as the words sounded strong and level in his ears, 'welcome to the twenty-second annual Life Matters Conference, and thank you for inviting me to speak. Some of you will be aware of my work in fraudulent claims investigation. Today I will share with you the secrets to faking your own death. You know, just in case you ever need to disappear.'

There was a smatter of laughter from the audience and Gregory flashed a smile. 'You'll know I have devoted my career to finding the people who try to defraud my company by pretending a calamity has befouled them, even as they sip a cocktail on a beach in French Polynesia.' He paused, he could almost taste the Piña Colada and feel the water lap his toes.

'And I have been exceptionally good at my job,' he bragged, but his tone remained humble. 'There is nothing I don't know about vanishing into the ether,' he twerked his eyebrows and grinned. The audience smiled back at him. He had them in the palm of his hand, hanging onto his every word. There was a reason he was so liked by so many.

No one tried to find him. Not that they would have known where to look. He was being modest when he boasted about his prowess: the truth is he was better at this than anyone. Plus, he'd been making plans for a long time, ever since he discovered two of the guys he went to camp with had died within months of each other. He watched as the others ostensibly overdosed, fell victim to home invasion, or had a heart attack in the sauna. He knew Freya would come for him and when she turned up at the Barcelona Hilton bar he knew it was time.

Eight months later, in a tiny thatched-roof bar on the pristine white sands of Bora Bora, he orders a Mai-Tai and asks the proprietor if he can borrow the apparently discarded copy of *The New Yorker* by his elbow.

'Sure,' he says. 'Those ladies left it,' he points to the receding group of three women: one blonde; one brunette and vaguely familiar to him, like he had seen her once before; and one with long black hair and bright floral tattoos covering her torso.

Gregory flicks through it. The corner of one page has been folded over and a familiar face stares back at him.

'Fuck,' he whispers under his breath as he reads the headline.

How to Slay at Work

For years, Freya Ellwood-Winter was one of the darlings of the beauty industry. Intelligent, attractive, and extremely self-assured; she was considered something of an icon. Or, in the words of one of her former employees, 'she slayed!'

Perhaps a poor choice of words given the current predicament Freya finds herself in. Tomorrow, she will appear in court charged with the murder of more than thirty-six individuals.

She was apprehended following a gun-related incident in the Caesar's Palace Hotel and Casino in Las Vegas, in which she shot the CEO of Serendipity plc. Freya was also injured in the attack, requiring eight hours of surgery to repair the damage caused by a gunshot wound inflicted by her brother, Kieran Lucas. Mr Lucas has also been apprehended and faces charges as an accessory and for a litany of fraud offences.

At first the Vegas incident was assumed to be an argument taken too far, or a simple misunderstanding. Until the gruesome truth began to emerge. Freya had been using the cover of extensive business travel to commit a series of atrocities across the globe. Or at least that is the accusation, one apparently corroborated by a small group of key witnesses believed to be Serendipity employees.

Serendipity, the favoured beauty brand of the nation's teenagers, has barely been out of the headlines recently. The company was also the subject of a recent scandal involving founders Connor and Liam Weedon. An investigation into the company's start-up capital exposed inconsistencies in the origin of the funds, resulting in the revelation of an early investor, Millicent Brooks. It is not yet known what role Ms Brooks intends to play in Serendipity's future, but rumours of a significant out of court settlement have been gaining traction.

Gregory turns the page and finds a Post-it stuck below a dated looking photo of a girl wearing a Camp North Creek T-shirt. A few lines are scrawled on the note:

Gregory, it is time for Verity to get justice. Be the witness you
should have been back then.

'Do you think Gregory will do it?' Lissa asks as they walk across the
brilliant white Polynesian sand towards the villa they've rented.
There's trepidation in her voice.

'Yes.' Sam is adamant. She's studied Gregory and learnt everything she can about him. The bottom line is he's a coward; he ran to
Bora Bora to hide from Freya, but she's no longer a threat. Sam
hopes he'll come forward as a witness of his own accord. But, if he
doesn't, she has plenty of ammunition against him, more than
enough to frighten him into submission. He will take the stand in
Freya's trial, tell the world what she did to her baby sister, and make
sure she spends the rest of her life rotting in prison.

Millie pauses for a moment and looks out over the turquoise
ocean. The sun is warm on her skin and she feels a sense of peace
wash over her. Yes, there is work still to be done – to be fair, when is
there not? But for now she can relax and enjoy the moment. Justice
will be served on Freya. Kieran will find himself convicted as an
accessory and face a long sentence. In some ways she feels for him,
Freya lied to him too, but her sympathy is tempered by the fact he
was prepared to throw her to the wolves after she broke up
with him.

She steals a glance at Lissa. They are no longer the women
Connor and Liam Weedon destroyed. They are the women who
took on Connor and Liam Weedon and won. The brothers have
been forced to admit Millie's early involvement in Serendipity and
paid an out of court settlement. Millie still can't quite wrap her
head around the number of zeros on the cheque.

She doesn't know what happens next, where the story will take her, take them. A smile tugs at the corner of Lissa's mouth as Sam whispers something in her ear, their fingers intertwining. Lissa looks happy and Millie's heart soars. This is why she did it. And she would do it all again – in a heartbeat.

ACKNOWLEDGEMENTS

Firstly, a huge thank you to my brilliant agent, Hannah Sheppard. I'm so privileged to have such an amazing champion for my writing and your tireless support makes all the difference.

To Francesca Best for your enthusiasm for this book, for your editorial insight, and for everything else you do to make my publishing dreams a reality. To Amanda Ridout, Nia Beynon, Isabelle Flynn, Leila Mauger, Hayley Russell, Sue Lamprell, Ben Wilson, Paul Martin, Arbaiah Aird, and Justinia Baird-Murray for all your work in bringing Millie's story to readers. And to the whole team at Boldwood for your warm welcome and support. I can't wait to see where the future takes us together!

To my family and friends for everything you do. Special mention to Mum for being an eternal cheerleader and a well of endless positivity in my writing. To my wonderful husband for being a brilliant sounding board and plot solver, for providing snacks, for listening to my rants, and generally having my back. I couldn't do this without you. And of course to Lily for just being adorable.

And finally to all the other authors, reviewers, bloggers, and readers. Bookish people really are the best people!

ABOUT THE AUTHOR

Sarah Bonner is the author of bestselling psychological thrillers, including *Her Perfect Twin*. She lives in West Sussex with her husband and very spoiled rescue dog.

Sign up to Sarah Bonner's newsletter for news, competitions and updates on future books.

Follow Sarah on social media here:

𝕏 x.com/sarahbonner101

f facebook.com/sarah.bonner.35574

○ instagram.com/sarahbonner101

♪ tiktok.com/@sarahbonner101

THE

Murder

LIST

THE MURDER LIST IS A NEWSLETTER DEDICATED TO ALL THINGS CRIME AND THRILLER FICTION!

SIGN UP TO MAKE SURE YOU'RE ON OUR HIT LIST FOR GRIPPING PAGE-TURNERS AND HEARTSTOPPING READS.

SIGN UP TO OUR
NEWSLETTER

BIT.LY/THEMURDERLISTNEWS

Boldwood

Boldwood Books is an award-winning fiction publishing company seeking out the best stories from around the world.

Find out more at www.boldwoodbooks.com

Join our reader community for brilliant books, competitions and offers!

Follow us
@BoldwoodBooks
@TheBoldBookClub

Sign up to our weekly deals newsletter

https://bit.ly/BoldwoodBNewsletter

Milton Keynes UK
Ingram Content Group UK Ltd.
UKHW040625150824
446763UK00002B/8